THE
EMPEROR

THE EMPEROR

Dark Verse Book 3

RUNYX

The Emperor

Dark Verse #3

RuNyx

Copyright © 2021 by RuNyx

runyxwrites.com

Cover Design by Nelly R.

For any queries/information, please direct it to runyxwrites@gmail.com

table of content

To every survivor,

*whether you carry your scars on your flesh or in your soul,
whether you've seen the worst of humankind or fought the worst
of fates, you're still here.*

This is for you.

author's note

This is the third book of the Dark Verse series and while it deals with a single couple and their relationship over a long span of years, there are characters and events mentioned from the previous two books. If you have not read The Predator and The Reaper, I highly recommend doing so for a complete reading experience.

If you've read the first two books, I feel I should mention that this one gets much darker. This book contains explicit, graphic scenes of violence and sexual nature.

There are also a few trigger warnings I feel would be fair to warn you about in case you are sensitive to these subjects – panic attack, post-traumatic stress disorder, sexual assault against a minor, violence against a minor, murder, mentions of rape and torture, mentions of human slavery and trafficking.

If any of these subject matters make you uncomfortable, please take heed. Your mental health is of utmost importance and if any of these affect you adversely, I urge you to pause. If you do continue to read the book, I sincerely hope you enjoy the journey. Thank you.

acknowledgment

Dante and Amara took me on a journey of my own inside myself. Some parts were extremely hard to write and some like water. But I wouldn't be here, much less doing something I love so much, without the immense support of these people.

First and foremost, to my readers, the ones who have been with me through the beginning – thank you. Thank you for believing in me and for giving me something to live for. Knowing you are there to catch my characters when they fall is the best feeling in the world.

Second, to my parents – your endless love for me is the reason I am who I am today. Your love across distance and time is my pillar and every day, I am grateful to be yours. Thank you.

I also want to thank the entire book community that has welcomed me and accepted my characters. To all the bloggers and bookstragrammers, to all the graphic editors and photographers, to the friends I've made and the connections I've established, thank you. To those who freaked out with me and celebrated my book, thank you. I initially wrote a special shoutout and realized it got to a thousand words so I'll just say, THANK YOU to everyone who picked up my babies and took a chance on me and recommended them to others, to everyone who has been kind to me and the few who have become close friends. You know who you are and how important you are to me. Thank you!

And to Nelly. There will never be enough words in my heart to thank you for what you do for me. Your art and vision and generosity truly makes me feel like the luckiest person. Thank you for giving my words the perfect visuals and for tolerating my annoying ass. I love you.

And Rachel, thank you for being my eagle eyes when I got squinty. I appreciate you and your friendship so much!

To my friends. Thank you for being so patient with me when I disappeared for days with messages unread and sometimes read and was a shitty friend basically. I love you.

To my tribe of readers, the gifts you have honored me with leave me speechless. The abundance you shower upon me fills my life every damn day. Thank you so, so much. You make my world a better place.

Most importantly, I want to thank you, the one reading this, for picking up my book and choosing to read me. If you've made it this far, I'm eternally grateful to you. I hope you enjoyed it but even if you didn't, thank you for choosing it. I appreciate you taking the time so much. Please consider leaving a review before jumping into your next bookish world.

Thank you so much!

playlist

Prisoner - Raphael Lake ft. Aaron Levy | The Night We Met - Lord Huron

Back to You - Selena Gomez | i hate u, I love u - gnash ft. Olivia O'Brian

Far From Home (The Raven) - Sam Tinnesz | The Scientist - Coldplay

The Beginning of the End - Klergy ft. Valerie Broussard

Say Something - A Great Big World ft. Christina Aguilara

Little Do You Know - Alex & Sierra | A Thousand Years - Christina Perri

Chasing Cars - Snow Patrol | Cry for Me - Camila Cabello

Set Fire to the Third Bar - Snow Patrol ft. Martha Wainwright

Satellite/Stealing Time - Above & Beyond

A Drop in the Ocean - Ron Pope | Back in Time - VV Brown

In the Air Tonight - Natalie Taylor | Shadow Preachers - Zella Day

My Songs Know What You Did in the Dark - Fall Out Boy

Next to Me - Imagine Dragons | Love's to Blame - Joel & Luke

Movement – Hozier | Graveyard - Halsey

i love you - Billie Eilish | Skin - Rag 'n' Bone Man

Go to War - Nothing More | Already Gone - Sleeping at Last

Cross Your Mind - Sabrina Claudio| Control - Halsey

Dogs of War - Blues Saraceno | New Divide - Linkin Park

Here Without You - 3 Doors Down | Survivor - 2WEI ft. Edda Hayes

Bad - Royal Deluxe | Wolves - Sam Tinnesz ft. Silverberg

Hurts Like Hell – Fleurie | Fire on Fire - Sam Smith

Distance - Christina Perri | Helium - Sia

Carry You - Jeffrey James | Between - Courier

When It's All Over – RAIGN | Don't Deserve You - Plumb

Holding On and Letting Go - Ross Copperman | Kryptonite - 3 Doors Down

Easier – Mansionair | Rescue Me - OneRepublic

In Need - Gert Taberner | Stay - Gracie Abrams

Boomerang - Imagine Dragons | Eclipse (All Yours) - Metric

Please Don't Say You Love Me - Alessia Mamino | Say You Love Me - Jessie Ware

Poison and Wine - The Civil Wars | Here She Comes Again - Royksopp

Vertigo - Raphael Lake ft. Ben Fisher | Starboy - The Weeknd ft. Daft Punk

exile - Taylor Swift ft. Bon Iver | Find My Way Back - Cody Fry

Fuck it I Love You - Lana Del Rey | Fall for You - Secondhand Serenade

I Just Want You - Castle OST | Legend - The Score

One Last Night – Vaults | Rolling in the Deep (Acapella) - Adele

Shattered - Trading Yesterday | Summertime Sadness - Lana Del Rey

Rise - John Dreamer | I Should Go - Levi Kris

Playlist is available on on Spotify & YouTube

preface

The house was old.

The morning was cold.

And the stories, told.

But never loud enough to reach ears that could help.

The man stood by the tree, a tree he'd been using to watch the home for over two weeks. The lone house surrounded by land and mist was eerie enough in itself. Woods at the back, river a mile away, the nearest road two miles, it was truly a home of nightmares. From the outside, it looked like a home he'd once known – with thin, dilapidated walls that never silenced the screams, the rot on the inside enveloped in the stone.

He saw the young boy at the window, early in the morning, his curious eyes trying to find something in the thick fog. He knew that if discovered, the boy would take a severe punishment. But the kid was brave, or maybe desperate. The man didn't know.

He should probably feel bad about using him. He didn't.

The man flicked on the lighter in his hand and raised it to signal the boy. He saw the little eyes notice his arm, quickly looking back to check if anyone was coming. Satisfied, the boy nodded twice. Two very slow, precise nods, just in case the man missed it. The man lowered his arm, getting the answer he'd come for.

Brave little shit had been more help than he'd hoped.

He watched as the kid went back to the room, away from the window, and hoped he didn't die. That none of them died before they were found. That'd be such a waste.

Getting the answer he'd been rooting for, the man stepped back into the fog he'd come from, disappearing from sight.

They weren't ready.

None of them.

PART 1

breeze

"*In the middle of the journey of our life*
I found myself within a dark wood
where the straight way was lost."
Dante Alighieri, Inferno

1

Amara

10 YEARS

They were kissing.

Amara watched with wide eyes from behind the tree as Mr. Maroni's son and the pretty girl with pink hair stood with their mouths joined. She had *pink hair*. Amara has never seen anyone with pink hair.

Tilting her little head to the side, she tried to see exactly what they were doing. She'd seen the heroes and heroines kiss in movies, but never in real life. Since her father wasn't with them, she hadn't seen him kiss her ma either.

Wait, were they eating each other's lips?

Ew.

Nose wrinkling, Amara swiped her tongue over her lips just to test how it felt. Wet. *Icky.* Making a face, she kept watching, trying to understand with her tiny mind exactly why they were enjoying it so much. It wasn't like she'd come to spy on them. Not at all. She'd just been walking in the woods *(which she absolutely should not have been doing alone)* when she'd come across a little shack. Curious, she had walked over to see it, and hidden behind a tree after seeing Mr. Maroni's son and the girl.

The *outside* girl.

Amara was young but she knew the rules well enough to know that outsiders weren't allowed on the compound. That was a new word she'd just learned last week – compound. *Caum-paau-nd.* That's what they all lived on. She was allowed because her ma worked at the big house on top of the hill. But this outside girl? She really wasn't supposed to be there. She could warn them. But why? Maybe they had permission. She was with Mr. Maroni's son, after all.

And they were kissing again. Weren't they getting tired? It looked so *boring* after the first few seconds.

Done with the show, Amara decided to go back home since it was already pretty late. The sun was almost set, the sky about to get dark, and the woods could get scary without light. And she was not supposed to roam on the compound after six 'o'clock; she'd get in trouble.

With that thought in mind, she started to run on her little feet back where the woods ended and the buildings began. The sky darkened and Amara panted, getting scared. She didn't like the dark. She shouldn't have stayed out so late. Her small body started to shake as she reached the edge of the woods, and tripping over her own feet, she went down hard.

Ouch, it hurt.

Amara looked down at her knee below the hem of her skirt, bruised and throbbing, and winced. Ma said her pain threshold was low. That meant she felt more pain when she got hurt. Threshold was a new word for her too. *Thresh-hold,* she repeated in her head, seeing a drop of blood well up on the skin of her knee. Feeling sick, she looked up at the dark sky to not see the blood.

"Who's there?" the voice of a man came from a distance, reminding her she had to hurry back home. She wasn't supposed to be out on the grounds after dark, especially not on these parts of the compound.

Standing up, her injured knee wobbly, Amara hurried over to the building where she lived with her mother. As she went downhill towards her home, feeling the throb in her leg, Amara hated the Maroni grounds. Why did it have to be so big, and on a mountain? Hills were hard to climb and get down on.

"Sneaking out again, 'Mara?" a boy's voice from behind her startled her.

Almost falling on her behind again, Amara barely balanced and stopped in her tracks to greet Vin. He was her best friend, her only friend actually. And for some reason, he could never say her name right. She had always been 'Mara to him.

"Vinnie! What are you doing sneaking around?" she demanded. Vin was just one year older than her – a fact he never forgot to remind her of – and he was wandering even though he wasn't supposed to either.

Vin came beside her, an inch shorter than she was. She liked to tease him about that until he reminded her he was going to grow tall in a few years and she'd stay the same. Ugh, he annoyed her.

"I was training," he said quietly, starting the walk downhill, taking her arm to help her. Okay, he was less annoying when he was being nice.

"What do you do in training?" she asked for the hundredth time, genuinely curious. He had begun 'training' – whatever that was – a week ago, the day after his eleventh birthday. She knew it had something to do with the big guns she saw the guards carrying, but nothing more. And Vin didn't tell her what he did, no matter how many times she asked him.

He shrugged, glancing at the dark training building to the right, where he'd come from. Amara saw the building in the distance, seeing another boy limping down the hill but in the opposite direction, towards the lake. The new boy. Even though he'd been staying there for as long as she could remember, everyone still called him the 'new boy'. She'd never met him, but from the way everyone talked about him, she knew he was dangerous.

"Have you talked to the new boy?" she couldn't contain herself from asking.

"He's been here five years, 'Mara," Vin reminded her. "He's not new anymore."

"I know," she stepped over a stone. They were almost home now. "That's just what everyone calls him."

The light from the building showed Vin's dark, floppy hair and dark eyes, his front tooth slightly crooked as he spoke. "He doesn't talk to anyone. The kids don't train with him."

"He's a kid too," climbing the steps, Amara pointed out.

Vin shook his head, the hair on his forehead swaying. "He's not like any of us. Stay away from him, okay?"

Amara looked at the lake in the distance. She'd never been to that part of the compound. Thinking of the angry boy who lived there, she didn't even want to go. On the landing of the huge building where she and Vin lived – she on the ground floor and Vin on the third – she stopped him, excited to share her little finding from the day.

"I found a little shed in the woods today," she told him, trying to keep her voice low so nobody would hear.

Vin, who had been looking up at the stars, looked at her with wide eyes. "You went to the woods alone? Are you *crazy?*"

"Shh," she looked around, scared someone older would hear him. If the news got to her ma, she'd be grounded. She *hated* being grounded. After a second, when no one came, she relaxed slightly.

"The woods are dangerous," Vin reminded her softly. That's something every single adult around them had told every kid. *Don't go into the woods.*

Amara rolled her eyes. "I didn't go in deep."

"But-"

"Oof," Amara exclaimed in annoyance, punching his arm to shut him up. "I wasn't the only one there. Mr. Maroni's son was there too. With a girl," she whispered, remembering the thrill of going into the woods, only to stumble upon the two teenagers.

Vin blinked, his eyes widening in excitement. "With a girl? An outsider?"

Amara nodded, grinning. Vin whistled. Or tried to. He practiced every day.

"They were *kissing,*" Amara informed him, her voice dropping even lower. "Kissing! Can you imagine? He was kissing an outside girl!"

Vin tugged at his collar, looking at the entrance door, looking uncomfortable. "That's cool."

Amara grinned. "Are you blushing?"

His chubby face flushed even more. "Of course not."

Laughing, she nudged his side with her elbow and hobbled to the door. Ma always told her to never make people uncomfortable. Though Vin was her best friend, he was uncomfortable, so she stopped.

"Don't go there alone again, okay?" he told her, entering the building behind her.

She went straight to her door and smiled at him. "Good night, Vinnie."

He shook his head, heading towards the stairs, already knowing her well enough to know she would sneak out again. Amara watched his back under the lights in the hallway, seeing the bruise on his leg under his shorts turning a nasty color, but he wasn't limping. She didn't know what they were doing to train him, but she didn't like it. Not one bit.

Angry at the thought of something hurting her friend, she opened the door to her apartment and entered the dim living room. It was late and her mother was most likely already asleep, tired from all the work she did during the day.

Her ma was the head housekeeper at the big mansion. She had joined as a cook in the kitchen and over the years gotten promoted. Now, she overlooked the entire kitchen and cleaning staff *and* the gardeners. And there were lots of them because the grounds were so big. It was one of the highest positions for the staff, which was why she had such a lovely apartment with three big bedrooms, even though it was just her and her mother. Her father had left them years ago. She remembered him sometimes, but she had always loved her mother more. As long as she had her ma, she was happy.

Making her way to the bathroom next to the living room where the first-aid kid was kept, Amara turned on the light.

"And where were you, young lady?"

Amara looked up at her ma, only a few inches taller than herself, her pleated hair falling over one shoulder. People said she looked like her – same dark green eyes, same inky black hair, same sun-kissed skin.

"I was walking with Vin," Amara told her the half-truth, knowing her mother trusted Vin.

Ma shook her head, sighing, before her eyes fell to her knee. "Oh Mumu, what happened?" she asked, reverting to the little nickname she loved.

"I just fell, Ma," she sat on the closed toilet seat, already knowing her mother would clean the little wound. As she thought, her mother quickly took out the box and got on her knees, putting Amara's feet on her lap.

"Does it hurt, Mumu?" her ma asked her quietly. It did hurt. Amara shook her head. After her father left them, she had become her mother's whole world. Any pain of hers, any happiness of hers, anything she felt, Ma felt. She was her other best friend.

"Ma?" Amara broke the silence as her mother put ointment on her wound, wondering if she should voice her question.

"Hmm?" her mother started putting the box away.

"You know Mr. Maroni's son?" she asked finally, feeling her face heat oddly.

Her mother's green eyes, so like her own, came to her. "Little Damien?"

Amara shook her head. "No, the older one."

"Dante?"

Amara nodded, her heart thumping. Hopping down from the seat, she walked out to her bedroom as her mother followed, turning down the lights behind her. Amara walked to her closet and picked out her nightdress. She didn't like to wear shorts or pants. Even for school, she preferred skirts and flowing dresses.

"Of course I know him," her mother said. "Why?"

She sat on her bed as Amara stripped to her underwear with the pretty blue flowers and put on the simple cotton nightdress.

"I just saw him today, that's all," Amara tried to be casual as she climbed on her bed and sat in front of her mother. "You never speak of him."

Feeling her mother's hands in her long hair, Amara tilted her head back as the nightly braiding started. Braiding the hair at night, her mother always told her, made it more beautiful and healthy in the morning. For as long as she could remember, her mother had been braiding her hair every night, and every morning they were wavy and pretty.

"He's a good boy, that one," her mother told her, her hands moving.

Amara had seen him from a distance for as long as she'd lived. He had always been there, but she had never focused on how soft his hair looked or how tall he already was. She felt a little flutter in her belly and rubbed it to shoo it away.

"How old is he?" she asked, tugging at the hem of her nightdress.

"Fifteen," her mother replied. "Poor boy lost his ma so young. He's taken care of his brother since then. And Mr. Maroni is… a very strict man."

Amara stared at the chest of drawers across from her, imagining how not having a mother must feel to him. Not very nice, she supposed. Kids should always have mothers like she did. Well, she could share hers.

"You should make him some sweets, Ma," Amara commented, feeling the wisdom in her idea. "Cookies. The chocolate ones. Yes, he'd like that I think."

Finished with the hair, her mother moved off the bed, letting Amara climb in. Pulling the covers over her, tucking them around her just as she liked, her mother smiled softly. It put a little dimple on her cheek that Amara wished she had. Vin told her she'd get one if she poked her finger into her cheek. So far, it hadn't worked.

"That's very thoughtful of you, Mumu," she stroked her cheek softly. "I'll do that tomorrow."

Amara smiled, taking a hold of her ma's right hand. It was rough and slender and not too big. She loved it. "Make me some too."

Chuckling, her mother dropped a kiss to her forehead. "Don't ever lose your heart, my baby."

Amara didn't really understand what that meant. How could someone lose their heart? Wouldn't they die? It was such a strange thing to say. But she just smiled as her mother left the room, feeling happy and safe and loved.

Staring up at the ceiling, she blinked, remembering the kiss she'd seen. It had looked icky, but maybe doing it was more fun. Maybe that was why they had just kept kissing. Why would people kiss if it was boring, right? She must have been missing something.

The room was quiet, only the little melody of her nightlight beside her. Amara settled in and closed her eyes, deciding to read more about kissing to understand why people enjoyed it. Then, maybe one day, when she grew up and looked beautiful, she could ask Mr. Maroni's son to give her one. He was very handsome. Maybe, he'd be nice and kiss her, after she became pretty enough to match his handsomeness.

His name was handsome too. Could names be handsome? In that quiet of the room, in that dark of the night, Amara giggled at the thought and tasted his name for the first time on her lips.

Yes, she decided. He would be her first kiss.

Dante

16 YEARS

Fuck, he hated this little fucker.

Dante cracked his jaw, keeping his eyes on the fourteen-year-old kid with the biggest chip on his shoulder. Deliberately keeping a little smirk on his face that hurt his bruised cheek, Dante pulled back his fist and punched the boy on his side.

He barely grunted, twisting around in a neat little move that his shorter body wouldn't have been capable of without intensive training, and his elbow connected to Dante's back in a hard move.

Fuck.

That one really hurt, but Dante chuckled. "C'mon, little man," he said, deliberately goading him. God, was it too much to ask for a reaction? He'd been working on his little project to chip away at this guy's defenses for over a year, and all he'd gotten were blank looks and dead blue eyes. Annoying as it was, Dante liked him, especially because it screwed with his old man. Anything that screwed with Bloodhound Maroni was fucking golden in his books.

The punch to his jaw came out of nowhere, followed by a quick punch to his nose.

Motherfucker.

Dante heard the crunch before he felt the searing pain of his skull being blown. Grabbing his nose, feeling the blood gush out, Dante felt a laugh bubble out of him, blinking the stars from his eyes. Jesus, the guy was good. Served him right for needling him.

Taking out the handkerchief he always kept in his pocket, a habit his beautiful mother had drilled into him, even in the frayed jeans that would have his mother probably roll over in her grave, he held it over his nose to stem the bleeding.

"You know I'm not going anywhere, right?" Dante mumbled through the fabric over his mouth, and finally, after a year of drilling, the younger guy spoke.

"Piss off."

Gold.

He'd hit *gold.*

Dante grinned behind the handkerchief. "Nice to meet you too, Tristan. You're my little buddy now."

Tristan narrowed his blue eyes slightly, before walking out of the training center. Or torture center, as Dante referred to it. Bloodhound Maroni had built an entire structure on his property devoted to training his soldiers and their children – training in self-defense, weapons, and torture, both to give and take it. The building had three levels – the ground floor devoted to hand-to-hand combat and weapons training, the first floor devoted to pain-tolerance training, and a basement devoted to interrogations. And though anyone underage wasn't allowed there since usually, it held outside enemies, Dante had been down there multiple times. The perks of being a Maroni.

Satisfied with the progress he'd made with Tristan, even though it was barely a centimeter, Dante walked out of the training center, nodding to the two guards posted outside whose only job was to make sure nobody who wasn't supposed to be there got in. They nodded back with respect.

Dante walked across the well-manicured lawns, uphill towards the mansion. It was such a monstrosity atop the lush green hill, but Dante loved it. His great-great-grandfather had been the one to build it. He'd been a merchant of glass, a well-respected member of the community, and a loner. That was the reason he'd bought the entire hill a little away from town, for his wife and family to live under one roof. Slowly, as the years had passed, more structures had been added to the property. But Dante loved that mansion, for the history and love it had been made with. Only if half the pit of vipers living in it now could somehow jump off the damn hill.

As he walked, the men patrolling the ground gave him respectful nods. As expected. He was the oldest son of Lorenzo 'Bloodhound' Maroni, the grandson of Antonio 'The Iceman' Maroni, who had been the founder of the Tenebrae Outfit and one of the most notorious leaders of the underworld. Dante was the heir to the empire. He was expected to continue the legacy in his blood, and he fucking hated it.

He was his mother's son more than his father's. And he couldn't understand how someone like his mother had ever been with someone like his father. He didn't know how they met because she had never mentioned it. And Dante remembered everything about her.

'You're my most precious art, my little hell-raiser, my Dante.'

That's what she'd called him. Her protector in the hell she had tried to survive, the one who would brave this hell and come out. Yes, he knew why she'd named him 'Dante'. It was after the poet who went through the seven circles of hell and got out. Dante would be lucky if he survived the first.

She'd been a painter, his mother, with the wild, curly brown hair, sad brown eyes, and soft, wide smile. Streaks of paint on her cheek, a poem in her throat, she would recite poetry or even hum songs while he would play with the clay she bought him, and his little toddler brother would be doing whatever toddlers did. She had nurtured the artist inside him, occasionally coming to guide his small hands as he molded the soft clay.

She'd taken a room for herself on the top floor of the mansion. The sunsets were the prettiest from there, she'd said. As a child, he had loved spending hours with her as she worked with her paints and he made little sculptures of clay for her.

It was also the room he'd found her in, her wrists slit open as red pooled around her, her canvas fallen to the side on the floor, soaking in her blood, her last masterpiece.

Shaking off his thoughts, Dante climbed up the low steps to the back of the mansion, walking to the side with a view of the lake, and removed his white handkerchief, now stained crimson. The green went as far as the eyes could see, only obliterated by the occasional structure. God, he loved this fucking hill even though he wished half the people got off it.

Moving his facial muscles, he tested the severity of his injuries. Little bastard got him good. It hurt, but he'd live.

Something barreled into him from the side, hitting him right where Tristan had elbowed him. Gritting his teeth, he spared a glance to the kid who'd slammed into him, now flat on her butt.

"Watch where you're going, squirt," he told her absently, calling her what he called his younger brother. Fuck, he needed a cigarette. He wasn't a smoker per se, but he liked the occasional puff. Taking one out from his pocket, he flicked open his metal lighter and took a deep drag. Smoke coiled inside his lungs, giving him a momentary reprieve from any other sensation. That was until he heard a feminine cough from his side.

Chuckling, he looked at the girl properly, seeing her back on her feet, in a simple blue dress, her black hair in a ponytail, and her large green eyes on him. He'd seen those eyes somewhere.

"Are you supposed to be in this area?" he asked, taking a little drag of the cigarette, watching her cute nose wrinkle.

"I'm hiding from my friend," she told him, her eyes drifting to the ground. "I think I should go now. Bye."

Surprised at the abrupt change, Dante threw his smoke to the ground. "Whoa, whoa, whoa. Hold up, squirt."

She whirled around, her ponytail hitting his chest, her eyes blazing with more fire than her little body was capable of. "Stop calling me that!"

Amused, Dante bowed his head slightly as he would to a lady. "My apologies, queen."

She liked that, he could tell.

"How old are you?" he asked, curious, trying to place her.

"How old are you?" she fired back.

Dante grinned. "Sixteen."

"I'm eleven," she declared proudly. "It was my birthday last month. I told my ma to send some of my birthday cake to you."

Dante suddenly realized who she was – their housekeeper's daughter. They had the same green eyes. He didn't know their housekeeper's name, but he had started calling her Zia after she'd started feeding him home-made cookies. While he didn't talk much to Zia, he lived for those sweet treats. His mother hadn't cooked much either, so Zia's desserts were something he'd started to cherish. He looked forward to having them all the time. And she was such a nice woman. Dante liked her.

The young girl, her daughter, was too far from the staff quarters. She'd be in too much trouble if his father, or worse his uncle, saw her there.

"You should go," he nodded to where she'd come from, not wanting her or her mother in the crosshairs of anyone at the mansion.

The girl blinked once, before giving him a little smile, almost shy. "You have really pretty eyes," she told him. Before he could respond, she turned away and ran down the hill, back to the staff wing.

'You have the prettiest eyes, Dante. Be careful with them.'

His mother's words came back to him, the only person before this girl to have told him so. His memory filled with her beautiful but sad brown eyes. Running his hand through his hair, he bent down, picking up the half-smoked cigarette, put it to his lips, and lighted it again. Exhaling through his broken nose hurt like a bitch, but he welcomed the pain, looking down towards the lake and the cottage beside it.

He'd never thought he'd find anyone on this planet who hated his father more than him – until Tristan. Though just fourteen, the younger boy would one day pull the trigger on the old man, and Dante would happily give him the gun. He just had to bide his time, until he was ready, until the world was ready.

"You have to make a run to the city tomorrow."

Speak of the devil.

Dante ignored him.

Suddenly, his father came before him, his voice agitated, "What's all this blood? Did someone hit you?"

Dante didn't turn as his father's voice thundered through the grounds on the last word. The power play had begun. His father would flex his muscles, remind everyone who had authority there, just in case anyone could forget the suffocating fact, and everyone would go to their stations a little more fearful of Lorenzo Maroni.

Flicking the ashes to the ground, Dante stayed silent, continuing to smoke.

"Don't you dare ignore me, boy. Did someone hit you?"

"It's nothing," Dante stated. But it was useless. His father wasn't hearing him.

He shouted, calling to Al, his right-hand man, commanding everyone on the compound to gather on the ground.

Dante gritted his teeth, trying to watch the gorgeous sunset as minutes passed and people nervously gathered, silent but stinking of fear. That's how his father ruled – fear. And the only way to piss him off was to not react to it.

Finally throwing the cigarette on the ground, Dante crushed it under his shoe, his eyes glancing over the crowd. He spotted Zia holding her daughter, the young girl with the green eyes who had just told him he had pretty eyes. She was watching not his father but him.

He gave her a little wink, watching her flush and quickly look away, and he wanted to laugh in the middle of the shitshow. Moving his eyes over the group, he saw Tristan standing at the far side, slightly removed from everyone else, a blank expression on his face. If he thought Dante was going to rat him out, he had another thought coming.

"Who hit my son?" his father barked. He paused for dramatic effect, his eyes going over the gathering. When no one responded and looked adequately fearful, his father continued his tirade. "Who dare hit my heir? A Maroni! Tell me now or you will be punished. Tell me who did this. Attacking a Maroni on this compound is the biggest insult to me."

Nervous glances were exchanged. Hushed whispers rolled over. The sun slowly set.

"You stand on my land, and insult my blood," his father went on. "Tell me now, or the consequences will be severe for everyone."

A movement from the side drew everyone's eyes. Dante watched, surprised, as Tristan stepped out from the gathering, his eyes steady on Bloodhound.

"You," his father sputtered, marching up to Tristan. "You did this? You disgraceful little bastard. I own you. Everything you do here, I control. You cannot-"

Dante saw, adrenaline pouring in this system, as a young boy inches shorter than his father, stepped right into his face, nothing in his expression, and uttered his first words in public.

"You ever try to leash me, I'll fucking strangle you with it."

If angels could sing, that was the moment Dante heard the whole freaking choir.

Someone in the crowd gasped but Dante kept his eyes on Tristan. He had been right to trust his gut when it came to him. The younger boy stared his father down for a second, before turning on his heel and walking away without another word, leaving behind a speechless, seething Lorenzo Maroni.

Oh, this was going to be *good.*

Tristan had just sealed his fate.

Dante grinned. They were going to be buddies if it killed him.

3

Amara

13 YEARS

Amara had a problem and his name was Dante Maroni.
It was official.
It was done.

And she was absolutely miserable. Why? Because while he knew vaguely of her existence, she was nowhere, absolutely *nowhere* on his radar. And she? She had a crush the size of Antarctica but hotter. Way hotter. And she tried to stop. Really stop. But her heart was like a rubber-band where he was concerned. The more she pulled away mentally, the harder she felt the tug to go back to her original place.

It was all wrong. He was already eighteen-years-old, a fact that everyone in the entire city, the entire country, the entire underworld knew because him becoming an adult was a very big deal to a lot of people – some who wanted to back him, some who wanted to cut him. Dante already had enemies. How did Amara know all this already? She paid attention. It was amazing how much people tended to talk around the help without once realizing they were people with ears instead of moving furniture.

Amara wasn't really an employee of the Maronis, but she liked to help her ma out after school and on weekends. She used to spend that time with Vin but since he started training, his schedule and hers stopped matching. They did catch up every other day though. He had recently hit his growth spurt while Amara had barely moved an inch up.

She looked up at him from her spot sitting against the tree, her novel open on her lap but her eyes on her friend as he sparred with an older Dante. They did this almost once a week because according to the rumor mill, two kids in training were incredible with knives – Vin and Tristan, the new boy whom she'd started to refer to with his name after the Incident. She still remembered the shock that had coursed through her when he had laid out Mr. Maroni without any fear. Ma had told her that night that the boy had a death wish. Amara didn't disagree.

However, the reason Dante trained every other week with the knives with Vin instead of Tristan was because Vin was more cheerful and less likely to seriously kill him out of annoyance. They liked to train outdoors, in a little clearing right in front of Tristan's cottage by the lake. And every other week, Amara came with a book and her friend and planted herself quietly in front of a tree to watch the show.

If Dante thought it odd, he never commented. In fact, he rarely said a word to her after that first time she'd bumped into him. But he didn't ignore her either. She was just there. Some days, he'd give her a little nod and her heart would flutter like an overexcited hummingbird. Some days, he'd look at her and grin and her entire stomach would roll with butterflies. And some days, rare days, when he said a cordial 'hey', Amara would save his voice in her memory and squeal on the inside while planning their babies' names.

Ugh, she was *hopeless.*

Her mother didn't know what she did when she came to watch the boys. She thought Amara just went out in the sun to read during the summer break. Amara never corrected her. Not that her mother would stop her from going; she just wasn't ready to share this with anyone yet. Whatever this was because it passed a simple crush a while ago. And she was ninety-nine percent sure he didn't actually know her name.

The clang of metal on metal broke her out of her reverie. With all her adolescent heart, she focused on the man of her infatuations, watching his tall, very tall form move swiftly as a shorter, younger Vin attacked him.

Dante Maroni was a piece of art – a very fine, very exquisite piece of art. Every time she saw him, she wanted to do a chef's kiss gesture to the sky. Yeah, he was that good. From his dark, untamed, slightly overlong hair that framed an absolutely stunning face – a face that got more and more chiseled as he grew older – to that jawline Amara traced with her fingers in her daydreams, to his deep chocolate eyes that she still found the prettiest, to his arms that flexed with muscles as he moved… yup, she was a goner. It was pathetic.

Annoyed with herself, Amara looked down at the book she'd borrowed from the school library.

'The very instant that I saw you did my heart fly to your service…'

Okay, she needed to get some non-romantic poetry because Shakespeare wasn't really helping. Unable to focus, Amara looked up again to see the boys wrapping up their session. They always did that with Dante giving Vin some pointers. Vin, her chubby best friend who wasn't so chubby anymore, always listened seriously. Amara was pretty sure Vin had a man-crush on Dante. Who could blame him though?

Although in all honesty, Amara didn't even know if what she felt was even a crush anymore. A crush was supposed to die a natural death in a few months. At least that's what she heard the girls at her school say. She wasn't really close to them, or anyone at school. Outside kids treated the compound kids very weirdly. And all the other kids at the compound were either too younger or too older than she was. Only she and Vin were close in age, and that was why they'd just stuck together as soon as they could walk.

Vin nodded to Dante before walking to her, his dark hair cut much shorter now. Dropping down beside her, he took a sip of water from the bottle she handed him, both of them watching as Dante climbed the steps to Tristan's cottage and walked in the door without knocking.

"Damn," Vin whistled beside her, finally able to whistle properly. "He's got some big balls."

Ew. Amara did not want to think about Dante or his proverbial balls. Her love for him was very pure and sanitized at this point.

"I didn't need that picture in my head," she made a disgusted face. They had studied male and female reproductive systems at school last year. While that had been very clinical, the extra workshop their entire grade had had over the last month on sexual diseases, prevention, and contraception had been a lot to process. Amara knew Plug A went into Slot B but she didn't want to imagine anything related to that yet.

Vin chuckled. "With the way you stare at him, that's hard to believe."

That brought her up short. "What do you mean?" she asked, her voice coming out high as her heartbeat picked up. Ugh, she needed to work on her pitch. Her music teacher at school kept telling her she had a great voice but her pitch was totally off.

Vin shrugged. "You just look at him like he's Zia's best batch of cookies and you've been hungry for a month. Like he's fresh out of the oven and you're waiting for him to cool before eating."

Her stomach grumbled at that very vivid visual.

Okay. This wasn't good. This wasn't good at all. No one was supposed to know.

Amara swallowed. "Do you think he noticed?"

"It's kinda hard not to," Vin pointed out, clearly amused. "You come here every time and it's not to read your book."

Amara groaned. "Vinnie?"

"Hmm?"

"Kill me, please."

Her friend chuckled. "Oh, don't be so dramatic. It's not that bad. Plus, it's a phase. You'll grow out of it."

Amara shook her head. "I can't help it. Trust me, I've tried. My eyes are traitors."

Vin huffed a laugh before drawing his knees up, his hands dangling over them. "A crush is fine. Hell, it's even natural. But don't want more than that."

Amara turned to look at his profile as he stared at the cottage, feeling the sun on her skin. "Why?" she asked softly.

"Because he's Dante Maroni, 'Mara," Vin replied, equally soft. "We're young right now and it doesn't feel like anything. But he's going to be a king. He'll have enemies. Hell, he already does. He'll be everything dark and you're afraid of the dark, remember? You don't belong in that world. You deserve better."

The lump in her throat was lodged there tightly. Even though Amara never imagined anything, she knew Vin was right. Dante

Maroni was destined to rule the underworld. And she was the furniture people like him forgot about.

Breathing out through her mouth, Amara rested her head on Vin's shoulder, finding comfort in knowing he was someone who knew her, loved her as fully as she did.

"Will you be dark too, Vinnie?" she asked him quietly, wondering about where his fate was taking him. If his training, his father's life was anything to go by, it wasn't a good place.

"I don't know," he sighed. "But I'll never be dark for you."

Amara smiled slightly. "I'll love you anyway, you know."

"Yeah, me too," Vin nodded. "Please don't get mushy on me now."

Chuckling, Amara hit him lightly with her book, and they both watched as Dante Maroni came out of the cottage. He nodded to them, before climbing back up to his castle, a king in the making, while she stayed on the ground.

4

Dante

19 YEARS

The only good thing about becoming an adult was moving out of the main house and into his own wing. And although his brother at fifteen wasn't allowed, Dante sure as hell wasn't going to leave him behind.

Not a lot of people outside of the compound knew about Damien. The reason for that was pretty simple – Damien was Lorenzo Maroni's imperfect child. Somehow, he'd had the umbilical cord wrapped around his neck during his birth, which cut off his supply of oxygen for a few precious seconds, a few seconds too many. That had cost Damien his ability to gauge the world. Dante was sure he was on some spectrum of autism, especially because his mind was too high-functioning for his age while his social skills weren't good. It had never been properly diagnosed though, so he couldn't be sure.

Bloodhound Maroni could not accept that his younger son could have a mental condition that required some help. While he had the abundance of resources to get Damien help anytime, he turned a blind eye to his younger son. Even though he was a great kid, Dante knew he had issues expressing himself, certain behaviors that were not appropriate in the world but appropriate for him. Dante knew that Damien would never, ever find acceptance and love in the world he lived in, and he deserved both those things.

Dante wasn't even sure exactly what it was – trauma from his birth or the fact that he had been in the room when Dante found their mother pooled in her own blood or just one of those things. Some of that blood had been on a five-year-old Damien, and Dante at all of eight-years had stepped into the blood, scooped up his brother, and walked out of the room. Somehow, he had known his mother had been dead just by looking. Some days, he hated her so much for abandoning her children like a coward.

Dante took a deep breath, his fingers itching to pull out a cigarette but he refrained. Flexing his fingers, he watched the building from behind his expensive shades, taking measure as his pink-haired girlfriend, Roni, clung to his arm.

Morning Star Home for Lost Boys

He had heard about this place through the grapevine. One of their soldiers had a nephew who had been diagnosed with a low-functioning spectrum of autism and he said this place had helped the boy. While Dante was old enough to take care of his brother as he had been for a long time, he wanted Damien to get the help he needed and deserved. More importantly, the compound was not a good place mentally for any of them. Dante had already started going out of the city for trips and business, and every time his mind kept going back to Damien and his safety. Even though it lodged a rock on his chest, this was for the best.

"This place is creepy," Roni muttered, her delicate fingers curling over his bicep. She wasn't entirely wrong. Even though the place was a well-kept stone mansion with manicured lawns, it looked like something out of a thriller movie. Or maybe it was just the fog coming in with the approaching winter.

"Let's go," Dante shook off the feeling, pushing open the wrought iron gate with one palm, the cold of the metal sending a little shiver down his spine.

With the other hand, he guided his girlfriend of three years over the threshold. Roni was a little thing, like a pixie almost. Barely came to his neck, hair colored a bright pink and cut short, full of life. She was an outsider who knew about him and his family, and somehow she didn't care. Maybe it was the rebel in her, thrilling at the idea of him. Dante knew that's what it was for him.

He had spent so many nights sneaking out to see her, sneaking her into the compound. One time one of his father's men had caught them and he'd given him a finger, laughing the incident off. Had it been immature? Yes. Had he cared? Not really. He cared about Roni, felt affection for her, definitely loved having sex with her, but he wasn't in love. Roni was a way of rebelling against his father, and she knew it too, having accompanied him more than once as he'd sneaked her into the compound. Theirs was a relationship of mutual rebellion.

Walking down the small path towards the main entrance, Dante looked around with sharp eyes, noticing a few kids in the windows, all of different ages, peering down at them – some with curiosity, others with mild hostility. Dante wondered the kind of picture he must make to them – tall, ripped, dressed in an all-black expensive turtleneck, leather jacket, and jeans, hair carelessly around his face, with a pink-haired pixie on his side.

He smirked at the mental image as the door opened and an elderly woman greeted them, already expecting them, and took them on the tour.

One of the best parts about having his wing on the compound was privacy. Zia always came to the house once a week with staff to stack groceries and clean everything up, mostly when he was out training or in the city learning the business. Apart from that, he lived alone, and he liked it that way.

He'd set up the top floor of his house as his art room, just like his mother had done in the main house. The view from there was pretty fucking spectacular. He had a direct view of the lake, Tristan's cottage, and the sprawling hills covered with the woods beyond that. This early in the morning, when the sky was a fiery shade swallowing the black night, he loved to come to the room.

Setting his steaming mug of coffee on the work table, Dante looked at the pieces he had made over the last few years. The earliest pieces were pottery, practice pieces until his technique was refined. He started to play with masks after that; people's faces that he had seen, those that had somehow caught his attention. Most were pretty terrible and he wanted to smash them, but seeing them was an exercise in improvement. And Dante was determined to improve.

Sitting down on the bench, he got out the new box of clay he had bought from a supply store in the city and started to wet it as the audiobook for *Harry Potter and the Half-Blood Prince* played in the background. He enjoyed working at the early hours of the morning to the sound of words and the natural light of the sun filling his studio, in nothing but his boxers.

And he fucking loved *Harry Potter*. He hadn't read it for the longest time but finally gave in, and now he was hooked. One of the things he liked most about the series was how human it was, even in a magical world. Like Harry and Hermione's friendship, for example. It actually reminded him a lot of the relationship he saw between young Vin and Zia's daughter. For years, he's seen her accompany Vin whenever they trained in the open, and he was envious of that friendship.

He wanted a friend like that for himself. Even though he was surrounded by people, Dante didn't have one person who was his. His brother, though he loved him to pieces, wasn't his friend. Neither was Roni. And even though he'd been working on Tristan for years, neither was he. Tristan tolerated him at best, was indifferent to him at worst – although after breaking his nose, he had mellowed down a little where he was concerned. His last name didn't allow him any friends on the compound. Kings, as his father constantly reminded him, didn't have friends. They had enemies.

Fuck, he sounded like a sorry little bitch.

Shaking his head, Dante put a pile of wet clay before him, before kneading it with his hands, focusing on the stretch of the mass between his fingers. It was still too tight, and gauging when it got loose enough to mold was one of the most important things.

A knock on his backdoor had him pausing. There weren't many people who would come to his door that early in the morning unless it was an emergency. Getting up swiftly from the bench, Dante washed his hands and grabbed a pair of jeans before making his way down.

Descending the stairs, he pushed his hair back from his face, cut through the spacious kitchen, and opened the backdoor, freezing at the sight of Zia's daughter standing there in the chill.

Her eyes roamed over the exposed expanse of his chest, down his stomach, before she flushed and looked him in the eyes. Dante stifled a huff of amusement at her reaction. He knew the girl had a crush on him. She had a habit of staring at him whenever he was in the vicinity. It was flattering but it only amused him. She was too young, and he already had a girlfriend.

He liked to tease her though. Sometimes, when he caught her staring, he'd give her a wink and she'd blush and look away. Sometimes, when he caught her sitting with a book, he'd just ask her the name because he knew she loved reading romance and that made her blush. Or sometimes, she'd laugh with Vin and he'd just watch her, thinking how she'd grow up to be a stunner, he had no doubt, especially with her eyes.

"I'm so sorry to bother you," she spoke in a sweet voice, her nerves making the pitch a little high. Dante felt himself soften, wanting to ease her nerves.

"That's okay," he deliberately spoke in the comforting tone that always worked on calming Damien. "Are you fine?"

She blinked, before nodding. "Oh yeah, yeah. I'm good. Ma told me to give you this before I left for school." She trailed off and handed him foil wrapped tray.

Dante took it, careful not to brush her hands in the process, and lifted the foil. The scent of freshly baked cookies assaulted his nose, almost making him roll his eyes to the back of his head.

"She usually just brings these over herself," Dante commented, looking around to see if she had come too.

"Um," the girl nervously bit her lip, her skin turning a darker shade of red. "I wanted to bring them myself. It's, well, it's my birthday."

Dante grinned. "Happy birthday, um," his smile faltered, realizing he didn't know her name.

"Amara," she smiled shyly, the brazen kid who had once asked him his age hidden behind the young girl she was growing into. She had softened over the years.

"Well, happy birthday, Amara," he told her softly and saw her blush again. God, her crush was intense, but he wasn't going to call her out on it. His mother didn't raise him to be an asshole to women, as long as she'd been alive.

Giving him a little nod, she quickly went down the low steps and onto the lawns, heading back to the staff quarters situated about a few hundred meters away. What was she now? Fourteen? Fifteen? Dante watched her go, her form already tall for her age, her inky hair in a high ponytail that swayed in the morning wind.

He was about to shut the door when he saw Tristan heading into the woods quietly. Well, well, well, who was he to turn down such an invitation?

Even though he shouldn't leave his tools and clay out, Dante couldn't pass up the opportunity. Grabbing the leather jacket he'd thrown on the kitchen chair the previous night and pushing his feet into the heavy shoes by the door, Dante locked the door and sprinted out to the woods, determined to find out what his little buddy was up to. He wasn't really little anymore though. Tristan at sixteen was already filling out pretty solidly, his body a witness to his harsh training.

Dante wondered sometimes if he wouldn't have been the same in his shoes. Though he'd been training for years, Dante had yet to make his first kill. He had seen people executed, he had interrogated many of them himself, but the actual kill? He still had to take a life.

Maybe that left a mark on the soul. Maybe that was why Tristan was as he was. Killing, that too his own father, at such a young age after losing his sister. Some days, Dante wanted to give the bastard a hug. But he was pretty sure he'd come back missing a limb if he even tried.

After trying to find him for a few minutes, Dante realized he'd lost the guy. More likely, Tristan had shaken him off his trail. Sighing, he decided to head back and have some cookies, taking some over to Damien. At least his brother liked his company.

"You like the cookies?" Dante asked Damien as they sat in the gazebo behind the mansion, playing chess. Damien loved to play chess and Dante loved to play with him.

Damien's foot tapped in sets of three as he moved the knight, nodding. "These cookies taste better than last time. Her sugar content is lower this time."

Tap, tap, tap.

Tap, tap, tap.

Dante grinned. Trust his brother to note the technicalities in a cookie.

"Zia is nice. Her daughter brought me the cookies this morning," Dante informed him. "She has really nice green eyes that I think you'll like."

Damien looked up towards Dante's neck. He didn't like eye contact. "Did you know green eyes are the rarest in the world? Less than 2% of the entire population has them. What shade are hers?"

Dante recalled the eyes he'd seen that morning. "Um, forest green I think? Like the color of rainforest trees."

Movement from the side had him watching Tristan coming out of the woods. The younger boy stopped in his tracks, watching both Dante and Damien for a long minute, before walking off towards his cottage.

"They're the only eye color that can change shades depending on mood and light as well," Damien continued as Dante focused back on the chess, moved his piece, taking out a pawn. "It's called the Rayleigh effect. Does it happen to your Green Eye Girl?"

"Her name is Amara," Dante helpfully supplied but his brother had found his new little passion.

"Green Eye Girl-"

"And no, I don't think her eyes change color."

"-has an even rarer shade even in the spectrum of green eyes. If hers are the ones that don't change the color or follow the Rayleigh, that's even rarer. Fascinating-"

Dante smiled as Damien continued about the green eyes, playing chess.

Something was wrong.

Dante had made the arrangements for his brother to live at the home for a year, under the care of psychiatrists who could hopefully guide him into understanding himself and give him the tools he needed to navigate the world. He had spent the last hour talking to Damien about it too. While people underestimated Damien's intelligence, he was a keen boy. He understood that he needed more help than he got at the compound, and accepted a little trip out of the place as long as

Dante promised to visit him regularly. There wasn't a chance he wouldn't. He loved the little fucker.

But something was wrong. He didn't know what, couldn't put a finger on it. But there was a weight in his gut, an age-old voiceless scream at his protective instincts.

Could it be separation anxiety, perhaps? After all, it was the first time he'd be away from his brother.

'Your heart will always know your truth, Dante. Trust it.'

Was he lying to himself? God, this was a mess. No, it was the best for his brother to get away from this place and get a shot at a normal life.

The ringing of his phone brought him out of his conflict.

Father calling.

Peachy.

"Yes, father?" Dante addressed him as he always did, barely able to suppress his loathing for the man.

"Come to the shack."

End tone.

Gritting his teeth at the order, Dante walked out of the mansion, down the hill, to the shack in the woods. Once upon a time, the little shack had been a hunting shed. It was barely bigger than a few square feet, and mostly abandoned. Nobody really went there so it had been a pretty good place for his little trysts over the years.

Frowning as to why his father would call him that far out, Dante breathed evenly and adopted the little mask he usually wore around the older man. As much as he despised him, Dante admitted that he was a powerful leader and he didn't get to that place by being dumb. He was sharp and he scented weakness before anyone even knew about it.

There was both pride and shame in him for having that blood in his veins.

He saw his father standing outside the shed, dressed in a suit, his beard starting to show little greys here and there. And he was smoking a cigar. Not a good sign.

"You called?" Dante asked, joining him, realizing that he was taller than the other man now, much more casually dressed though. His father didn't like his attire. He didn't want Dante in ripped jeans and leather jackets, looking like the quintessential bad boy. No, he wanted Dante in suits and ties, looking like a good bad man.

Bloodhound Maroni smiled. "Yes. It's time."

Dante's stomach dropped, even as he kept his face even. It was time for the kill.

Taking a cigarette out of his pocket, he lit it up, and exhaled a cloud of smoke, seeing it swirl up at the cloudy sky. Usually, Dante loved the winters in Tenebrae. It got cold, wet, and snowy, and it made him love the summers even more. Not today though. Today, the clouds seemed gloomy, foreboding.

That feeling returned tenfold.

"Who is it?"

Lorenzo Maroni smiled again, a smile that made the back of Dante's neck prickle and went to the shack's door. Dante threw his cigarette to the side, crushing it under his boot before slowly approaching the door, to see who was inside.

Roni.

No.

Fuck, no.

She sat tied to a chair, tape over her mouth, her eyes red and swollen from tears as Al and Leo stood behind her.

Tension knotting on his shoulders, he turned to look at his father, his spine rigid as his hands fisted. "What the fuck is this?" he demanded.

"This," his father said with a theatrical flourish, "is what you created, my son. You thought you would get involved with an outsider, a common girl, and I would do nothing?"

He hadn't thought of what his father would do. He might be indispensable but she wasn't. He should have thought of it. Fuck, he should have.

"Let her go," he told the older man, his voice firm. "I won't see her again."

Lorenzo Maroni shook his head, finally putting out his own cigar. "This is a lesson, son. A lesson you need to remember. Love has no place in our world."

Dante locked his jaw. "You loved mama," he reminded the man.

His father laughed. "No, I didn't. I wanted her, so I took her. That's what men like us do. You're too soft and I've let it go on too long."

"What do you mean you took her?" Dante stared at his father, surprise filling him, followed by disgust at the implication. He had never imagined what his father was hinting at.

"Took. Snatched. I saw her and took her right from her car, brought her here, married her," his father said, almost proudly.

Dante thought of his mother, beautiful, warm, but always sad, acid in his stomach. "Did you rape her?"

"Why does it matter?"

He had.

Disgust filled Dante, bile rising his throat as he swallowed it down. He looked away from the man who had sired him, perhaps forcefully, on his mother, and his skin crawled.

Roni whimpered, making him look at her small form. She didn't deserve this. She really didn't deserve this. She was an amazing girl, and the closest thing he had to a true friend. His first lover. She made him laugh. She didn't deserve these ropes and tape.

His heart clenched, processing everything he had been told and everything he was seeing. He had to get her out. Somehow.

"Leo tells me you've gotten excellent with knives," his father's voice cut to the desperation filling him. Dante focused on his words, his heart slamming as the words dawned on him.

"Let her go, father," he looked to the man, his eyes burning. "I swear fealty to you. I swear to follow every command you make. I swear to never see her again. Just please, let her go. I'm begging you."

"Don't beg!" his father yelled at him, grabbing him by the arm. "You are a Maroni! Maroni's don't beg, not even on their deathbeds. Do you understand?"

Dante nodded, letting his father shake his arm. Fear filled him at how the situation was unfolding. Huffing out a breath, his father cooled himself down, looking back at Dante again.

"Take this as another lesson," he continued speaking, almost in a gentle voice. "Always have the upper hand when you're bargaining. Right now, you have nothing. I am the one holding the power. What happens to this girl is under my control. What happens to your brother is under my control. You want him to get the help he needs? Kill the girl. A life for a life."

Dante breathed out slowly, his mind racing to find a way, find a loophole, something, anything.

Nothing.

Fuck.

There had to be something.

Roni whimpered again.

Dante went to kneel before her, in a way he had kneeled before her countless times and saw her tears drench her face, words trapped between them. His head dropped to her lap, his hands gripping her chair.

"You don't kill her," his father's voice said in that same even tone, "I'll give her to the men who will have her first and kill her later. She will suffer. You, on the other hand, can give her mercy, my boy."

No.

No.

He couldn't. This was his fault. He never should have gotten involved with her. So many years they had spent together, and this is what it had come to.

"You have two minutes to choose."

Two minutes.

One hundred and twenty seconds.

Suddenly, Dante could hear every beat of his heart pounding in his head, the blood rushing to his ears, ticking like a time bomb, every second closer to detonation.

He looked up at the wide, frightened blue eyes of the young girl who had dared to stay with him, knowing what he would choose. He couldn't let her suffer, not at the hands of his father's men. He couldn't let her die like that.

He couldn't do shit. He was a helpless little asshole who'd thought he could get away with playing with fire, without burning himself or his lover.

"Motherfucker!" he screamed in helpless frustration, getting up to pick an empty chair, throwing it across the room.

He looked back at his father, his heart racing. "Don't make me do this."

"One minute," came the reply.

Grabbing fistfuls of his hair, Dante shook, howling at the ceiling in his helplessness, not wanting to do the one thing he knew he had to do to spare her.

"Thirty seconds."

Tension climbed up in the room.

Exhaling out a deep breath, Dante slowly let a sense of calm wash over him. Without a word, he walked to his father and took the knife from the inside of his coat pocket, the little weight feeling like a rock in his hand. "You unleash this beast, father, do it knowing that one day, it will kill you too. This is your last chance to stop this madness."

His father almost smiled proudly. The man was fucking *fucked* in the head.

"Time's up, son."

Closing his eyes for an instant, Dante was tempted to slice him with the knife. But it wouldn't solve anything – Roni would still die and the underworld would get thrown into chaos he wasn't ready to handle yet.

Taking the knife, he went back to his kneeling position, and removed the tape from her mouth, wet with her tears.

"There has to be a way, Dante," Roni's voice shook, trembling with her body. "Please don't do this."

Dante looked her in the eyes, his own burning, throat tight. "Forgive me, Roni," he could hear his voice roughened with pain.

With that, he thrust the blade right into her heart.

Her scream penetrated the air, her throat gurgling as blood seeped out from the stab wound. Hands shaking, he pulled the blade out and put it on her neck – the same neck he had kissed so many times – slitting her carotid artery, giving her as instant a death as he could. She didn't deserve this. This, this was on him.

Through it all, he held her eyes, seeing the life slowly seep from her body as his own changed with every passing second, his heart hardening.

"Dan…" she choked on her blood one last time, before going limp.

It was over in seconds.

Dante kept looking at her vacant face, feeling her blood pool around them, something cold, cold settling into his heart. He hadn't been able to protect her. His first lover, his first kill.

Someone clapped him on the back. His father.

Dante looked at his hands stained with her blood, felt the rage for the man simmer, and took a deep breath.

Now isn't the time.

One day. He would make him pay, for his mother, for his brother, for Roni. One day. He just had to wait. He just had to wait and patiently dig his grave. He just had to play not in the open like he had been playing, but in the shadows where Bloodhound Maroni wouldn't scent him.

One day.

"Bury her," he heard his father order Al.

No.

Dante shook his head, his heart heavy, his body covered in her blood. "I'll do it."

After a pause, his father nodded to the men to clean up the shack and left. Dante stood, his arms slightly shaking as he cut through the ropes tying her, and hauled her up. Her body felt heavy, heavier than it had when he'd carried her before.

Without looking at the men, he walked out of the shack and deeper into the woods, the silence, the cold, and her body his only company. He felt the first tear escape his eyes and tightened his jaw, blinking to clear his vision as he edged closer to the lake. No. He wouldn't cry. His father was right – this was a lesson, a lesson to never, ever expose any weakness, anything that could be used against him, at least not where anyone could see. That was where he'd failed Roni.

He was smart, he was sharp, and he was cunning. And going forward, he was going to use every single one of those things to his favor, while letting his father think he was on a leash. A mask. He would wear a mask.

"Here."

Dante turned at the voice, to see Tristan standing in a small clearing with a shovel and a pile of clothes beside him, a hole in the ground between them. He looked at the younger boy, surprised, but stayed silent.

Quietly, Tristan took out a cotton sheet and laid it on the ground, indicating for Dante to place Roni's body on it. Dante did, almost on autopilot, looking one last time at another lifeless body of a woman he had cared for. Tristan wrapped up her corpse, tying the sheets in precise knots that had Dante clenching his jaw.

"Your clothes too," the younger boy said briskly. Dante realized he was right. The clothes were covered in blood. They needed to go.

Taking off his leather jacket, Dante held it in his hands for a second, realizing he would probably never wear one again, and threw it in the hole. Stripping off the rest of his clothes, standing in the freezing wind naked, he felt the cold seep deep into his bones, to his heart.

"Go clean up," Tristan nodded to the lake, and Dante, for some reason, listened to the boy. His mind wasn't working. The water was frigid, but the cold didn't penetrate this brain. As he took the water and rubbed at his skin, he realized things inside him were shifting. After everything that had happened in the last hour, Dante was not the same. Though he was washing the blood off his skin, it had already seeped into his pores, mixing with his veins, a scar on his heart every time it beat.

Clean as he could be, Dante walked back to the grave, to see Tristan almost finished with covering it up. It was unexpected, this little assistance. Considerate, even. He never would have described the boy like that.

Swooping down to pick up the clothes in a pile beside him, Dante found his own white sweater and jeans and shoes. Frowning, he looked at the seventeen-year-old dedicatedly covering the ground.

"Did you break into my house?" he asked, mildly surprised.

Tristan shrugged, a fine sheen of sweat on his face. "Wasn't hard to break into."

Dante shook his head. Quickly dressing, he went to sit down by the lake, and looked up at the mansion on the hill, crowned above the woods, flexing his fingers. Tristan came to sit beside him after a few minutes, throwing the shovel to the side, handing him a bottle of Jack Daniels from Dante's stash.

Dante almost chuckled at that, before sobering. "Are we friends now?"

"No."

"So what's this? You watch my back and I watch yours kinda deal?"

"Fuck off, asshole."

What he expected.

Taking a swig from the bottle, he passed it to Tristan even though they were underage for it. They were underage for a lot of shit they did. What was the right age to kill someone, after all?

"That shouldn't have happened," Tristan spoke after a long beat of silence.

"No," Dante agreed. "It shouldn't have."

"You gonna do something about it?" the other boy asked, the most he had said in a conversation with Dante.

"Yeah," Dante nodded, his eyes on the mansion lights turning on. "But not today."

"Good."

The clouds got darker, the wind chillier as night approached. Minutes went by.

"How do you move past it?" Dante asked him quietly. "How do you forget?"

"You don't."

Yeah, he didn't think they could.

"Thanks," Dante muttered after taking another swig from the bottle. "I appreciate this."

He was met with silence, but for once, it was companionable.

And so they sat that night, two young killers, one fresh and one seasoned, swallowing down alcohol to drown the chaos inside them, and knowing that love truly didn't have a place in their lives.

Amara

15 YEARS

She never told anyone about the body.

That day, walking deep in the woods, Amara had witnessed the two big boys burying a young girl, the same pink-haired girl she had seen Dante kissing all those years ago. Scared out of her mind, she had run home and stayed in bed for a week after that, worried that someone would come after her for seeing what she had seen.

Nobody had. Her mother had simply thought it had been a bad period, and let her stay indoors. She hadn't gone to school, hadn't even met Vin that week, giving him the same excuse. However, after a week of anxiety and a whole lot of nothing, she had finally accepted that nobody had seen her and slowly gone about her life.

Her feelings for Dante though? Conflicted.

She didn't know what it said about her. On the one hand, she didn't understand what kind of a man – and he was a man now – would bury the body of his lover. On the other hand, she still found him attractive, more attractive in fact, as time went by. Perhaps, it was because she had grown up on the compound, and had always known that the people around her weren't morally white. Hell, she was seeing her own best friend training himself into a weapon. She saw his bruises, saw his muscles build over time because he was being conditioned.

What was morality, anyway? That night had triggered her into giving that some serious thought. Being a good person and doing good things weren't always the same. As she was growing older, Amara realized there was a very fine line between them. Her hero could be the villain in someone else's story. Though she hated blood, if one day someone threatened her mother or even Vin, would she not hurt them? Was she incapable of taking another life?

People weren't black and white, and sadly, neither were emotions.

She knew her thoughts were not that of a fifteen-year-old, but what she had witnessed had impacted her. She stopped going to the outdoor training sessions after that and started avoiding Dante. She never went to his door again, and now if he came to Vin while she was there, she simply excused herself and left. Her feelings for him were pretty much all over the place.

He had noticed her behavior. One time, she'd heard him corner Vin and ask 'is Amara ignoring me?' and she'd run in the opposite direction. One time she'd stumbled upon him playing chess with his brother in the gazebo behind the house and ran away. Not one of her finest moments, she admitted. He'd tried to corner her a few times too over the past year, and she had eluded him every time. She knew she should just tell him it was nothing, but he freaked her out a bit. He didn't scare her or anything, but he'd become a little more intense over the past year and Amara had become a bit of a worrywart.

"Mumu?" her mother called her from the kitchen, and Amara put down the book she'd been reading, placing her handmade bookmark to mark her page, and walked out of her room.

"Yes, Ma?" she asked, suddenly coming to a halt at seeing a big, big Dante Maroni standing in the space of her small kitchen. He had never, not in all the time she'd harbored her crush on him, come to their little apartment.

Her heart, the traitorous little thing, started to thump extra hard breathing the same air as he was.

Not the time for this.

"Dante wants to talk to you," her mother informed her, her deep green eyes alight with curiosity and a little apprehension. Amara was certain hers mirrored the same expression. There was no reason for him to want to talk to her, not like this. Not unless he somehow knew that she knew about the body.

Her heart sank.

Oh god.

Swallowing, Amara nodded and indicated the backdoor, silently asking him to talk outside. The backdoor of the staff building opened right to the edge of the woods. No chances of anyone overhearing the conversation out there.

Grabbing the cashmere wrap Vin had gifted her for her birthday a week ago, Amara draped it over her shoulders, pushing her stocking-clad feet into warm boots by the door, and walked out into the bright, cold morning. He followed her, closing the door behind him.

The cool wind blew around her, bringing the scent of the trees and the soil and cologne. Cologne? Amara sniffed softly and realized it was indeed cologne. He was wearing it, the scent woodsy and musky and reminding her of fire crackling over wood and twisted sheets. Yeah, her thoughts weren't so pure anymore.

Down, girl.

"Mumu?" he asked her, his tone slightly amused, his long legs matching her pace. Though she was tall at five feet eight inches – thanks to a sudden growth spurt that had given her inches and stopped – surprisingly, she only reached his chin.

Amara wrapped her arms around herself, forcing a small smile to cut through the tension in her head. "Yeah, I used to call my mother ma and myself Mu when I was a kid. It stuck."

Dante nodded. "My brother used to do something similar."

"I never see him around here anymore," Amara commented before biting her tongue. She shouldn't have said that.

"He's not here. He visits sometimes."

Leaving it at that, since it wasn't her place, Amara stopped at the edge of the woods and turned to face him, taking in his form. After that night with the dead body, unless he'd been training shirtless with Vin, Amara had only seen Dante wearing crisp button-down shirts and pants. A heavy metal watch glinted on his strong wrist, his jacket tailored for his body. And the cologne, Not to forget the cologne. She seriously felt underdressed in her plain grey woolen dress and wild hair.

His hair swayed in the gentle breeze as his dark, soulful eyes regarded her steadily.

"Is something going on?" he asked, his voice matching the warm chocolate of his eyes, making her want to cuddle up with a cat and a book. Then, his words penetrated.

Amara forced herself to hold his gaze as her hands gripped her elbows under the wrap. "What do you mean?"

He quirked a dark eyebrow, thrusting his hands in his pockets. "You've been acting weird."

Amara felt her hackles rise, her brows coming down even as her heart raced. "No offense, Mr. Maroni, but you don't know me well enough to know how I'm acting."

Her words had some sort of an effect on him. Amara didn't know what that was exactly but something cackled between them, something electric, raising the little hairs on the back of her neck and arms with its intensity as she held his haze.

After a long moment of silence, his other eyebrow joined its companion on his forehead. "I just wanted to check if you were okay. I have a feeling you've been deliberately avoiding me for some reason for a while now, and I don't know why. I don't like it."

He really shouldn't have added that last part. Her poor heart started working double-time to keep up. Amara focused on the first part of his sentence. She couldn't very well say, *'because I saw you bury the body of a girl I saw you kiss once upon a time',* could she? No.

"You shouldn't even be noticing that, Mr. Maroni," she pointed out, her pitch starting to climb again before she leashed it. "I'm of no consequence to you."

Dante tilted his head to the side, seeing her. Like *seeing her,* seeing her. *Really* seeing her. Uh-oh.

"It's odd you'd say that. My mother used to often tell me," he mused quietly after a moment, his eyes on hers. "People are like chess pieces. Anyone on the board is of consequence."

Amara shook off the little tremor that started at the base of her spine. "And you think I'm on the board?"

"I don't know yet," he said softly, still watching her avidly.

There was silence after that. What did one even say to something like that? Amara broke their stare and looked down at the scuffed toes of her boots, in front of the shining shoes he had on. The mud at the bottom of those expensive shoes just screamed how usual they were for him. They weren't for her. Her usual was thrift stores and second-hand books and used furniture. Though the Maronis paid well, she and her mother lived modestly. Mostly, her mother put savings in the bank for their future. Gazing down at the differences between their lives laid out at their feet, Amara wondered why he was even talking to her.

Clearing her throat, Amara looked up at the man she had been infatuated with since before she knew the word and accepted a healthy dose of reality. He might be nice enough to check in on her but he was also the man who owned this entire hill they were standing on, the man who had buried a girl he'd been intimate with. They existed in different planes. Guys like him didn't have an interest in girls like her. They liked the daughters of their rich business partners, elegant beauties they could have on their arms and make soft, sensual love with while playing power games with their families.

She needed to get over this, whatever this was.

"If that's all, Mr. Maroni?"

"Dante," he corrected almost absently. "Seriously, why are you avoiding me?"

Amara shook her head, sighing. "I'm not."

"Liar," his eyes darkened, his gaze lasered on her. "It bothers me."

Amara felt herself becoming surprised at that, but she stayed on track. "I don't know what you want me to say. It's very nice of you to check in on me, but unnecessary. Have a good day."

With that, she left him standing there and simply walked to her door without looking back at him, her emotions in turmoil in her chest. She entered the house and closed the door behind her, leaning against it and taking a deep, long breath.

"Everything okay?" her mother asked, looking up at her from the dough she was kneading.

Amara nodded, taking the wrap off her shoulders.

"You want to talk about it?" her mother asked, voice gentle. Amara went around the counter and hugged her from the back, taller than her by a few inches. Burying her nose in her mother's skin, she smelled the clean scent of the citrus soap she used, the moisturizer, and the sugar. She smelled of home.

Feeling something inside herself unknot at the scent, Amara reassured her. "There's nothing to talk about, Ma."

"Of course," her mother chuckled, continuing to push the dough. "Not like you fancy him or anything."

Amara pulled back, disbelieving. "Did Vin tell you that?" her voice came out a little too high for her comfort. *Pitch control,* her music teacher's voice reprimanded in her head.

"He didn't have to," her ma shrugged, giving her a little look. "Pass the cinnamon."

Amara absently took it out from the shelf, handing it over silently. "Then how did you know?"

"I'm your mother," her ma stated, as though that was explanation enough. It was, in a way. Her mother saw too much where she was concerned.

"It's just a crush, Ma," Amara said casually. "It'll pass." She really, truly hoped so.

Her mother didn't call her out on the fact that it hadn't passed in five years, and for that, Amara loved her a little bit more.

A few days later, she came out the back door of the mansion with some supplies for the gardener when she saw him sitting with his usually absent brother in the gazebo, playing chess of all things. She started to spin on her heels when suddenly he called her out.

"Amara, come meet my brother."

Amara sighed. While she really kind of didn't want to stay in his space, it would have been very impolite, outright rude, to his brother whom she'd never met. Pasting a smile on her face, she walked forward towards the gazebo and immediately noticed the similarities between the two boys – the same dark hair, the same tall build, the same cut of the jaw. They were brothers, alright.

She also noticed that his brother hunched over slightly, keeping his gaze super focused on the chessboard.

"This is Damien," Dante said in that voice that sent butterflies rolling in her tummy. "Damien, this is Amara."

"Green Eye Girl," Damien said in an almost toneless voice.

Dante chuckled, turning to the side, casually leaning against the marble pillar. "Yeah, Green Eye Girl."

"Hello, Green Eye Girl," Damien said in that same toneless voice, moving a piece. "Are her eyes really the color of forests?"

"Why don't you see for yourself?" Dante dared him and looked at the board.

Damien glanced up at her, his dark eyes fleetingly coming to hers for two seconds, before he looked back at the board again, tapping his foot on the ground in sets of three.

Dante looked at him in surprise, before glancing at her. "He looked you in the eye."

Amara felt a little awkward but amused. Before she could say anything, the gardener called her from the back. She said her goodbyes and ran back, happy for the escape from his company.

It was the noise that made her do it.

There was a party at the mansion celebrating something, and it was an all-hands-on-deck kind of event. Since it was the weekend, she had pitched in to help out her mother and run around getting everything organized. Parties were the worst to execute. It left her mother so tired afterward, and the idiot Maronis didn't have the bright idea of hiring someone to split duties with her mother. Not like they couldn't afford it.

Amara walked down the mansion's corridor, her hands full of crisp, white, freshly laundered, and ironed sheets when she heard the noise.

After the last time she'd seen something she shouldn't have, Amara really didn't want to investigate. There was no sense borrowing trouble, and the mansion was creepy enough as it was when it was empty.

Determined to ignore it, Amara started on her way when the noise came again, halting her in her tracks. It came from behind one of the closed doors.

Amara looked up and down the corridor, trying to see if anyone was coming that way. It was the third floor and it was deserted.

Taking a deep breath, she put the clothes on a table by the wall, nudging a crystal vase aside. Who the hell kept a crystal vase on the third floor in an abandoned corridor? Crazy rich people.

Hushed voices came from behind the door, and Amara tiptoed forward, bending down to peek inside the keyhole.

Mr. Maroni, the older Mr. Maroni, stood over a man, a gun held to his temple.

"Will you give your masters the message or should I send one with your body?" he asked quietly as the man in the chair whimpered. That was the noise she'd heard. Whimpering.

Amara felt her heartbeat in her throat as she cast a quick look around the corridor again, ensuring it was empty, before watching what was happening inside. She saw Mr. Maroni's brother – or was he the cousin? – come into view, his back to Amara's vantage.

"I think we should talk to them ourselves, Lorenzo," he spoke in a gravelly voice that sent a shiver down Amara's spine. "The Syndicate won't care if this cunt goes missing, not if they get their delivery on time."

"I want in, Leo," Lorenzo Maroni said. "It's been years since they stopped us. X says we can try again and I want it to be a powerful message. Would he deliver that message alive or dead?"

"I think you should talk to X," Leo suggested.

The man in the chair cried out. "You know that's not how they do things. After what happened with your first shipment, they won't let you. You messed up and now rumors say your son…"

"…is out of the picture," Lorenzo Maroni stated with finality. "Dante can never know about this."

Know what?

His cousin spoke again. "The shipment will go out in three days from the old warehouse, with or without him. We don't need this guy."

RUNYX

There was silence in the room. Amara barely dared to breathe, her hands gripping the side of the doorframe so she didn't lose her balance. She should go. She really should. But her feet stayed glued to the spot, her one eye looking into the room.

"Let's send him back with the message," Lorenzo Maroni nodded, before suddenly pointing the gun at the man's shoulder and pulling the trigger.

The loud noise ricocheted in the room, startling Amara. A yelp left her before she could stop it. Clapping a hand over her mouth, she stumbled back from the door, hurriedly picking up the laundry and running down the hallway. Her heart hammered in her chest as she heard the door behind her open, and she sprinted down the stairs, her feet going as fast as they could.

One floor down.

Two floors down.

Amara hit the ground level and ran to the kitchen, the area bustling with staff getting everything ready for the party. Shoving the laundry in the hands of one of the surprised servants, she ran down the gallery towards the back entrance.

Only to collide into a brick wall.

Shaking, Amara looked up to see Dante Maroni holding her by the arms, keeping her upright, a look of concern on his face.

"Hey, hey, are you okay?"

Amara looked at him with wide eyes and nodded. Mr. Maroni had said he couldn't know. She didn't even know what it was but she

82

couldn't tell him. What would be the point? What she witnessed in that room wasn't anything new in this world. She was the one who was having a hard time processing it.

"Yeah, um," she floundered for words, panting. "I think I left the oven on at home. I just- I just need to check it."

She started to pull away when his grip on her arms tightened a fraction, not enough to hurt but enough to keep her in place.

"Look at me," he said in a tone she'd never heard from him before. Commanding her attention. Unwittingly, her eyes went to his dark browns, to see them studying her.

"What the *fuck* is going on with you?" he demanded, his gaze steady on hers, alert.

Amara straightened her spine, knowing she had to push him off. Nobody could know she'd seen anything, for her and her mother's safety. "It doesn't concern you. Will you let go of my arms?"

Dante's fingers stayed wrapped around her biceps, almost entirely encircling them, his touch burning through the fabric of her top. The tension from earlier built between them again as they stared the other down, one that hadn't been there in any of their previous interactions. His fingers flexed once, jaw visibly clenching before he released her. Amara swallowed and walked out of the mansion at a fast clip.

Heart still pounding, she looked back to see him still standing at the same spot, watching her leave. She wanted to tell him, but it was nothing compared to what he probably saw every day. And she didn't even know the man. She had grown up crushing on him but she didn't know who he was.

It was better she never say anything to anyone.

Amara gulped the secret down, shoving it to the recesses of her mind, and kept walking back to her house.

"Damn, you clean up nice!" Amara exclaimed, looking at Vin as he came out from the store. He looked very dashing in an ironed black button-down shirt tucked into black pants, a simple belt around his narrow waist. At sixteen, he was already filling out like a heartbreaker.

They had come to the city because Vin had needed something more formal for the party, and since he could already drive, he had borrowed his dad's car and they'd made it a trip. Amara had needed the excursion to get her head right. And buying a beautiful dress had only helped with that.

It was a gorgeous dark green dress with a modest neckline and full sleeves. The color brought out her eyes, the hemline fell to her knees. Amara had seen it and fallen in love.

They had both decided to get ready at the store itself, so they could go straight to the party. Vin had patrolling duty with the other security staff, which was a big deal since boys his age were never allowed that job. And Amara had decided to help her mother out so while she would be at the party, she would be working.

"Yeah, yeah," her friend tugged at his collar, his tell for when he got uncomfortable, and Amara grinned. Walking to the car through the empty lot, Amara pulled her hair into a high ponytail, so it wouldn't get in the way.

"Do you think I should try wearing lipstick tonight?" she asked Vin, who groaned at her question.

"You need girlfriends to talk that shit with, 'Mara," he told her, pulling the car keys out of his pocket.

Amara linked her arm with his. "But I've got you. Will I look pretty with lipstick?" she teased him, and he gave her a droll look.

"You forget I've seen you with snot on your face too many times," he rolled his eyes. "And licking the wall-"

"Hey, that was just one time and I was three!"

"-and you'll look nice," he finished over her. "If you want to, wear the damn lipstick."

Amara laughed, elbowing him in the ribs. "You're so bad. So, how was training today?"

The evening got colder as they walked closer to the car.

"Good," Vin replied, shoving his hands in his pockets. "Dante asked me about you today."

Amara almost tripped over her feet but kept gripping his arm. Trying to aim for nonchalance, she casually asked. "Really? What did he ask?"

"If you and I were a thing," Vin's voice had the same cringe she felt. She could see why people would assume that given they were joined at the hip, but neither of them was into each other that way. Ew. "I think he's into you."

"Did you correct him?" Amara asked as they came to a stop at the dark sedan they had driven in, ignoring his last sentence.

"I asked him why he wanted to know," Vin informed her, walking around to the driver's side with the bag holding their old clothes. "I mean you're my best friend, and we know the score. But I think he's weirded out that you don't pay attention to him anymore. And if thinking you're with me is any protection for you, let him think whatever."

And this was why she loved this guy. Her hero.

She gave him a smile over the roof of the car. "You're a sweetheart, Vinnie."

"Fuck, will you not call me that out in the open?" he quickly looked around, making Amara laugh.

Her laughter cut off before it was even out.

Before she could say anything, a hand slammed over her mouth, snatching her violently away from the car. A truck came screeching into the parking lot as one man went over to Vin's side, both of them getting into a hand-to-hand fight before the older, larger guy held Vin down, one putting a hand over his mouth as well.

Amara watched, horrified, as the man slammed him to the hard concrete on his stomach, incapacitating him.

"Take the girl."

Amara yelled behind her captor's hand, the smell of raw tobacco drowning in her nostrils as she struggled against him. She brought the heel of her ballet flats down on the man's toes, enough to make him grunt but not enough to loosen his hold. The man started to drag her back towards the waiting truck and she kicked her feet, one of her flats coming free in the tussle.

She saw the man over Vin hit him over the head with an elbow, saw Vin go limp on the ground, and started to wrestle against her captor with all her might, her heart slamming at a furious pace inside her chest.

"Fuckin' bitch won't stop moving," the man behind her complained to his companion. Damn right, she wasn't going to stop moving. Somehow, she managed to trap some skin of his hand between her teeth and bit down as hard as she could.

The man yelled, pulling his hand away enough for her to scream.

"Help!"

A cloth filled her mouth, gagging her, muffling any sound she tried to make.

"Get her in the truck," one of the men said and Amara struggled harder, her lungs starting to burn from the exertion.

She looked with wide eyes as the masked man facing her grunted in pain and turned around.

Vin stood behind the guy, coming at him with the knife he always kept on him. Her eyes tracked them feverishly, seeing Vin go from attack to defense. The other guy was clearly not just bigger, but also more experienced than her friend.

He grabbed ahold of Vin's knife hand, snapping his wrist, making her friend grunt in pain. Amara thrashed against the man holding her, trying to get to him. She watched in horror as the man took the knife and slashed her friend's face open.

It was Vin's loud howl of agony that had the man cursing and throwing the knife to the ground.

"We gotta hurry," he told the guy holding her and they began to drag her back towards the running vehicle. Amara saw someone running towards Vin as the men pushed her into the trunk, and everything went dark.

Amara

15 YEARS

A mara blinked her eyes open, disoriented as she came to in an unfamiliar room.

It looked like the inside of a prison cell, only cleaner, almost sterile. The walls were a weird shade of off white she had never really seen on walls before. The door in front of her was wooden, heavy, and brown. A smaller door was to her right. And it was dark, not enough to be pitch black since there was enough light coming from under the door to allow her visibility. But it was dark enough to make her uncomfortable.

Amara pulled her arm up to rub the bleariness out of her eyes, only to stop short as she felt the heavy metal around her wrists.

Slightly more alert, she looked down at her hands, to see manacles, actual manacles, locking her in place, attached to chains, hooked to the wall behind her.

Heart starting to beat faster as memories came flooding in, Amara looked around the room, trying to find a weapon, a key, anything that could help her escape. There was nothing – no windows in the room, no furniture except an empty table against the wall opposite her. She was sitting on the ground.

And even though her mouth felt full of cotton, she didn't actually have anything gagging her.

Swallowing down her dry throat, Amara contemplated making a noise. She didn't know anything about her attackers. She didn't know who they were or why they had come for her. Could it be accidental? Maybe they had mistaken her for someone else? She was the housekeeper's daughter and not important at all. It didn't make sense.

On the tail of that thought, the door unlocked and swung open, light flooding the room, momentarily blinding her. Amara blinked a few times to let her eyes adjust as the man who had slashed Vin's face entered the room with a bottle of water. In the shadows, Amara could barely see him clearly, while he could see her completely since the light fell on her. The only things she could make out – he was heavyset, possibly bearded.

"Morning, bitch," the man hopped on the table opposite her, making the wood creak under his weight. "Sleep well?"

Amara gulped, staying silent. God, she hoped they didn't hurt her. She couldn't stand the pain. She'd never been able to. *Please let this be a misunderstanding.*

The man threw the small bottle beside her. The plastic crashed into the wall before rolling towards her. Was it drugged?

"Not drugged," the man clarified, evidently reading her thoughts. "We're gonna have a little chat, that's all."

She didn't believe him. There was something in the tone of his voice, something too casual in the way he'd framed that sentence that made Amara very wary. Looking down at the bottle, Amara felt tempted to pick it up but refrained. She was thirsty but she'd rather stay conscious.

After seeing she wasn't picking the bottle up, the man asked, "You know who we work for?"

She had zero ideas. She shook her head, not knowing if that was the smart thing to do.

"Good, that's very good," the man nodded encouragingly, and Amara took a breath in relief. Okay, ignorance was the good thing.

"Do you know why you're here?"

Amara shook her head again, pulling down at the hem of her dress as nerves assaulted her, blood rushing to her ears.

The man leaned forward, putting his elbows on his knees, still too much in the dark for her to make out his features. "You're here to give us some answers. You do that, nobody is going to get hurt, and we let you go. Got that?"

A shiver started at the base of her spine, lead settling in her gut. He was lying. She could tell. They weren't going to let her go.

But she nodded in reply.

"You know Lorenzo Maroni?" the man asked, taking out a cigarette and putting it to his mouth. He lit a match, momentarily throwing a little light on his features, before taking a huge puff. The smoke didn't smell like the usual cigarette; it was sweet, almost cloyingly so as she inhaled it.

"I...I know of him," Amara stuttered, her body filling with adrenaline as her heartbeat spiked. God, why was she there? It didn't make any sense. She didn't know what this man wanted from her.

"You've never seen him?"

"Just in passing," Amara said, her voice climbing as her nerves attacked her, her habit coming to the fore under the tremendous strain on her mind.

The man nodded, taking out his phone and showing her the image of a man. "Can you see him?"

Amara squinted slightly, looking at the picture. It was the photo of a bald man wearing glasses. He seemed familiar but she didn't recognize him. It was possible she'd seen him on the compound.

"Ever seen him?"

Amara shook her head. "I think you have the wrong person," she said hopefully, trying to reason with him. "Please just let me go. I don't know anything."

She heard him laugh, and Amara's blood chilled.

"Oh, I have the right person," he assured her, his voice setting all her alarm bells ringing. "Tell me about Dante Maroni."

Amara felt her heart stop for a second, before continuing the hard rhythm. "He's Lorenzo Maroni's son."

"Yes. He's a mean fucker, that one," the man huffed out. "He ever talk business with you?"

She shook her head. "I barely know Dante."

"That's not what a little birdie told me," the man sing-songed. "In fact, I heard you two looked awfully cozy with each other, if you know what I mean."

A vigorous shiver wracked her.

"No," she empathically denied. "I don't know him. I don't know anything. Please just let me go."

The man laughed. "You're cute."

No. *No.*

Her skin crawled. Amara made sure her dress still covered her knees and folded in on herself, to make her body as small as possible.

"Okay, so you ain't talking Dante Maroni," the man leaned back, straightening, the wood groaning under his weight. "Know anything about a Syndicate?"

Amara's mind flashed back to the room at the Maroni mansion. Lorenzo Maroni's cousin had mentioned it. She shook her head.

The man nodded. "Know anything about a shipment?"

'The shipment goes out in three days.'

Amara denied it.

"Stubborn bitch," the man laughed. "I'll break you yet."

Amara shivered, from the cold or the fear invading her entire being, she didn't know. "You're going to kill me, aren't you?" she asked, her voice breaking as her eyes welled up.

The man hopped off the table. "Sorry, sweets. My boys and me, we don't leave witnesses."

With that, he went out of the door, leaving it open this time. He returned in a few minutes with a bag, placing it on the table. Taking out a large key from his pocket, he came towards her.

Amara shrank into the wall, backing away from him.

"No," she begged, desperation leaking into her voice. "Please, let me go. I'll never tell anyone anything."

The man chuckled, as though she amused him. The scent of tobacco, motor oil, and that overly sweet smoke invaded her space as he unshackled her wrists. "Rest up. Be back soon."

He took the bag and walked out again, locking the door, leaving her in the dark.

As soon as the man had left, Amara had explored the other closed door for a weapon. It had been a bathroom with nothing but a toilet, a sink, and liquid soap. Out in the room, there was nothing except the table and the chains that were bolted to the wall, so she couldn't use them either. Defeated, scared, Amara had simply walked to the corner and huddled in on herself, praying for someone, anyone, to come to her rescue. She didn't know how long it was, or what time it was, when the man returned, this time with both his companions.

Heart in her throat, she looked up to see them blocking the light from the door.

"I don't know anything," she pleaded again, her voice cracking. "Please. If you want money, I can get you some. Please, let me go."

They ignored her. One of them dragged a chair into the room. The second man came to her, pulling her up roughly by the arm, and threw her into the chair. Amara looked at them frantically, her eyes coming to a halt at the first man laying down a coil of rope, a knife, and a container on the table.

He put on gloves.

Her breathing escalated.

No.

"I don't know *anything!*" she didn't care how her voice broke on that last word. Her fear eclipsed everything.

"We still gonna chat, girl," he informed her, as her gut tightened.

He took the rope, dipping it in the container. Amara heard the slight sizzle and her body began to tremble. He spoke. "You don't wanna have these acid ropes around those pretty wrists, do you?"

She shook her head frantically, tears streaming down her face.

"Very good. Then tell me about the compound. Is there any entry from the woods?"

"I don't know," Amara said, even though she knew there was. "Kids aren't...aren't allowed to go in the woods," she stumbled upon the words in her nervousness. She'd come across it on one of her walks and though it was fenced, it was still there. But she wasn't going to tell them that. Not when it was her home.

"See," the man nodded. "That was a test question and you passed. Good. Is there any underground entrance?"

Amara shook her head, her eyes on the rope. "I'm sorry, I don't know anything."

The man stepped closer, the acrid scent of acid coming with him. Amara clenched her teeth to keep her jaw from trembling.

"And you know nothing about the Syndicate?"

She denied it.

"Lorenzo Maroni has a weakness outside that you know about?"

Why were they asking her these absurd questions?

"Dante Maroni have anyone in his life outside?" the man asked, leaning closer to her. "Someone we can use against him?"

His brother.

Amara shook her head no, silent, trembling all over, panic, real panic setting in as the man brought the rope closer.

He smiled. "This will be fun."

And so began the screams.

*

They had the wrong girl. It didn't make sense. She was nobody.

Minutes blurred.

Heartbeats blurred.

Questions blurred.

Was it day? Was it night?

Everything blurred but the burn.

Her hands. Her back. Her feet. Everything burned.

And she screamed.

*

"What do you know about the syndicate?"

Breathe.

"Does Dante Maroni have anyone that can be used against him?"

Focus.

"Is there a shipment you know anything about?"

Live.

"When do the guards take their patrol break at night?"

Survive.

"Should we tell Maroni his little girlfriend is here?"

Scream.

*

Focus. Breathe. Live. Survive. Scream.

Breathe. Live. Survive. Scream.

Live. Survive. Scream.

Survive. Scream.

Scream.

*

She was alone.

Somehow, someway, her brain had sent her that message through the fog of pain.

Amara sat in the chair, wrists free but limp, her whole body shaking like a leaf as her skin burned.

She was alone.

And the door was open.

She blinked, barely able to see past the water in her eyes. Everything hurt. Everything was pain.

But she had to survive. She had barely lived her life. She had singing lessons to attend in summer, school to graduate, books to read, places to visit, a boy to kiss, babies to have. Her mother couldn't lose her. Vin couldn't mourn her.

She was alive. That was all that mattered. They hadn't broken her yet.

Gripping the sides of the chair with juddering arms, Amara somehow found the strength inside herself to push up. The burning in her wrist flared and she bit her lip hard to stifle any sound. She couldn't alert any of them.

Amara stood up, her legs unsteady, the soles of her feet burning with every step she took, circulation agitating the assaulted skin there, leaving prints of blood on the floor. Her eyes went to the open door. They thought her scared enough or weak enough to not try anything. They didn't know. Fear was sister to desperation. And she was *desperate* to escape this hell.

With soft steps, stifling every whimper, tears running down her cheeks, hair matted around her face, Amara edged towards the open door cautiously, getting out into some kind of corridor. Looking left, and then right, she headed to the latter, going down a set of stairs, every step feeling like a pit of fire. She breathed through it somehow, her need to escape greater than anything else, and came to an empty office room of some sort with an EXIT door. She heard the men who had abducted her somewhere, watching a game.

Her only goal was to escape.

Spying the door, Amara felt a burst of adrenaline shoot down her body, filling her with energy, and worse, hope. She limped towards the door, panting, and exited into a garage of some kind with shuttered doors. Unlocked shuttered doors.

Desperate to just get away, she made a beeline towards it, only to be suddenly yanked by her hair. Pain exploded in her scalp, a cry leaving her lips as the first man dragged her to the truck in the garage and shoved her over the hood.

"You still got fight in you, bitch?" he spat out against her ear, pressing into her from behind.

Bile rose up her throat, her skin crawling with revulsion.

Amara saw his companions come out into the garage.

"Please, no," she begged. "Please."

They laughed.

"Fucking slut," the man held her down.

Her clothes went first.

And she screamed,

and screamed,

and screamed...

until she couldn't anymore.

There was a little spider on the floor.

It was pretty too.

Amara lay on her side in the garage, her eyes watching the spider as it tried to climb up the wall. He fell down. It reminded her of that story ma used to tell her, of a king in a cave after a battle, watching the spider climb and fall a hundred times. Or was it a queen? Was it a hundred times, or fifty? This little spider had only climbed up twice, before moving on. Maybe, the stories were wrong.

Itsy, bitsy spider, Amara hummed in her mind.

God, she was tired. She didn't even hurt anymore. She just wanted to sleep. Her whole body wanted to sleep. Her arms were already asleep. She tried to move them and only twitched her fingers. Why was she staying awake anyway? There was nothing for her to stay awake for.

The little spider returned.

Itsy, bitsy spider, she continued humming, watching with swollen eyes as he took another route, and began his climb again.

She almost smiled, rooting for him to make it to the top.

"Jesus, fuck!"

The sound penetrated from somewhere behind her but Amara didn't bother focusing on it.

Hands touched her arms, slowly turning her on her back.

Fire flared again in slices down her flesh.

Something covered her.

It smelled nice.

Amara blinked up and saw blue, blue eyes looking down at her. She recognized those eyes from somewhere. It reminded her of clear skies and pretty clouds. She wanted to float there.

"I'm going to lift you up, okay?" the boy spoke quietly, his voice pulling her back to the ground. He had a nice voice. She wanted to wrap herself in it and never leave.

Recognition dawned through the haze in her mind.

The new boy. Tristan. What was he doing there? Or was she hallucinating? Had her mind truly splintered?

Amara opened her mouth to answer him, but something was burning her throat. No sound came out. Panic cleared the haze a little more.

"It's okay, you're safe now," he reassured her. "No one will lay a finger on you. I promise."

She believed him for some reason. He should have made his promise before though.

"Please," she somehow rasped out.

He leaned forward to hear her better.

"Don't...don't tell...any...one," she got the words out, barely, through the pain in her throat. Tea. She needed her ma's hot herbal tea.

The boy simply looked at her for a moment, something powerful in his eyes, before picking her up, careful with the injuries on her back, and placing her on a table. Setting her down gently, he wrapped the jacket, his jacket, more snugly around her.

"You doing okay?" he asked, in a voice so gentle, it made her lips tremble.

Amara shook her head. She didn't think she'd ever be okay again.

"Hang in there, yeah?" he said softly.

What for, Amara wanted to ask but couldn't get her throat to cooperate. Tea. She needed tea.

"Dante, I have her," she heard the boy say and felt herself drifting off suddenly, her lids getting heavier.

She heard more voices but her eyes wouldn't open.

And for some reason, somehow believing Tristan's promise that she was safe, Amara let go and fell into blessed oblivion.

Amara

15 YEARS

She couldn't move.

Amara blinked her eyes open to an unfamiliar room, déjà-vu hitting her hard, as her heartbeat escalated in panic. The sudden sound of beeping had her looking to the side, to see some kind of monitor with wires, the kind that she'd seen in movies.

Hospital.

She was in the hospital.

Memories assaulted her and she took a deep breath, pushing them back into a vault.

Not now. Not now. Not now.

"Mumu?"

The voice had her eyes flying to see her mother at the door, her eyes wet and swollen, and Amara felt a noise leave her chest. Her mother ran to her, careful of the tubes going in her body, and hugged her tight to her chest, petting her hair like she always did.

Amara broke.

Wailing, her body remembering the pain and her mind remembering the moment it splintered, Amara sobbed as her mother held her, gentling her with kisses to her head, murmuring soft words to her that didn't make any sense. They didn't have to. Her mother was there and Amara was safe and loved and that was all that mattered. She could feel her mother crying with her and it was that which made her pull back to really see her. Her green eyes were shimmering with pain for her daughter, her mouth still in a gentle line, her ma looked exhausted and heartbroken and so, so loving.

Amara took a deep breath as her mother wiped her tears with her hand.

"We'll get through this, Mumu," her mother told her gently.

She opened her mouth to speak when a throat cleared from the door and a woman her mother's age, clearly the doctor, entered the room.

"I'm glad to see you're awake, Amara," the doctor gave her a gentle smile. "How are you feeling?"

Amara started to speak when the doctor shook her head. "No, don't speak yet. Just nod or shake your head, okay?"

She felt her mother squeeze her hand. Confused, Amara agreed.

"Do you know what day it is?" the doctor asked.

Amara shook her head.

"It's January 6th," the lady informed her.

Amara's mind went reeling. Her last memory before her abduction had been in December. How? Her confusion must have been evident on her face as the doctor spoke again. "You were taken for over three days. And you've been here for two weeks under an induced coma."

Shock filtered through her system.

"Your body was severely traumatized and needed to begin its healing process," the doctor went on. "We felt under the circumstances, it would be best for both your mind and body to rest for a bit."

Amara grit her teeth, processing everything she was being told.

"Your mother mentioned you've always had a low pain threshold?"

Amara nodded. She had never realized how low of a threshold it had been until the monsters had her.

The doctor continued with sympathy in her eyes. "That is probably why some of your injuries had such severe reactions. I'm sorry for everything you went through, Amara. But there is more I need to tell you. Is it alright if I continue?"

Amara liked the fact that the doctor asked her the question, giving her a choice. She looked at her mother, sitting strong beside her, and gave the doctor a nod.

"You have some acid burns and cuts on your back, sides, and feet that will more than likely scar," the doctor went on. "The worst of the scarring will be over your wrists. The good news is that they're all healing very well. You can have cosmetic surgery down the line to minimize them if you want."

Amara looked down at her wrists and feet, wrapped in white gauze. She was probably on pain killers since she couldn't feel anything more than a twinge.

"Amara?" the doctor called, calling her attention back to herself, her eyes even more sympathetic. "You cannot use your voice for at least the next month. Your screaming severely damaged your vocal cords, to the point we had to do surgery. It happens in extremely rare cases but I feel your low pain threshold resulted in that."

Amara swallowed, panic filling her again as she squeezed her mother's hand.

"It's okay, baby," her mother comforted from the side, her tone telling her she already knew all of this.

She opened her mouth and closed it again.

"You'll be able to speak again once it's all healed, don't worry," the doctor reassured her. "But it is more than likely that your pitch range will be limited."

Amara took a deep breath, taking it all in.

The doctor continued. "We also tested you for sexual assault and filed a report, as we have to in cases like this. Police will want to talk to you once you're ready. But no one outside your mother knows here. Do you want me to inform anyone else?"

No. No, she absolutely didn't want anyone to know. The shame curled inside her like a snake, and she shook her head vigorously.

The doctor gave a small smile in understanding. "Okay. But I recommend you talk to a therapist about everything. Your body will heal but your mind needs to as well. You've been through something traumatic and therapy can genuinely help you. I'll leave the contact information for someone who specializes in such cases with your mother. Would you consider that?"

She didn't know, but she nodded nonetheless. The doctor gave her a soft smile and told her to rest, before leaving her with her mother.

She wondered if her mother had reached out to her father about any of it.

Her mother pushed her hair back from her face in a gesture Amara knew in her bones.

"There were a few people here to see you. Vin was outside too," her mother told her softly. "Do you want me to tell him anything?"

He would already carry the guilt of the incident on his shoulders. He didn't need to know she'd been violated as well. She shook her head.

Her mother smiled. "I'll send him in when he's back, and then you rest, okay?"

She nodded.

"Don't lose your heart, my baby," her mother told her, and Amara felt her eyes burn as the meaning of the words finally dawned upon her.

When the door opened a few minutes later, Amara turned her head expecting to see her friend, and instead found a somber, deadly boy with blue eyes standing there, the boy who had saved her. Tristan.

Swallowing, she watched as he entered the room, closing the door behind him, and went to the wall opposite her, maybe to make her feel not crowded. He should have known that after everything he had done for her, she trusted him with her life.

He was dressed in a simple black t-shirt and jeans and as he leaned against the wall, he pushed his hands into the pockets, his eyes considering her quietly.

She wanted to thank him – for coming to look for her, for finding her, for covering her with the jacket off his back, for getting her to safety. She wanted to say so many things to him but couldn't, so she simply gave him a little smile.

He watched the smile for a moment before speaking, his tone still as gentle as it had been when he found her. "Have the doctors told you what happened?"

That was the most words she'd heard from him. Amara nodded.

"Your mother knows everything?"

She nodded again.

"Are they treating you okay?"

The hospital, he meant. It was almost sweet of him to ask. Amara mutely said yes.

"Good," he pushed off from the wall, heading to the door.

Amara must have made some kind of noise because he paused with his hand on the knob, and looked at her. She didn't want anyone to know everything besides her mother. He knew and she pleaded with him silently to reassure her that he'd keep it between them.

"I won't tell anyone," he told her softly, before walking out the door.

She trusted that. If he said he would keep her secret, it would go to the grave with him.

Vin had come into her room after her Tristan left, a bandage on his cheek where he'd been cut, and Amara had tried to smile for him. And for the first time, she'd seen her friend break down at her feet, hiccupping 'I'm sorry' over and over.

Amara had wanted to tell him it wasn't his fault, that he had nothing to be sorry about, but had simply settled for squeezing his hand until he had calmed down and told her she was going to heal if it killed him.

She'd almost smiled at that.

Now, alone in the room since visiting hours were over, Amara stared up at the ceiling and tried not to let memories penetrate her mind. It was hard. So hard. She felt filthy, like her skin wasn't her own anymore, like the guilt and pain and shame she felt for something that wasn't her fault would never leave her alone. It was hard to ignore the memories, but she tried. Maybe, the doctor was right. Maybe talking to a therapist could help her keep the demons at bay.

The door to the room opened, and Amara kept staring up, waiting for the medication to lull her back to sleep. It was probably just the nurse coming in to check her vitals as she'd been coming every two hours. After a long minute, when she didn't hear anything, Amara turned her head to the side.

And felt her heart stop.

Dante Maroni sat on the chair in the room, looking absolutely *wrecked.* His tie was askew, his shirt crushed, his hair in disarray, and his eyes wild. Her breath caught in her chest. She'd never seen him look like this before.

Her heart started to pound and the monitor beeped, matching its rhythm, embarrassingly telling both of them that she was affected by his presence. She didn't want him to see her like this, not lying in a hospital bed, wounded and broken and not herself. She didn't even know who 'herself' was anymore. It was probably a good thing she couldn't talk at the moment. She wouldn't know what to say. Memories of him over the years threaded with the memories of questions she'd been asked about him, over and over again, questions she had refused to answer.

Him kissing the pink-haired girl – *does he have anyone that could be used against him?*

Him burying her dead body – *should we tell him his little girlfriend is here?*

Him standing shirtless early morning at his door – *does he talk any business with you?*

Him holding her arms, asking her what was wrong – *does Dante Maroni have a weakness?*

Memories after memories, linking, shifting, changing.

Amara focused on his gaze, trying to root herself in the room so she wouldn't lose herself in her head.

The storm in his eyes focused on her – not her bandages, not her neck, but on her eyes.

She didn't know what he was trying to find inside her, what he was seeing in that moment. Her own storm, perhaps. She was a heartbeat away from dispersing into the thin air, pieces of her lost forever on the winds.

"They're dead."

His voice jerked her back to the moment.

The words penetrated the space between them.

They were dead.

They. Were. Dead.

Gone.

She didn't know how. She didn't know when. She didn't care.

They had paid.

Her vision blurred.

Something raw, visceral trapped itself in her chest.

They had paid.

Her breathing escalated, lips trembling with a scream lodged in her damaged throat. She wanted to howl in agony, in vindication, so loud everyone in the world would hear her.

They. Had. Paid.

Her hands started to shake.

He saw it. He saw it and stood up swiftly from the chair, coming to her in three strides. Going down on his haunches, he took her small, gauze-wrapped hand in his larger one, holding her eyes with an intensity she had never felt in her life.

He looked at her hands, tracing the bandages, then at her feet wrapped in the same, before bringing those dark, dark eyes back to her.

"You're not going to walk through life, Amara," he uttered roughly, each word a vow that cemented itself in her heart. "You'll dance through it. And I'll *fucking remove* anyone who tries to break your rhythm. I promise you."

Amara felt a tear slip out the side of her eye, his words seeping into her soul, wrapping around her in a fierce, warm, protective cocoon. She didn't know why he was there, or why he had felt the need to vindicate her, or why she was important enough for him to make that promise, or why he had come to tell her that himself, but in that moment, she was just a girl and he was just a boy, and somehow, their broken pieces matched.

PART 2

gust

"So, I wait for you like a lonely house
till you will see me again and live in me.
Till then my windows ache."
Pablo Neruda, 100 Love Sonnets

8

Dante

20 YEARS

It had begun when she started avoiding him.

The girl had somehow always been there, on the sides. Every week during his training with Vin, every time Zia spoke of her daughter, every time she quickly looked away whenever he glanced at her. She had always been there, and Dante had never noticed like a man never noticed the light of the sun until he went blind. Not until she had stepped back. Suddenly, he became aware of her absence by the tree, aware of how she changed her course if she happened to see him coming, aware of how she went out of her way to get out of his presence.

In the beginning, he had chalked it down to her getting over her crush. But it had continued, for over a year before he had realized it could have been something else.

He had gone to visit Damien and told him about it, just wondering what the hell had been going on, and Damien – his brother who had never looked anyone in the eye except her – had said, "Maybe she doesn't like you anymore."

Looking at her sleeping, her young body a witness to nightmares she should never have witnessed but had somehow survived, Dante knew she was on his chessboard. He still didn't know how and what her role was, but he had learned to trust the voice inside him after everything that had happened with Roni. Her death taught him never to rebel with an outsider again.

And that voice told her this sleeping girl was important. It had become an insistent whisper a year ago. Now, it was a roar.

She was important and he was not going to ignore that.

They had just brought her home from the hospital, and since she'd fallen asleep on the way, Dante had carried her to her room and placed her under her covers. He knew he had become more subdued on the outside after Roni's death – the perfect prince to the imperfect kingdom – even as he rebelled on the inside. He'd just learned to hide it better.

Amara's abduction had shaken him. He had known something had been wrong with her that evening of the party, and he'd let her go, even as his gut had wanted to keep insisting she tell him. He had let her go and she had been taken, brutalized, and he carried a part of that on himself. They had searched for three days when Tristan had given him a call, telling him he'd found her a few miles out of the city.

Dante would never forget the moment he had run inside that garage, the lead in his stomach as the sight of her had hit him, covered in bruises and burns and blood, wrapped in Tristan's jacket, slumped on the table. The rage he had felt, still felt, had been a black hole inside his body, sucking everything into itself, expanding, until it was the only thing flowing through his veins. He had asked Tristan what had happened to her and the other boy had simply told him to take her to the hospital quickly. Dante had picked her up carefully, and she had opened those beautiful green eyes of hers for a second, glazed in pain but recognizing him, before collapsing on his chest with a trust that had unmanned him.

Yeah, she was fucking important to him.

Dante pushed her hair away from her face and leaving her to her slumber, he walked out of the bedroom into the cozy living room, to see his housekeeper standing by the window, looking out.

Dante joined her there, his eyes taking in the view of the falling dusk and the mansion.

"Who did this?" she asked after a long time, finally now that they were alone and away from ears.

Dante thought back to the interrogation he had subjected her abductor to while Tristan had violently taken care of his minions. It had taken hours for Dante to break him but he had, with that black rage and vengeance for that important girl with the forest eyes driving him. All he got was one name – Gilbert – before the man had died. Tristan and Dante had agreed to keep it to themselves. Until they knew the truth, they were telling everyone that it had been a rival family trying their luck. Though it didn't sit well with him since she deserved the truth, Dante lied. "It was a rival gang. Amara had been in the wrong place at the wrong time."

Zia took a deep breath before asking him, "Should we leave this place? A part of me wants to take her away from here."

Dante shook his head. "It's too late. You've lived here too long. It's safer for both of you to stay here on the compound."

She accepted that, having already thought of it. "The boy at the cottage, the one who saved my baby," she asked. "Do you think he would like it if I took care of his place?"

Dante felt a smile curl his lips, imagining Tristan seeing the maternal housekeeper on his doorstep. "Yeah, I think he'd like that."

She nodded, turning to look at him with the odd, beautiful green eyes her daughter had inherited from her. "Thank you, Dante. You didn't have to do any of this for us, but I am grateful."

Dante put a hand on her shoulder, giving her a slight squeeze. "She's going to need all of us."

Her mother shook her head. "She will appreciate all of us but all she needs is her heart. Amara has always been strong but so kind in a way I didn't think people could be. I used to think strength had to be jaded until she taught me otherwise. She is strong like water is strong

– it doesn't appear that way because it's adaptable, but it can seep into the smallest of cracks and break open the largest of rocks over time. She'll be fine."

Dante didn't say anything, because he didn't know her. But he wanted to know this girl with endless strength. He knew she was gentle, he knew she smiled big, he knew she had the most unique, beautiful eyes that the artist in him admired, and he knew she probably didn't know her own strength. He had seen tough men break and seen their mind splinter, sometimes having been the one to break them. However, her three days at the hands of her captors, with the torture they put her through, hadn't destroyed her. Beat her, yes, but she was still there, alive and visceral, vibrating with a force she probably didn't realize she was emanating.

"She's the one who told me to give you cookies years ago, you know," her mother smiled. "I told her about your mama's death and that's what she said – to give you sweets. I never thought of it before that. You were just a young boy too. And somehow, she saw it. Her heart has always amazed me."

Dante remembered the first time Zia had come to him with cookies. He had been surprised and a little suspicious, but by the last bite, he'd felt better than he had in years.

And she'd done that for him, that slumbering, broken girl.

Yeah, she was important alright. Perhaps, she always had been and Dante just hadn't seen it. He was just realizing that.

'Fate is always weaving its threads, Dante. We just don't see them until our eyes open.'

His mother's words came back to him, a smile on her face as she said the words looking out at the sunset. He didn't know if anything like fate existed beyond the books. But standing there, he could feel his eyes opening, thin threads stretching out from him and going beyond the room, hooking him to the sleeping girl inside.

Dante sat in front of his father in the study, keeping his face clear of all expression except a little smirk. While he let Lorenzo Maroni think he was on a leash, behaving like the good son that he was, that little smirk was his middle finger to his sire.

"Your brother is being moved. There was a fire at the home, so they're relocating," the bastard said, his eyes gauging Dante's reaction. If he thought Dante was unaware of anything happening with his brother, the man was dumber than he'd given him credit for.

"Where?" Dante asked, leaning back in the chair.

As much as he hated his father, he had to admit the man had class. The older Dante grew, the more he realized he liked classy things, and this study was a prime example of that. Polished wooden furniture that matched the wooden panels behind his father's chair, a bookshelf on the opposite corner filled with books he doubted his father had ever read; windows to his left with patterned draperies that somehow went with the stone and wood theme, and a huge desk that dominated this corner of the room. Cherry on top were the small chandeliers hanging from the ceiling.

Classy motherfucker.

Dante hated that he got that from him, at least on the outside. Deep down, it was his mother who'd taught him class.

"Another location," Bloodhound Maroni told him, holding that piece of information for leverage. Information, as his father had taught him, was the key. Dante smirked, already one step ahead of his game.

He could see that the smirk bothered the older man before he shook it off. "The girl, is she going to be a problem?"

Dante felt his shoulders tighten at the words. No way was she getting in his father's crosshairs. She already had enough shit to last a lifetime.

"I don't think so," Dante informed him casually. He'd learned over the years that dealing with his father was pretty simple – appease him, stroke his ego, and let him stay complacent on his throne. Those made him overlook anything under his nose while outright rebellion honed him in.

"Who took her?"

"Still looking into it."

His father nodded. "Pay off the mother and the girl to keep their mouths shut. We don't want our enemies on the ground thinking they can pick anyone off the compound. Keep an eye on her."

Yeah, they were keeping it low-key. Surprisingly, not many in the underworld even knew there had been an abduction, at least not to his knowledge. Or maybe, it wasn't that surprising. Her last name wasn't consequential enough. He frowned slightly, trying to remember if he even knew her last name.

Dante nodded, swiftly getting up from the chair and straightening his suit jacket.

"Oh, and a woman is coming into the fold," his father informed him, taking his phone out to show him the photo of a beautiful, dark-haired woman. "Her father used to be a soldier before he folded, and she's been making some waves lately. Her name is Nerea. Keep an eye on her too."

Dante narrowed his eyes, his senses tingling. This was off, very off. There was no way his father was just letting a woman come into the fold because she was 'making waves'. An equal opportunity believer his father was not. Women were whores to him. This absolutely did not go with his personality, even if she was sleeping with him. There was no way she could talk her way from his bed into the Outfit.

Nevertheless, he nodded, striding out of the room and into the corridor, taking his phone out. Dialing his only partner in crime, he put it to his ear and went out of the mansion.

"Where are you?" he asked as soon as the call was answered.

"Out," came Tristan's succinct response.

Dante rolled his eyes. "Oh, come on."

There was silence for a second before he said, "Lincoln's. 205."

The hotel? What the hell was Tristan's ass doing at a luxury hotel in the city?

"Be there in 20."

Dante cut the call and headed to his black Range Rover that he'd bought the year he got his Outfit tattoo on his bicep. Hopping in, he drove out onto the long, winding driveway, down the hill, coming to the compound gates manned by four guards. Nodding to each one of them, he shot out of the property at a speed he shouldn't have and headed to the city where the hotel was.

The view never stopped to amaze him – rolling green hills, endless skies, a winding river, and the huge city in the distance. Fuck, he loved this place.

Pulling into the hotel parking in record time, Dante stepped out and took the spacious elevator straight to the second floor. The hotel, plush and catering to luxurious tastes, was an odd location for his little buddy to be in. Going down the corridor to the room, Dante saw a woman give him an appreciative look, an invitation evident in her eyes, and he simply smiled at her, continuing on his way.

Tristan opened the door before he could knock, walking into a single bedroom, a laptop open on the bed.

"Hello to you too, buddy," Dante closed the door behind him, his eyes on the laptop. There was a black and white feed on the screen of a restaurant.

"Is that the hotel restaurant?" he asked, taking a seat on the chair as Tristan sat on the bed. The younger boy hesitated for a second before nodding once.

Interesting.

Dante focused on the screen, seeing the camera recording a particular table where three men and a young girl sat.

Gabriel Vitalio was in the city.

Dante watched as the girl, wearing glasses, looked out the window. Morana Vitalio. Fuck.

"Are you fucking kidding me?" his eyes flew to Tristan, surprise filling his system as he saw the evidence of Tristan's past thrown in his face. He knew the bloody history he had with the Vitalios but he had never, not once, thought that Tristan would be watching the girl. Given his intense personality, he probably should have.

Tristan didn't say a word, just continued to stare as the girl, not older than thirteen or fourteen, pushed her glasses up her nose and stole a glance at her father, before looking out the window again, bored out of her mind. One of the men stole a glance at her and Dante's skin crawled. Tristan's hand fisted.

"Don't let me kill him," Tristan muttered and suddenly, Dante knew why he was there. He was there to contain him. Watching the creep, Dante didn't mind that one fucking bit.

126

An hour later, the lunch wrapped up, and Vitalio party got up to leave. Tristan shut the laptop, threw it in his bag, his body vibrating with tension.

"Let's go," Dante said, leading the way out of the hotel room, down the corridor, down the elevator, and out to the side where the restaurant opened into the alley. Clocking the man who had stared a little too long at young Morana Vitalio, both he and Tristan followed him as he took out a cigarette to smoke.

Dante hung back, letting Tristan take the lead and take whatever frustration he had out on him. The younger boy went behind the man and put him in a headlock.

Dante watched them tussle, itching to take a smoke himself, when he felt eyes watching him. Turning to the side, he saw a man limping at the mouth of the alley, watching the entire scene.

Dante waited for a second, thinking he would pass, but he didn't. He stayed, and he stared.

The limping dude was weird.

Dante let Tristan handle the creep, his own eyes on the bearded man at the other end of the alley, watching him watch them. Was he one of Gabriel's guys?

Dante headed to him, and he started to limp away, relying heavily on his cane.

"Wait," Dante called out, on the main street now, though it was mostly deserted at this time of the night. "Who are you? Why were you watching us?"

The man stopped, turning to look at him from behind his glasses. He put a hand inside his pocket, pulling out a piece of paper.

"I'm not a threat to you, Mr. Maroni. But one day, you'll have questions," the man told him quietly. "Call me then."

Dante took the paper, suspicious.

"And take care of him. He's important."

With that, the man limped away, and Dante watched, weirded the fuck out.

But he kept the paper. And then he intervened before Tristan killed the fucker.

"Roses?" he carried Amara through the woods to the little spot beside the lake where she'd used to sit with her book. It was a beautiful day, and while she wasn't allowed to put pressure on her feet by walking yet, Dante knew she liked getting out of the house.

His little bundle shook her head, a small smile on her lips.

Dante chuckled, setting her down gently against the tree, taking a seat beside her.

"What woman doesn't like roses?" Dante huffed, mock-scandalized.

She shrugged, closing her eyes, soaking in the rays of the sun.

Dante looked at her, trying to wrap his head around everything that had happened within the last few weeks. Mostly, he was working and trying to process everything this girl was causing to happen inside him.

Where before he had been a man not appreciating the sun until he went blind, now he was a blind man blessed with vision seeing the sunlight in all its glory. Amara wasn't sunlight of clear skies; she was the sun hiding behind dark clouds, muted but powerful enough to still light the world.

Beautiful Amara who had begun to heal but still couldn't speak or walk. That would heal in time. It was her mind that was scaring him if he admitted.

He had made it a point to visit her every day at least once, just to check up on her. At first, she hadn't really responded to anything, lost inside her own head, but slowly, she had begun to give him small smiles even when her eyes miles away. She fought it, wherever her head was, he could tell. Sometimes, she spaced out in the middle of a sentence he was saying, before shaking herself and coming back. Sometimes, she started to breathe rapidly before he had to call her name and bring her to the present.

The doctor had told him she would more than likely need therapy just to come to terms with her entire experience. Dante was beginning to admit she was right. But until she could talk, he had vowed to himself to be there for her. He felt responsible for her for some reason. Maybe it was the terror he had felt when Vin had called him. Maybe it was the panic he'd felt when he'd run into the garage to see her body so broken. Maybe it was the relief at the sign of life he'd felt when he picked her up in his arms and took her to the hospital. He didn't know what or why it was, but he was coming to terms with the idea of not knowing. Sometimes, things didn't really have a reason. Sometimes, they just were.

He had actually started reading up on trauma and torture survivors to understand her psyche better, so he could help her in any way she needed to heal. He was just grateful she hadn't been violated in any other way. When the doctor had recounted her injuries, Dante remembered holding his breath and nearly collapsing from relief. She was a strong little thing.

"Do you even like flowers?" Dante asked, continuing their conversation, looking up at the sky, letting the sun warm him.

She shrugged again in his peripheral vision, holding up two slender fingers. Two flowers.

"Let me guess," he looked at her in her purple dress and scarf and boots, trying to imagine what flowers she liked. "Orchids?"

She just gave a small smile. The frustrating girl was deliberately being thick. Dante had gotten used to reading her responses and what they meant in these conversations he had with her.

He rolled his eyes, looking down at her hands. The bandages had been removed a few days ago, the wounds airing out. In the bright sunlight, he could see the gruesome scars that went around her wrists.

Black rage filled him as he saw it, the need to raise those fuckers from the grave just to kill them again acute inside him.

He started to touch her hand but stopped himself. Carrying her was one thing, it was necessary to hold her then. But touching her skin like this in the open, where anyone could see was not something she needed.

Taking a deep breath in, he fisted his hand and pulled it back, turning his head up to the sky, and continued their chat as nothing had happened.

"Wildflowers?"

A small smile while her eyes were in a nightmare.

Days passed.

He went to see her every day, just to keep an eye on her, or that's what he told himself.

He carried her out in the sun when it was out. He stayed in and watched movies with her when it wasn't.

He took at least two hours every day to spend with her, even though she didn't talk to him. But she communicated. She communicated with her eyes and her soft smiles and her hands.

Some days, she'd zone out and struggle. Some days, she'd give him her entire attention.

Dante went to see her every day, and after a while, he realized she wanted him to.

Weeks passed.

He saw her every day, and then he skipped.

For four days, he went out of town to see his brother.

For the next three, he and Tristan chased down the lead for her attack.

A week later he went to her.

She glared at him, threw him a pillow, and cried a little. He sat down beside her, and she hit him in the chest. It was the first time she touched him voluntarily before retreating into her blankets.

That was progress.

Months passed.

His hunt for Gilbert wasn't panning out, but he kept at it. It was disastrous how many people were named Gilbert and without the last name, they were at a loss. The search for him also became a side project as he learned more of the business.

She started homeschooling. She started therapy. She started healing.

She hung out with Vin, occasionally with Tristan, and read romance books.

Every day, he knew a little more about her.

Every day, she saw a little more of him.

Every day, her scars solidified a little more on her skin.

But she didn't talk to him.

Her mother said she had started to whisper little sentences. Vin told him she'd started to whisper little questions. Even fucking Tristan had said she'd started to whisper little words to him.

But not with Dante.

That *fucking bugged* him.

Years passed.

She became his person.

He would usually finish his day by going to her house and spending a few hours with her. She listened when he talked and communicated if she had questions. She made him watch movies and indulged him when he just wanted to be.

Sometimes he would see her flinch in the middle of nothing and he wondered if her torture had ever become another kind of violation. But the doctors had said nothing and she said nothing and Dante didn't know if he should assume just because of the shit in his head.

His father never questioned him about her, but Dante kept him in the loop, saying he was keeping an eye on her. He knew he was being reckless. He knew he was being rebellious again. But he was a grown man and not a boy, and he could keep her safe.

Vin came outright and asked him what his intentions were with her, while Dante demanded he confirm he was nothing but her best friend. He confirmed and Dante was relieved.

The thing between them grew, feeling the sun and the water, feeling the nurture and the affection. They began to feel more like magnets than puzzle pieces, finding their way to each other, close but not close enough, as the tension between them built and built and built.

She became his person.

She became his.

Amara

1 7 Y E A R S

id he possibly have a girlfriend?

Amara didn't know why it jolted her out of her reverie, but it did. As she watched him lead the beautiful woman across the floor in a dance, Amara realized she'd somehow fallen into the safety of the time he spent with her.

Over the last year, Dante had become something like the sun. She waited every day to feel his warmth, if only just for a few minutes before the clouds returned. But as long as she had the sun, the clouds were bearable.

She didn't know what she felt for him anymore, everything inside her convoluted in the way he'd been weaved into her life. But she did know that he'd become important to her, very important. And watching him dance closely with a pretty woman? It kinda hurt.

Okay, it *really* hurt.

But it made sense. He was older and more mature and needed someone who could compliment that. And it wasn't a traumatized seventeen-year-old girl in therapy who never spoke a word to him. While she had begun speaking to a few people, she didn't to him. It wasn't like she didn't want to. She did. But god, she *hated* her new voice. And she really, really didn't want him to hate it.

Taking a deep breath, Amara walked the edge of the dance floor at the mansion, heading towards the kitchen where her mother was. There was a party at the big house for Mr. Maroni's 50th birthday, and while Amara wasn't supposed to attend, she had needed something out of her routine.

The compound had started to suffocate her, to the point where she actually looked forward to her therapy sessions in the city. Yeah, she was going to therapy, had been going for a year. And she'd been homeschooling with the same tutors who came to teach Tristan, helping her with her education.

But she honestly didn't care anymore.

She didn't recognize herself anymore.

Things she once cared about seemed pointless to her. She knew the people around her cared for her, and after a few weeks, she'd realized she couldn't hurt them as she hurt. So, she had put a smile on her face and listened to them talk, and lived on, pretending something very, very wrong, very ugly hadn't taken root inside her.

She didn't know how to push it out. She didn't want to talk to people, didn't like the sound of her own voice, didn't like the look of her skin. She felt the scars under her feet every time she put on her shoes, felt the slight twinge in her back every time fabric slid across her flesh to cover it up. Worse, she saw the ugly, mottled skin on her wrists, vertical lines on the sides of her stomach, and that one surgical slit across her neck.

Her torture had been written on her skin and stained on her mind. And she hated who she was at that point – lost, adrift, clueless.

The ballet flats she wore as she made her way through the people reminded her she probably could never wear heels. Her sense of balance had been a little off since the incident. There wasn't any physical reason for it, as her doctor had reminded her kindly. It was psychological. A lot of things were psychological with her.

God, she hated her brain some days for not shielding her, not blacking out the entire memory, and leaving her with a clean slate. That would've been better. Some days, anger at herself made her want to do something drastic. Some days, the knife on the kitchen counter looked friendly. Some days, all she wanted was to let go, but only knowing how much the people around her would hurt stopped her every time. She took hot showers to clean her skin but the filth stayed buried in, no matter how hard she scrubbed.

"Ma," she called out to her mother, her new voice barely louder than a high whisper, and felt the eyes of the staff come to her. She ignored the awkward looks they gave her. Yeah, that was a new development – the staring, the whispers, the gossip. She had become a pariah. Boo-fucking-hoo.

Her mother looked up from where she was talking to two waiters, a smile on her face.

Amara swore her mother was a superhero at this point. She saved her, every single day, without even knowing. Just by giving her the same smile she used to give her before, loving her the same way she used to love her before. When everything around her had changed, her mother had been her constant through it all.

"I'm heading home," she told her ma, feeling the strain in her throat as she spoke. The doctor had told her it would get better over time as her cords healed completely, but this would be her voice now.

At least, she'd never have to listen to her own screams again.

"I'll walk you out," the feminine voice beside her had her looking up at another new development in her life. Her half-sister, Nerea.

She had shown up one day out of the blue, with attitude for everyone else except Amara, and Amara really didn't know how to deal with that. She already had too much on her plate without adding an older half-sibling she'd never known about.

And she wanted to be alone.

Giving Nerea a small smile, she shook her head. "It's okay, enjoy the party."

God, her voice.

"Are you sure?" Nerea asked, looking concerned. "I'd love to spend some time getting to connect with you."

"Me too," Amara reassured her. "But another time?"

Nerea nodded.

Leaving the staff to their duties attending to the party and her half-sister standing there, Amara walked out the back door, exiting into the lawns. Wrapping her scarf around her, even though it wasn't cold, she looked up at the clear sky, watching the stars twinkle, and headed to the lake.

A few people milled outside, the noise from the party loud on the wind as Amara kept her head down and made her way down the hill.

This was another development over the year. While she still had her social graces, she didn't like being around many people anymore. They always stared and not because she had grown up to become beautiful. She didn't feel beautiful. She felt ugly and rotten on the inside. Where they just saw a tall girl of seventeen with wild black hair framing a face with pretty features and dark green eyes, she saw a girl who didn't know who she was under that skin.

Who was she?

Coming to a stop by the lake, she looked up at the sky, hoping for an answer she knew wasn't coming.

Someone came to stand by her side.

Amara turned her face, slightly surprised to see Tristan standing there, looking up at the stars too. This was another new development.

For some reason, after the incident, he'd just become more present in her life. He never spoke to her, not much, but he was always there in the periphery, lingering, letting her know he was there.

And he never stared at her.

Amara looked at him, wondering how he did it. She had heard of his screams over the years from the staff. Sheknew he had scars of his own, and she wondered how he lived like this with all the memories in his head.

"How do you do it?" she voiced the question to him, hating the way her sound didn't even come out properly. "How do you forget?"

He was silent for a beat, his eyes on the stars. "You don't."

Amara swallowed, looking back up at the sky.

"You need to find something or someone to live for," he spoke quietly beside her, his tone the same gentle one he always used with her. "Something or someone who makes you want to push through all the shit the world will throw at you."

Amara paused for a beat, considering his words. "You have someone you live for?"

"Yeah."

With that, Tristan turned and left her alone, mulling over his advice. He was right. That's what she was missing – something to live for, something that was just hers.

Inhaling the crisp, fresh air of the night, she shook off her morose thoughts and headed back towards the staff quarters which were mostly empty since everyone was at the party.

Dante's dark house made her pause.

Even though he had become a constant in her life, she had never actually been inside his house. The closest had been years ago when she'd brought him cookies early in the morning and he had answered the door in all his shirtless glory. God, she'd been a fool for him then.

She was still a fool for him, just a more traumatized fool.

Curious, Amara looked around her to see no one was around and climbed the steps to his door. Her hand went on the knob and for the first time in a long time, she felt a thrill shoot up her spine. Checking one final time to see if anyone saw her, she turned the knob and sneaked into the darkened house, quietly shutting the door behind her.

She probably shouldn't be invading his privacy like she was, but her curiosity overrode her common sense. There was just one light turned on in the kitchen area, and Amara looked around, seeing the space in its entirety.

The kitchen was about the size of her living room, with wooden panels and granite countertops, the island some kind of stone with four stools on one side. There was also a small dining table for four people off to the side before the backdoor. Though clean, the place looked cozy, lived in.

Inquisitive, she walked deeper into the house guided by the single light, coming to a stop at the stairs. Pausing briefly, telling herself everyone was at the party, Amara ascended quietly, her eyes exploring on the way. There were two rooms on the floor, both with their doors shut, and knowing one of them was his bedroom, Amara stayed clear, not wanting to invade his privacy to that extent.

A small set of stairs to the side went higher up to an open space she couldn't see.

She climbed up, letting her eyes adjust to the dark the higher she went.

It smelled different in there – like wet earth and wax. It was quite pleasant actually.

Running her hands up the wall, she came to a switch and flicked the light on, turning to face the room.

And froze.

Sculptures, dozens of them, littered the area.

Amara felt her eyes widen as the surprise hit her, her gaze taking in everything in the room. There was a workbench with tools, and a window, and nothing but sculptures. So many sculptures – some finished, some half-done, some with a plastic sheet over them. There was everything from small vases to busts to two full-blown statues, all varying in degrees of skill.

Dazed, she walked forward towards one of the busts, a woman with a half-finished face, taking in the rough textures over the skin that had yet to be polished. She raised her hand to touch it, to feel what it felt like when suddenly, she became aware that she wasn't alone.

Spinning on spot, her eyes flew to the entrance to see Dante Maroni leaning casually against the doorjamb with his hands in his pant pockets, still dressed in the beautiful tux he'd worn for the party, his hair swiped back from his face, pushing his cheekbones and jawline into sharp relief, his dark eyes on her.

Amara swallowed, her heart pounding as a flush covered her face. She almost opened her mouth to speak before biting her tongue, remembering she couldn't let him hear her voice. Eyes to the floor, she rushed towards the exit, hoping to simply get out. She expected him to step to the side so she could pass, as he had done countless times before.

He didn't. He stayed exactly as he was, forcing her to stop or barrel into him.

Amara felt her blood rushing to her ears, her chest starting to heave as her breathing escalated.

"Look at me," came the soft command from above her.

Amara closed her eyes for a second, before giving him her eyes, to find him watching her with an intensity that had become harder and harder to ignore as the weeks went by. He looked at her like that more often, like a condemned soul being offered salvation, like a blind man seeing the sun. That look always flared in his eyes before he caged it in. Usually, he was charming and easy-going with everyone else that she saw him interacting with, but with her, there was that intensity she never saw him have with anyone else either. Just with her. And every time she felt his eyes on her, she knew the look she'd find in them.

"Are you scared?" he asked her, his voice rough, his words rolling over her in the quiet of the room.

No, she wasn't scared. She was hungry for something she shouldn't be.

Amara shook her head.

He straightened, taking a step closer to her, close enough that she could feel dwarfed in his presence. Amara loved that about him, that he was the only man she knew who could make her feel so small, so protected.

She watched as he slowly raised his hand, slow enough that she could stop him if she wanted, and hooked his index finger in her scarf, tugging it down her neck.

The skin underneath exposed.

Her breasts heaved.

Heart hammering inside her chest, Amara fisted the sides of her dress to keep her hands from doing anything they shouldn't. She watched him, his dark eyes never wavering from hers even as he exposed her scar to the light in the room, the scar she always hid from everyone.

His gaze never flickered down to it, their eyes locked on each other as he touched the skin with his index finger.

A soft, barely-there touch.

It seared her, from the point of his finger to her flesh, burning and not in a way that was painful. No. It was decadent, like the warmest of fires that seeped into her cold soul, kindling her chilled bones, warming her from the inside out.

His dark eyes, still the most beautiful she had ever seen, focused on her own as he deliberately brushed her scar again, almost as though he was learning its texture.

A small shiver went down her spine, raising goosebumps on her arms and making her breasts feel heavy for the first time with such wild arousal. It was a heady sensation – almost enough to want to make her close her eyes and luxuriate in the feel of the body she usually hated so much.

"Say something."

The soft command made her lips part, as he continued to lightly rub her scar with his fingers. She looked up at him, seeing for the first time how much her silence had affected him. She swallowed once and he felt it, her throat bobbing against his touch, and his gaze darkened.

There was something in that moment – a vulnerability she had never experienced before, one that she didn't mind with him, interspersing with the tension that had layered between them, thickening over the years. He had seen her at her worst, continued to see her at her worst, and he still looked at her as though she was something precious.

The words left her lips before she knew it, in her new, raspy voice not louder than a whisper – words he felt on his hands before they filled the space between them.

"Kiss me."

Silence.

Heavy silence, punctuated just with their breathing.

Something flared in his eyes and she broke their gaze, her eyes moving to his mouth, to trace his lips and his jaw, as her toes curled in her shoes.

She closed her eyes, unable to believe she'd voiced that to the boy she had been half in love with most of her life, the young man who had become something so important she didn't even have a name for it anymore.

She felt the air between them change, the woodsy scent of his signature cologne that she loved permeating the space between them. His breath brushed over her face – warm and whiskeyed. Her breaths stuttered in response. His hand went to the back of her neck to hold her in place, tilting her face up, and her heart thundered, waiting for the kiss, knowing she would cherish it in her heart for eternity.

She should have known not to expect a normal first kiss from Dante Maroni.

His lips came, landing softly on the skin of her neck, right over her scar.

He kissed it once, twice, and Amara felt her lips tremble, the significance of what he was doing not lost on her.

"We shouldn't do this," he whispered against her neck.

"No, we shouldn't," Amara whispered back.

He kissed the full horizontal length of her scar again, and inhaling the line of her neck, he stepped back.

Amara blinked her eyes open, her heart thumping, his dark orbs blazing on hers.

It was over in seconds. It felt like lifetimes.

"I will kiss you and brand myself upon your heart, Amara," he told her quietly. "Just make sure you're ready for me to."

He turned his back to her and Amara walked out on shaky legs, her neck tingling with the memory of his lips. She went down the stairs, out of the house, across the lawn, replaying the scene over and over in her head, a small laugh bubbling out of her throat by the time she entered her apartment, remembering the first time she'd seen Dante kissing a girl years ago.

Back then, she'd thought to herself he'd be her first kiss. He had been in a way.

And while her lips were still famished for his, the ugliness inside her didn't feel so ugly anymore.

"If he had a girlfriend, how would you feel about that?" her therapist Dr. Das, a gorgeous woman in her late thirties, asked Amara, looking at her with solemn eyes behind round glasses.

How did she feel about that?

"Angry," Amara told her in her new voice and looked around the room that had become a sanctuary of sorts for her over the last year. Dr. Das saw her clients – she didn't like calling them patients – in the study of her brownstone house in South Tenebrae.

It was a room contrary to Amara's expectations of what therapist offices looked like. The walls were white, the windows covered with bright green and yellow drapes, letting in an abundance of natural light, a huge Mandala wall-hanging in brown and black taking an entire wall opposite the door. The adjacent wall had stacks of shelves housing numerous books. There was no desk, just a comfortable couch, and armchair with a small table in between. It belonged more to a bohemian yoga instructor than an acclaimed psychologist.

"And why does it make you angry?" Dr. Das asked in her neutral voice that Amara somehow found soothing.

Because he's mine.

Amara didn't voice that, just stared at a spot on the wall.

"Okay," Dr. Das moved on, understanding she wasn't going to answer. "Do you feel any bouts of depression still? Not wanting to get out of the bed, any suicidal thoughts?"

"Very occasionally," Amara admitted. She probably would have felt it more had she not had the people around her, holding her up all the way through. She didn't know how women who didn't have anyone believe them or support them did it. Just the thought of speaking her truth and having people reject it made her stomach knot.

"Panic attacks? Anxiety?"

Yeah, those were there. She nodded.

"What triggers them?"

Amara paused, thinking of every time over the last year that she'd felt the beginning of an incoming attack. "I don't know," she rasped out.

Clearing her throat, she spoke again softly, wishing her new voice could magically change. "Sometimes, I just smell raw tobacco somewhere and everything comes flashing back. I just freeze and no matter how much I try to bring myself back to the present, it doesn't work until the flashes are done. And the entire thing exhausts me. Sometimes, it's thinking about the future and not knowing anything. The unknown scares me. And sometimes, it's knowing I want Dante but knowing I'll probably never have him."

Throat dry, she leaned forward and picked up the glass of water, gulping it down.

"And why can't you have him?"

Amara shrugged. "We belong in different worlds. Girls like me don't get happy endings with guys like him."

"Yet, you asked him to kiss you last night," Dr. Das pointed out. "You spoke to him for the first time since the abduction. You initiated, or rather invited, a physical intimacy. And now, you are able to identify some of your triggers. That's tremendous progress, Amara."

Amara stared at the older woman, realizing it was true. It was progress. She wasn't stuck in the same hole she had been when she first came to therapy.

"And how do you feel after last night?"

She looked down at her printed dress, picking at it. "Good. I... I want more."

"With a boy?" the other woman asked over her framed glasses.

"With him," Amara clarified.

"Him specifically?"

She gave a helpless shrug. "It's always been him."

"Could it be that you've only known him since childhood, so you naturally associate any budding romantic or sexual attraction with him?"

Amara was shaking her head before the other woman finished speaking. "If that was the case, I should have had these feelings for Vin. He's been more constant in my life for longer. I love him but platonically."

"And what about your sexual fantasies?" Dr. Das asked, getting back to the topic they had been working on for the last few weeks.

"I fantasize about him. Dante, I mean," Amara admitted, looking down at the table. "Sometimes, he'll carry me out to sit in the sun and I imagine how it'd feel if he picked me up for more naughty reasons. Or sometimes, when he's talking, I look at his lips and imagine how they'd feel moving on my skin. I just look at him and imagine what he'd do if I kissed him. I mean I did ask him to kiss me and he didn't so I'm not sure how…" she trailed off.

"But he didn't reject you," Dr. Das pointed out.

Amara shook her head, sipping more water. No, he hadn't rejected her. "I think he's being careful with me."

"That's considerate of him," the older woman noted. "But you don't sound too happy about it."

"I mean," Amara bit her lip. "I like that he's thoughtful because I don't know how I'll react in a situation like that. But I just want him to do it, you know. It makes me anxious. Can we not talk about this?"

Dr. Das nodded, tucking a stray curl back in place, making a note in her journal. "Okay. What about Nerea? How are you dealing with her?"

Amara thought of the woman and bit her lip. "I'm not really thinking about it, honestly. It's conflicting."

"Why?" Dr. Das asked.

Amara leaned back on the comfortable couch, staring up at the ceiling. It had a nice abstract pattern. "My father has never been in my life. It's just been Ma and I and I've never felt anything was missing. But knowing he had another kid he actually raised, and we never even knew. It's just too odd. I mean, I'm not jealous or anything. She's actually really nice to me. It's just weird. I always wanted a sister, but I don't know if I'm projecting that desire to see her affection, or if she's truly affectionate for me. I don't want to hinder any potential relationship we can have but I also don't want to trust too easily."

"Fair enough," Dr. Das spoke from her chair. "Seems like you want her to earn your trust."

"Yes," Amara agreed.

The other woman stood up, indicating their time was ending. "I want you to think about two things for me this week, Amara."

Amara nodded. She liked the direction Dr. Das gave her. While she knew a lot of people in their world didn't believe in therapy, Amara knew her time with Dr. Das was one of the main things keeping her together.

"You're seventeen so I want you to think about the two things any average teenager would think about at your age," Dr. Das told her as they walked out towards the main door. "First – think specifically about not what you wanted to do with your life, but what you can see yourself doing now. What is something you could get passionate about, something you could truly believe in doing? Think about that."

Amara nodded, willing to work on that. She wanted to know herself and learn this new girl she had become, whoever she was.

"And?" she asked, opening the door to the house, knowing Vin would be waiting to drive her back home. She wasn't comfortable driving yet.

"And I want you to think about the young man waiting for you."

Amara frowned, turning her neck to see who she was talking about.

Dante. Dante in a suit, leaning against the side of his Range Rover, eyes hidden behind shades, waiting for her.

He was waiting for *her*.

"I specifically want you to think about what you feel for him."

Amara watched him standing there in the middle of the day, the boy who had been her dream, the man who had become her reality, the one who had carried her into the light every single day when her body couldn't move, the one who had made her smile through her nightmare time and time again, the one who had kissed her scar and looked at her like she was a treasure. Amara looked at him, waiting for her, and she knew.

She was in love with Dante Maroni.

"You're unusually quiet," Dante noted as he drove them back. "The session went okay?"

Amara glanced at him. Dante drove the same way he did everything else – confidently, with ease, like he'd been born to it. She had been on the passenger side of his car a grand total of two times and she already loved being chauffeured by him.

"Yes," she answered him, keeping her eyes on his profile. God, he was a stunning specimen of the male variety – strong nose, high cheekbones, defined jawline, proportioned full lips, that vein that went down the side of his neck and into his collar, and those dark, fathomless eyes she had called pretty as a kid. She was intensely, insanely attracted to the physicality of him, but Amara knew she would have loved him even if he had been disfigured and ugly. It was who he was on the inside, who he was with her, that made her soft for him.

"We just talked about how to navigate sex," she said, partly answering him.

She saw him cast a glance at her from the corner of his eyes, his jaw clenching. "I didn't know you were sleeping with anyone," he said casually. *Too casually*. "Anyone I know?"

He'd probably break the fictional guy's bones. God, he was easy to rile.

Although he had never really made a move on her, Dante was possessive of her, but in a weird way. It had started out as protectiveness of her after her abduction, and somewhere down the line, possessiveness seeped in. He didn't mind that she had a very hot guy best friend. In fact, he loved her friendship with Vin and her nascent bond with Tristan. But he watched with dark eyes that burned when they were alone, stamping her entire being just with a look. When anyone was around, he somehow toned that look down, hiding it with the charm that had become second skin to him. But she knew. He had already branded her heart deep.

Amara rolled her eyes. "I'm not. But eventually, I probably will."

His hands tightened on the wheel, that vein at the side popping. "Any candidates?" he asked, his voice a little rough.

Amara looked down at her hands, seeing the scars on her wrists she usually hid with bracelets.

"You."

Her word shot through the tension in the car like a bullet, notching it higher and higher, until she could feel blood rushing to her face, unable to look at him.

He swerved the car to the shoulder suddenly, making her look up and grab the door handle to keep from falling to the side, her eyes taking in the little dirt road he pulled into.

"What-" before she could voice her question, she was out of her seat, straddling a very hot Dante Maroni, his hands spearing into her hair, his mouth crashing on hers.

His mouth crashed on hers, and the tension that had built between them through the years snapped, the recoil of it exploding her senses.

She shivered from the suddenness of it, feeling, truly feeling, him under her, one of his hands holding the back of her head, the other sliding down to the small of her back, pulling her flush against him. She gripped his hair, pulling him closer still, her breasts crushed against his shoulders, her core burning, unashamed of the pleasure just the kiss brought her.

She deserved this pleasure. She shouldn't have to be ashamed of her body for wanting it. Even as she knew this logically, she fought the curl of shame that beckoned her, telling her anything pleasurable after everything her body had been through was wrong, that her desire for any man to penetrate her was wrong.

No, no, it wasn't wrong. Her wanting this man wasn't wrong. Her wanting to have sex and feel pleasure wasn't wrong.

He groaned against her mouth, his tongue flicking at her closed lips, parting them, swooping in to lick at her tongue, and she felt it between her legs, right where his bulge was pressing into her. Slanting her face to the side with his hand in her hair, he deepened the kiss.

Her heart pounded, tasting him.

He pulled back to catch his breath, his eyes pools of darkness that made her feel safe, his lips wet from her mouth.

"You're the beat to my heart, Amara," he whispered against her mouth, pressing his forehead to hers, and something that had been wilted inside Amara unfurled, opening, soaking, blooming in the emotion she could see in his eyes.

She was the beat to his heart and he was the beat to hers, both of them pulsing together.

Maybe, they were both the same beats.

Maybe, theirs was the same heart.

10

Amara

Kissing Dante had become one of Amara's favorite things. It wasn't boring at all like her ten-year-old self had thought. No. Kissing him was heaven. Kissing him was sin. It was everything in between, and she was addicted.

Some days, they'd go for a walk in the woods and he'd press her up against a tree, slanting his lips over hers. Some days, he'd pick her up from her appointments and they'd pull into the same dirt road, making out for hours in his car. Some days, she'd sneak over to his house, feeling his mouth dance with hers in perfect rhythm.

They kissed a lot, but Dante never, not once took it further. His hands stayed above her waist, his lips above her neck, and even though she felt him get hard every time, she never, not once, felt unsafe with him.

They also did a lot of non-kissing things. Some mornings, Amara got up at the crack of dawn and climbed up to his studio, watching him work on his sculptures while listening to books with him. Audiobooks weren't really her thing, but she enjoyed the time she spent listening to them with him. While his tastes were wide, Amara loved romance. One time, she had him play a romantic novel and the narrator reading the steamy parts left them both pretty hot and bothered. That part had been like listening to classy erotica.

On Sundays, Dante had also taken to teaching her dance to help with her sense of balance. He would bring her to his studio and spend two hours playing music and leading her around the room, holding her upright when her knees shook, catching her if she fell, to the point she would literally close her eyes and trust him blindly, and he would always keep her safe.

Her self-esteem got a bit better but it was still on shaky ground.

"I don't know why you'd spend time with me, Dante," she'd told him one day. "I'm young and damaged and nobody. I have scars and a broken voice and my head isn't right. You're the heir to the Outfit and have your pick of people. Sometimes, I feel like you'll open your eyes and see you have better choices and I'll be left alone." To that, Dante had dragged her close and kissed her hard, reassuring her that she was it for him.

Things were getting better all around. Vin was recovered and initiated into the soldier ranks. Her mother had less of a workload because the Maroni's had finally hired another housekeeper to split. Nerea was growing on her, with her devil-may-care attitude and kind smiles to Amara. Amara had actually begun to really like her, and respect her for being a lone woman in an Outfit of men.

Just yesterday, her half-sister had come to her with a beautiful pair of boots.

"What's this for?" Amara had asked, smiling at the gift.

Nerea had shrugged with a small grin. "I've never had a sister so let me spoil you, okay?"

Yeah, she was growing on her, alright.

The only people Amara had gone out of her way to avoid had been Mr. Maroni and his cousin, Leo.

This was why when the messenger came calling her to Mr. Maroni's office, it punched her in the chest.

It was her birthday, and Mr. Maroni had called her to the mansion.

Amara gulped as the messenger, a maid at the main house, left after giving her the message. She doubted he wanted her presence to wish her a happy adulthood day. In all the time she had lived on the compound, something like this – a messenger coming from the mansion to call someone from the staff quarters – had never happened.

Palms clammy, Amara felt the beginnings of an anxiety attack, a pit opening in her stomach, and breathed out slowly, counting backward in her head as Dr. Das had told her. Straightening her dress,

Amara wrapped a scarf around her neck and put on boots, before following the maid up the hill.

"Did he say why he wanted to see me?" Amara asked, unable to contain her nerves.

The maid looked back at her before continuing. "No. He just asked me to call you."

"By my name?" Amara asked, and had her voice been normal, it would have escalated to a high pitch.

"Yeah," the maid left her at the entrance. "He's in his study."

Amara knew the room since she'd been in the mansion helping her mother many times. Taking a deep breath in, Amara headed into the mansion, turning right from the huge foyer, each step she took closer to the study sinking her stomach to her knees.

The wooden door seemed foreboding as she stood before it, gathering the courage to knock.

"Come in," came the heavy voice as she rapped twice on the door.

Pushing it open, Amara looked at the intimidating man sitting behind a huge desk, and older version of Dante, his dark eyes coming to her. His face slashed in a brief smile that Amara didn't like, not one bit.

"Ah, Amara," he said as though he'd known her all his life. "Have a seat. And please close the door behind you."

With a sweaty palm, Amara closed the door, and quietly sat down in the chair before the desk.

Mr. Maroni ran a thick hand through his prominent salt-and-pepper beard, and watching him closely, Amara could see where Dante got some of his features from. His mother must have been a beauty too.

"How are you doing?" he asked pleasantly. Too pleasantly.

"I'm fine, Mr. Maroni," Amara spoke as evenly as she could, pinching the inside of her wrist to keep her nerves at bay.

"Very good," he nodded. "Your mother tells me you'll get your graduation degree this month?"

Amara nodded but stayed silent.

"Have you thought about what you'd like to pursue as a career?" he asked, leaning his elbows on his desk, the picture of sincerity. God, he was good.

"Psychology," Amara informed him, her voice thankfully steady.

"Any specialization?"

Amara hesitated for a second before responding. "Cognitive Behavioral Therapy, specializing in trauma."

"Ah," he smiled, his white teeth gleaming against his beard. "Turning your experience into something positive. Very inspiring for a girl your age. I actually called you here because I feel responsible for what happened years ago. You live on my property and it was very wrong."

God, he almost convinced her of that bullshit.

Amara simply stared at him, waiting for him to continue. Her silence made people uncomfortable, but Lorenzo Maroni simply measured her with those sharp eyes.

Standing up, he went to the wet bar at the corner. "The University of Shadow Port has an excellent Department of Psychology. They also have an accelerated program that allows students to finish credits and get their degrees in two years instead of four. Hard work, but plausible," he said, pouring himself some whiskey from the crystal decanter, before turning to her. "I have an offer for you, Amara. I'll pay for your entire education at one of the best universities in the country. In return, you simply stay there after your graduation and cut all ties with my son."

Amara blinked at the man, her heart starting to pound – not at the offer but the fact that he wanted her out of Dante's life.

She swallowed, fear infiltrating her system, making her breathing choppy as she slowly stood up. "With all due respect, Mr. Maroni," she rasped out quietly, "I'll decline."

She turned to leave the room when his voice stopped her in her tracks. "Or your mother dies, Amara."

She spun around on the spot, looking at him in shock.

He gazed back at her calmly. "This is for your own good, girl. My son might fancy you for now but in a month, a year, a few years at the max? He won't. He'll fuck you and he'll be done. And one day, he will marry someone who fits him and take over the entire Outfit." His voice almost gentled as every word hit her chest like a bullet. "I'm giving you a chance to choose a future for yourself, make a life for yourself, a clean slate."

"And if I don't make the choice you want," Amara huffed in disbelieving laughter, "you kill my mother."

"Yes," he stated, with no remorse. "Take the weekend to think about it. I'll book your tickets for the night of your graduation. You'll have an apartment, a car, everything you need waiting for you. Except for your mother, who will stay here as insurance."

Amara felt her eyes burn.

"Oh, and don't think of telling my son," Mr. Maroni continued, taking a sip of his drink, his face a mask of kindness. "You know his brother? He's in a mental home. Dante loves him. You tell Dante and his brother will disappear and that, my dear, will be on you."

Amara had thought she'd seen the worst of humanity when they had taken her. Looking at Lorenzo Maroni, she realized she hadn't. True evil was like air pollution, inhaled without thought, seeping into the lungs, rotting from the inside out. It was invisible. Insidious. Sadistic. And Lorenzo Maroni was true evil.

Amara pushed her tongue to the roof of her mouth to keep her tears contained. Leaving the room, she walked out of the mansion into the bright day, her entire life changed in the span of a few minutes.

Amara looked at her mother across the kitchen island, gripping her hands. Her mother's eyes reflected the same pain and rage she felt inside her bones.

"We can leave, Mumu," her mother squeezed her hands. "Start somewhere fresh. We have enough savings."

Amara shook her head, wiping her tear across her cheek. "The threat is for your life, Ma. It won't matter where we go."

A tear slid down her mother's aging face. "You love him."

Amara felt her own eyes water. "Yes," she whispered softly, a secret just shared between the two of them.

"You always loved him," her mother stated.

"Not like this," Amara looked down at their joined hands, hers softer, younger, her mother's rougher, more wrinkled. "He always had a bit of my heart, but I'm not that girl anymore. My heart isn't the same anymore. This new heart, it doesn't just love him, Ma. It beats for him." Tears streamed down her face. "He came into this new heart to help me rebuild it, day after day, and he just never left."

Her mother came around the counter to her side, wrapping Amara in her arms, cocooning her in that feeling of safety that always came with her, pressing kisses to her head. Amara broke down, knowing she had no choice. Her mother's life, his brother's life, they were precious. She couldn't be selfish.

"You need to tell him, Mumu," her mother spoke into her hair.

Amara pulled back. "I can't risk his brother's life."

The older woman cupped her face, looking down at her firmly. "Dante is not a boy, Amara," her mother said, using her given name, conveying her seriousness. "He's been playing this game for a long time. He knows his father better than you do. Tell him the truth, tell him everything, and let him handle it."

Amara bit her lip, so, so tempted. "But his brother-"

"Trust him," her mother interrupted her. "He has been here for you, for years. That boy loves you. Don't deny him the chance to handle this."

Maybe her mother was right. Maybe he could do something about it.

Nodding, she hiccupped, deciding to talk to him about it soon.

Vin came to her soon after sunset, his body tall and strong and nothing like his old chubby self, holding a package in his hands.

"Have you been crying?" he asked, his eyes knowing her too well.

"I'm aging now," Amara rolled her eyes, taking the package from him. "What's this?"

Vin smiled, shaking his head. "Just get dressed. I have orders to get you out in 30 minutes."

Amara frowned at that, taking the package to her room, tearing it open. It was a dress, a gorgeous dress. Quickly stripping down to her underwear, Amara slipped into the dress, looking at her reflection in the full-length mirror. The dress was forest color, shimmering in greens if she turned one way and metallic if she twisted another. It had a high neck and full sleeves, coming down to her wrists, the hem falling down to her ankles, with one slit on the right that came mid-thigh.

Taking a deep breath, she tied her hair in a high ponytail that would show off the shape of her neck without showing off the skin and swiped a little red lipstick over her mouth.

She couldn't see a single of her scars in the dress. Just like that, she looked like a genetically blessed woman with slightly heavy breasts and ass that was balanced out by her height. She looked beautiful. And for one night, she could pretend.

Sliding her feet into flats that didn't really go with the entire outfit, she exited the room to see her mother and Vin look up. Vin grinned, giving her a little whistle that boosted her shaky confidence. Her mother tried to smile, her eyes still pained from what she'd told her.

No. Tonight she would pretend.

Giving her ma a little kiss on her cheek, Amara smiled and let Vin escort her up to the waiting car.

"Thanks for the dress," she told him as they neared the car.

Vin chuckled. "Not my gift."

Amara frowned. "What do you mean?"

He just chuckled and got in the car. Amara buckled herself in as they drove out of the property towards the city. "Where are we going?"

"It's a surprise."

Accepting that he wouldn't say anything else, Amara let herself enjoy the ride, watching the lights of the city as they twinkled closer and closer. The possibility of having to leave that place, of losing the city she had come to love had Amara drinking in the sights even more.

Not tonight.

Vin drove to a deserted street, towards an empty multi-story building near Dr. Das's house, stopping the car right outside the entrance.

"He's waiting for you."

Amara looked at her friend, her heart starting to pound as it dawned on her.

Dante.

"He asked you to drive me here?" she asked, her voice low, slightly rough.

He nodded. "For your safety. Go up to the top floor. Happy birthday, 'Mara."

Amara leaned across the console to hug him tightly, her chest heavy. "I love you, Vinnie."

Vin pat her back. "Love you too, 'Mara. Though if you tell anyone I got mushy, we're gonna have a problem."

She choked on a laugh and jumped out of the car. Inhaling deeply, she entered the dark building, spotting the elevator on the right, and took it to the top floor, her stomach in knots. No music came on and Amara exhaled.

"Relax," she told herself softly. "It's just Dante."

After moments, the elevator dinged and the door parted to reveal a huge, open, dimly lit space. Amara took a step inside, looking around the single, huge room, seeing beautiful sculptures displayed around the room. She spotted different variations – from mythology-inspired sculptures to custom art she had never seen before.

As her eyes took in everything in the room, she felt him at her back.

Amara stilled, the new-found instinct inside flooding panic into her system with a presence at her back, flashbacks lingering on the fringes of her mind, waiting for her to open the floodgates.

She locked it shut tight, exhaling, urging her mind to feel safe. Dante was behind her. Dante, not anyone else. Her Dante, who would never hurt her. She trusted him.

But it wouldn't leave, that feeling of being invaded. He didn't know, or he'd never do it. And she couldn't tell him, not without wanting to curl up into that ball of shame, even though she knew logically it wasn't her fault. Sadly, emotion didn't leave space for logic.

Swallowing, she simply stepped away from him, seemingly casual as she walked to one of the art pieces, a grey bowl with veins of gold running beautifully through it.

"That's the ancient art of *kintsugi*," his voice, that warm, husky, masculine voice of sinful chocolate and twisted sheets can from her side. "It's the art of putting cracked or broken pieces of pottery together, repairing them with gold, and making a stronger, more stunning piece than the one before."

Amara stared at the bowl, seeing the splendor of it. What she had thought artful veins of gold were, in fact, cracks where the bowl had broken. It was highlighting the cracks instead of hiding them.

"What place is this?" she asked him softly. She wasn't entirely comfortable using her voice with him yet, but over the last few months, she had begun talking to him.

"It's an art gallery. I'm going to buy it one day," he replied in a tone that matched hers, his hot presence at her side. Feeling nothing behind her back had her relaxing a fraction more.

"And why are we here?" she moved her eyes from the bowl to look at him, surprised to see him dressed in a tux, holding a medium-sized box in his hands.

He looked down at her, the look in his eyes making her heart begin to pound for a different reason. The light from the outside fell on one side of his face, and her palms itched to trace the line of his jaw, to feel if it was as smooth as it looked or rough against her skin.

Surprising the hell out of her, he went down on one knee beside her.

What the hell was he doing?

Amara bit her lip as he opened the box, his eyes on hers, and revealed a pair of beautiful golden stilettos. They were gorgeous, with an ankle strap that crossed over the top, the thin heel a solid three inches.

She gulped. "It's beautiful... but... I can't wear heels," she lilted through the words, explaining it to him.

"Trust me," his eyes stayed on hers, fierce yet somehow soft.

Wiping her palms on the dress, she nodded.

He took the shoes out, placing the box to the side, and held her right ankle. Amara felt a current shoot up from the spot to her core, tingling her body in a way she had only felt with him before. He placed her foot on this knee, the slit of her dress gaping open, exposing her entire leg to him.

Amara saw his eyes rove over the exposed skin, before coming to hers, the heat in them knocking her breath out of her lungs.

"Ask me to kiss you," he told her, his voice rough, grating over her skin in the most delicious friction.

Her toes curled on his thigh in reaction, her throat dry. God, she loved him and right then, she wanted him to take his fill, to touch, to devour. Every sexual fantasy she'd harbored for him in secret came to the fore of her mind. She didn't know where he would kiss her if she asked, kneeling as he was, but she wanted it. She wanted him.

"Kiss me," she whispered in the space between them, her heart racing.

His fingers tightened around her ankle fractionally, his eyes breaking their gaze to trace the line of her leg, stopping at the single, small scar from the knife in the middle of her thigh. He leaned forward, his mouth pressing to the spot, and Amara felt her head tip back, her breath coming out in a rush as all the blood in her body rushed to the spot to greet his lips. She tightened her grip on his shoulder, feeling his tongue softly lick the little scar. Her heart stuttered, the action causing wetness to pool between her legs, the significance of it causing her eyes to burn.

He pulled back, squeezing her ankle to get her eyes on his, his gaze so hot, so hungry it created a riot erupt her insides, his face so, so close to her mound she knew could scent her arousal.

"Ask me to kiss you," he uttered again, his Adam's apple bobbing over his collar, his jaw clenching once. She knew what he was asking. She knew exactly where his mouth would go if she asked him again, and though she should stop this madness, she couldn't. Her body, while still hers, followed his commands.

She swallowed, feeling the heaviness in her breasts, her nipples standing to attention even though his eyes never wavered to them. Gliding her hands over his broad shoulders, feeling the muscles covered with his jacket under her palms, Amara slid her fingers into his hair for the first time, thrilling at being able to touch him like this.

"Kiss me, Dante."

His eyes blazed as he put his left hand on the small of her back, steadying her, and tugged her ankle up, placing her knee over his shoulder. Amara felt herself lean back against the wall, her heart pounding as he widened her legs enough for the slit of her dress to gape. She felt him move, placing a soft kiss on the inside of her thigh, right where her thigh met her pussy, and for a second, she felt apprehension crawl over her skin.

Her palms began to sweat in what she identified as one of the first signs of her anxiety attack.

No.

Not now. Please, not right now.

Her chest got tight, her heartbeats spiking for another reason altogether. Her breaths started to come faster. Black crawled the edges of her vision, tar dripping into her lungs, weighing them down too heavily she couldn't breathe.

Dr. Das's voice entered her head.

Sex is natural, Amara. Your introduction to it was traumatic, so of course, that impacted you. You can enjoy sex but communicate with your partner. Let them know what's working and not working.

What if he never wanted to do this again?

She closed her eyes, blinking rapidly.

"No," she wasn't even aware of the word leaving her as blackness swept over her vision.

He stopped immediately, his eyes coming to her. He took in her face, and whatever he saw there must have affected him because his gaze softened. He pressed a soft kiss to the side of her knee before putting her leg down.

Dante took off her flat, his fingers stroking over the arch of her feet, going to the underside, tracing the scars she had there, before slipping the shoe on her and placing her foot back on the ground.

Sense of balance shaken, for more than one reason, Amara held his shoulders for support as he did the same with the other foot, putting her flats in the box to the side.

Amara stood still beside the wall, her knees slightly shaking at the elevated height, as he straightened. Damn if the fact that he still towered over her didn't have her lady bits tingling. She didn't understand what had just happened. She wanted this man. She wanted to do naughty, wicked things to him and have him do naughty, wicked things to her. Her panic didn't make sense. But then, it rarely did.

"I'm sorry," Amara whispered, feeling her stomach twist, hating that she didn't know if her refusal would make this her last opportunity to experience something like this with him.

She should have known not to underestimate the man Dante Maroni had become.

"You have nothing to be sorry about, Amara," he took a hold of her fingers and tugged her towards the center of the room on her tottering heels, supporting her weight, tapping something on his phone before pocketing it. "That's not how this works."

The opening trails of a song filled the room as he pulled her in, pressing her flush against his body, one hand holding hers, the other on the small of her back, in a familiar way he held her when they danced.

"How does this work?" she swallowed, asking his shoulder.

"It works with you stopping me when you need to, and me stopping. Or you telling me to keep going, and me going on. Simple as that."

"And if I keep stopping you?" she voiced the one fear she had.

"Then I stop. No questions."

Amara pressed her nose into his shoulder, inhaling that woodsy fire scent of his that she loved, feeling heady, feeling beautiful, feeling loved.

He began to sway them softly at first, and she tightened her hold on his shoulder to keep her balance.

"Let go, Amara," he lined his lips with her ear, speaking the words against her lobe, his mouth brushing her skin, sending a shiver down her spine.

"Let go of everything inside your head," he continued speaking, guiding her forward, then back. "Feel. Just close your eyes and feel. The music. This moment. Me."

Amara felt her eyes flutter close, her heart racing. "What if I get hurt?" she whispered into his jacket.

He pulled back so she could see him, his eyes solemn, soft, sincere on hers. His face dipped closer and he pressed a soft kiss to her mouth.

"Then, I'll kiss your scars."

And just like that, the little of her heart she'd been holding onto was his.

That night, they danced. That night, they talked.

He told her how he wanted to buy the gallery one day in honor of his mother. She told him of her dream, of helping people heal. He told her about the pink-haired girl he'd had to kill. She told him she'd seen him bury the body. He told her about his brother and his love for building things. She told him about Nerea and how she was slowly accepting her.

He didn't kiss her below the neck again. She didn't ask him to.

That night was perfect.

And then, the morning came.

Amara waited in the woods, outside the shack where she had seen him years ago.

She was going to tell him about his father's offer and let him handle it, as her mother had said.

She saw him walk out of the path, dressed in perfectly ironed grey pants and a black button-up, his sleeves folded over his forearms, his eyes on the shack behind her. Something dark passed in them before he looked at her, his face more stoic than she was used to.

"What happened?"

The hope inside her fluttered a little, but she pushed it down. "Your father made me an offer yesterday."

She saw him frown before nodding at her to go on. She did, recounting the whole meeting, the offer, the threat, everything. With each word, something dark fell over his face. With each word, the vein on the side of his neck throbbed. With each word, his beautiful dark eyes got more and more closed.

He shoved his hands in his pockets, his eyes on the shack behind her, silent once she was done.

Realization dawned on her. It was the same place he'd had to kill Roni. Shit.

A strong wind moved through the trees, pushing her hair around, chilling her arms. The clouds remained overhead, casting everything around her in a gloomy glow. Amara pulled at her scarf out of nervous habit, before stopping herself, the silence making her antsy.

Dante clenched his jaw, before finally spearing her with a look she had never seen from him.

And she knew.

He was going to break her heart. After all the promises, after everything, he was going to be the one to break her.

"It's a good offer," he said simply, and Amara felt something in her chest splinter.

She took a deep breath, looking down at the ground, her hands fisting at her sides.

"Even if I could risk my brother, which I can't, my father's right," he told her, his words chipping small, little pieces inside her, "I'm young right now. One day, I'll have to take over and marry someone more suitable for my status. That's not a future for you. You can have a better life away from this place, Amara."

How many times did people break before they stopped mending? The pain in her heart enveloped her body. He wasn't telling her anything she didn't know herself. But god, it hurt. And while Amara wasn't a stranger to pain, this one was another kind entirely, the kind that made her want to drop to her knees and howl at the unfairness of this, the kind that made her want to slap him across the face for daring to make her hope.

She stayed standing, hands fisted at her sides, keeping her eyes glued to the ground, the thin layer of snow, and the plants that were suffocating under it.

"I'm sorry, but I think we both lost sight of that," his voice was harsh as he continued, but she didn't look up. She couldn't look up. *Now right now.* "We're not a love story. We're a tragedy in the making. There's no happy ending for us. I feel that you have a better future ahead of you, and you should take it."

Each word hit the nail harder, not into her coffin but into her flesh, leaving it bleeding and raw and open.

Darkness frayed around the edges of her vision, her jaw hurting from keeping it closed tight. Amara closed her eyes, pushing her tongue to the roof of her mouth, willing the little trick to work.

Don't let him see. Don't let him see. Don't break.

She should have known. She should have known they were too good to be true. Hadn't she said to herself that girls like her didn't end with guys like him? She should have never let herself believe the madness he had weaved into her soul.

"You should leave," he told her.

She was going to. She was going to leave and never see him again.

Keeping her face to the ground, Amara walked away from the clearing without a word, wondering if there would ever be an end to the pain, realizing that there wasn't much difference between true evil and true love. They snuck up on the vulnerable, gripped them by the throat, and left a realm of ruin behind.

Dante

23 YEARS

D ante had been to Shadow Port previously for work and he was going again in two days, but it was the first time Tristan wanted to accompany him. He said it was because he wanted to look at some property in the city, but Dante knew he wanted to spy on the little Vitalio. Over the years, he had seen the man fall deeper and deeper into an obsession that would have been unhealthy had it not been the only thing sustaining him.

Dante's own obsession, though not as mad as Tristan's, burned just as hot, even if there was a difference. Morana Vitalio didn't even know Tristan existed, and his girl had existed with Dante in her life for as long as he could remember. Where Tristan's obsession was a visible thunderstorm, Dante's was more like the wind – ever-present and life-sustaining but invisible. It could go from a comforting breeze that gave relief to the relentless wind that fanned the flames.

His obsession was born of an emotion he had not thought himself capable of. When it began, he didn't know. Maybe it was the second she collided into him and fearlessly demanded his attention, or maybe it was when he held her broken body in his arms after searching for her for days, or maybe it was when she looked at him with mindless pain before slumping in relief; or maybe it was when he saw her trying to walk on her hurting feet, fall and push herself up again.

Dante didn't know when he fell in love with Amara. He just did.

This was exactly why he sat in the Outfit restaurant in his city, watching as the mustached man across him, the man he'd finally located after four years of searching. The man swallowed his food, his eyes nervous. He should be very nervous.

"It was years ago, man," the jackass said, his eyes shifty. "We just got the order to take the girl. I can't remember anything else."

Something that had always bothered Dante about Amara's abduction had been the lack of logic behind it. Had it been a normal kidnapping with the ransom, he could've understood that still. But with the level of torture she had endured, and from what her kidnappers had told him before he killed them, he knew she'd been targeted specifically. And it didn't make sense. If someone had wanted Outfit secrets, Vin had been a better choice to take, instead of the young girl who wasn't in the fold. Also, the fact that her kidnappers had been professionals, the kind that chewed on cyanide capsules in their teeth rather than give information.

Dante used the spoon in his left hand to twine the spaghetti on the fork, before putting the bite in his mouth, chewing slowly to both enjoy the taste and let the asshole in front of him sweat. They were seated in a corner away from the main part of the restaurant, and Dante liked that. Cleanup would be less of a headache. Although, nobody would dare come to them, not with his gun openly visible on the table.

Swallowing down his bite, he deliberately picked up his glass of wine, a decadent red, and swirled it in his hand, his eyes on Gilbert, the man he'd finally found. What the fuck kind of a douche name was Gilbert?

"I swear I don't know anything, Mr. Maroni," the man swore profusely and Dante shook his head.

"See, Gilbert," Dante took a sip of the wine. *Ah, so good.* "I don't like people who lie to my face. I know the hit went from you to those boys. So, I'm giving you one more chance. Who told your boys to kidnap the girl?"

Gilbert slugged down his drink, wiping his hand on his palm. "Look, I really don't know."

Dante pursed his lips, indicating the man's drink. "You know the whiskey you just enjoyed so much? It's poisoned."

"What?!"

Dante calmly twined another forkful of spaghetti and continued talking. "It's an extremely rare blend of venoms. Very hard to acquire, to the point I actually had to hire a very skilled thief to get it for me, especially for occasions like this. But that's beside the point. Three little drops. I'd say you have five, maybe ten minutes top."

"What do you mean?" the man panicked, his face sweating.

"Unless of course, you get an antidote," Dante helpfully pointed out, "which happens to be in my jacket pocket."

The man in front of him adjusted on the chair, breathing heavily.

"In about two minutes your system will start to shut down," Dante picked up his glass again, leaning back in his chair. "You don't have a lot of time, Gilbert. If I were you, I'd be singing like a canary."

"It was a phone call," the man huffed out, squirming on the chair now. "He didn't give his name, just transferred all the money and told us to interrogate the girl."

"Interrogate her about what?" Dante asked calmly as the man tugged at his collar.

"Everything. He said she had some information and we had to break her by any means possible and call him back with the info."

"And did you?" Dante looked down at his watch. "Call him back?"

"No," the man started to shake. "She didn't break."

Fuck, no, she didn't break. Not his fierce warrior queen.

Dante didn't ask for the number. After so many years playing the game, he knew well enough how things worked. The number would be a dead end.

"You gotta give me something if you want to live," Dante said in a singsong voice, seeing the hands on his metal watch.

"I just know he worked for a group, alright?" the man panted, sweating profusely. "Some kind of guild or syndicate or something. Give me the antidote, please!"

A few patrons in the restaurant looked at the table, at both the men and the gun on the table, before looking away. They all knew this was an Outfit establishment.

Dante chuckled. "See, that's where you're wrong, Gilbert. You gave your boys the permission to torture a fifteen-year-old kid." He leaned forward, the rage inside him simmering. "Did you know she was mine?"

The other man's eyes widened as he sputtered. "No, no. I swear I didn't know she was yours. I never would have taken the job if I knew."

Dante picked up his napkin and wiped his mouth. "Well, at least you know exactly why you're dying. Goodbye, asshole."

He saw the man shake, spasm, and fall over the table, a white froth coming from the side of his mouth. Dante nodded to the manager, dropping a wad of cash for the wide-eyed waiter. "Tell the chef the food was fabulous. And keep the change."

While the men involved in her torture were all dead, the man who had ordered it was still at large. And Dante wasn't going to rest until he found him.

A month passed.

Dante didn't see her again, at least not where she could see him. He went to Shadow Port, vetted the apartment she would stay in and her neighborhood, the classes she would be taking, and her professors. He got a flat in Tristan's building and told him to keep an eye on her when he was in the city. Satisfied, he came home, hoping to see her around the compound before she left.

But she rarely got out of her apartment that last month. He knew she ached for him, not knowing his ache bled worse. It was only through her mother that he knew the day she got her degree and packed her bags. He saw her mother and Vin drop her at the airport, checked to see when her flight landed on his phone and called the guy he had planted in the apartment across hers, confirming that she had arrived safely.

He would not see her again. He would let her go and let her live her life. But he would be damned if he ever let anyone crush her spirit.

And once she was physically away from his father's wrath, Dante went to bargain with the devil.

"Where's Damien?" Dante barged into his father's study, slamming his palms down upon his desk.

His father frowned at him. "What do you mean?"

He built rage inside him, black, bitter. "Cut the shit. Where is he?"

Lorenzo Maroni blinked at him, leaning back against his chair. "I have no idea what you're talking about."

Dante breathed in, calling for all his patience. "I went to see him, only to get there while a fire burned the fucking property down. Why does every home he's in burn down, huh? I've spent hours searching for him, through bodies and survivors, and he wasn't there. So, dear father, where the fuck is my brother?!"

He saw his father grab his phone from the table, standing up as he dialed someone and started to pace. Dante waited, the acid inside his veins just looking at the man eating him alive.

"Damien Maroni," his father barked into the phone. "Where is he?" Pause. "No, he's not at the facility. There was a fire." Pause. "Yes, I want him found."

He turned towards Dante, his eyes steady. "I don't know where he is but he will be found."

Dante leaned forward, his eyes deadest on the man. "You better hope so, father. Or you and I are going to be having a very different conversation."

"Don't you dare threaten me."

Dante stayed silent, letting his eyes talk, every ounce of hatred he felt for the man and for himself becoming visible to him.

"You don't find my brother, you have nothing to hold over my head," Dante told him quietly.

"I have her," his father told him. "You're foolishly attached to her. And I have her, son."

Dante deliberately gave him a little smirk. "Good. And you better make sure nothing happens to her."

"Or?"

"Or I walk."

The silence between them loaded with tension. Dante had never made that threat before. But he hadn't been ready before. He was now.

"You can't walk away," Bloodhound Maroni stepped into his space, his finger pointed at his chest, his eyes disbelieving.

"I can and I will," he told his father, taking a hold of his finger and pushing it down. "A hair on her head gets harmed, I'm out. Your entire legacy crumbles. Lorenzo Bloodhound Maroni becomes nothing but fodder for gossip without an heir."

"I would kill you before that."

As expected. "And there would be nothing standing between you and Tristan," Dante informed his father. "Now that he's a grown adult, why do you think you're still alive, father?"

That shook him. He could see that.

Dante pat his shoulder. "Thinking she was a pawn was your biggest mistake, old man. So, tell your watchdogs to keep her safe. She gets so much as a paper cut, it's your reputation and your neck on the line."

"I will not have you sullying our blood with a common little whore."

What a pompous prick.

"That 'common little whore' is going to be the mother of my children one day, father," Dante smiled at the man. "Your grandchildren. The future Maronis."

"You get with her, I will slit her and her mother's throats," the older man spat out.

Triumph rolled through him. He had maneuvered his father exactly where he had wanted him. "So, as long as I stay away from her, you leave her alone?"

"She was going to meet with an accident," his father said, making Dante's gut clench. He had already suspected that though. "But you've learned to bargain, son. I won't touch her as long as you put her out of your head. Find someone else to fuck."

Dante gritted his teeth, knowing now wasn't the time to tip the scales of this precarious balance. With that, he turned around to leave and paused. "Oh, and as of today, her mother is my employee, not yours. The same rules apply to her. Now, I'll leave you to find my brother."

He knew what his father would find – a burned corpse of a teenage boy by the edge of the property. Dante doubted it would occur to his father that he had been played. His brother was across the ocean, safe in a wonderful house with friends he had made in the facility, living a good life away from these games, no longer a pawn on the board. Dante could never see him again, never risk having anything trace him back to Damien, for his own safety.

Dante had known, as soon as Amara had told him about his father's generous offer, that her life was forfeit. His father was going to break her rhythm and that, he fucking couldn't allow. So he had removed the only leverage his father had had over him for years, planning his brother's fake death and protecting the woman who had his heart, even as he broke hers.

Something clogged in his chest, remembering the last time he had seen his brother a few weeks ago, almost as tall as he was, intelligent enough to understand what Dante was telling him. Damien understood his brother loved him, which was why he had to let him go. He would always watch over him, but until the old man died, they couldn't see each other again.

With Amara, he had to lay low. Her life hung in the precarious balance between his father's threat and Dante's promise. It was a sacrifice worth the wait. She was worth the wait.

Although he imagined she'd tell him to go to hell if he showed up, her voice low and raspy and fucking messing with his heartbeat like it always did. He didn't think she knew how much he loved her voice. In his world of gunshots and screams, her voice was a gentle prayer, evidence that there was life after the endless noise.

There would be life after this.

The old man couldn't die, not yet. There were too many variables that would impact a lot of lives if he was killed.

Dante imagined killing him a lot, torturing him in different ways for everything he'd done to his mother, his brother, to Roni, to Amara. He wanted to sneak up to his room and slit his throat in his sleep. He wanted to march into his office and put a bullet between his eyes. He wanted to drag him to the interrogation room and make him bleed for hours.

Dante nurtured the hatred he felt for the man, cloaking it under an easy smile, all the while planning to take his kingdom apart, bit by bit, moving the pieces until nothing remained but the bare foundations of the empire that Dante would build.

It wasn't time yet.

But one day, it would be.

And that day, Dante would smoke a fucking cigarette as he watched him bleed, and he would come home to fuck the woman he loved.

Amara

18/19 YEARS

The new city was a stranger, made worse by the fact that she was completely alone.

She missed her mother, her best friend, her half-sister.

She missed the hills, the woods, the views.

She missed *him.*

She missed his kisses, his eyes, his voice. That little grin he gave her, that polished look on his face, that fire in his endless eyes. She missed the sculptures and conversations and books, the dances and the drives and the dreams.

After years of spending every day together, the separation felt more brutal. But she'd make it. She had to.

*

"Hi, I'm Daphne!"

The bright girl in her class came towards her. First week of school and it had been slightly overwhelming. The campus was beautiful and the classes were interesting.

Amara smiled. "Hi," she whispered in her soft voice.

The girl frowned. "Why are you whispering?"

The smile stuttered.

*

"I don't know how to connect with anyone," Amara told her new therapist, a nice middle-aged black man with an office close to the university campus. "People always ask why I can't speak normally and I can't really tell them that I screamed too much now, can I? I don't think torture is a part of the polite conversation!"

Dr. Nelson watched her quietly, letting her vent the acid out.

"I can't go out without the bracelets or scarves because one time this boy saw my wrists and asked me what happened. Can people not see it's something traumatic? Can they not be more sensitive? I miss being myself. I miss being able to just be myself without feeling that I'm broken."

*

She stared at the ceiling, watching the fan move slowly, heart thundering after waking up from a nightmare. Her studio apartment was dark, and she was alone. Anyone could break-in. Anyone could take her from her bed. And she wouldn't be able to even scream for help.

She watched the ceiling, wondering why she was even there, wondering how high the fan was from the floor, wondering if it could hold enough weight.

Then she flushed those thoughts out.

*

"Do you want me to come to visit you?" Nerea asked on the phone. "We can have a weekend of fun. You can show me around the city."

"I'd love that, Nerea," Amara whispered into her phone. "You'll like the museum here."

"Do I look like someone who'd enjoy a museum?" Nerea chuckled.

They made plans. Nerea came to see her and for a weekend, Amara felt amazing.

On Monday, loneliness encroached again.

She woke up, went to classes, came back to a dark apartment, studied, and slept.

Rinse and repeat.

Some nights she woke up shaking with nightmares, some she fell into an exhausted sleep. She always aimed for the latter, working and studying and tiring her mind.

*

A noise made her pause, her key in her door, her hand on the handle.

The noise came again, from behind the plant at the side of her door.

Amara bent down, hitching her bag higher on her shoulder, and placed the books in her hands on the floor, her bracelets jingling with the movement, and noise came again. A mewl.

She looked behind the plant to see a tiny little cream-colored kitten with the biggest olive green eyes mewling quietly.

Her heart melted. Picking her up carefully in her palm, Amara brought her up close to her face, a true smile on her lips after so long.

"You lost, baby?" she asked in a small baby voice. "How did you get here?"

The kitten blinked up at her, mewling again, before putting her head on her hand in a motion that made Amara a puddle.

She straightened, unlocked the door, and brought her companion in loneliness home.

"So, what do we call you, huh? Pixie?"

Stare.

"Pogo?"

Stare.

"Stardust?"

Stare.

"Lola?"

Stare.

"Lulu?

Meow.

"Lulu it is."

Months passed.

It wasn't easy living alone. It took her some time to get used to the idea. Having Lulu helped.

Amara hadn't realized how safe living on the compound had made her feel. She missed her mother, missed her best friend, and even missed the bastard who had broken her heart. Though she still loved him for everything he had been through with her, she was glad to not see him since that day in the woods months ago. After the breakup of a relationship that had never been, Amara had swallowed the bitter pill, asked Vin to drive her to Dr. Das, and cried like a baby while the older woman had listened to her vent without any judgment.

'You're brave to open your heart to him after everything you have been through, Amara. While it is sad that he doesn't reciprocate your affection, it could be a good thing. You'll be able to explore more once you go to university.'

Yeah, the only problem with that? Amara couldn't trust anyone for shit. She gave the men a wide berth, somehow always wary if one of them would pick her up and put her in a truck. The girls she didn't know what to do with. There were a few who simply ignored her, and the few who had tried to talk to her Amara realized were normal girls. They hadn't lived their whole lives on a mafia compound, with a best friend who was a mafia soldier, and an ex-something who was an underworld prince. Her normal and their normal did not match and Amara couldn't find herself talking beyond a certain point with anyone.

The only good things about her new life were the accelerated classes that she really enjoyed, Dr. Nelson – the therapist in the city Dr. Das had recommended, and Lulu, the fluffy little thing who had immediately curled up against her with such trust, Amara had fallen in love.

Amara looked at Alex, her TA who kept asking her out until she said yes, as he danced against her. She had given him every excuse in the world, especially the fact that with her accelerated modules she had to finish in two years, she didn't have time to date. He had been persistent.

The lights in the club he had brought her to flickered neon all around her, the music loud and throbbing and all wrong. Amara had thought he'd take her out to a restaurant or something for the date. Instead, he'd brought her to the hub of hedonism and it wasn't her scene.

She swayed on her heels, not accepting any drinks from him no matter how much he tried, to the point she started getting annoyed. "Dance, Amara" he shouted over the music, stepping into her personal space. Amara involuntarily stepped back, hitting a wall, her nerves shot but pasted a smile on her face.

He stepped closer to her, backing her into the wall, and her palms started to get clammy. She didn't like this. "Step back, Alex," she said but her voice got drowned in the music. He leaned closer to hear her, the scent of vodka strong on his body, and Amara's gut churned.

She just wanted to go home to Lulu.

"Gonna kiss you, yeah," he said, caging her in.

"You're not owed a kiss for a date," she told him, inhaling deeply to keep her nerves at bay. "I said step back." But it was fruitless. The music was too loud. She gave him a shove, clearly indicating her displeasure, hoping he'd give her space.

He didn't. Evidently, entitled assholery afflicted men out in the normal world too.

Amara kneed him in the groin in a move Vin had taught her, pushing him off. Alex cupped his balls, gritting his teeth, his face turning red. "What the fuck!"

She ran to the side door, pushing bodies out of her way, and exited into a narrow, secluded side entrance of some kind. A red bulb hung over the wall, lighting the stairs that led up and out into the street hopefully.

Amara leaned against the wall, holding her stomach, trying to catch her breath. She didn't have anyone she could call in the city, who would drop everything and pick her up and take her home. She was a big girl but she didn't trust people. The cab she got into could drive off the path. The driver could be a psycho and take her somewhere else. Scenarios like that always ran through her head, making her anxious, and she needed to keep calm.

The side door opened, and Amara looked at it, suddenly alert, ready to run up the stairs if need be.

Only to feel her heart stop.

Dantes Maroni stood in the narrow corridor, making it seem smaller, dressed in a crisp dark shirt and dark pants, his dark eyes on hers, not saying a word.

Months.

She hadn't seen him in months and he dared to stare at her with that possessive look in his eyes, had the *fucking audacity* to stand in front of her like no time had passed, to make the need in her heart so acute it hurt.

Amara glared at him, her chin starting to tremble as her eyes burned, rage enveloping her as she just looked at him.

She closed the space between them, her hands shoving his chest, all the pain and hurt and loneliness she'd kept inside herself for months bubbling to the surface. Red edged around her vision, her body quivering from the force of her emotions, and she shoved him again, her sight blurring with tears. She punched him in the chest, little sounds of aggression leaving her, almost feral, and he let her, not stopping her until she was spent.

"Get away from me," she pushed him on his solid muscles that didn't even move, glaring at him through her tears, her body shaking. Fuck, she was having an emotional breakdown.

"Amara," he said softly, taking a hold of her wrists in his hands, his fingers going right over her bracelets that covered her scars.

"You didn't fight for me," her mouth trembled as she pulled but his grip didn't loosen. "You didn't fight for me, Dante!"

He tugged her close, until she tipped into his chest, holding both her wrists with one hand while cupping her face with the other, his eyes wild on hers. "I fight for you every fucking day, Amara."

God, she hated him for meaning it. She loved him too, even after all this time.

A tear escaped her eye and Dante leaned in, kissing it from her cheek like he still had the right.

"You need to let me go," she told him, her voice breaking, meaning more than her hands. "I can still feel you haunting me here. I can feel you and I can't live like that. You need to stop. Please. Let me go. Please, let me go," she started sobbing against him, not realizing when his arms came around her, holding her tight. "Let me go. Let me go. Please. Please," she hiccupped.

He pressed his forehead against hers. "You're in my blood, beating in my fucking heart. The only way you go is when the heart stops."

God, he couldn't say shit like that to her. Falling with him was so easy, so exhilarating. It was the crash that scared her.

Wiping her cheeks, Amara straightened, looking at his tie slightly askew because of her shoving. Taking hold of it, she set it straight, putting her hand over his heart, and looked him in the eyes. "I'm in love with you, Dante," she confessed to him, although they both knew. "But I won't let you waltz in and out of my life as you please. You say you're fighting for me, and you might even win the battle, but you will lose me. End our suffering right now."

Dante clenched his jaw. "Go to your apartment. I'll come to talk in a few days."

Amara nodded, took a deep breath, and stepped back from him, turning to go up the stairs.

A hand suddenly spun her around and his mouth lingering close to hers, inches from her, so close she could feel the warmth of his breath over her lips, the air between them hard, intense, electric, making her tingle from the root of her hair to the tips of her curling toes. She leaned into him, soaking up the tension, the magnetism, the physicality she had missed so much, a hello and a goodbye all at once, before pulling back and walking away.

He needed to make his choice.

Dante Maroni was an idiot and she was an even bigger idiot for goading him.

A week later, Amara opened the door to her little studio apartment, getting in and locking it behind her, throwing her wedges to the side.

"Is he a good kisser?" the voice from the darkness of her living room area startled her.

Amara shrieked, spinning on the spot to see the man she hadn't seen in a week, the man who owned her every waking thought, sitting casually on her couch, sipping from the wine bottle she kept in her cabinet, Lulu curled around his feet.

Lulu, slightly bigger than when Amara had found her and even more adorable with the softest cream fur and the prettiest green eyes. She was also a traitor, napping against the man she had no idea what to do with.

"What are you doing here?" she asked him quietly, turning on the lights in her small but cozy apartment, putting her clutch on the side table. She threw off her keys to the side, and padded barefoot to her bedroom, taking her earrings off, appearing casual even as her heart thundered in her chest. After a few days of waiting for Dante and him not showing up, Amara had gone out on another date with a guy from her Psychology of Art class. Had she half-hoped it would make him react? Yes, yes she had.

Lulu lifted her head at the sound of her voice, her flat face perking up at seeing her, and she prodded up to rub against her legs before going on her merry way. Lulu was a stray like her, alone in the big city, her baby now.

Amara dropped her earrings in the bowl on the dresser, her neck prickling with the presence that came to her back. She looked up at the mirror, seeing him behind her, his jaw clean-shaven, a bruise on his temple that hadn't been there before, his tall, wide form eclipsing her own.

The butterflies that had been dead in her belly during her entire date fluttered to life just at the presence of this man who didn't feel for her as she did for him.

"You didn't answer me, Amara," he murmured softly, his dark, chocolate eyes tracking her own body, from the red dress she'd worn to the little denim jacket and the scarf she'd paired it with. His eyes took in every inch of her, as though they had missed roving over her skin, and goosebumps broke out over her arms.

"It's none of your business, Dante," she rasped out quietly, watching as his eyes darkened in the reflection. He was at her back and while it usually triggered her, being able to see him in the mirror had her mind pausing from the knee-jerk reaction.

She saw his hand rise up in the reflection, coming around to her neck, a finger looping into the silk scarf, tugging it down. Her breathing hitched as she watched him expose her scar to their reflection slowly, his thumb brushing the horizontal mark, his face leaning down to brush his lips against her ear.

"Did he kiss you, Amara?"

Her nipples pebbled. Breathing heavily, her chest heaving, their gazes locked, something heady pulsing between them, Amara shook her head. Dante pressed his lips to her lobe again, the possessive fire in his eyes so familiar yet so foreign.

"Ask me to kiss you."

Her lips tingled, the memory of the last time she'd asked him for a kiss throbbing between them. She knew if she asked this time, it would change things. They had gone for months without seeing each other, without speaking to each other, living their lives. He had no right to come barging into hers, only to walk away as he pleased. She wouldn't let herself be a pushover, not for the whim of a man, even if he was the one for her.

Taking a step away from him, Amara threw off her jacket, her temperature too hot. "You don't have the right to demand anything, Dante. I'm not yours. You gave me up, remember?"

He was in her space before she had spoken the last word, his hands spearing into her hair, tilting her face up, his mouth breaths away from hers.

"You and I, Amara, we will never be anyone else's," he murmured, his words ghosting over her lips. "We could fuck a hundred other people but *this*, this will never go away. Do you feel it pulsing between us?"

Her heart was thundering by the time he finished speaking, his chest an inch away from her heaving breasts. She did feel it, much stronger than it had ever been before. Amara looked up at his lips, the mouth she had tasted on hers in so many different ways, just a command away.

"Are you going to fight for us?" she whispered, the wound of his words still bleeding in her chest.

"I am, Amara," he told her, his eyes burning, taking in her face. "But I can't give you more than that right now. I tried staying away, letting you live your life. Fuck, I've tried-" he pressed his forehead to hers. "I can't, Amara. You're the beat to my fucking heart."

And he was hers.

Amara felt her eyes burning, remembering the feeling of love and safety she'd felt him, the deep pain of loneliness that had become her constant over the last few months, her nose twitching.

She believed him. For whatever reason, her heart had known even when breaking that he'd not done it out of disregard. And watching him, the anguish on his face, she believed him.

But she didn't know if this meant anything, or what tomorrow would bring. But she knew she wanted him, wanted everything with this man.

Swallowing down her nerves, her face still cupped in his large, warm palms, Amara stood up on her toes, her nose brushing hers, and spoke the words out.

"Kiss me."

His lips crashed on hers before she had finished speaking, swallowing the last of her word.

Finally.

Her body trembled.

Amara stretched higher on her toes, the pressure of his mouth making a shiver run down her spine. He tilted her head to the side, slashing his lips more firmly across hers, and licked at the seams of her closed mouth, the taste of him – smoke and wine and him – filling the gnawing hunger inside her. She felt her lips part on a soft moan, and he took the invitation, swooping in, tangling his tongue with hers.

Dante's kiss was fire through her veins, not the kind that burned her down to cinders and ashes, but the kind that warmed her from the inside out in places she hadn't known she'd been cold and shivering. It lit up the corners in her being that had been shrouded in darkness, forcing everything malefic to the shadows as she basked in the warmth.

He guided her mouth and she followed, this dance of a different kind, one they'd danced so many times before.

He pulled back, and she opened her eyes, taking in his lips, painted the shade of hers, wet from her mouth. It sent a tendril of something possessive dispersing inside her, watching him wear the evidence of herself on his flesh. She wanted him to be marked with her, just as he had marked her on the inside.

He moved his thumb over her lips, the touch rough.

Before she knew what she was doing, she opened her mouth and sucked it in.

His eyes darkened. "You need to stop if you don't want to be fucked, Amara."

Heat snaked inside her body, coiling low in her belly, melting her insides.

She wanted to be fucked. She wanted to be fucked by him. But she didn't want to panic in the middle of it.

She bit down on his thumb, keeping her eyes steady on his. "Go slow, please."

His eyes flared and suddenly, she was flat on her back on the bed, her legs dangling over the edge, Dante kneeling between them, his gaze on hers, his mouth a heartbeat away from her panties.

"Do you want me to stop?"

She shook her head mutely, her heart hammering in a way that sent wetness pooling between her legs.

He took a hold of her panties, pulling them down her legs and throwing them on the bed, his fingers finding her folds. "Fuck, you're drenched."

His rough, hard voice noting that with his rough, hard fingers on her flesh just made her wetter. She pushed a hand in his hair, moaning. "Dante."

She felt his hands get a hold under her knees, pushing her legs back towards her on the bed, splaying her wide open to his eyes. "I'm going to eat this pussy until they bury me in the ground," he stated, his mouth falling on her folds.

Amara arched off the bed, her hands gripping his hair, liquid heat moving through her body, spiraling to the spot his mouth devoured her. And he devoured her, his tongue plunging inside, tasting her, learning her spots, one of his hands coming down on her little nub of flesh, his thumb rubbing her vigorously as he ate her out like it was his sole purpose in life.

It was her first time being eaten out, and god she loved it. This pleasure was nothing like anything she'd felt before, not even the few times she'd tried to touch herself since the assault. She had never been this wet; the orgasm had never been this close. Writhing against his face, noises of pleasure escaping her throat, Amara pulled his mouth closer, never wanting him to move away.

"That's it, baby," he encouraged her, making out with her pussy like it was the last time he would have it. "Ride my face. Fuck, you taste so good. Use my tongue."

God, he was a talker. A dirty, nasty talker under those suits. It turned her on even more.

His tongue swirled around her clit, side to side, round and round, diagonally, every which way, and Amara felt a wave so intense crash over her it made her scream, the cords in her throat straining as pleasure flooded her, her legs spasming out of control as she came all over him.

He held her down through it all, letting her ride the wave, keeping her rooted to the bed as she slowly came down.

She felt limp. Heavy, like her bones weighed a ton, but in the best way.

Blinking, she looked up as he hovered over her, between her legs, still in his suit, looking down at her with a look so visceral it made something in her heart clench.

"Hi," she whispered, her chest heaving.

His lips, still wet from her, tilted upwards. "Hi. You okay?"

She licked her lips. She could feel the bulge in his pants pressed against her naked heat and knew she was probably leaving a wet spot over him. And while the evidence of his arousal itself made memories want to resurface, she wanted nothing more than this man, buried as deep as he could be inside her, one with her in every way he could be.

She had to do this. She needed to do this. Keeping their gazes locked, strengthened by the possessive heat in those brown eyes, knowing he would rather cut off his arm than physically hurt her, she knew he would let her.

"Two things-" she told him softly "-don't ever take me from behind, and don't call me a slut."

He raised his eyebrows slightly, and he hesitated for a second. "Is there something I should know before we do this?"

Amara felt her palms get clammy. "No." She could never tell him, not when that shame still curled in her gut.

"You sure?"

She nodded. Raising her hands, she slowly started to undo the buttons on his shirt, exposing inch after inch of delicious male flesh he hid under those expensive suits of his until he hovered over her with his jacket on and shirt gaping open, his chest covered by a sparse smattering of hair, trailing down to solid abs, down to his belt and the bulge under it.

She pushed on his shoulders. "Lie back," she told him quietly and saw his lips pull up in his typical smirk.

"As you wish, my lady."

A laugh escaped her. "Did you just quote *The Princess Bride* while I'm trying to seduce you?"

"You never have to try, Amara," he murmured, tracing her lips with his fingers before laying back, linking his arms behind his head. "In my defense, you did make me watch that movie twice."

"You liked it," Amara pointed out.

"I loved it," he said, his gaze surprisingly sober on hers. "I believe in true love, and I believe in waiting for it. Would you have waited, Amara? If it had been you in the movie, would you have waited on a promise, not knowing why or when or how?"

She knew they weren't talking about the movie anymore. She climbed over him, straddling his waist, his erection pressing right into her core.

"Is my true love trying to find me, be with me, in the movie?" she asked, her heart pounding as she unzipped him, feeling his cock in her hands for the first time.

She saw his abs flex at her touch, but he stayed still, watching her. "Every single day."

Her heart stuttered. She couldn't keep her walls up against him, not when he said shit like that and actually meant it.

Ignoring how his word affected her, she wrapped her fingers around him, or tried to, the feel of him soft but hard, heavy, in her palm. With her other hand, she pat one of his pant pockets, taking out his leather wallet, hoping there was a condom in it.

There was. Taking it out, she squirmed back, ripping it open with her teeth, and finally looking down at his cock, the first cock she had actually seen outside of porn.

It was big. *Big.* Fuck.

Panic started to seep into the edges. She couldn't take it in. She wouldn't be able to take it in. It would hurt.

God, it couldn't hurt.

Her hand trembled, and she felt him take the condom from her, rolling it over his erection in a smooth motion.

That cleared some of the haze of her panic. She wasn't doing this with some random stranger who would push into her without any thought or possibly hurt her. This was Dante. The man who had picked up her body when it had been at its most broken and held her soul when she had thought it beyond repair, giving her gold to fill her cracks every day for three years. He was the most dangerous man that she knew, but also the noblest in a way. She knew he would never she was at her safest when she was with him. And if she told him to stop, he would stop.

Taking a deep breath in, she looked into his eyes, opening her legs wider, feeling his tip touch her nether lips.

"I would wait for you for an eternity, Dante Maroni," she whispered to him, slowly lowering herself on his erection, feeling her walls stretch to accommodate his thickness. A breath whooshed out of her and she pulled her dress off, exposing every inch of her body to his hungry gaze. "But that eternity would be spent alone, wouldn't it?"

211

His hands came up to cup her breasts, squeezing them hard and she sank an inch deeper on him, trying to rotate her hips to lessen the burn. He pulled her forward so she leaned down, her nipples brushing over his chest, as his hands slid into her hair, his jaw clenched, his eyes fierce on hers.

"One day, I'm going to put my ring on that finger, Amara," he grit out, pushing up another inch into her. "One day, I'm going to put my babies inside you. Just wait for me, baby. Please wait for me."

Amara felt her breath hitch, her heart stuttering as she finally sank all the way down on his length, feeling full but not invaded, her eyes holding his gaze. "What about-" she asked him, her voice soft, squirming as he throbbed inside her. "-you being Dante Maroni. One day, you'll have to find yourself a mafia princess and put your ring on her and your babies inside her." God, just the thought of that hurt. She already hated his future wife. "Remember what you said? We're not a love story. We're a tragedy waiting to happen."

Suddenly, she was on her back as he loomed over her, pushing inside her deeper than she'd thought possible, his mouth a fraction away from hers. "Then, let's make it a good one."

He placed her knees over his elbows, opening her wider as he pulled out of her, leaning back completely. Amara felt herself moan as her walls clenched, empty of him, wanting him back, and within a second, he thrust back in. The power of his thrust pushed her up on the bed, her breasts bouncing, and he leaned down, taking one of her nipples into her mouth. The suction sent a shot of pleasure to her core, making her muscles squeeze around him, her hands gripping her sheets beside her.

This felt like nothing she could have imagined, nothing from her nightmares.

"Fuck, you feel so good," he said on another hard thrust, his teeth tugging on her nipple, his thumb settling on her clit, rubbing between her legs. "So tight and wet and mine. This pussy has been mine, hasn't it Amara?"

She was getting mindless with pleasure, her neck straining to the side as she tried to hold back the wave from crashing into her.

"Let go, baby," she heard him whisper into her ear, her legs completely pressing back as he leaned over her, licking her neck, his chest rubbing against her nipples in friction that sent heat spiraling through her.

"Come for me, Amara."

Thrust. Rub. Lick.

"Grip my cock with your pussy."

Thrust. Rub. Nip.

"Feel that?"

Thrust. Rub. Bite.

"You dirty girl, so wet for me."

Thrust. Rub. Lick.

"You're making a puddle on the sheets."

And she *came.*

Like a rocket that shot up into the sky and splintered apart in a million pieces of fire and smoke, evaporating into nothingness in seconds. She came so, so hard her teeth punctured her lips, a strangled cry leaving her throat, her body jerking in his arms as he held her down, still moving inside her, still fucking her like she was his dirty girl and her pussy his to plunder.

"Look at me," he grit out, pushing his hands into her hair, gripping her head to keep it still as she slowly came down to the ground.

"You" *thrust* "are" *thrust* "mine".

With that he picked up the pace, hammering his hips against her, his pelvis pushing her clit on every downward motion, his eyes, those beautiful, dark eyes, steady on hers, seeing her completely laid bare and naked and vulnerable and open in every way that she could be. He saw it and he took it, and she gave and gave and gave, the intimacy of their bodies, their gazes, their hearts all connecting in one tandem until she didn't know where she ended and where he began. That look in his eyes – pure unadulterated desire for *everything* – pushed her over the edge again.

She felt him jerk inside her, his growl rough as he came, his cock pushing as deep into her as it could go, making her walls weep around him.

Their bodies came down from the high of their orgasm slowly, sweaty, and spent. He got up and went to the bathroom, and she just lay there unmoving, staring at the ceiling, waiting for her heart to gradually calm down.

The feel of something wet between her legs had her looking down, to see him cleaning her with a wet towel, and she felt her heart squeeze in her chest. Why did he have to be so perfect for her?

He threw the towel to the side, stripping out of his clothes, exposing his entire body to her eyes for the first time up close.

Amara watched the muscles and ridges on his body – the broad shoulders she'd held on to multiple times as he carried her, the strong arms that made her feel the safest she'd ever felt, the beautiful chest she wanted to use as a pillow for the rest of her life. She watched him – from his big, beautiful feet to his muscled thighs, to his semi-hard cock, to his happy trail, to his abs, to his pecs, to his neck, and finally, to his eyes.

He leaned down and kissed her softly, stretching out beside her.

"You okay, baby?" he asked against her lips as she cupped his jaw. She went from 'dirty girl' to 'baby' and she loved it. The brain was such a weird thing. She would've thought being called a dirty girl would have possibly triggered her. But when he said it like that, in his voice of warm chocolate and twisted sheets, his dark eyes worshipping her skin, 'dirty girl' felt like 'goddess'. She loved it. How could she ever stand a chance against this man when he made her feel like this?

She nodded to his question. "How is my mom?"

"Safe. Enjoying the challenge of trying to get into Tristan's house. Mine is pretty boring for her."

Amara huffed a laugh, imagining it vividly. "How is he doing?"

"Same old," he told her, playing with her hair, his fingers holding a wild curl. "He actually bought a property in the city."

"In Tenebrae?"

He shook his head. "In Shadow Port. It's not that far from here. You should go sometime. I think he'll like that."

Amara felt a flutter of excitement in her system, her heart aching at the thought of having a friend in the city, even though Tristan wasn't a conventional one. "Does that mean he'll be here often?"

"I think he'll be here a lot," he said, his eyes taking a measure of her. "You know Gabriel Vitalio?"

She nodded. Of course, she knew the infamous Vitalio. She was in his city.

"He has a daughter – Morana," he hesitated. "Tristan has a history with her. Let's leave it at that for now."

Amara knew he wanted to share, but she didn't push, knowing he would tell her if he wanted to. Changing the topic, she asked, "What about your brother? How is he?"

There was silence for a beat before he pulled her leg over his hip, their bodies pressed together, his eyes on the ceiling. "Damien is doing good. He's almost your age but his brain is extraordinary. His Asperger's diagnosis has been confirmed by another doctor so they're making special learning modules for him."

Amara rubbed the line of his chest. "Is he safe?"

"Yeah," Dante took her hand, interlinking their fingers together. "I faked his death so my fucking father wouldn't use him as a pawn anymore. But I can't see him for a long time. Not until Daddy dearest is dead."

Amara felt her heart pound, her mind absorbing the lengths this man could go to, to protect the people he loved. She forgot sometimes, in moments like this when he was soft with her, that he was still the same ruthless Dante Maroni who was rumored to have interrogated a guy for thirty hours without getting a speck of blood on his clothes. Without his clothes, naked as he was now, Amara saw him in his entirety – the man and the beast.

"What's that look for?" he asked quietly, tracing the palm of her smaller hand with his thumb.

"Is it the same with me?" she asked her voice nothing more than a whisper. "That I'm off the board until your father is dead?" Yeah, she felt no remorse for thinking about the death of that man.

Dante turned back to the ceiling, his mouth curling. "You remember what I told you about chess pieces? That I didn't know what piece you were?"

"Yes."

He turned his neck to put his eyes on hers. "You're the queen on the board, Amara. You're my most powerful piece, but my most vulnerable. They get you, they get me, and the game is over. So, I'll do whatever I need to make sure they never get you. Even if that means hiding you like my dirty little secret for the time being."

Amara swallowed, her heart in her throat. Could she live like that? "So, what now?"

"Now, we deflect," he told her. "We move on with our lives. I take a mafia princess or two on a date. You take a guy or two on a date. I go about taking over the business. You go about your classes and therapy. Any eyes watching us see that we're over. But we go home alone." His eyes blazed on hers. "Nobody touches you, Amara, or I'll spend a lot of time cleaning up a lot of blood."

"And same goes for you?" she asked, just wanting to confirm.

"I'm not a hypocrite, baby," he brushed her hair back from her face. "I'm not asking you to do anything I won't be doing myself. Nobody touches me either, just you. I have an apartment in Tristan's building. When we're in the city, I'll sneak away to come to see you. No phones or anywhere online, it's all traceable. If we happen to meet during the day, you're someone I used to know and I'm someone who broke your heart. My father can never get a whiff of the real thing."

Amara went up on an elbow, her heart thundering as she processed everything he was saying. He hadn't given up on them, he had just played them all like the master manipulator he was. Could she trust him to not play her? "And in between? If you get horny?"

He held her jaw in his hand, the gesture one of such dominance it sent fire licking at her bones. "Then, I wrap my fist around my cock and remember how tight your pussy felt, and I come."

His other hand slid down her body, cupping her between her legs, the heat of his palm stark against her wetness. "It's that simple, baby. I'm not a slave to my desires, they're a slave to me."

Amara processed that, looking at the sincerity and openness on his face, the kind she'd rarely seen him give to anyone for a long time. He had perfected his mask of a charming, easy-going, easily underestimated guy. Laying bare as he was, she could see how much he hid – the manipulation, the shrewdness, the sincerity.

His eyes moved over her face. "What I'm offering is not what you deserve, but for your own safety I can't give more than this right now. I don't even know when I could give you what you do deserve. There's no timeline to this, so it won't be easy. But you get to choose. If you don't want this, tell me now. I'll walk away and I'll stay away, and you'll never have to deal with me again."

She didn't want that. She wanted him. She wanted a future with him even if she didn't know what it looked like. It was a risk and if it backfired, Amara didn't think she'd be able to recover from that loss.

"And if I want this?" she asked him softly, hand fingers wrapped around his wrist, feeling his steady pulse under her palm. "What then? What do we do for now?"

"We hide in the shadows for now." Dante gave her that little grin, the one that always sent butterflies fluttering in her belly, and whispered against her lips, "So, will you play with me, my queen?"

Amara looked into the eyes of the man she loved, saw that same love reflected back at her, and sealed their fates.

"Yes, I will, my king."

*

They made love one more time before sunrise.

Amara woke up to see him getting dressed, her throat tightening even as her heart felt joy. She saw as he gave Lulu a head rub and came to her, leaning on his hands beside her face.

"I have to leave," he told her, his eyes soft, his mouth swollen from their kisses.

Amara nodded.

He bent to press a kiss to her lips, then presses their foreheads together for a long second.

And then he straightened and walked out, leaving her in her bed, with a smile on her face and a hope in her heart.

Days became weeks.

He came to see her five times those first few weeks. She wrapped them away in her memories.

She saw more of him on the internet, sometimes alone, sometimes with a woman. She ignored it as he asked.

It chipped away little pieces of her.

Weeks became months.

She finished school with accelerated classes, started her master's degree, began her therapy training. Made friends with books, talked to Lulu, continued with her own therapy. Embraced her demons in the morning, grew into herself in the afternoon, found pleasure in her body at night.

He came many times.

He left every time.

Chip, chip, chip.

Months became years.

She celebrated her twenty-second birthday with him.

She finished her accelerated Master's, got on her Doctorate, and studied her ass off. She spoke to her mother every other day, kept in touch with Vin and Nerea, and went to Tristan's penthouse occasionally.

He started spending a few days at a time with her, risking everything for one time.

He had to force himself to leave every damn time, saving everything for next time.

Chip, chip, chip.

Years became six.

With her professional evolution and personal therapy, twenty-five knocked on her door with blooming confidence. She finished her doctorate, started her business, got new clients, moved into an apartment she bought herself. She went out on dates, covered her scars, and wore her heels, and came home alone.

Some days, she felt she was weak for waiting for him. Other days, she felt she was strong for waiting for him. The coin kept flipping, the only constant her deepening love for him and his maddening love for her.

He rose in the ranks, became a true heir to the throne, and Amara felt proud.

He never touched another woman, his heart and body and soul all hers, and Amara felt loved.

He loved coming to her, holding her for long minutes like his arms had been famished.

He hated leaving her, pressing his forehead to hers as her eyes burned.

They hid in the shadows.

Chip, chip, chip.

Six years became seven.

They became the roots of a tree, buried deep underground, out of sight, twined together, entangled together, strengthening each other, weakening each other, taking all the love like nourishment, storing it in secret places, all the while waiting for the tree that had been violently cut to sprout leaves again.

It took time for forests to grow, kingdoms to build, and empires to exist. Where one was being broken, another was being molded to take its place.

They were lovers and friends, strangers and acquaintances, all those things, none of those things.

They just were.

Waiting.

Chip, chip, chip.

Her exile never ended.

They never truly began.

But empires took more time to break than people, and slowly it cracked.

PART 3

tempest

(Present Day)

*"I'll follow you
and make a heaven out of hell,
and I'll die by your hand, which I love so well."*
William Shakespeare, A Midsummer Night's Dream

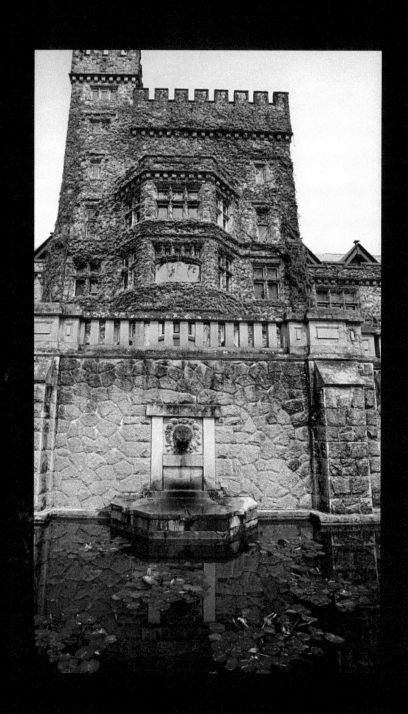

13

Amara

She knew something was wrong the moment she saw him at her door in the middle of the day. He never came to her during the day.

"Dante-" his mouth was on hers before she could utter more, the urgency in his kiss infusing her blood, the taste of him after weeks, weeks of not seeing him, aphrodisiac in her veins. She hadn't seen him since the night they had the heated falling out over her telling Morana the truth about Tristan. He had come to her that night, both their tempers high, and fucked her all night through in anger that had blown into exhaustion.

He pushed her into her new apartment – the one she'd bought herself three months ago – pushing the door close with his foot, turning her to press her against it, hard. Her balance tottered in her heels – heels she'd come to love because of how confident and powerful they made her feel, but also because every time she put one on, it reminded her of that first time.

Before she could catch a breath, he was on his knees, her legs over his broad shoulders, her panties a scrap of fabric in his hands, ripped and discarded, and his mouth was between her legs.

A man who ate his girl out solely for his pleasure was a different breed of dangerous, and Dante Maroni was the most dangerous of all. In all the years they had been doing this, Amara had lost count of how many times she'd woken up with his mouth between her thighs, how many times he'd bent her over just to taste her, how many times he'd pushed her against the wall to make out with her pussy. He did it for no other reason than he loved it, and he'd made her addicted to his skilled mouth, ravishing her tryst after tryst, orgasm after orgasm, hour after hour, just because he could.

Her pussy knew him, recognized him, and drenched for him within seconds. Amara pushed her head back against the wall, his hands the only things holding her upright, and saw Lulu watching them curiously from the doorway.

A strangled laugh escaped her, ending on a moan as he pushed his tongue inside her, his hand wrapping around her thigh to rub her clit. Fuck, he was good. So, so good.

Amara bit her lip, grinding against his mouth, chasing her pleasure, unashamed of her body's desire after so long with him. Some days, she still felt a twinge of guilt for never having told him the extent of her assault, or how it still affected her, how she still woke some nights drenched in sweat, a heartbeat away from screaming, and how Lulu – her sweet, loving Lulu who had grown up to her full furry body – always climbed on her chest and started purring like a motor to calm her down, her big green eyes on Amara.

"Lulu is watching us," she told him, tugging at his hair.

"Let her watch," he growled, looking up at her, the sight of him on his knees before her making her melt. "Let her watch how I'm going to fuck her mom hard against the door."

Oh my.

With that, he straightened to his full height, having grown a few inches taller somehow, broader, more filled out, still towering over her in her heels. Dante Maroni as a boy had been her unrequited; Dante Maroni as a man was her undoing.

His hands went under her ass as she unzipped his pants, taking out his hard, familiar length, feeling the heavy weight throb in her palm. He lifted her easily, lined himself up against her, and thrust home.

Home.

He felt like *home.*

Amara felt her eyes burn and closed them, her body shuddering with the pleasure of connecting with him, her heart weeping knowing he would leave after. She shouldn't keep doing this. She couldn't stop doing this.

His mouth took hers, her taste on his lips making her clench around his cock, the kiss wet, sloppy, perfect. He pulled out an inch before pistoning his cock in, her walls fluttering around him in greeting, gripping him tight, keeping him.

"Missed you," he pressed his forehead into hers, his eyes dark and heavy on hers. "I missed you so fucking much, dirty girl."

Amara felt a lump in her throat. "I missed you too," she whispered, and his eyes roved over her face, as though memorizing her, trying to trace if anything had changed since the last time he'd seen her. The last time they'd been in the same space, tempers had been high and she'd called him a coward in her frustration of being stuck in the same loop with him because he either wasn't moving them forward or wasn't telling her. They hadn't talked much that night.

"I'm sorry," she murmured, taking in the slash of his dark brows, the wide forehead, his strong nose, shaven jaw, swollen mouth, his hair that was usually slicked back from his face falling forward as he fucked her. She took every part of him in, seeing how much he'd changed physically from a decade ago, from the twenty-year-old boy who had rooted himself in her life to the thirty-year-old man he had become.

She knew he understood what she meant. But something was wrong. His eyes were too dark, too heavy. She'd spent enough time learning the browns in them – how the sunlight hit every fleck, turning them to burnished gold; how night made them black holes, sucking everything they saw into themselves. She knew his eyes like the scars on her wrist – every little bit memorized, imprinted on her heart.

"Dante," she rasped out.

He kissed her, silencing any question on her lips, picking up his pace, lifting her higher so he hit that magical spot deep inside her, turning her liquid in his arms. Tilting her head back, she gripped his shoulders as he kissed down her neck, licking her scar like he loved to do, his mouth wrecking her heart. Over the years, he had kissed every inch of her body, seen every one of her physical scars, and lavished them with love like they were the most beautiful badges of bravery. They were her veins of gold, he'd said so many times.

Losing herself to the pleasure, Amara felt the tingling start in her toes, heat scorching the base of her spine as the friction drove her deeper and deeper into the abyss.

"Fuck, your pussy has been hungry," Dante muttered, his own pleasure loosening the filthy thoughts in his head. "She's missed me, hasn't she?"

"Yeah," Amara panted, trying to push back against him but he kept her pinned in place, hammering into her, the door shaking behind her with each thrust.

"Fuck yeah," he licked the line of her neck, biting her pulse point, sending sparks of ecstasy through her bloodstream. "So horny, you're dripping all over me."

Dirty-talking Dante was her kryptonite. She went crazy when he talked like that.

"What are you going to do about it?" she challenged, clamping her walls deliberately around him as he entered her again.

He bit her jaw in retaliation. "Own this pussy," he grit out, changing the angle, the speed. "Own you. Fucking all of you. So deep you won't get me out."

Fat chance of that.

She bit her lips as he lifted her higher, taking her hardened nipple into his mouth through her dress, the fabric rubbing wet against her sensitive flesh. Her nerves caught fire.

"Oh god," she whimpered, her voice straining as he hit her g-spot again, and she exploded all around him, gasping for breath, her walls clenching and squeezing him, her body shaking as he kept thrusting in and out, over and over.

"Just like that," he groaned, burying his face in her neck, his motion roughening. "Come on my cock, baby. Fucking soak me. Mark me."

She kept coming as he hit her spot, over and over again, before he exploded inside her, soaking her walls with his seed, pushing in as deep as he could go.

They stayed there for a few seconds, catching their breaths, the intensity of the experience still making her shiver as he stayed lodged inside her, his face in her neck, pressing soft, sweet kisses to her skin. This, this was exactly why she had been waiting for him, for so many years. Months of separations dissolved in the moments of connection, so true, so raw, so pure, she knew she would never have it again. There was no other Dante for her, and she knew there was no other Amara for him.

He lifted his head, cupping her face, his eyes moving over her. "I'm sorry too. I have to go."

The abruptness of it made her heart sink. She hated it when he left, and truthfully, she hated him a little for leaving every time, even as she understood it. Usually, he stayed a little longer though. She didn't understand what was causing this rapid shift.

And she saw something in his eyes, something she had never seen before. Fear.

That brought her up short. "Dante-"

"Ask me to kiss you, Amara," he commanded, something he hadn't said to her in ages, his eyes so heavy, so dark, his pupils and irises merging to make a black hole, absorbing everything that she was into them.

Warning bells began to ring in her ears.

"Kiss me," she told him and he held her face, pulling her up to her toes, pressing his mouth to hers in the softest, most soulful kisses he'd ever given her. He stayed that way for a long minute, before pulling out of her, pulling away from her, and adjusting his attire.

Amara watched with silent eyes as he left, as quickly as he'd come. Like a tornado without a warning, he'd blown in, shaken her foundations, wrecked everything inside her, and left her standing in her living room with a probably-traumatized cat, hickeys on her neck, and a leaking pussy.

She got the news two weeks later.

She saw the news two weeks later.

Dante Maroni was dead.

Dante

She had disappeared.

He was doing this for her, for them, and she had fucking vanished. God, he couldn't wait to get back so he could look for her himself.

Dante tugged at the cap on his head, missing the feeling of the watch on his hand and the suit on his body. The t-shirt, while soft, wasn't really him in public. But that was the point.

Dante Maroni was dead, and he was a ghost. For years, he had been building towards this point, working from the inside to this end.

Daddy dearest's closet was finally open, and the monsters inside sunk their claws into him.

He didn't want to fake his death, but it had all come to a head with a phone call from the man across from him – the same weirdo who'd been watching Tristan and him beat up a creep years ago. With a heavy beard and hazel eyes that were a hundred percent Morana, the man had given him evidence of his father's true evil.

For years, Dante had known there had been something more to the business, but he'd never been able to nail it. Not until his search for Amara's abductors had led him to a name.

The Syndicate.

He had remembered the name. And when Morana came up with the same name again searching for any trace of the missing children twenty years ago, it put him on high alert.

But the Syndicate was a ghost – no one knew anything about it, hadn't heard about it, didn't even know it existed. So to catch a ghost, he crossed over to the other side and became one himself.

The man passed him the envelope. He didn't know the man's name, never had, but soon after getting his brother out and Amara's exile, Dante had contacted him. They'd been working together ever since, taking over his father's empire piece by piece, from the fringes, readying the entire system for his takeover on his terms – although Dante was amazed he hadn't realized this guy had set Tristan up by stealing the codes until later. But the man had asked Dante not to let them know, and while Dante wouldn't have agreed usually, he was Morana's father. So, Dante respected that.

"This is the address?" Dante asked, sinking deeper into the shadows of the hole-in-the-wall bar in Tenebrae, where the worst of humanity hung around, drinking cheap booze and finding cheaper pussy. Nobody in the world would recognize him here, not with his scruff and cap and loose clothes.

"Yes," the man replied, rubbing his knee that Dante knew had been injured courtesy of his father. The Reaper was a strong man to survive what he did and to live as he did, just to protect his child who didn't even know of his existence. And Dante had grown fond of Morana, so he knew this would hit her hard. But still, he respected strength, and the strongest person he knew was in the winds.

Where the fuck was she?

"That's your in," the man continued, speaking in low tones despite the noise in the place. "I have information that two members of the Syndicate will be there. They all have a little S tattooed between their thumb and forefinger. Find them. Befriend them or interrogate them, it's your call."

He nodded.

He was going to infiltrate the Syndicate, the ghost organization that didn't exist. He didn't know who all were involved in it, or exactly what they did, but fuck if he let this shit run the show in his city while he took over. His father, from what Dante had inferred, either partnered with the organization in some way or did their bidding. He wasn't involved, because he didn't have a tattoo on his hand, and Dante had checked.

"Take a backup. A few men," the Reaper told him, his hazel eyes serious on Dante, older, more experienced. Dante knew the man would kill his father one day, and honestly, if anyone deserved to kill the asshole, it was this man.

"I'll take Tristan," Dante nodded again, throwing some cash on the table out of habit, and got up, keeping his head low, walking out of the bar. It was an art, to blend with the crowd and the shadows especially with his height and build.

Walking to the pavement, Dante began to walk down the dark street, sending Tristan a text with the address and time through the disposable burner phone, knowing he would get there.

While teen Tristan had been a raging storm, adult Tristan had become the calm before it. He alone was enough of a backup, and Dante trusted the bastard to watch him. Tristan still barely tolerated him, but he was fond of Amara and knowing Amara loved his sorry ass was a point in his favor. Plus thankfully, Morana being fond of Dante had softened him, to the point that now Dante could make a quip and Tristan would just sigh and let it go. Sigh. The man never sighed. But Dante knew what love – and good sex – with the woman of one's heart did for a man. He had known it for years, had survived for years because of it, had found strength in the darkest pits of hell because of it, because of her.

Amara.

A decade ago, Dante had loved the girl she'd been. Now, he was awed by the woman she had become.

He had seen her, every time he saw her, growing into her skin, glowing with her scars, becoming a woman who would one day rule by his side.

Dante had never known softness and strength could coexist together in such balance before her. Despite being through everything she'd been through, walking through hell and fighting the demons in her mind, she still had a love for life that unmanned him. The most generous of hearts, the most steely of spines, Amara was a woman of beauty, a warrior of blood, a queen of scars.

And he was one fucking lucky bastard that she felt an ounce of affection for him, enough to wait on his promises even as it hurt her.

Most people weren't capable of that kind of love – to give so much without losing themselves. Yet, she did. With him, with her cat, with Tristan, and now with Morana, Amara gave.

He had dropped that cat Lulu - *what the fuck kind of name was Lulu?* – outside her apartment immediately after her exile, back when he'd thought he could let her go and stay away from her. He hadn't wanted her to be completely alone and somehow, knowing she had a companion he gave her, made him feel closer to her. Although, she still didn't know Lulu had been Dante's gift to her. She said Lulu was her miracle at a time she'd needed it the most, and Dante let her believe that. One of them needed to keep believing in miracles.

Where are you, baby?

Fuck, he missed her. And he had no shame admitting how completely, utterly in love with her he was. If there was one thing his mother had taught him right at the beginning of his life, it was emotions and that feelings were powerful. And a man who denied them out of a misbegotten sense of societal norm was a fool. There was nothing more forceful than emotion, and Dante was witness to that. Hate for his father, revenge for his mother, justice for his brother and Roni, and love for Amara – all pure, unadulterated emotions in his veins, driving him to plan, plot, and plunder, piece by piece.

And after years, it was slowly coming to a head.

The address was a farmhouse eighty miles out of the city, deep in the country, registered under the name of one Alessandro Villanova. Dante had no idea who this guy was but as he and Tristan entered the property, his eyes took in the simple exterior. Too simple. It was a house one would pass on the highway without once taking a second look at. Dante knew how deceptive exteriors could be, and these simple grey walls were meant to deceive.

"Tell me you have a bad feeling about this," Dante muttered to a silent Tristan, his stomach turning. Tristan's jaw clenched. Answer enough. He believed his feelings now. If his gut said something was off, then something was off.

They sneaked around the shadows, weapons in hand, ready to attack or defend as needed.

Sounds coming from a room had them exchanging a look before they cautiously proceeded to it. Having worked together seamlessly for years, they were well in sync. Nodding on the count of three, Dante slowly extended his hand and pushed the door open, his heart calm but gut churning.

He and Tristan watched the four adults in the room, and suddenly, Dante knew exactly what the Syndicate was about.

Children.

Tristan's fist slammed on the guy's already swelling face. Dante stood to the side, letting him take his rage out. Dante knew seeing the girl, the red-headed little girl, in that place, in that position, had unlocked a slew of demons in Tristan's head.

They had stumbled upon the scene and for the first time, Dante saw Tristan's face break, knowing his own reflected the same. While they were murderers and monsters, there were some lines they could never, ever even imagine crossing. What they witnessed had been true monstrosity.

Somehow, they'd grabbed the first asshole who had left the room, the asshole with the S tattooed on his hand, and brought him to one of their warehouses to interrogate.

If Tristan's hits were anything to go by, he wouldn't be able to talk, much less give any coherent information. *Time to step in.*

Throwing his cigarette away, Dante put a hand on the younger man's heaving shoulder.

"I'll take it from here," he looked at the man he had come to consider a brother-in-arms, a man who was on the verge of losing his shit. Dante knew that every day that went without any news on Luna was another weight on his shoulder.

"Go to Morana," he told Tristan quietly, not worried about their captive listening. He wouldn't be making it out alive anyway. "Be with her. I'll handle this motherfucker."

Tristan hesitated before giving him a tight nod and walking out of the warehouse.

Dante grabbed a chair and turned it, taking a seat in front of the bastard, wishing he could take him to the interrogation basement at the compound. He had better infrastructure there. Well, he'd improvise.

Taking out another cigarette, because this was a fucking stressful situation and he needed to keep as calm as possible, Dante lit it up slowly, keeping his eyes on the man. Dark-haired, medium built, averagely dressed, he could pass on the street for just another guy.

He stayed silent, simply smoking and watching him. That was his primary tactic. People always underestimated how powerful mastering silence could be, especially because human beings always tried to fill it. It was a psychological torture tactic – one of Dante's personal favorites and one that the artist in him appreciated – because it let their imaginations run wild. Would he kill them? How would he do that? With a bullet, a knife, or a wire? Would he torture them? Break their bones? Pull their nails? Or something worse?

It was his favorite because before he even asked them a question, they scared themselves on their own enough to show him a crack. And then, Dante put a nail on the crack and hammered, and hammered, until it split.

He took in a deep drag, letting his emotions simmer under his skin, watching the man's face swell.

"What do you want?"

Crack.

Dante simply sat there, watching him steadily. He knew that freaked them out – this huge dude just smoking calmly, no response, no crazy look, nothing.

"Look, I don't even know who you are."

Lie. The man had recognized him, paling like he'd seen a ghost.

Dante blew out a cloud of smoke. Feeling a little evil, he started making smoke rings in the air, seeing them float towards the man.

The guy pissed in his pants. Dante didn't react, still sitting five feet away from him, even as the stench filled the room.

"I'll tell you what you want to know," he blubbered. "I have a wife, kids. I love them. Please let me go."

Yeah, and a pig was flying overhead. The fucker couldn't be serious.

Dante crossed one ankle over his knee, placing his hand with the cigarette down over the other.

"Syndicate," he uttered one word.

The guy swallowed. "I... I don't know what you're talking 'bout."

Dante didn't respond, just kept watching him silently. One minute passed. Two. More. After a few minutes, the guy squirmed.

"I just got drafted into the organization last month," the man admitted. "Today was my... um, induction party."

Fucking sleazy slimeball.

Dante inhaled another drag.

"That's all I know."

Not likely.

"What's your name?" Dante asked.

"Um, Martin."

"Martin, how did you get to know about them?" Dante asked. The guy swallowed but stayed silent. Dante gave him a deliberate smirk, the one that really got to people after his silence, fueling their imaginations some more.

"I... you only get in through... reference," he confessed after a few seconds.

Dante nodded. "Very good, Martin. And who was yours?"

"A... a guy I met in a ... chatroom online."

"And what did this guy tell you about the Syndicate?"

The guy shivered. "Just that... they were an organization that catered to... what I was looking for."

"Kids, you mean," Dante grit out, feeling the rage pulse in his blood.

The guy looked away, apparently ashamed. Yeah, the fucker had had a hard-on a few hours ago, so Dante didn't feel an ounce of sympathy for him.

"And this guy," Dante redirected the interrogation back on track. "He was recruiting? How does it work?"

"If I tell you, will you let me go?" he straightened in his chair, trying to be brave.

"Depends on what you tell me, Martin," Dante drawled out, leaning back in his chair. "I get in a good mood, you get out of here." In a body bag, Dante didn't add.

The man nodded, believing him. "I'll tell you everything I know."

Good.

"The guy," Martin began, looking to his feet. "I just know him by his username. MrX. He said he was a part of a group that could arrange... what I wanted for me. All I had to do was show up to the induction and show them I was serious, get the tattoo, and they'd give me the instructions later. I just got the tattoo today. I don't know anything else."

"And this MrX," Dante asked, his mind working to put the pieces in place. "Have you ever seen him?"

The guy shook his blown-up head. "No. The guys tonight were all inductees and a tattoo guy. MrX had cameras they said they'd be watching us with."

Dante believed him. He tilted his head to the side. "And during the entire month as an inductee-in-waiting, did you ever hear anything you think I'd be interested in? Bonus information always puts me in a very good mood, Martin."

Martin hesitated.

"Don't make me stand up, Martin," Dante warned.

The guy was a wuss. "There was one thing," he stuttered. "I don't think MrX wanted to let it slip."

"What?"

"About a Shadowman," the guy said. "We were just talking about it and he said this Shadowman or whatever kind of kept his eyes on the Syndicate, so to be careful of my day-to-day activity."

Shadowman.

Fuck.

Dante had heard about him, whoever he was, only in rumors. Even in his side of the underworld, the name was a frightening legend. And if the guy was on the Syndicate's tail, then he had a deep, deep knowledge of their world. Dante had just hit the tip of the iceberg, and this guy was already deep in the ocean. He'd never had the reason to try and find the person, but that could change now.

"Anything else? What about MrX?" Dante asked.

The guy thought for a second before his eyes blinked. "I don't really know, I swear. He just mentioned he had retired as a recruiter. He used to be a handler of some sort."

Dante felt his gut tighten. He stayed quiet, waiting.

"He...," the man swallowed. "There was this one story he told me, warning me about what happened to rats. It's... he's kind of pretty well-known in the group."

Dante just blinked, flexing his fingers.

"Said he had a girl interrogated fifteen years ago in your city... because she heard some shit she wasn't supposed to. He hired the guys and they kept her for four days, I think he said."

"Three days," Dante corrected, red slowly creeping at the edges of his vision, his blood rushing to his ear as the vein beside his neck began to throb.

"Y...yeah," the guy stuttered. "He... was warning me. Telling me he had them torture and rape her just to see if she knew anything, and then had her rescued by an anonymous tip."

Torture and rape her.

Torture. And. Rape. Her.

Rape her.

Amara.

His Amara.

At *fifteen fucking years old.*

All his doubts over the years solidified and suddenly memories flashed through his mind – her stiffening if he came up behind her, her hesitation the first time she'd undressed him, the panic that hit her out of nowhere in the middle of fucking sometimes. Dante had always chalked it up to her post-traumatic stress, well aware that the experience of her physical torture would never entirely leave her. He had had his doubts sometimes, but never, not once, knew she'd been violated like that. The doctor had never said a word about it during the days he'd spent at the hospital, the police report had nothing about it. She had never said a word. Not. One. Word. Every time he had been with her, fucking her brains out or eating her pussy or talking dirty to her, she had never shared something that he should have known.

And now she had vanished.

It all crashed around him, shaking his trust in the one woman he had trusted more than anything else.

Dante pulled his gun, aimed it at the man's head, and shot. His finger didn't leave the trigger, shot after shot ringing out until the gun ran out of bullets and the man's body ran out of place.

It was time.

Time for him to take the throne.

Time for him to find MrX.

Time for his queen to come home.

Lorenzo Maroni's countdown had begun.

15

Amara

mara looked at her first client in the new city, a giant dark-haired man – and she meant giant, even bigger than Dante, who was the largest man she knew – and tried to keep her facial expression serene. Because this guy wasn't just a giant, he was a scarred, one-eyed giant. And he had a real eye patch over his right eye. She'd never seen anyone with an eye patch.

She suddenly had flashbacks to the bodice rippers she used to read in her teenage years, of sexy, dashing pirates and damsels in distresses. He was definitely sexy, in a rough, dangerous way that as a woman Amara could appreciate.

She opened her door wider, pasted a polite smile on her face, and welcomed him into the office.

"I hope you didn't have any trouble finding the place, Mr. Villanova," she sat down on her comfortable armchair, the view outside the window lush, tropical green.

The man took a seat across her in the matching cream armchair, watching her with one eye such a light hazel it almost looked golden. She had never seen anyone with that shade of eye color either. His other eye, the one with the eye patch, had a wicked-looking scar going under it, from the side of his skull to the edge of his lip, pulling it down in a permanent half frown.

"Call me Alpha," he spoke smoothly, his voice rough.

Amara felt her eyebrows go up at his name. Well, she'd never known an Alpha either. Seemed like this city was going to be a lot of firsts for her.

"Alpha," Amara corrected herself. "I'm Dr. Mara Rossi. What can I do for you?"

"May I call you Mara?" he asked, looking around her medium-sized office. After selling her apartment in Shadow Port and grabbing Lulu, Amara had packed up her stuff and asked her half-sister Nerea to arrange a fake passport for her under a fake name that was close enough that she'd still recognize it, just so she could travel to a location unknown. She had ended up traveling down south to the tropical big city of Los Fortis, a place she'd researched well before for any connections to Tenebrae or the Outfit. There were none.

She needed to put her old life behind, everything except her mother, whom she still called every other day through a burner phone, swearing her to secrecy. Her mother, she knew, would keep her secret this time. And though a huge part of Amara wanted to call Vin or Tristan or Morana, she knew a clean break was for the best. Especially from Dante. They were through.

"Of course," Amara replied to the man, focusing on him. After getting her degree and serving her clinical hours under the supervision of the University counselor, Amara had been a practicing licensed therapist for six months. And she hadn't even advertised after moving to Los Fortis, so getting the call from this man to schedule an appointment had been a surprise.

"I'm not here for therapy, Mara," the man told her, and suddenly, Amara felt her palms begin to sweat. His size and form, which she had appreciated a second ago, became more threatening.

She stayed calm, practicing her counting. "Then, why are you here?"

He leaned back in the chair, observing her, before speaking quietly. "I'm not going to hurt you."

Amara swallowed but stayed silent, her heart pounding.

"I want to know who you are," he put his hand on his chin. "You see, this is my city. I keep a very close eye on anyone who comes or goes from certain high profile locations such as Shadow Port. And this building is mine. I had your documents checked and they're fake. A very good fake, but fake nonetheless. So, who are you, and why are you in my city?"

Amara felt her breath whoosh out of her slightly. Getting up on her feet, Amara walked on her heels to the desk in the room and took out a file from the drawer. Walking back to the man, she slowly handed it to him so he could see her degrees for himself.

"I'm not here to cause you any trouble, Alpha," she told him, her voice raspy. "I am a licensed therapist. My name is Amara. And I'm in your city to set down roots. I like the moderate climate and the nearness to the forest. It... it reminds me of home."

She watched him hand the file back to her without looking. "I can't read."

Amara felt herself flush. "Oh, I'm so sorry," she apologized, taking the file back.

He shook his head. "I'm good at reading people though. In my line of work, you have to be. Shadow Port doesn't have any forests. Where's your home?"

Amara cursed herself for that slip. She hesitated, but seeing his one eye considering her, she answered truthfully. "Tenebrae City."

He nodded. "You're a far way from home, Amara. Any particular reason?"

She took in a deep breath, walking to the window, looking out at the city line and the forest beyond it, so similar to Tenebrae except on the other side of the hemisphere.

"I'm pregnant."

The man stayed silent on the chair for a long minute. "And the father?"

She simply shook her head. How could she explain? The years of knowing him, loving him, being loved by him, only for him to walk in one day, fuck her without a condom, and fake his death with no warning to her. She had had an alert set on her phone for his name, so if anything about him hit the internet, she got a notification. She remembered getting the notification, sitting with Lulu on her lap as she watched a movie, remembered opening her phone, remembered seeing the headline.

Heir to the Maroni empire dead in an explosion.

She remembered the cry that had left her mouth, her eyes unable to believe the news. She remembered calling Morana with shaking fingers. She remembered that he had faked his brother's death in a fire too. The truth had dawned upon her and it had been cruel. Dante hadn't told her, not even given her a hint, nothing to prepare her.

And she had been carrying their child already. Although it had been too soon for a test confirmation, Amara had known. Her breasts had become sensitive and she had missed her period, and Amara never missed her periods. They came like clockwork. And Lulu had started poking her nose into her stomach. She had known that day they had made a baby.

And that had changed everything.

"Well," Alpha stood from the armchair, breaking her out of his thoughts. "In that case, Amara, you're welcome here at Los Fortis. You and your child will be safe here."

He pushed a hand into his jeans pocket and brought out a card, putting it on her table. "This is my contact. You have any trouble, or anyone gives you shit, you call me."

Amara looked down at the card, a plain black piece of paper with silver embossing, and stared at him, touched by his kindness. "Thank you," she croaked out, emotional that someone had cared enough.

Alpha nodded, walking to the door. "Is the father alive?"

Amara laughed at the irony of the question. Not knowing how to answer, since he was dead to the world at the moment, she simply told him her truth. "He and I, we are doomed to bleed from a wound that will never heal."

The large man considered her for a long moment. "You have strength, Amara. I can see that. And the strong don't have bleeding wounds; they have scars that heal."

Yeah, she shared that with him apparently.

Giving her a sharp nod, his dark hair falling on his face, his black eye patch stark against his scar, Alpha walked out, leaving her standing there with her thoughts.

Amara pat down her stomach, shaking her head.

"Your Daddy is a bastard," she told the baby, chuckling at herself. "But we still love him, don't we?"

Yeah, she was doomed, alright.

Los Fortis was an incredible city. Built in the 50s with a rubber and mineral industry boom, it was located close enough to the Amazon to have an incredible view of endless green vistas right outside the city limits. With a population of over five million people, the city was a hub for everything. Most importantly, though crime existed, she couldn't find any visible links to the underworld and that was a relief.

Her child was her priority now.

Amara had rented the office five minutes away from where she'd bought a tiny house but big enough for two people, with a beautiful garden that she was excited to get into. While gardening had never been something she'd allowed herself to explore, it had always fascinated her – the art of growing and nurturing life.

Her neighborhood was one of the reasons the property had been on the pricey end – it was the safest area in the entire city. There were rows of houses like hers, with families and the elderly, and it was a gated community with guards and cameras. She liked that. She wanted that extra blanket of security.

She walked to her house, a cute little thing painted a bright yellow on the outside and white on the inside, hitching her bag higher on her shoulder, the silk scarf around her neck fluttering in the wind. A thin sheen of sweat covered her body from the mild humidity, and she looked around at the other houses, nodding at one of her neighbors who had been super friendly to her when she moved it a few weeks ago.

The balls of her feet aching from the short walk in her two-inch heels, the skin around the scars on her feet tingling, Amara unlocked her door and opened it.

"Lulu," she called out, dropping her keys on the side table and kicking her heels to the side, locking the door behind her. "I'm home."

A flash of cream fur dashed at her, twining around her legs, and Amara bent to pick her up in her arms.

Lulu's big green eyes watched her as she let out an enthusiastic 'meow'.

Amara smiled. "I'm happy to see you too. Did you miss me, huh?" she asked, walking towards the kitchen.

'Meow' she got in response. Her heart softened.

Lulu had been Amara's one true companion through all her years in exile, and Amara was grateful for her, especially because she was an incredibly affectionate cat. Of course, she had her moments where she swished her tail and walked off to do whatever cats did, but she loved being around Amara. Her therapist in Shadow Port had told her how much pets could help with anxiety and she believed that. She'd lost the count of how many times she'd been on the verge of an attack when Lulu had just jumped on her and started her purring, the vibration from her warm, furry body enough to bring her back to the moment.

It had been Lulu who had sensed Amara's pregnancy before she had looked for signs, Lulu who had butted her head against her stomach and started licking at it when she'd never done it before.

Squeezing her fur baby, she let her go and got herself a glass of water, pulling out her old-school burner phone from her loose pant pocket. While she usually disliked wearing pants, loose pants had become her work uniform over the years. They helped her dissociate enough from herself that she could focus on her clients.

Dialing her mother's number, she put the phone to her ear, heard it ring five times before her mother picked it up.

"Hi, Ma," she spoke softly on the phone, her heart aching to meet her again. She didn't know how, but someday, she'd get her mother to Los Fortis and take care of her.

"Mumu," her mother's voice came through the line, the smile in her voice filling Amara with warmth. "How are you? Have you settled in?"

"Yes, Ma," Amara said, opening a can of tuna and putting it in Lulu's bowl. "The house is set, and it's so nice here. I can't wait for you to come."

"Me too," her mother sighed. "It's too soon right now. In a few months, it'll be more natural."

Amara agreed.

"Have you seen a doctor yet?"

"No, I will this week," Amara sat down on the dining table chair. The kitchen didn't have an island but it was spacious and opened into the back garden, which she loved. Continuing the conversation, she told her mother, "I have an appointment with a therapist Dr. Neiman referred for me on Wednesday. And I meet the gynecologist on Friday."

"Good, good," her mother said, the sound of pots coming from behind her. "Dante is alive."

Big surprise there.

"I told you your precious boy was too smart to die," Amara had told her mother that countless times. "He played everyone."

"Yes," her mother's voice lowered. "Mr. Maroni is dead though."

That stopped Amara.

"Really dead?" she asked, her heart pounding.

"Really dead," her mother confirmed. "Dante is getting things organized for his takeover."

He was taking over.

He was finally fucking taking over.

Lorenzo Maroni was dead.

Amara smiled, pride filling her at the man she loved, knowing his years of work and strategy had brought him to the top. He finally had the reigns to the kingdom.

"Shouldn't you tell him, Mumu?" her mother asked her, as she always did, hoping Amara would simply tell Dante she was expecting their baby, and they would live happily ever after.

'I can't be with you, for your safety, until my father is dead'.

Things were more complicated than that. She loved Dante but his lack of a warning to her had cut her deep. Through the years, she'd always felt they were a team. He'd confided secrets in her – about his mother and his father's possible kidnapping and marital rape of her, about his brother and where he'd hidden him and how it hurt not being able to see him, about Tristan and his hatred for Morana coming from his murder of his father, about what he was doing. Though Amara had never been directly involved in the things he did over the years, she had been in the loop – he had come to her when troubled, shared things about the people in their world, asked for her advice in situations that had him conflicted. She had always been a part of his quest.

It had led her to believe they could play everyone else but they couldn't play each other. Almost seven years she spent keeping them in the shadows, waiting months for minutes with him, living her life in the meantime, not for him to go die without giving her any warning. No, she deserved better than that. Love be damned, she deserved better than that. She had trusted him with her life and her heart, and though she still trusted him with her life, her heart was hurting.

He was an asshole, and she probably would have forgiven him once he apologized, had she not been pregnant. The prospect of becoming a mother had every protective instinct inside her raring to the surface. Her child, their child, deserved a father who wasn't a guest. More importantly, he or she deserved not to be born in that world without protection. Just being Dante Maroni's child would put the baby in danger. No. She'd raise her baby with all the love her mother had raised her with, and all the protection she could provide in their anonymity.

"There's no point, Ma," she told her mother. "I have been his secret for so long, he maybe forgot what bringing me to light would do. Especially now, with him taking over, he'll need to marry someone with power, who can stabilize the Outfit. Bringing me into the picture will only make him look weak. And I can't be his secret anymore, Ma. And I won't let my child be. So, it's better if he never knows about it."

"I understand, baby. I did the same for you. But Dante is different. I still think you should tell him, Amara," her mother tried to convince her, using her given name to sound firm. Amara knew the tactic well. "He loves you. And with Mr. Maroni gone, he could give you and my grandchild what you need."

Amara was tempted, so, so tempted.

"Just promise me you'll think about it," her mother beseeched her. "He… he's changed since he's come back, Mumu. He's darker. I can't explain it. I'm worried about him."

Her heart started to pound, her hand gripping the phone tight as the need to find him, comfort him, let him share his demons with her, washed over her. She tamped it down.

"I promise I'll consider it," Amara told her mother. They chat for a few minutes about other things, before Amara cut the call and stared at Lulu eating.

"You think I should tell him too, don't you?"

Lulu looked at her, then kept eating.

"Of course you do. You love him, you little traitor."

Nom nom nom.

"But he really behaved like a dick, you know."

Cronch.

"You and I and the baby are going to be happy here, Lulu."

A doubtful look.

"Don't give me that face. I'm not entirely mad at him. This is for the best."

Lulu ignored her.

Amara sighed and started preparing her dinner.

He settled between her legs. God, she loved when he did that. She writhed against him, feeling his shoulders spread her thighs open, his mouth descending on her mound.

He spread soft kisses on her waxed skin, his scruff rasping against her sensitive flesh.

Wait, why did he have a scruff?

"I'm so fucking pissed at you, dirty girl," he growled, still kissing her mound, not going where she needed his lips.

Why was he pissed at her? She was the one angry at him.

"This pussy knows me even in sleep, doesn't she, baby?"

Oh yeah. She was getting so wet, anticipating the pleasure she knew he would bring her. She flexed her hips, trying to get him to hurry. Ah, she missed him, missed his touch, missed that dirty-talking mouth. And she loved this dream.

A finger swiped through her folds and she felt her hips come off the bed. It felt so real.

"You're coming home with me, baby," he told her. She'd love that. She missed the compound, the woods, the hills, the people. It had been so long since she'd seen it. She wanted to go home.

"Wake up, Amara," he commanded her.

No, if she woke up she'd lose him. She didn't want to wake up, not just yet.

His tongue licked at her folds once. God, it felt so good. Too good.

Amara blinked her eyes open, staring up the ceiling fan moving at full speed, aware of the wind caressing her hardened, exposed nipples, feeling wet between her naked thighs. It took her a second to process everything – the black silk baby doll she'd worn to bed thrown to the side, Lulu napping on the floor near the door, the room dark with the street light from outside filtering her window, and a very angry, gloriously shirtless, slightly bearded Dante Maroni between her legs.

What the hell?

Heart racing, she suddenly grappled with the sheets and tried to scatter backward, only to be stopped by his strong grip around her thighs.

"What are you- oh shit," her words ended on a moan as he pulled her forward, pushing her thighs back, and dove in.

Amara gripped his hair with one hand, the other going to the sheets beside her, her breath coming out too fast as his tongue pushed into her. Dear gods of cunnilingus had blessed this man with a mouth he knew how to use *so good.*

She bit her lip, pulling his head closer, mindless as she felt a wave of pleasure crest inside her.

"Yes," she panted. "God, Dante, please."

He built her up higher and higher, his thumb stroking her clit slowly, oh so slowly, bringing her right to the edge before suddenly, he stopped.

"I swear to god, D-"

His hand suddenly came over her mouth, quieting her, and he shook his head once. Heart pounding, Amara watched with wide eyes as he stayed still over her, his head tilted to the side, a vein in his neck throbbing as he listened.

Amara couldn't hear anything but she looked to the door, to see Lulu was perked up too, her ears twitching.

A clock ticked in the house. A dog barked somewhere outside. Critters spoke in their nightly ritual. But they were all usual sounds, nothing to alert both the feline and the man.

Lulu padded out the door to investigate and Dante moved off her, putting his fingers to his lips to warn her to stay silent, throwing his blue shirt towards her. Amara nodded, quickly buttoning up the shirt, glad for Dante's height once again because it fell almost to her knees, and grabbed her discarded panties, pulling them on.

She saw Dante bend down to scoop up his jacket, pulling out a gun.

Lulu meowed from outside. Dante went to the door, his form quiet as he waited, almost unmoving, alert. Amara watched, the silence suffocating, a knot of anxiety tightening in her gut. She pressed her palm to her stomach, willing her heartbeat to calm down, to keep breathing normally. This was not the time to panic.

Swallowing, she tiptoed to the side of the bed, taking out the taser she kept in her drawer, feeling better about arming herself. Though she could have had a gun, Amara didn't like them. She didn't like death, as necessary as it was in their world, and she didn't want to take a life. But it was probably something she should think about, arming herself, now that she was more vulnerable.

Her eyes traced her man, the two tattoos on his back flexing as he moved. It had always fascinated her, those tattoos of his — a giant black dragon taking up the entire left side of his spine, its tail curled and head turned back, watching as a flock of ravens emerged from its wings and flew away diagonally to the right. Knowing him and his artistry, Amara knew it had some significance to him, but he'd never told her.

She saw as he went out into the dark living room, heard a gunshot, heard a scuffle and masculine grunts. Blood rushing in her ears, Amara tried to keep her breathing contained and her arm ready for anyone who came through the door.

They came through the window, and before she could make a sound, everything blacked out.

Amara

She came to with the sound of her name being called.

Blinking her eyes open, she shook her head to clear the grogginess, unable to move. Looking down, she realized why. Her hands were tied to the arms of a chair, the roped binding her wrists to the wood right over her scars.

Her stomach sank.

No.

No.

She started to struggle to get free, chafing her wrists against the rope, her breathing escalating. This couldn't be happening again. She couldn't survive it again.

God, please. No.

"Amara!"

The loud, masculine voice calling her name had her looking up.

Dante.

He was there, across from her, tied to a chair, with ropes going across his chest, his hands, and his feet. He was still shirtless. Why was he shirtless?

Amara pushed her tongue to the roof of her mouth, a long-term habit that somehow always calmed her down a bit. Inhaling deeply, still feeling the greasy fingers of black stroking her mind, Amara looked around the room, trying to distract herself.

And felt her heart plummet.

It was the same room.

The same room she'd been in a decade ago for three days, tied to a chair, her bloody footprints on the floor as she tried to escape. All the therapy over the years could not have prepared her for the mental assault of this place. The walls started to close in on her.

'Does Dante Maroni have anyone we can use against him?'

He had her. He had a baby he didn't even know about. She had to tell him. God, she needed to tell him.

Amara opened her mouth but her eyes stayed glued to the wall over his head, where the chains still hung free. Her throat locked. The greasy fingers came over her consciousness, dripping tar into her lungs, weighing her down.

"God damn it, look at me!"

A shout penetrated the fog.

"Amara, baby, look at me," a man called from the distance. "Give me your beautiful eyes."

Beautiful eyes. She knew that voice – that voice of smoke and chocolate and twisted sheets.

Dante.

She looked at him, confused for a second as to why he was there. He hadn't been there the last time. She'd been in this room, all alone, scared. She was scared now – so, so scared. Her hands started to shake.

"Amara," his dark eyes locked on hers, fierce and intense and blazing. "I am going to kill every single man in this building for this. Not one of them will get close to touching you. I promise. Trust me, baby."

She started to tremble.

She trusted him, but her memories kept clashing with his words. Amara tried to calm her heart down, tried every trick in the book to shut the door in her mind, but it crept in. She was stuck in a thick marsh of pain, wanting to move out, move forward, but stuck.

'Should we tell Maroni we have his little girlfriend here?'
The laughter. The jeers. The pain. The blood.

Amara closed her eyes, the ropes on her wrist brandishing her, the scar on her neck feeling like a noose, the marks on her feet flashing back to slipping in her own blood as she limped away.

"I'm here with you, Amara," the words came, dragging her back to the present. She focused on him, on the ropes cutting into his chest as he leaned towards her, on the one tattoo he had on his chest, a tattoo she had licked countless times.

Win.

Dante said a few battles were worth losing deliberately if it meant winning the war, and he would always win. She would win too. She needed to win. Against the assholes who had victimized her, against the demons who had possessed her, against the people who hadn't accepted her. She needed to win.

Keeping her eyes glued to his chest, she let out a long breath, gripping the hands of the chair, and took in a deep breath.

"That's it, baby," he encouraged her. "Calm yourself down. I'm right here with you. You're not alone again. I'm right here. That's it, take in another breath."

His voice soothed her, other memories seeping in, replacing the ugly ones – his fierce promise to her besides her hospital bed, his months of carrying one-sided conversations with her every day when she couldn't talk, his dirty words whispered into her skin every time they connected, his murmured secrets into her ear as they lay in bed, his voice a connecting thread through the years, carrying so many beautiful memories. That voice of smoke and chocolate and twisted sheets.

Amara let it wash over her, feeling her heart slowly come down.

She opened her mouth to speak but words didn't come. She swallowed.

"It's okay," he told her. "Don't talk. You okay now?"

She nodded mutely, her eyes locking with his dark browns.

"If my suspicion is correct," he began conversationally, as though they were hanging out in some café, "someone from the Outfit leaked that I was coming to Los Fortis to see you to the Syndicate."

'Do you know anything about the Syndicate?'

The ugly voice whispered, ready to drag her back down again.

"They're who I've been investigating underground over the last few weeks," he informed her, watching her closely. "I'll tell you the whole story once we're out of here. And we will get out of here, Amara."

The confidence with which he stated that eased some of her nerves.

She saw him, really saw him, and the ways he'd changed over the weeks. For one, he had the dark scruff on his face, something she'd never seen him with before. It made him look wilder, more dangerous, and she wasn't entirely sure she minded that. But it was his eyes that gave her pause. There was something darker in them, in his entire aura, and that gave her pause. She wasn't sure if it was because of his father's death or him taking over or his time undercover, but it hardened him, even in private, in ways she hadn't seen before.

"Why did you run?" he asked her, his gaze steady on hers, holding hers, anchoring hers. "You knew I wasn't dead."

Amara swallowed. She had to tell him. But she needed to ask him her own question first. "Why didn't you tell me?" she croaked out in a barely-there whisper.

His eyebrows pulled down slightly before understanding dawned in his eyes. "You're mad at me."

God, she wanted to hit him.

Amara felt herself begin to shake, the rawness of her emotions overpowering her, the pain she had been suppressing for years bubbling to the surface, mixing with the rage of being in this place, mixing with the agony of that one moment she had thought him dead, mixing with the hurt of being alone for so long, mixing with the guilt of not telling him about the baby, mixing with the panic that still infused her. It all fused together in an amalgamation of emotions until she couldn't differentiate one from the other, her entire body beginning to quiver in the chair as her eyes burned.

"Amara," she heard his voice from the distance, every syllable getting farther and farther as she lost herself to the sea of emotions, drowning in every single one of them, closing her eyes.

She couldn't breathe.

"Can you loosen your ropes?"

The random question filtered through the fog.

She opened her eyes to see him looking at her calmly.

"They didn't spend time tying you up," he informed her. "You were unconscious and they wanted to contain me, so they didn't focus. I'm assuming your knots are pretty sloppy. And with the scars on your wrists, the skin would give you more space to pull it out. You think you can do that?"

Amara looked down at her bonds, the fog in her mind slowly dissipating with his words. He was right. The skin on her wrist with the scars was slightly sunken, giving her hand more room. Testing the rope, she calmly tried to pull her hand instead of struggling as she'd been, and felt it get to the base of her thumb.

"Yeah," she told him, looking up to see him looking at her thighs with furrowed brows.

"Are you starting your period? It's not your time."

The absurd question gave her pause in her act of tugging on the rope.

Of course, she didn't start her period. Following his gaze, she bent her head down and saw it.

Blood.

Just a little, but there, between her thighs.

No.

No, no, no, no.

"No, no, no," she started chanting, shaking her head, staring in horror at the little stain of red on her skin, panic cloying in her chest.

"Amara, what-"

"I haven't had my period in weeks," she whispered, her horrified eyes coming to see him.

She saw him absorb her words. He knew she was extremely regular, he knew her cycles. Hell, he used to time his visits according to them. The implication of the words dawned upon him. She could see it click in place, the last time they had been together, and a fire blazed in his eyes she had never, not in the entire time she'd known him, seen.

He didn't say a word, just absorbed all the information his brain was processing, his eyes never moving from hers.

"Calm yourself," he finally spoke, his voice a hard command. "Get out of your ropes and I will get us out of here. Not one motherfucker in this place is touching you or my child. But you need to stop stressing."

Amara knew that too. She also knew he was pissed to be cursing like that. Dante Maroni didn't curse in the company of ladies; he was too well-mannered for that.

She swallowed, closing her eyes, taking a deep breath, and nodding.

"Were you never going to tell me?" he asked after a few minutes of silence, his entire body still, on the edge.

"I probably would have in a while," she admitted. "I just-"

"You just what?" he grit out.

"Excuse me for protecting my child while you were off playing dead without a word of warning to me, you bastard!" she burst out, her throat straining, her anger matching his, years of frustration bleeding out in her tone. "Do you think it's easy, Dante? Living alone in a city on enemy territory, without friends, without protection, without anything but a promise for years – did you really think I'd let my child go through that?"

"Our child," he growled. "And did you think it was easy for me, Amara?" he asked her, his voice calm, his eyes anything but. "Did you think I was having the time of my life 'playing dead'? That I was having a blast all these years living like this? That I was not working and bleeding every damn day to make a future for us?"

Amara felt her lips tremble, her heart aching to reach out to him. "It wasn't easy for either of us, Dante. That was exactly why I wanted it to be easy for our child. He or she shouldn't have to pay for our choices. For years, you and I waited for each other, but I feel like somewhere, we lost our way. The goal became so much more important we forgot about the journey."

Her honesty silenced him for a long minute.

"I had my father killed," he told her quietly. "I watched him bleed out like a slaughtered pig, and I smoked. For years, that had been my goal. Turning the fringes of his empire in my favor, manipulating people, making a name for myself – all so one day, when he was gone, I could give you and our children everything you deserved."

Her heart clenched at the sincerity of his words. That was one of the things she'd always loved about Dante – he never shied from his emotions. He felt what he felt and gave zero fucks if anyone called him anything, and nobody dared because Dante Maroni was a legend already, the most masculine of men in their toxic society, the most powerful because he knew exactly what he felt and didn't lie to himself about it.

"As soon as we are out of here," he told her, his voice firm, his eyes heated, "you and I are going to have a long due conversation about keeping shit from each other."

Uh oh. Something in his tone prickled at the back of her neck, raising the hair there. She looked into his eyes closely, seeing the pain and rage there, but also an anguish she didn't think had anything to do with their conversation. Heart stuttering, she inhaled deeply. "Dante-"

"You didn't tell me, Amara," he spoke, his jaw clenching.

He knew.

She didn't know how, but he knew.

"For years," he continued, the fury on his face matching the fire in her veins, "you took me inside your body, welcomed me to your bed, let me have you every way possible. But. You. Never. Told. Me."

Tears escaped her eyes.

"And I suspected something. I should've fucking asked. You know why I didn't? Because I trusted you. I trusted that you'd tell me if anything like that had happened. And you never did, so I never

277

assumed, because I didn't want to insult the memory of your experience."

He was killing her. "Dante-"

"We both fucked up, Amara," he told her, his eyes blazing. "And we're both going to own up to it. And we're both going to talk about this and forgive and move on. I'm not giving you a choice here. I didn't work my ass off all these years for something trivial as lack of communication to break us."

"It isn't trivial," Amara murmured.

"Yes, it is," he told her. "We get out of here. We fucking reconnect. Did you really think I was going to let you go? After fighting for us for a decade, did you really think that, Amara?"

Amara fisted her hands. "You hurt me."

"Yeah, well, I'm a dick."

A reluctant chuckle escaped her at the way he said that.

His lips twitched before he sobered again. "Did you know," he went on, searing her with his dark gaze, "that while Tristan and I killed the assholes who took you, I've been searching for the guy who gave the order for years? It's been my side project and going undercover just made me realize I should have given it more time. Because it's all connected and I was too focused on Bloodhound Maroni. Fucking dead bastard."

God, she hurt. She hurt for him, for herself, for everything they had been through because of one man. For the second time in her life, Amara was glad of someone's death.

"You couldn't have known, Dante," she told him softly, wanting to ease the pain she could feel emanating from him. "What he did isn't on you. Who he was isn't on you."

"I am a Maroni, Amara," he told her, and she realized the change in his demeanor taking over had already brought. He had been an heir, a prince, who now sat on the throne. "I am his blood."

"Yes," she nodded, holding his stare. "But it's not what you're given that makes you who are. It's what you do with it. It's not the weapon but the one who wields it that holds the power, and you, Dante Maroni are a powerful man."

"Fuck, I want to kiss you right now," he cursed out, his eyes fire on hers.

Amara felt her breath catch, and for the first time, felt her lips twitch. "Get yourself out of the chair first, badass."

His lips mirrored hers for a second before he spoke again. "You really think they have me here against my will? That I'd be foolish enough to risk myself if this wasn't my plan?"

Amara felt her heart begin to race, her eyes looking down at the ropes secured tightly around him. "What do you mean?"

"My father was working with the Syndicate for a long time," he explained to her. "And he wasn't alone. The organization wouldn't want someone disagreeable in power in the Outfit. Whoever their mole is would have been waiting for an opportunity to eliminate me."

"So, you handed it to them on a platter by traveling alone to Los Fortis," Amara finished, comprehending exactly what he was saying.

God, how could she have forgotten he was such a good player? Something akin to pride filled her.

"I hadn't anticipated them taking you."

"Still well played, my king," she whispered, a small smile on her face. "What are you waiting for now?"

"For them to come to the room, to interrogate me," he told her calmly. "I'll be leading them. Though they'll probably hit me a little, I need you to stay calm and keep working on the ropes. Had I been alone, I wouldn't have worried. But you and-"

"I know," the smile dipped from her face, her stomach turning. "I'll try. It's just this place, I can't control my responses."

"This hell is my kingdom now, Amara," he told her, his eyes solemn. "As long as I'm alive, it won't touch you. And I intend to live a very long, very happy life with you."

The knot she'd been holding inside her melted a bit. Even in the middle of her hell, Amara felt a feeling of safety wash over her.

Taking a deep breath in, she nodded and began to work on the ropes.

Dante

She was trying. Dante could see the toll it was taking on her mind, being in this place, tied to a chair, pregnant with their child.

Pregnant.

She was fucking pregnant and she hadn't told him. Albeit he'd been playing dead for most of the time, it enraged him. That last time he'd gone to see her had been an impulse. He'd wanted to be with her, touch her, just one more time in case he actually died and never got that chance again. He hadn't meant to see her, much less push her against the wall, fuck her raw, and leave. That had been a dick move, he admitted that. But they'd made a baby, their baby. Fuck, that did things to him, knowing the queen of his heart was going to be the mother of his child.

And what an amazing mother she would be. She had been raised by a loving woman and magnified it tenfold within her. Amara was a woman born with an instinct to nurture – the weak, the innocent, the helpless. She was soft and so fucking forgiving, or else she would have kicked his ass to the curb a long time ago. The fact that she had packed up and moved thousands of miles away to protect their child filled him with pride and warmth. She was a tigress with her cubs. Finding her in Los Fortis, knowing this time he was keeping her, knowing he didn't have to leave her again, had been the single-most rewarding moment of his life.

But that little blood on her thighs worried him. He knew there could be a little spotting, and this was an incredibly stressful situation, but fuck, Dante hated putting her through this. He hadn't anticipated that they would take her, or that they would bring them to this location.

Although why had they brought them to this specific location? Something about that bugged Dante.

Hopefully, Morana already had the mole singled out. She'd been monitoring every outgoing call and message from the compound since he'd been back. He just hoped the fuckers who abducted them came to interrogate him soon so he could get Amara out of the place. Knowing everything that had happened to her here, he couldn't even imagine everything happening inside her mind right then. Her eyes kept zoning in and out as she fought her demons, the scar on her neck stark against her paling skin, her hands gripping the chair with white knuckles.

Dante watched her closely. Knowing she was pregnant changed things. If he saw the slightest sign of things becoming too much, he'd have to figure some way out. The idiots hadn't even checked him for weapons, assuming he'd been unarmed since he'd been in bed shirtless. He had a nasty little surprise waiting for them.

As if on cue, the door to the room opened. Amara's eyes flew to it as she jumped a bit, her grip on the chair tightening before she visibly took a deep breath.

Hold on, baby. Just a little longer, Dante urged her silently.

Her breasts heaved under his shirt as she worked on her breathing, her eyes on the man who entered the room. Dante let his eyes go from her and focused on the man, switching gears in his mind. This was his interrogation.

Relaxing in the chair, he stayed silent as the stranger came in, wearing a black t-shirt and cargo pants and combat boots, a 9mm visible on his hip. It was a classic tactic – show the captive you were armed to instill fear of death. Dante was well-versed in these maneuvers. He stayed silent, watching the guy.

He squat down a few feet from him, ignoring Amara for now, focusing on him, which was good. He didn't want them paying her any attention.

"Dante Maroni," the man said in a singsong tone, the hint of an accent in his voice on the 't'. "In the flesh."

"Oh, you're a fan?" Dante chuckled easily. "You'll have to free my hands for an autograph." Let him think he had the power.

The man gave a grin, a fake gold tooth glinting on the side. Dante wished some stereotypes weren't so cliché. "My bosses aren't a fan. In fact, they aren't very happy with you right now. You're interfering with the business."

Just the opening he needed. "You know, this is why people think mobsters don't have manners. They could just have booked an appointment if they wanted to talk," he drawled out casually.

The man tilted his head to the side. "Alright, so that's how we're playing this." He straightened, walking towards Amara. Dante forced himself to stay relaxed as the man squat before her.

"You're a pretty one," he said conversationally. "I heard they did terrible things to you right here in this place. How does it feel to be back?"

Dante watched Amara still, watching him like a hawk, her gaze never straying from the man. "You guys need to stop tying women up. It's getting old."

That's my girl. Dante felt pride fill him as he watched her play, hyper-focused on the man.

The man laughed. "Feisty. You think your boyfriend here will give me answers if I do things to you, hmm?"

"Oh, he's not my boyfriend," Amara told the guy, staying calmer than Dante had hoped. "We just fuck occasionally."

Like hell they did.

284

The man leaned closer to her. Dante tensed.

"In that case, fucking me in front of him shouldn't be an issue."

Oh, the bastard was good. But his girl was better.

"It would be," Amara shrugged. "I'm allergic to assholes. Trauma and all, you know."

The man let out a laugh, turning to look back at Dante. "I like her. Too bad I'll have to hurt her to get you talking."

Dante stayed silent, giving him a little smirk, ready to distract him so Amara could work on her knot inconspicuously. "You're good, I'll give you that. Bringing us both here, using her to threaten me. Nice."

The man stood up, walking to a table on the side, with a toolbox. Dante watched as Amara paled, a fine sheen of sweat on her face as she watched the table. He watched her take a quick breath, and slowly tug her hands against the ropes, loosening them even more. His gut tightened. He needed to speed it up.

"So," he started casually. "What do you want to know?"

The man turned to look at him, his eyebrows up his forehead in surprise. "My bosses had a warehouse of... goods in your city. Last week, it burned to the ground."

Dante frowned. "That wasn't me."

The man nodded. "Didn't seem like it. That's actually someone else's MO. But Tenebrae is an important center for our business, and your lack of cooperation has led to a lot of heavy losses for a lot of very important people. However, thanks to the goodwill of your father and his work for us, my bosses are willing to offer you a deal."

Dante raised an eyebrow. "Again, you couldn't have taken an appointment for this? You had to drag me out of bed and tie me up for that?"

The man shrugged. "We didn't know how well you'd cooperate. She-" he nodded towards a slightly terrified, slightly determined Amara, who paused in her silent struggle to loosen the knot on her hands "-was just insurance. She's been that for a long time."

Dante quickly brought his attention back, leaving Amara to work on her ropes. Her wrists were slender and her scars made the skin around it smooth. She had a fair chance of slipping her hand out.

"What do you mean?" Dante asked, keeping him engaged.

The guy just smiled.

Dante felt his mind reeling, and he filed the information for later. He didn't directly look at Amara but he could see in his periphery that she was gaining some momentum in her struggle.

"Okay," he told the guy, keeping him focused on himself. "So, what's the deal your bosses wanna give me?"

The guy smiled and squat down in front of him again, his hand in a fist. "Work with us and live. Simple."

"What kind of work?" Dante asked, already knowing the answer.

"Your father was pretty active in the business," the man went on. "You don't have to be. Just allow us storage and transport through the city and we have a deal."

"Storage and transport of kids?" Dante asked, his gut tightening.

"Smart man," the man nodded.

"And if I refuse?"

"Then I take that piece of prime pussy over there out to my men until you're more… agreeable."

Dante clenched his jaw but didn't say a word, his hands fisting on the chair.

"Hey asshole," the soft voice from behind made the guy turn. Dante saw Amara swing up the toolbox, her arms shaking with the weight as she smacked the man across the face with it.

The guy roared in pain, falling to the floor, clutching the bleeding gash on his head.

"You can't afford this piece of prime pussy," Amara heaved the metal toolbox again and brought it down hard on his skull, the sound of the loud crunch making Dante wince. The guy passed out, the wound on his head probably fatal. She stood there shaking, her chest heaving, hair wild around her face, rage flashing in her green eyes, cloaked in nothing but his shirt, looking like an avenging goddess. Fuck, he was such a goner.

"Amara," he called out to her. "C'mon, baby. Others might be coming."

She looked up at him with wide eyes, putting the toolbox to the side, her entire frame trembling from the adrenaline he could feel surging to the fore inside him. Hopping over the unconscious guy, she quickly came to him, her long, slender fingers shaking as she tried to undo the knot on his wrist.

"Give me those beautiful eyes," he told her gently, knowing he needed to guide them out of it.

She stilled in her efforts, looking up at him.

"Good girl," he praised her softly. "There's a knife in my right sock. Raise up my pant leg and take it out."

She leaned down, his shirt gaping open and even though it wasn't the time to notice, he was a man. His eyes went there, took her in, satisfied that this was his woman. He felt her fingers doing the task nimbly before she straightened and started to cut at the rope under his wrist. He just needed one hand free before he wrecked these bastards.

This close, he could hear her loud breathing as she both panicked and tried to keep it down, and said the one thing he knew would distract her thoughts from the fear.

"I can't wait to fuck you."

Amara paused, looking up at him with bewildered eyes. "Are you serious?! This is not the time for dirty talk, Dante Maroni."

He gave her a little grin deliberately, staying calm and unaffected because he knew it would relax her. And he needed her to relax.

Amara muttered something under her breath before venting. "Why do they make this look so easy in the movies? You're tied to this freaking chair with these ropes that just won't cut and I'm one second away from a panic attack."

"You're doing great," he told her, looking down at the scars on her wrists that were rubbed raw from her struggle, her knuckles white as she made progress with the blade. The rope was barely holding together with a few strands that would snap any second.

"Hey!"

A loud voice from the door jerked Amara. She spun around and Dante leaned to the side, to see one burly guy looking at them angrily. He came towards her, and Dante snapped his arm out, feeling the tension in the rope cut through his forearm, took the knife from her limp hand, throwing it across the room. His aim hit true, the blade lodging itself in the man's neck as blood spurted out, him falling to his knees.

Amara scattered back a few steps even though she was clear of the blood, her face a mask of shock. He just hoped her mind survived their night together.

Undoing the knot on his other hand deftly, Dante quickly got out of the ropes, standing up and shaking his limbs and jumping twice to get the blood flowing.

First things first, he crossed the space between him and his girl, grabbed her beautiful face in his hands, and kissed her deep. "You are a fucking warrior queen, and I'm so proud of you," he told her softly, seeing the effect his words had on her.

Her lips trembled in a slight smile. "You make me strong."

Fuck, he liked that.

Giving her a smile, he pressed their foreheads together, his ears open to any external noise. "As soon as we walk out that door, you're going to see a side of me tonight you've never seen before. I'm going to slaughter them, and you'll have to see that. Think you'll love me after?"

She gripped his wrists, nodding. "In sickness in health, in life in death, in murder in mayhem, isn't that how it goes?"

He chuckled, giving her a small kiss, giving her the affection he knew she craved in her bones but rarely voiced, and pulled back. Leaning down, he stripped the 9mm from the first guy and his knife from the other, handing the gun to her.

"Keep this," he told her as she took the weapon, her hands shaking. "It's loaded and unlocked. Stay behind me. You see anyone coming at you, aim and fire. Space your legs apart so your frame is steady. The recoil is a bitch, so be prepared for that. You okay?"

"Won't you need this?" she asked him, holding the gun with both hands.

He smiled, waving the sharp knife. "I'm good. Let's get out of this hellhole."

The biggest disadvantage was not knowing exactly how many people were on the premises once they got out the door. It could be two or ten or twenty, and while on his own it wouldn't have mattered, he was protecting precious cargo and anything getting to her would make him very, very angry.

Heading to the door, he quickly leaned out to check both sides of the corridor.

"There's a staircase to the right," came the soft words from behind him. "It goes down to an office of sorts and opens into... a garage," her voice hitched on that last word. That's where he'd found her and Tristan, in the garage. That's where he'd picked her up in his arms and she'd fluttered her eyes open, anchoring herself to his heart with the trust in them. He doubted she remembered any of that, but he never forgot it, the way her small body had shuddered and her pained breathing had assaulted his chest like bullets. He knew what talking about this place, reliving her memories of escape was doing to her. And yet, she did it. Terrified as she was, she did it.

He didn't understand how she could ever think herself weak.

Nodding once in acknowledgment of the information, Dante switched the gears in his mind, his body honed with years of training in tune with his mental commands, and stepped out into the barely-lit corridor. Trusting her to stay behind him, he crept forward, coming to a stop at seeing one guy near the top of the staircase. Prowling on quiet feet, he stepped behind the man, muffling his mouth with his hand, and slit his throat, laying the body quietly on the ground.

Jumping over the body to the stairs, he saw Amara staring at the dead guy, and gave her a hand to jump over him. She landed behind him and nodded at him to go on, and he turned around, descending the steps silently, senses on high alert.

He heard the noise at the bottom of the stairs, clocked two men, and swiftly came at one from the back, hitting the top of his skull with his elbow. Before the other guy could react, he leaned to the side, kicking him in the throat, while jabbing the first man in his femoral artery, letting him bleed. The second man raised his gun and Dante twisted, swiping at his knee with his feet, putting the blade with his mouth as he got a grip of the guy's head and broke his neck. It happened within seconds, the speed and surprise in his favor, as he entered the office.

Two more guys disarmed and dead, he helped his woman over their bodies, looking out the glass on the exit door and into the garage.

There were at least six men that he could see, all similarly dressed in black as the others had been, and Dante took note of their positions, mentally mapping out the strategy to take them out.

"Dante," the quiet, almost terrified whisper had him turning his neck to look at wide, green eyes. Following her gaze, he looked at the blood on her fingers, not understanding why that would scare her. Not until he saw her look down between her legs.

She was bleeding, and it wasn't a drop this time.

His heart began to pound as she stared up at him, her eyes shimmering with tears.

No.

The baby.

Fuck, no.

"Hang in there for me, Amara," he gripped the side of her face with his free hand, smearing blood onto her skin, his voice coming out rough to his own ears. "We're almost out, okay? I know this is stressful but you fucking *hang in here with me.*"

"Y…yes," she stuttered, wiping her fingers on his shirt that she was wearing, exhaling out deeply. "Just get us out of here, Dante. We'll be fine."

They had to be.

He couldn't lose their baby, not just minutes after knowing about him or her. But he knew he needed to get them out soon before they were in danger. If he opened the door, it would alert the men and while he could take a lot of them out with the knife, there was still a risk of someone getting to Amara. If he took the gun and quickly shot out a few and coupled it with the knife, it minimized the risk.

"Give me the gun, and shield your body with mine," he instructed her. "If they somehow get me, get out of here. No matter what, Amara. Get yourself out."

He saw the first tear fall, saw that she wanted to tell him no, but she understood. If she got out, she could get their child to safety and contact Tristan. She nodded through her tears.

He pressed his forehead to hers for a second, saying the words he'd told her countless times over the years. "You're the beat to my heart, Amara."

"And you're mine," she replied, her voice barely audible, her words tattooed on his skin.

Urgency infusing his bloodstream, Dante pulled away, embracing the adrenaline, and opened the door a fraction, enough to slip out. He snuck up behind the guy closest to him, cut his jugular open, and muffled his mouth, laying him down.

One guy looked over and Dante aimed, shooting him between the eyes, immediately taking a shot at another guy's head, another's knee, and another's spleen. Two of the men ducked behind cars once the shots rang out.

Dante hid behind a pillar, leaving Amara with the gun again, indicating her to stay in place behind the pillar. She nodded and he slinked out, staying low, walking around the edges of the big garage to where he'd seen the men duck behind a blue Ford. Keeping his body alert but loose, he padded over the side, the knife gripped in his hand like an extension of his limb and came behind the car just to see one guy. A bullet zapped through his side, barely a graze but burning like a fucker, but Dante barely let it stop him, slashing the guy open, feeling the blood on his torso.

He straightened to find the last guy, only to feel him at his back.

He turned, throwing the knife at him as the guy fired. Falling to the floor and rolling to evade, the wound on his side burning, he heard another shot ring out and his stomach tightened.

Straightening, he saw the last guy on the floor, a knife in his chest and a bullet in his head, and looked up to see Amara standing behind him, shaking like a leaf with the gun in her hand.

She had just shot the guy to save his ass. She had protected him. His terrified Amara.

Fuck.

He strode to her just as her knees gave out, her cheeks wet with tears. Taking the gun from her juddering hands, he picked her up and put her over his shoulder in a fireman carry, uncaring of all the blood except the one between her legs, and walked to the Ford.

Opening the door, he put her in the passenger seat, watching as the adrenaline and stress sent her body into shock, and sprinted around, hotwiring the car. Reversing out, going over one of the bodies, he turned to look at Amara, to see her staring blankly out the windshield.

"Amara," he called her, watching as her eyes came to him.

"How're you holding up baby?" he asked her, keeping his voice soft and his eyes on the road, déjà-vu hitting him as he took the same route to the hospital that he'd taken fifteen years ago.

"You have so much blood on you," she remarked, her voice slightly strained.

"I look hot in blood, don't I?" he joked, slightly relieved as she cracked a smile. "Although if it comes to liquid, I prefer the chocolate syrup you covered me in that one time and then went 69."

The distraction was working, her mind like clay in his hands, gullible to his suggestions, molding in the direction he wanted it to go.

"We had fun that night," she remembered, her eyes softening on him.

Oh yeah, that had been an incredible night. "We can try it again later."

She stayed silent for a long second as they sped by. "We're losing the baby, Dante."

His grip tightened on the steering wheel as he pushed the car to the limit, his chest caving in at her words. "Don't say that, Amara."

"I'm bleeding too much," her tone resigned, defeated, and it cut him.

"Yeah, and you will be fine," he grit out. "Don't you dare give up. Not now. Not after all this."

"I'm so tired, Dante," she whispered, and something in her voice made his gut clench.

"I know, baby."

"I just want to sleep."

No, this wasn't good. "Just stay awake a little longer, yeah? Keep me company. We're almost there."

"You know," she began. "I used to have nightmares in the beginning about that place. That someone would drag me there again, and I wanted to die before it ever happened."

Fuck, he wanted to murder every asshole who had been involved all over again.

"But I never understood why they took me," she mused, her fingers playing with the hem of the bloodied shirt. "I was no one. And yet, they kept asking me questions like I knew so much."

He let her talk, glad that she was staying awake.

"They asked me if they should tell you your little girlfriend was there," she huffed a laugh. "I wasn't anything to you then."

She was wrong. "You were always something to me. I just didn't know what it was."

"I don't even know when my feelings for you changed," she continued, adjusting in her seat. "I used to dream you would be my first kiss, you know. But it was a dream. You were so far away."

"I'm not anymore," he pointed out, and she turned her head to look at him, her green eyes somber.

"You saved me from my nightmares then, and you saved me from them now," she said, putting a hand on his arm. "Thank you."

Hit by the emotion in her voice, Dante kept his eyes on the road, taking her bloody hand and kissing it. "You're mine, Amara. Mine to cherish, mine to protect, mine to love. We may not be husband and wife to the world but I have been married to you in my heart for eight years. And no matter what comes at us, we will get through it together. We build our empire together. No more running. Promise me."

"Even if we lose the baby and I can't give you any more?"

He tightened his grip on her hand. "Even then."

Swallowing, she pressed a kiss to his shoulder. "No more running."

With that, he swerved into the hospital emergency parking and prayed for both his woman and his child to be safe.

Amara

They lost a baby.

They didn't lose another.

It was in the hospital, lying on white sheets while Dante got his side stitched, refusing to leave her when the middle-aged female doctor had come in with the news.

She'd been eight-week pregnant with twins, and one of them had latched onto her strong enough to make it through the ordeal while the other hadn't made it.

She was still pregnant but she had lost a baby.

She didn't know what to feel.

The doctor said it was a phenomenon called the 'vanishing twin syndrome' that wasn't as rare as people believed. It was odd, the sense of loss interlinked with the sense of euphoria she was feeling. Looking at Dante, she saw the same reflected back at her, the emotion intense on his face, his eyes on her stomach as the doctor checked her with a stethoscope.

"It's too early to know the gender," the doctor told them. "But the ultrasound showed this little one doing well. However, I have to urge you to be careful throughout the whole pregnancy. The miscarriage puts you at high risk."

Amara nodded, still processing the grief and the relief.

"Anything specific we should be doing, doctor?" Dante asked from her side, his hand holding hers, his gaze determined.

"For now, I would suggest refraining from any strenuous physical or mental exertion," the doctor said. "We'll keep monitoring as we go."

Dante nodded. "And sex?"

Amara felt her face flush as the doctor smiled. "It should be okay. Just be careful not to put any pressure on her stomach or be too wild."

Dante stood up, still shirtless but completely clean, a bandage on his side, wearing scrub pants he'd taken from a male nurse. He'd drawn a line at donning a gown and the female nurse hadn't minded too much, not with the way her eyes had been drinking in his torso. It had made Amara both laugh and sympathize with the woman. She knew how it felt.

"Oh my god, are you okay?!"

The feminine voice from the door had Amara turning to see Morana standing there, her hair in a loopy bun, wearing black leggings and a yellow billowy top, her rectangular glasses on her nose, her hazel eyes wide with concern, and a very rigid Tristan looming behind her.

Lips turning up in a smile at seeing two of her favorite people, she waved them in as the doctor left.

Morana rushed to perch herself on the space by her bed, her eyes going to Dante's shirtless chest that he deliberately flexed because he knew it would rile Tristan up.

On cue, Tristan glared at him. "Don't you have a shirt?"

Dante grinned. "Actually, no, I don't Tristan."

Tristan sighed, and Amara chuckled as Morana leaned forward to hug her.

"I'm here for anything you need, okay?" she whispered in Amara's ear.

Amara squeezed her back, her heart full, glad every single day that she'd trusted this girl, both for her sake and Tristan's.

Tristan leaned down and gave her a kiss on the cheek, something he had never done before, and focused his blue eyes on her. "Don't disappear again like that."

Those five words were enough to let her know that he'd been worried. Over the years, while he had never spoken much to her, he had been there for her time and time again, keeping that promise he'd made to her in the garage. Amara blinked back her tears, nodding.

"Did you find anything?" Dante's voice broke their moment, his demeanor grave.

Morana pushed up her glasses and exchanged a look with Tristan.

"We did," she answered. "I flagged two calls right after you left for Los Fortis. One was made by Vin, and one by Nerea."

Dante tightened his fingers around Amara's. "Did Vin check out?"

Morana hesitated. "I think so. I mean he was in Shadow Port at the time so I kept an eye on him. He didn't do anything except make a call, but he's been cagey. I don't know."

Amara felt her head begin to shake before Morana had stopped speaking. "I don't care how cagey he's being, Vinnie would never, and I mean never, do anything like that."

"He was there, Amara," Tristan spoke quietly from the side. "When you were taken, he was there."

"And you didn't see him fight to save me," Amara countered, her voice straining. "It's not him. He might be shady with other people but he would never, ever hurt me."

"I believe that," Dante supported her claim. "I've known him for a long time, especially with Amara. He would lay his life for her."

Morana nodded. "I trust your judgments on this. And anyways, Nerea was being cagier than Vin."

Amara felt her heart drop. While she wasn't particularly close to Nerea, she was still her half-sister. Amara had come to care for the woman.

"What did she do?" Dante asked.

"What didn't she do?" Morana scoffed, leaning back against Tristan's thighs, and started counting off her fingers. "She made a shady call to an unknown number that I tried to track but it kept bouncing. Then, she left the compound and bought herself a ticket to Los Fortis, and had a meeting with a one-eyed man whom I had a hard time identifying because the missing eye, you know, but he's-"

"Alpha," Amara spoke, surprised.

"-Alessandro Villanova, also known as Alpha."

Dante and Tristan exchanged a hard look at the name.

Dante focused his dark gaze on her, the heaviness in them not of her lover's but the leader of the Outfit. "How do you know him?"

Amara looked at the seriousness on his face. "He came to see me after I moved to the city. Said the city was his and he monitored anyone coming from certain places, like Shadow Port. I got flagged because of my fake passport."

"Where did you get a fake passport?"

Amara felt her heart sink. "Nerea."

Dante nodded, turning to Tristan. "Call for a meeting of the Outfit leaders. It's time."

The other man nodded, brushing his hand over Morana's arm. She looked up at him, and Amara marveled at the way they communicated silently. They'd always been able to do that, just look and have entire conversations nobody in the room was privy to. That was some serious telekinetic shit. Had she not had an amazing man of her own, she would have been envious of that connection.

"Okie dokes," Morana turned to Amara, a smile on her face, "The big guy wants to go and I have to help him with some stuff, so I'll see you soon. We're staying in Tenebrae for a week before flying out so let's do dinner one night? Hopefully, not as tense as last time."

Amara hesitated, looking at Dante. Though he had found her, she didn't know what was going to happen now. Logistically, was she staying on the compound with him or what?

"We'll do a dinner Saturday night at the mansion," Dante stated. "Just the four of us."

Amara felt a breath she'd been holding whoosh out of her, as suddenly something hit her. "Lulu? Oh god, is she okay?"

"She's at the compound," Dante told her.

"Who's Lulu?" Morana asked at the same time.

"My cat."

"You have a cat?" Morana blinked. "That's adorable. Can we get a cat?" she looked up at Tristan.

"No."

Amara laughed at the expression on his face and the huff Morana gave, before they left.

"She's good for him," Dante noted, his eyes coming back to her, his lips tilted up.

"She makes him alive," Amara told him, stroking his hand with hers. "You didn't tell them about the baby."

His fingers brushed over her scars, his eyes going to her still-flat stomach. "I don't want to share her yet."

Her heart fluttered. "We don't know the gender yet."

He just shrugged, bending to press his face to her gown, right over the baby. "She's a fighter, a survivor like her momma. Aren't you, princess?"

Amara melted as he spoke in low, soft tones to her stomach. "Is it odd that I feel sad for the one we lost, even if I'm happy we have one?"

He shook his head. "You just feel as you feel, Amara. A part of me is broken for the baby we lost, but it's the most beautiful feeling to know one of them survived, that she clung through that hell and came out with us. Sometimes, mourning and celebration are two sides of the same coin."

She nodded. He was right. If they focused on the loss, it would be unfair to their child who had made it. They could be happy. They deserved to be happy. After everything they had been through, together and on their own, they deserved this little slice of joy.

"You ready to come home?"

Home.

She was finally going home.

Eyes wet, Amara nodded, and he kissed her hand, the man who had slain demons and men alike to bring her back.

She had missed this place – the rolling green hills, the winding roads, the giant mansion that dominated the view as the car climbed up. It felt odd, coming to the grounds knowing they belonged solely to the man driving her up, the king of the castle himself, and not to the man whose reign of terror and power had permeated the air. As an adult, it looked different than it had as a teenager – the hills were prettier, the roads were narrower, and the mansion less scary.

"My father's stuff at the house is being stored up in the attic," Dante said from beside her, dressed in a dark suit that he had one of his men bring over, along with a beautiful floral dress for her in blues and greens. Hair slicked back from his face, highlighting that impeccable bone structure she secretly hoped their child inherited, the dangerous scruff shrouding his jaw, eyes hidden behind dark shades, Dante looked formidable.

"Are you moved in?" she asked, tugging at the neckline of the dress, her boobs sensitive without a bra.

Dante's neck turned to see the movement, before he turned back, nodding at the guards to open the gates. The huge metal gates swung open and he drove into the compound. "I was more focused on finding you than moving. Although I did get the process started during my father's funeral, it'll take a few days more for it to be entirely complete."

Pulling up in front of the mansion, Dante got out, walked around to her side, and opened her door, giving her a hand. She took it, alighting from the vehicle, and looked up at him.

He cupped her face, brushing his thumb over her exposed neck scar. "Go see your mother," he said softly. "She's waiting for you at my old place. I'll get some stuff done here."

"Okay," she agreed, a zap of excitement going through her at the thought of meeting her mother.

His lips tilted up before he swooped in, crushing their mouths together, the kiss deep and wet and over in seconds.

Amara panted, blinking up at him. "What was that for?"

"Because I can kiss you whenever, wherever, however I want now," he stepped back. "And nobody can do shit about it." He gave her a light slap on the ass. "Now go."

"Bossy bastard," she muttered under her breath, a smile on her lips as she turned and started to walk quickly to his building in the distance. She saw a few patrolling guards stop and give her a look but she ignored them, barely containing the urge to run.

Standing on his porch, Amara lifted her hand and knocked on the door twice, bouncing on her toes in contained excitement.

The door opened and her mother, whom she hadn't seen in years, stood there, staring up at her.

"Mumu," her eyes filled and Amara went into her arms, snuggling in the crook of her neck in a habit that she never got over, her nose filling with the same familiar scent of citrus and sugar and warmth that she knew in her bones.

Her mother's arms tightened around her, holding her close for long minutes as they both just cried, the reunion sweet after years of torment. Amara pulled back, noting the wrinkles on her face, the greys in her hair, the softness of her skin.

They went in to Dante's living room and for hours, talked – about the babies, about what had happened, about everything. Her mother was overjoyed that Dante knew about the pregnancy and that she'd be a grandmother; she was heartbroken that one of them had passed away. Amara asked her about everything she had missed on the compound and her mother told her everything – about Mr. Maroni's funeral, about Dante's brother not wanting to return, about the change in management. And looking at her talk, Amara felt herself fall deeper in love with the man who had not just saved her time and again but protected the one person who was important to her with respect.

Dante Maroni was a remarkable man, and she was lucky he was hers.

Her mother left the house after a few hours, telling her she had some moving stuff to oversee at the main house, and Amara stayed behind, needing a few moments alone before she went out. Walking around his house again, she saw the boxes and stuff lined up beside the stairs. Curious, she climbed up, peeking into his almost empty bedroom, before dodging a box and going up higher into his studio.

As she ascended the last steps, the memories in this room hit her. That first kiss on her neck, right against the door, those stolen kisses after they got together, early morning moments of her listening to his audiobook and watching him sculpt. So many memories in this place and the fact that he was leaving it made her a little sad.

She walked into the large room, taking in the big windows and the plethora of sculptures around it, the workbench lit by a beam of sunlight. She knew many of those sculptures, the ones he had made initially, but a lot of them were new. His art had refined over the years, chiseled itself, and his creations had become something else.

She went to the one of a man's hand reaching out over the space to something, the tendons and veins, and ridges in the limb beautifully defined, the longing in the way it stretched palpable. Amara lifted her hand, touching her fingers to his smooth ones, feeling the cold of the clay against her fingertips, awed by the art with her tactile senses.

"I was drunk when I made that," the voice from the door had her turning around to see the creator himself, leaning against the wall, exactly as he'd been that night so many years ago. Amara felt her heartbeat race at the memory.

"It's beautiful," she told him softly, pulling her hand back, looking around the room. "What will you do with these?"

"They'll move to the mansion tomorrow," he told her, striding in with languid steps. "There's a room I've emptied for it."

"I'll miss this one," Amara confessed, stroking the hand again. "My adolescent self had a few fantasies in this place."

She felt him step beside her, his finger moving over the length of her exposed arms, his lips at her ear. "Do tell."

Amara felt wetness pool between her legs, her already-sensitive breasts tingling as her heart thundered. "Sometimes when… sometimes when I used to watch your hands on the clay…" she trailed off.

His finger trailed up her arm slowly, leaving goosebumps in its wake. "Yes?" he tugged her lobe between his teeth.

Amara felt herself arch, her hands fisting her dress. "I used to imagine you laying me on the bench, and using your hands on me."

His finger reached the strap of her dress, going under it, tugging it down.

"Dante-" It was the middle of the day. Anyone could walk in the door.

"And?" he asked, pulling the strap down enough to expose one swollen breast, his fingers going around the areola in maddening circles, her chest heaving as she gripped his forearm.

"That was it," she moaned as the circle grew inward, so close to her straining nipple, but he didn't touch it.

"Are you wet for me, dirty girl?" he whispered into her ear, his voice smooth and heady and making her eyes roll back in her head.

"Yes," she panted.

"How wet?" he asked, his teeth biting her lobe lightly, sending a shot of fire straight to her core. Amara moved one hand to relieve the ache between her legs, only to have him trap both her hands in one firm grip behind her, arching her exposed breast higher for his infuriating circles close to her nipple.

"Why don't you find out?" she goaded him, needing him to touch her.

"I will," he assured her. "But tell me first, are you leaking over your thighs?"

"Yes," she admitted, feeling the wetness pooling.

"And if I ate you out, you'd drip over my chin?"

Dear gods of foreplay, his filthy dirty mouth turned her on.

She nodded.

"Say it," he commanded.

"Yes, I'd drip over your chin," she spoke, the words, the visual, his finger driving her crazy.

She felt his scruff brush over the side of her face, the sensation new and thrilling, as he asked, "Does my dirty girl need a dirty fuck?"

God, yes. Yes, she needed one so bad. It had been months.

She nodded.

His finger completed another revolution around her nipple. "You know the best part? I'm going to fuck you bare and come deep inside you. Do you want that?"

"I do," she breathed.

He let her arms go and stepped back, leaving her slightly disoriented. Before she knew it, he pushed the other strap down, her dress falling to the floor, leaving her naked in broad daylight while he stayed fully dressed in his suit. He picked her up, put her on the table and taking a seat on the bench, pulled her right to the edge, pushing her thighs back and opening her up.

The sunlight fell on her skin, warming her, highlighting every single scar on her body in stark relief. She saw his dark eyes rove over every single one of them, before stopping between her legs.

Although they had done it a hundred times over, her heart still beat like a drum, her body ready and on edge for him. He bent his head, licking the length of her with the flat of his tongue, the sensation making her arch her back on the table.

"Oh god," she breathed out. "Don't stop."

He slowly dipped in again, his tongue diving inside her, tasting her, eating her like she was the finest dish and he was a man starved. Shivers coursed up and down her spine, her skin warming with the sun on the outside and burning with the heat he ignited from the inside, the dual sensation sending her racing towards the edge of the cliff, secure in the knowledge that he would catch her.

He started writing the alphabets on her nub with his tongue, pushing her closer and closer.

She crashed on the D.

Gripping his hair, her spine arching as she pushed her hips closer to him, she felt her orgasm roll over her – quick, hard, fast – quicker than it had ever been before.

Languid from the pleasure, she saw with hooded eyes as he straightened, unzipping his pants, his mouth wet from her juices, and gripped her under the knees, pushing her legs back until she was almost bent in half, her heart beating like crazy as he plunged into her.

A moan left her, her voice straining as his length speared her, his thickness stretching her walls, her inner muscles fluttering as he pulled back, sinking in deeper.

"Hold your legs open," he instructed her, and she placed her hands under her knees, obeying the command. He bent over her, weight on his forearms at the side of her head, careful to not put any pressure on her stomach, his pelvis rubbing against her in the position, his dark eyes on her face.

He pulled out and snapped again, sending her body slightly up on the table.

"You should've known not to run from me, crazy girl," he grit out, the rage in his eyes transferring to his movements. "I would chase you to the ends of this earth."

Amara felt her fingers tighten around her thighs, her muscles vibrating with the sexual and emotional hunger only this man satiated in her. His rage infused her blood as she let go of her thighs, hitting him in the chest. "You let me think you were dead, you dick! *Dead!* Do you know how that destroyed me?"

Her hands kept hitting him over and over, her body shaking with anger. He took a hold of her wrists, pinning them over her head, his eyes heated, enraged. "You knew I was faking soon enough, Amara. And you still ran, taking my child. Wanna know how *that* made me feel?" He leaned forward, his face an inch from hers, his cock pushing deeper inside her. "Pissed. So. Fucking. Pissed."

She stared at him, angry, annoyed, aroused, and clenched her inner muscles around him, really tightly.

He growled over her, his hips flexing, her anger, her annoyance, her arousal reflected back at her.

"I'm going to fuck my anger out on your pussy," he told her, his jaw clenching. "I'm going to use your body, and I'm going to be selfish as fuck."

She lifted her chin. "I'll use you back."

"Fuck, yes, you will."

With that, he straightened, held her hands above her head, and slammed deep inside her. Amara stretched her legs open again, trying to give him more room but unable to move with the way he had pinned her down. One hand holding both of her wrists, the other came to grip her jaw, his eyes dark on hers as he picked up speed, thrusting hard and deep inside her, the friction and the inability to move doing things to her body she couldn't understand.

He fucked her, hard, fast, deep, so deep, and maybe it was the pregnancy but Amara had never been as aware of every inch of him, of the depth of every thrust that bottomed him out, of the clench of every muscle, as she was in that moment.

His teeth came to her chin, biting her as he hit the spot inside her with his cock, and her eyes closed.

"Marry me, Amara."

The words had her lids opening, the fierce look on his face making her wetter as her heart clenched.

"Be my wife, be my dirty girl, be mine," he mumbled against her lips.

"You're a romantic," she huffed a laugh, a breath whooshing out of her.

He kissed her scar, moving inside her, his voice matching his harsh breathing. "Give me your dreams and your nightmares, your pleasure and your pain, your fantasies and your fears. Give me everything. Be my queen outside, and my filthy girl inside," he hammered his hips into hers, his words coming out rough, gritty, raw. "And make me fucking yours, so everyone who looks at my ring knows I have you finally. Say yes, Amara."

God, he was killing her.

Amara felt her neck arch as a current of pleasure shot through her, her mind becoming mushy.

"Marry me."

"Dante-" she whispered against his lips just as he smashed their mouths together, passion flaring hotter between them. For long minutes, there was the sound of their breathing, the creaking of the table, the slap of flesh hitting flesh. She came gushing within moments, he followed right after, pressing their foreheads together.

"Say yes, baby."

Amara fluttered her eyes open, seeing the man her soul recognized as own, and said 'yes'.

"We'll need to come up with a proposal story," Amara told him as she walked up the hill to the mansion, her hand in his. "I don't think that one will be appropriate for the baby."

He gave her a hot look, his lips turning up, but stayed silent.

The sun was setting over the horizon, the light falling on the stone walls of the mansion and setting them on fire. It felt surreal, the moment – being back on the grounds she had grown up on, the grounds that had seen her birth and her ruin, the grounds that had waited for her to return home. More surreal was walking on that ground, hand in hand with the boy she'd been infatuated with and the man she had fallen in love with, without secrecy or fear or shame. While she was aware of the few eyes that turned their way as they climbed the mansion steps, while she knew the lingering staff would feed the gossip with everything, there was something liberating about this kind of open affection, one that she had been denied for so long. She craved it like the dry soil that had burned and cracked, thirsting for one drop of rain. She soaked it up like she would never get it again, her cracks not gone but healing, and only desired more.

The sound of his phone ringing had them stopping in the entryway. A flash of fur had her looking down to see Lulu twining between Dante's legs, her fur marking the bottom of his pants.

"I should probably get some lint rollers, shouldn't I?" he said wryly, looking down at her fur baby. Dante bent to scoop Lulu up in one arm, bringing her to his face. "Don't shed on me where people can see. I have a reputation to protect."

Amara felt amusement crawl up her cheeks, seeing the huge man in the expensive suit and the tiny cat getting fur all over him, making her laugh. Dante turned to her, handing Lulu over. "Head on to the dining room, I'll make some calls."

Amara nodded, watching as he strode away, the dark jacket of his suit stretched across his wide back, a flutter of feminine appreciation making her sigh. She could ogle him now, as openly as she wanted to.

Feeling happy in a long time, Amara hugged her fur baby to her chest. "I'm glad you're okay, Lulu."

The cat squirmed in her arms, before settling. Lulu was a weird cat. Sometimes she fell asleep right in Amara's arms, and from experience, Amara knew she was settling in for a nap. She kissed the top of her head and walked towards the dining room.

Amara had only been in that room on a few occasions, mostly when she'd been helping her mother. She had never had a meal there. It felt surreal too, standing on the door, watching as the staff laid the table for dinner. Her instinct was to join them, helping them place everything, but she refrained. She didn't know how she was going to be the lady of the house when she had grown up serving them. It was an odd realization, and something she needed to think about. While she didn't want to be detached from the working members of the compound, as Dante Maroni's wife she would have to adhere to certain expectations.

The twelve-foot table was the focal point of the hall-like room, with tall windows with a stunning view of the darkening hills, and a huge crystal chandelier hanging from the high ceiling that glimmered in the sunset with different colors of the fire.

Amara watched from the sidelines as two of the girls who had been her juniors placed the cutlery on the long table, avoiding looking at her as she stood at the door with a napping Lulu.

Fuck expectations. Just because no one before her had been friendly with the staff didn't mean she couldn't start. Forgetting one's roots was one of the biggest mistakes she had seen people make. Roots were important for a tree to grow.

Putting a wide smile on her face, she headed into the room and noticed the five staff members pause.

"So, you're all just going to ignore me?" she asked them in a teasing tone.

One of the men smiled. "Welcome home, Amara. It's been a long time."

She smiled back. "It has been a very long time, Fabio. How is your knee?"

His smile widened. "Still twinges."

Amara turned to the woman who had been her mother's apprentice. "And you Maria, is your son still playing football?"

The older woman gave a stiff smile. "Yes, Miss Amara."

The stiffness of the smile made her own wobble a bit. Amara hugged Lulu closer and swallowed.

"Give us the room, please," a feminine voice from the door had Amara turning to look at Chiara Mancini, Leo Mancini's wife. While Amara had never had any interaction with her, she didn't like the woman one bit. Chiara was extraordinarily beautiful, perhaps one of the most beautiful women Amara had seen, but her soul was rotten. Rumor said she had been married by a much older Leo who had raped her in the marriage. Amara had been empathetic towards the woman until she had heard about her taste for younger boys. Tristan being her first extra-marital affair hadn't endeared her any either.

Amara didn't know if she had ever come onto Dante, but she straightened her spine as the room emptied.

Dressed in a stunning silver dress, Chiara strode in, a polite smile on her lips. "I don't think we have been introduced. I'm Chiara."

For a second Amara felt vulnerable, as though she was somewhere she wasn't supposed to be. But then she remembered the man who had walked through hell with her, the man she was going to spend the rest of her life with, and realized that dealing with people like Chiara would come with the package of them being open.

"Dr. Amara," she introduced herself politely, using the same confident tone she used with her clients.

Chiara's eyes flickered to the scar on her neck that she wasn't hiding anymore before she looked up at Amara. It was one of the rare occasions Amara thanked her height over the shorter woman.

"Well," the other woman began, looking down at the sleeping cat in her arms, her nose wrinkling slightly. "Are you Dante's girlfriend?"

Amara gave the woman a cool gaze. "I'm sorry, who are you?"

"I'm Dante's family," Chiara chimed, her eyes all innocent. "He's under such pressure. Being the leader is not easy, and he's so young yet. I'm just looking out for him."

"I appreciate that," Amara told her in her soft voice that she still hated on certain occasions like this one. People like Chiara heard her speak and immediately thought her weak. Soft did not equal strong in their vocabulary. Soft meant malleable, gullible, vulnerable. Only that was strong which was in-their-face. Morana was strong in her eyes probably, with her devil-may-care attitude and the spine of steel she wore in her eyes. Amara, with her flowery dress and furry cat and soft voice and scars, was a passing fancy, a poor little innocent, an easy target.

Maybe, her voice and her demeanor was a good thing. It let them underestimate her.

Keeping her expression deliberately pleasant, Amara thanked her. "It's nice of you to look out for him."

Chiara fell for it, hook, line, and sinker. "Someone has to. Hopefully, he'll marry one of the prospects soon."

"Prospects?" Amara asked, mildly curious, rocking Lulu in her arms.

"Oh, women he's been vetting for years," Chiara told her helpfully. "All girls from prominent families with good connections. He needs someone who adds to his power."

Amara felt her lips turn up at the not-so-subtle attack at herself. Amara of a week ago might even have agreed with Chiara, might have felt the doubts about her suitability. But the woman who had been tied up in her nightmare had struggled against her ropes, escaped them, and shot a man dead to protect the father of her child. This Amara had woken up into her nightmare and walked out, not unscathed but stronger. This Amara didn't let a dig get to her simply because if Dante had wanted to marry one of the more suitable girls, he would have. He didn't. He had given his crown to her.

Before Amara could give a response, she heard Morana's voice.

"Oh, look Tristan, it's your lizard ex," Morana exclaimed from the door, rolling her eyes behind the glasses. She was in such contrast to Chiara, in black jeans and a blue printed t-shirt with *Nerd Life = Thug Life'*. Amara felt her lips twitch at the quote and the way Morana openly glared at Chiara, coming to stand beside Amara in a clear show of support.

Tristan's lips twitched too.

Damn, Morana was good for him.

Chiara glared at them, before going to the windows, leaving them alone.

"Is this Lulu?" Morana whispered, looking down at the slumbering cat in awe.

Amara nodded. "You wanna hold her? She's very friendly."

"Oh, I can?" Morana grinned at her, slowly taking Lulu's soft body in her arms. The cat woke up in the transfer, turning to look at Amara.

"It's okay, baby," Amara cajoled her, rubbing between her eyes. "She's a friend. You like new people, remember?"

Lulu meowed and turned to stare at Morana.

"She's so soft," Morana uttered, amazed. Tristan came to stand behind her and Lulu, the little attention seeker that she was, tried to climb over Morana's shoulder to sniff him. Morana struggled to contain her.

"Traitor, I know he smells nice, but stay with me for a second!"

Lulu stretched towards Tristan. Tristan stared at the cat, before shaking his head and taking a step back.

"Get that thing away from me, please."

Amara felt Dante enter the room, her eyes immediately seeking him out, and smiled as he came towards them. He scooped Lulu up in his arms and turned to Tristan.

"This thing is a fucking cat, dude," he told the other man, rubbing Lulu behind the ear, so naturally Amara wondered if he'd ever had pets before. "She's a cute little thing."

"Can we get one, caveman?" Morana blinked up at him, putting a hand on his arm. "We'll adopt a stray."

Tristan sighed, sending a glare at Amara, and she burst out laughing.

It felt good. Life felt good.

Dinner had gone as well as one could hope, she supposed. Chiara had pretty much given her looks and her husband, Leo, had gazed off into the distance, clearly distracted by something. Another couple their age – she didn't know their names – had given her polite smiles, while their three kids had been quiet but stealing looks at her and Lulu napping at the base of a sitting man's statue. Dante had taken a seat at the head of the table – where his father had once sat – and had her seated on his left side. Tristan took the seat on his right, opposite

322

Amara, with Morana beside him. It was strategic, a silent message to everyone watching that this was how he was rolling the ball.

Amara had enjoyed the dinner after a long time and observed her man talking in quiet tones with Tristan, or turning to ask one of the kids a question. In between, he had just touched her foot with his shoe, giving her a bit more of that affection she craved from him. With his stubble that darkened his jaw, contrasting with his impeccably-dressed body, Dante Maroni was a vision of masculine beauty and primitive badassery, with a dark gaze that missed nothing and a light smile that hid everything. He was contradictions and balances complimenting each other in one specimen; a slow, deceptive, undetectable poison to everyone except the people close to his heart. Small doses of him over the years had made her stronger, a resilient survivor.

Now, standing in his study, the same study where Lorenzo Maroni had changed her life, Amara watched the king of the underworld on his throne, a glass of scotch in his hand, watching the two other people he trusted talk.

"The airport guy gave me an address," Morana spoke, sipping from her glass of scotch, sitting cross-legged on the couch, her eyes on Dante. "But when we got there, the house was empty. And just yesterday, I got an alert that it had burned down. Faulty wiring, they said."

Dante leaned back on the table, swirling the scotch in his glass, his eyes on Tristan. "We'll find her, Tristan."

Luna.

Tristan's little sister who had disappeared twenty years ago.

Amara felt her heart clench at the way he leaned against the window, rigid, looking down at the floor, and she walked to him. Hunched as he was, his head was the same height as hers. Amara put a hand on his bicep, giving him a squeeze, and he looked up at her with those focused blue eyes.

"Don't lose hope, yeah?" she whispered to him. "You worked so many years to get control. You have the reins now. You have Dante, who has the reins here. You have Morana, who does stuff I don't even understand. And you have me, who does nothing but for moral support. We'll find her."

His jaw clenched but he gave her a nod, straightening and walking to sit beside Morana, who snuggled into him like he was a bear instead of one of the most dangerous men in their world. But then, nobody knew how dangerous he was more than Morana.

Amara took Tristan's vacated space and leaned against the windowsill, as Dante spoke up. "You notice too many fires in buildings of late, Tristan?"

"Yeah, it's fishy."

"I agree," Dante took a sip of the drink. "So, we don't have any leads as of now?"

Morana shook her head. "I've contacted the airport guy again but haven't heard anything back yet."

Dante nodded. "Well, let me tell you what I know." Putting his drink to the side, he took out a cigarette from his pocket, and hesitated, his eyes coming to Amara. She nodded at him to go ahead, and he lit it up. She didn't have anything to contribute to the meeting per se, but Amara knew Dante wanted to keep her in the loop. She appreciated that, especially because if she was to be by his side, she wanted it to be a true partnership.

He inhaled deeply, telling her just by the action that it was stressful. "The Syndicate is deeper than we thought," he began. "I barely got through the surface and the filth is deep. They've been trading in children for at least twenty-years that we know of. Could be much more than that."

Amara felt her hand instinctively go to her stomach, before she breathed out, bile rising in her throat at what he was saying. It was ghastly. Children were a line never, ever to be crossed, and to hear they had been grossly violated for decades just made her skin crawl.

Why aren't you screaming anymore, slut?

The memory came out of nowhere, barreling into her consciousness. She had been a child too.

She pinched the inside of her wrist and exhaled, listening to Dante's voice, anchoring herself to the present.

"I don't know how many ways they operate," he went on. "But I did find one of them. They have recruiters of sorts who scour through chat rooms and forums where assholes who are into kids go, and that's where they find members to get into the organization."

"Factoring in at least twenty years, maybe more," Morana voiced, "this could mean they have over hundreds of thousands of members."

"Jesus," Tristan cursed, rubbing a hand over his face.

The kids. The poor kids.

Dante took another drag. "These members seem worthless though. We need to find more information about how deep this goes and who all are involved in this. The recruiter this guy told me about went by the username MrX." Dante hesitated, casting a small look at her, before speaking again, a tic in his jaw. "He's also the guy who ordered Amara's abduction fifteen years ago."

The strings of a conversation from long ago drifted back to her, triggered by that name.

'MrX is here.'
'Show me the girl.'

"He was there," Amara murmured, her brain still trying to recall more of a conversation she didn't even remember happening.

Dante turned to look at her, one eyebrow raised.

"That name triggered something," Amara frowned. "I think I wasn't fully conscious when I heard his name. But he was there for a moment."

Dante's eyes blazed as he looked back at Morana. "Tristan and I looked into the building back then and it was a dead end. I want you to look again, look deeper, to see if we missed anything. Amara's abduction never made any logical sense to me, and this MrX guy being connected to it… he's a lead to pursue."

Morana nodded. "I'll get on it. If they're hunting these forums, there would definitely be a trail on the dark web. But it won't be safe. I hadn't realized how much the Reaper – my father, I mean, had been shielding me down there. It might take a while for me to cloak myself but I can do it."

Amara was kind of in awe of Morana's brain and her confidence in her abilities. As a woman who had to rebuild herself from the ground up, and someone who still had days of self-loathing, that confidence seemed so unreachable to her. As a therapist, she knew that confidence was a well-made shield hiding a well of emotion.

"Good, but it shouldn't lead back to you," Dante pointed out. "We can't risk them closing the one door we found. Also, do me a favor and try to find something on the Shadowman, if you can."

"The Shadowman?"

"He's involved?"

The other couple spoke at the same time.

The Shadowman. That was an interesting name, especially given how they were earned in their world.

Dante looked at Tristan. "My interrogation told me the one person the Syndicate is careful of is the Shadowman. So, the enemy of my enemy is my friend. I want to meet my new friend and find out what he knows."

"Okay, but that's a badass name," Morana echoed Amara's thought. "Who is this guy?"

"No one knows," Tristan answered her, his arm over the back of the couch behind her. "There were whispers about him on the street out of nowhere. Big players turned up dead right in their homes, no signs of entry or exit, no break-in, dead by a bullet, garrote, poison, ice. He has no MO, no face, no name. That's why they started calling him the Shadowman." He turned to Dante. "But why would the Syndicate be careful of him? He's one man, they're an entire organization."

"Why indeed," Dante muttered, blowing out a cloud of smoke. "You feel like paying a visit to Alessandro Villanova tomorrow? We'll take the jet."

Tristan nodded. "Time?"

"Eight."

"Alpha," Amara spoke up from the side, seeing all eyes turn to her. "That's what he told me to call him. He was kind to me, especially given I was there under a false name. He even offered me protection."

"Did he now?" Dante stubbed the cigarette in an ashtray, his dark eyes on her, the possessive fire that had simmered in them over the years burning hot again. "Could it be because you were a beautiful woman all alone in his territory?"

Amara narrowed her eyes. "I'm not defending him. Just keep in mind that he was good to me when he didn't have to be."

Dante's jaw clenched before he turned to the other two in the room. "We're getting married."

Amara felt her jaw drop at his sudden announcement as Morana exclaimed an 'oh my god', and Tristan's eyebrows hit the roof. He looked between the two of them before a small smile curved his mouth. "Congratulations."

"This is amazing!" Morana leaned forward, her excitement so genuine it warmed Amara's heart. "Wait, where is her ring? Did you propose without a ring?"

"It wasn't planned. I'll get my ring on her, don't worry," Dante reassured her. "You need to send Vin back to the compound. I need him here. And keep your eyes on Nerea. Any suspicious movement, tell me immediately."

Morana nodded, still grinning. "Okay, but I'm helping you plan the wedding. I've never been to a wedding!"

Amara realized with surprise she hadn't either. The first wedding she was going to attend would be her own.

Tristan raised his glass. "To hope."

Coming from him, Amara truly felt it bubbling in her heart. Hope.

Dante

Alessandro 'Alpha' Villanova was one reclusive
motherfucker. Who the fuck stayed on the edge of the
fucking Amazon?

Dante felt the sweat collecting on his brow as he got out of the
black jeep that had picked them up from the airport and driven them
through Los Fortis to the outskirts of the city, to the point where he
had started to wonder if these guys meant to dispose of him and
Tristan in the jungle. He could see Tristan was on alert too, but silent
as they jumped out of the vehicle and onto one of the largest
compounds he had ever seen. Dante had thought his compound on
Tenebrae was big and green but this one felt endless, stretching as far
as the eyes could see, situated on a plateau that dipped into the vast

ocean of green on the east side, the only access road connecting to the city on the west.

"Follow me," one of the henchmen who had picked them up, a tall, lanky guy with African heritage led them up the concrete pavement closed by climbing trellises on the sides. The scents of tropical flowers infused the air around them, the sounds of birds chirping close by a musical cacophony.

Dante was impressed, and it wasn't easy to impress him. As a courtesy, as it was when any leader wanted to enter the territory of another, Dante had had a meeting arranged with this man, curious to meet him but wary. The fact that the property he and Tristan had infiltrated had been registered in his name didn't win him any points, but Dante also knew how easy it was to use something in someone else's name. Keeping his mind open for the moment, and ignoring the fact that he'd tried to possibly make a move on his woman, Dante gave Tristan a nod and both men followed the guy.

The trellises ended with the pavement and Dante came to a stop, his eyes looking upon one of the most spectacular creations he had ever seen. Just twenty minutes away from Los Fortis, Alessandro Villanova had built himself a compound the likes of which Dante had never seen.

There were three tiers to the entire compound, the bottom one with at least ten or more small brown cottages around the incline, with sloping, red-tiled roofs that had faded to a light sandstone color. A three-story grey building was to the side on that tier, the only flat-roofed structure in the place. The second tier had bigger and fewer cottages, in the same brown and red, spaced out by lush green flora with colorful flowers. And on the top tier was a huge grey mansion of bricks and glass, with wide terraces on either side of the mansion, and a large curved pool that started beside the terrace and probably extended to the back.

If places could give people hard-ons, this one would top the list. The seclusion, the exoticness, the views, the savage grandeur, it was all combined together to be a private sanctuary to a small army, an empire hidden from the plain eye.

"Fuck," Tristan muttered from his side, taking the place in, and Dante felt that. Shaking his head, he took in the various people milling about the first tier and climbed up the stone steps that led from the ground to the top. Just living here was one serious workout.

By the time they had climbed to the mansion, Dante could feel the sweat inside his suit. But fuck, just the view was worth it – the city in the distance on one side, and vast stretches of dark forest on the other.

The henchman led both him and Tristan to a seating arrangement on one of the terraces, and Dante clocked in the lack of any security on this level.

"He'll be with you in a minute," the henchman said and left them alone, descending the stairs they had just climbed. The stairs were the sole point of access that he could see.

"No security," Tristan commented, on the same page as him.

Dante nodded, pushing his hands in his pockets and staring at the view. The air at this level was cold but slightly humid. "How did we never know about this place?"

Tristan came to stand beside him. "It's pretty peaceful here. Reminds me of these honeymoon resorts Morana keeps showing me."

Honeymoon resorts. The guy was talking *honeymoon resorts.* Pigs really had to be flying somewhere in the world.

Dante turned to consider the other man. "You think you'll ever go on a honeymoon with her?"

Tristan stared out at the lush landscape. "I don't think she actually expects us to. Not right now, anyway. The thing with the Reaper hit her hard. For now, she's coping by distracting herself with travel plans after Luna, and I'm letting her. She's processing."

Dante felt his lips lift. "You're whipped."

"Fuck off, asshole."

Dante grinned, looking out at the cloudy sky. "I'm happy for you, you little shit. For both of you."

Tristan stayed silent for a beat. "You and Amara doing okay?"

"What, you're giving me relationship advice now?"

He shrugged. "Communication and shit are important in relationships."

Dante looked at him in surprise. "Who are you and what have you done with Tristan?"

He saw the fucker's lips twitch.

The sound of dogs barking had them both turning to see three large German Shepherds behind the glass doors, a giant man walking towards them. Dante rarely met anyone larger than he was, but this guy had a few inches over him, both in height and thickness. Dark black hair wavy around his fucked up face, an honest-to-god eye patch over one eye, the man screamed danger and dominance in ways that had Dante's predatory instincts come to the fore.

He put on the façade that had served him the best – the suave gentleman whom people tended to underestimate. People expected the Dante Maroni – the Wall of the Tenebrae Outfit, the son of Bloodhound Maroni, and grandson of Iceman Maroni – to be one vicious, arrogant, brutal motherfucker. He was all those things. But the suits, the manners, the charm always fooled them.

The giant guy nodded to them both, extending one large, scarred hand towards him.

"Alpha," he spoke in a gruff voice, his one eye a dark gold, assessing them both. "Welcome to Los Fortis."

Dante shook his hand firmly. "Dante Maroni. This is Tristan Caine."

Alpha nodded to Tristan and waved them both to the covered area on the terrace with bamboo furniture. They all sat down, the dogs inside settling against the glass, watching their master and the strangers.

"Quite a place you've built yourself here," Dante commented, breaking the silence.

Alpha just smiled, only one side of his lips and cheeks moving, the other permanently pulled down by the scar that ran under his eye patch. He was a survivor, this guy, and Dante had immediate respect for anyone who'd gone through shit to come out the other side.

An old lady with weathered skin came out with a tray from the other side of the terrace, carrying steaming mugs of coffee and snacks. She gave all three of them a smile, speaking in her lilting accent. "The coffee is a local specialty. Please let me know if you need anything else."

"Thank you, Leah," Alpha told her, his voice warming fractionally. Dante wondered for a second if he should drink or refuse, but Alpha told him. "I don't poison guests, Mr. Maroni. That's not my style."

Both he and Tristan took a steaming mug each and sipped. It was bitter but damn if it didn't taste incredible.

"Did your father finally tell you? Is that why you're here?" Alpha asked, relaxed in his chair. The fact that he was relaxed, that there was no security, that he and Tristan hadn't been stripped of weapons before meeting him told Dante exactly how lethal the man before him was. Unlike his father who had relied on his army of security to keep him safe, this man was a warrior king, who had amassed his army by fighting and winning.

"What do you mean?" Dante asked, taking a sip of his brew.

The man's golden eye sharpened on him. "We share a father, Mr. Maroni."

Dante's hand paused on the way to his mouth, his eyes honing in on the other man. "Excuse me?"

Alpha laughed. "The bastard didn't tell you."

Dante felt his fingers flex on the mug. He set it down on the table and leaned forward, his jaw clenching. "Explain."

The other man took pity on him. "My mother was a sex worker in Los Fortis, sending her younger sister to art school and keeping a roof over their heads. Lorenzo Maroni saw her one day on his visit to the city about thirty-three years ago, raped her, and left her pregnant. He also kidnapped her sister and took her with him. He married her."

Dante felt his heart cracking open, the ground beneath his feet shifting. He looked at the other man, truly looked at him, and saw the similarity – the dark hair, the jawline, the cheekbones, the nose, the build. He was looking at his half-brother.

The fucked-up stories of his father's selfish, monstrous actions made him want to raise the man from the grave and kill him again. One man's monstrosity destroyed so many lives and counting.

Fuck.

"I don't even know what to say," Dante shook his head, still trying to wrap his head around everything.

Alpha tilted his head to the side. "I thought you knew when I got the request for the meeting. Especially since one of your soldiers recently came to confirm the story with me."

"Nerea?" Dante asked. "She was here because she knew this? How?"

336

Alpha shrugged. "She said she was looking into your mother's past and came across me. I never had any intentions of telling you."

That brought him up short. "Why not? And why didn't you ever contact me?"

Alpha huffed a laugh, without amusement. "Oh, I did contact Lorenzo Maroni. When I was thirteen, on the streets, and my mother was dying, I needed money for her surgery, and as a last resort, I contacted him." He put the mug down on the table. "And I got nothing except confirmation that he was a rotten asshole and we were better without him."

Dante felt his teeth gnash, his hands fisting. All this time, he'd had an older brother, a true heir to the empire he'd never wanted, and his father had fucked him up.

"Anyways, why are you here, if not for a family reunion?"

"Do you own any property near Tenebrae, Alpha?" Tristan spoke up for the first time, his voice tight. Dante took a deep breath and walked to the edge of the terrace, needing to wrap his head around everything.

"No," Alpha answered. "I never wanted to get anywhere near Maroni territory."

Dante didn't know what to believe. While he could be telling the truth about his father, it could also be something to manipulate him and Tristan. If this man was in cahoots with the Syndicate, he could very well misdirect them.

"Do you know anything about the Syndicate?" Dante turned, pushing his hands into his pockets, focusing on the reason for their meeting.

Alpha stared at him evenly with one eye. It would intimidate a lesser man. "They trade children. But I have nothing to do with them. Why come to me?"

"Because we found a house registered in your name where the Syndicate was initiating new members by raping a little girl," Tristan stated, his hands fisted on his thighs.

"Which name? Alpha or Alessandro?"

"Alessandro," Dante chimed in.

He shook his head. "That's not possible. Nobody in the underworld knows my given name. Everything I have is under Alpha or Alpha Villanova. Nobody knows Alessandro except my sentinels."

"You told Amara both your names," Dante chimed in.

Alpha's eye came to him. "Ah, she's yours. Good woman, but I gave her both the names thinking there might be more there."

Dante's gut burned. Fuck, no. "She's mine."

Alpha grunted. "Point is, I don't know why anyone would buy a house in my given name and why the Syndicate would use it. I've heard of them, and in my business, we hear things. But I've never had contact with them."

"What is your business?" Dante asked, curious as to how a boy from the street with no money had amassed the compound he was standing upon.

"Security and retrieval," Alpha left it at that, and Dante almost smiled. Reclusive bastard.

"The Syndicate is responsible for a lot of shit we're just getting to know about," Dante walked back to the seat, taking off his suit jacket in the warm weather. "Our father was working with them in some capacity, I don't know how yet."

Pushing his jacket to the side, he leaned forward, looking his older brother in the eye. "Can I trust you, man to man?"

Alpha's eyebrow went up. "As long as you're not like your father, I have no problem with you."

Dante nodded. Good enough. Any man who hated his father had a point in his book.

"Twenty years ago," he began, "twenty-five girls were abducted from Tenebrae. One of them was Tristan's sister, Luna. We know Lorenzo Maroni and Gabriel Vitalio gave the kids to the Syndicate, but we don't know where she was sent. That's who we're looking for."

He saw Alpha's eyes go to Tristan, softening slightly. "That's hard. I hate to be the one to tell you this, but there is a high chance she's not alive. A lot of kids who go with the Syndicate don't survive. You have to be prepared for that possibility."

Tristan nodded, his jaw tight. "I am. But I want answers."

"And I want to know which motherfucker found my name and used me," Alpha stated.

"We have a hacker who can track that," Dante informed the older man. "In exchange, you give us a lead. Deal?"

Alpha considered him for a long second. "Okay, I'll see what I can find."

Dante stood up, taking his card out of his pocket, handing it to the other man, hesitating. "My mother slit her wrists open in the room she used to paint in with our younger brother there. He has Asperger's and he's living a great life far away from this world. I had to sacrifice seeing him to protect him and now he doesn't want to come back. I get that. He's found a good woman and works as an architect from home, and has told me to keep myself and this world away from his life. We talk on the phone sometimes but we're acquaintances. In protecting him as a brother, I failed him too. My point is, if you are my brother, I get why you didn't tell me anything, but going forward, you decide how we operate – as brothers or as acquaintances. The choice is yours."

With that, Dante gave the bigger man a nod and walked to the stairs, Tristan on his heels.

"Dante?"

He paused and turned to see the man.

"Congratulations on the baby."

Dante felt his lips curl, and with a nod, he descended, looking at Tristan. "You don't look surprised."

Tristan moved easily beside him. "Amara kept touching her stomach last night. I suspected."

Dante looked at the incredible vista laid at his feet, the realization that it belonged to his brother staggering. "Do you believe his story?"

"Yeah," Tristan said. "He resembles your father a bit, except that one eye."

"I've never seen anyone with one eye," Dante commented. "I hope he finds some leads for us. Have Morana look into him and the property deeply."

Tristan nodded just as his phone rang. Dante saw Morana's name flashing and knew it was important. Those two liked to text more than talk on the phone, from what he'd observed.

Tristan picked up. "Yes?"

Dante almost felt his eye roll at the way he answered the love of his life. Tristan stiffened, pausing his downward descent, and Dante stopped as well, alert.

"Send me the address. Dante and I will take the jet."

Dante waited for him to explain as he pocketed his phone. "The airport asshole sent her an address, telling her to get to it within 24 hours, or we'll miss it."

Adrenaline flushed into Dante's system. "Where?"

"70 miles out of Tenebrae," Tristan answered.

The men exchanged a look and sprinted down the stairs, ready to raise some hell.

Dante called for backup en route to the airport, glad to know Vin had returned and would bring three solid men to the airport at Tenebrae, from where they would all drive to the location. Maneuvering his Range Rover, Tristan at his side, Dante checked his rear-view mirror to see the two black SUVs from the compound tailing him as he drove out of the city limits, following the GPS directions.

"Take the next exit off Portsmouth Avenue," the robotic feminine voice said, and Dante followed, his shoulders in knots from five hours on the flight. He rotated his shoulders and cracked his neck, the sound loud in the silent vehicle. Stress balled in his gut, and it was from the unknown. Dante didn't know if they'd be walking into a trap or a genuine lead. Worse, he didn't know what kind of a lead. It could be anything from an abandoned place to a disastrous house like the last time.

"You ready, buddy?" he asked Tristan in a deliberately light voice, goading him, knowing he was more stressed.

Tristan just gave him a look but stayed silent, his hand holding his gun. Dante's own was on the dashboard, waiting to be picked up and fired.

"Turn left on Madison Boulevard," the navigation said, and he turned left onto a dirt road off the main highway. Acres of farmland surrounded the path for a few miles before the woods began. Night fell over the sky, darkening the land enough to make it eerie, a full moon glowing brightly in the midst.

"This feels like a gothic movie," Dante noted, checking the map on the dashboard GPS.

"Your destination is 2 miles ahead," the voice said.

Headlights shone their way as they entered the wooded area. A big, dilapidated wooden house came into view. The house was completely dark, abandoned.

Dante stopped the vehicle, picked up his gun, and jumped out, shutting his door, hearing all the car doors shutting as everyone got out. The chill in the air raised the hair on the back of his neck, something dark roiling inside his gut as he looked at the house. It wasn't just the setting or the house that was creepy, but the air around it was nefarious with screams unheard and stories untold. Dante had always kept his heart and senses open and they were all vibrating with tension at that moment.

Giving the men behind him a nod, he exchanged a look with Tristan and motioned him forward with two fingers. Tristan nodded back, and they hunched down, keeping the tall grass as cover as they crept forward.

A crooked board hung to the side of the house, its print faded. Dante squinted, trying to read the print but it was too faded to make out.

"I see shadows by the right window," Vin's voice whispered low from behind him. Dante looked and saw some dark movement as well. On quiet footsteps, he crossed the yard and went up the porch, the wooden boards groaning under his weight, giving him away.

Adrenaline pumping through his blood, Dante nodded back at his companions.

Stealth lost, he raised his hands and pointed the gun straight, unlocking it, and kicked the door in. The poor state of the wood made the door crash in.

Bullets fired from the inside and Dante took cover. His side was already grazed; he didn't want another on his body, thanks very much.

"Take them back," he ordered Vin and two other guys, who ran around the back of the house. Dante bent low and took off his jacket, holding it in his hand, waiting.

Another shot rang out from the inside, and pinning the location mentally, Dante straightened, throwing the jacket in the face of his assailant, blinding him momentarily, long enough to shoot out his knees.

He looked at the Outfit soldier behind Tristan and ordered, "Disarm him, drag him out, and keep him alive for interrogation."

"Yes, boss," the guy got to work, as Dante and Tristan went deeper into the dark house, only the moonlight coming in from the windows guiding them.

"One guy blew his face off," Vin's voice came from the other side. "Another ran into the woods. Liam and Alek are on him."

Dante nodded, body strung tight, ears open, listening for any untoward sound. It was eerily quiet, no natural sounds of the night, nothing except his regulated breathing and the blood in his ears. But he could sense they weren't alone. He felt eyes on himself, but couldn't pin from where.

"We have company," he muttered softly to Tristan and Vin. "Stay close."

Walking forward, deeper into the house, he came to a foyer of sorts, with a staircase that went up, and began to climb. On the first floor, he checked each door, careful not to miss anyone. Vin took the second floor while Tristan stayed on the ground. In a few minutes, the house was checked and empty.

"That was it?" Tristan asked softly. "We busted in for that guy outside? It doesn't make sense."

No, it didn't. They were missing something.

The sound of a glass breaking from the kitchen had them all alert and running in the direction. They came in, the entire space empty, a glass broken over the floor, pieces shattered right over a trapdoor.

Exchanging a glance with his companions, Dante squat down and gripped the metal handle which was surprisingly not cold to the touch, meaning someone had touched it recently and heaved it open.

And looked down at eight pairs of innocent, terrified eyes looking up at them.

"Jesus fucking Christ," Vin mumbled. "Those are boys."

Those were boys indeed – young, not older than ten, dirty boys.

"C'mon," he cajoled in a gentle voice even as his blood boiled, extending his hand to one of them, putting his gun down. "We're not going to hurt you."

One of the boys stuttered, "Will-will you take us home?"

Fuck, his heart was going to come out of his fucking chest.

"Yeah," Dante promised. "We'll send you boys home. C'mon out of there. It looks dirty."

"It smells bad too," another boy said. "How do we know you're telling the truth?"

Before Dante could reply, a third boy, one with bright eyes the color of which Dante couldn't make out, stated. "They are. He told me about the blue-eyed one," he said, pointing to Tristan.

"Who told you about him?" Dante asked, confused.

"The Shadowman."

20

Amara

A mara was surprised when she got the call at nine.

She and Morana had been lounging in Tristan's cottage, talking about their lives and spending a girl's night just being friends, chilling with another female companion, someone they had both never had in their lives.

Amara had talked to her about her arrangement with Dante over the years, her accelerated degrees that had allowed her to get into practicing therapy, and her reasons for running away. Morana had confessed about her father's situation, about how lost she felt some days and how Tristan anchored her, about how she wondered about Gabriel's actual daughter and her fate. They also talked about wedding plans while sipping on hot chocolate, and for the first time in her life, Amara felt how much having a true female friend did wonder for the soul. Morana was a true girlfriend of her heart, the kind who would drop everything and be there for her at any time of the day, the kind she could text the weirdest stuff and she would just text back weirder, the kind whom Amara could trust with her baby if one day something ever happened to her.

Her day had started so well, with Dante waking her with a soft kiss as he left, telling her Vin would be there for the day. She had spent her morning seeing her friend – her once-chubby now-hottie friend – and reconnecting with the man he had become, realizing that while he had hardened, he was still the same boy underneath she loved. He was another true friend of her heart, one who had made her day just by spending time with her.

So the call had surprised her. Now, sitting beside Morana in the passenger seat of one of the Outfit sedans as she drove to a location, Amara didn't know whether to be worried or not.

"I knew the airport guy had done us a solid this time," Morana told her.

"Yes, but why would Dante call me to come to the location? And ask me to call in my contact at social services?" Amara asked, baffled.

Morana shrugged, swerving, overtaking a car, going at a speed much higher than Amara was used to, but doing it confidently. "Who knows? Is your contact sending someone to the location?"

Amara checked her phone. "Yeah, they should be there in about twenty minutes."

"We'll be there in ten."

"The GPS doesn't show that," Amara pointed out, and her friend just gave her a grin, accelerating even more.

Amara laughed, holding the handle by the door. "Just don't get us in an accident, please. There's a baby the size of a bean on-board."

Morana gave her an amused look, slowing down a bit as they came to a turn. "I know. Tristan told me. He said you kept touching your stomach yesterday and I quote 'asshole probably knocked her up'."

Amara sputtered a laugh, not really surprised at Tristan's observation or comment.

"Any news on Nerea?" Amara asked.

"Nope," Morana sighed. "I've been keeping an eye on her movements but they've been clean so far."

Amara nodded. Just as she'd expected. They chat up the rest of the way about the baby, becoming silent as they turned on a dirt path lit by moonlight, and saw the woods.

"Is it just me or is this place straight out of a slasher flick?" Morana muttered quietly as she drove over the path, to the edge of the wooded area. The headlights lit the way, showing nothing but trees on both side, and darkness beyond.

"This is creepy," Amara agreed, watching the GPS show their destination just a mile ahead. "Are you sure we're on the right path?"

The answer came in the form of three SUVs, a police cruiser, an ambulance, and a creepy as fuck house lit up by the headlights of all the vehicles. Morana parked the vehicle beside the police cruiser and they both got out, exchanging a look before walking towards the front of the house where people were standing covering the front steps of the house.

The closer they got to the group, the more Amara realized there were small people sitting on the steps, huddled in blankets. Small boys.

Heart pounding, she watched as Morana split to the side of the house, where Tristan sat on the ground talking to one boy. Leaving them to it, she turned to see Dante standing with no jacket, his shirt sleeves folded over his forearms, hands on his hips as he listened to a cop say something. His eyes came to her, went over her from head to toe, before he extended his hand to her, calling her silently to his side.

Amara walked on her wedges to him, looking around the scene, questions in her eyes. Dante slid his arm around her waist, continuing his conversation with the middle-aged cop, balding.

"Five of them matched the missing person reports filed over the last year," the cop told them, ignoring her. "We've called their guardians; they should be here by the morning. We'll take their statements after."

Dante nodded, mindlessly rubbing the side of her hip, even as his focus was on the conversation along with hers. "What about the boys at the hospital?"

The cop shook his head. "We're trying to locate their files but nothing is coming up. Reckon we'll have to search the last five years or so. They're at the hospital for now. We have a man on them."

"Make it two," Dante ordered, and Amara wondered if he could actually order a cop. She knew the Maronis had a lot of the departments in their pockets, but she didn't know how deep it went.

"I'll have to call in social services on this one," the cop said.

"My woman here," he squeezed her hip, "is a licensed therapist with connections in the department. She's already made the call."

"They'll be here soon," Amara chimed in, her voice low.

The cop nodded. "Look, you can explain this away, but I'll have to file a report."

"Okay. What about that one?" Dante tilted his head to indicate the boy sitting with Tristan.

"No idea," the cop said. "We've gone back eight years, which the boy said was his age, but can't find a thing in our system. No missing person report. No contacts. We'll keep looking but the chances are slim on that one."

"Thanks, Derek," Dante gave the cop a nod. "Keep me posted."

The cop gave a sharp nod and turned to talk to the line of young boys sitting on the steps, where his partner was already talking while two paramedics checked them over. Tristan sat a few feet away, head lowered, as the boy with him talked, Morana watching them from the side.

"What's going on?" Amara asked her man, looking up at him, seeing the dark shadows fall over his face.

"We found the kids here," he told her, turning to look at the scene. "All kidnapped, ready to be shipped. Vin took one of the guys we caught to the Compound for interrogation. One died, the other is in the wind. Eight kids, Amara. Eight boys."

Amara pressed a kiss to his shoulder, letting him get it out.

They both watched as Tristan kept his head lowered, listening to whatever the boy was saying. Amara had never seen her friend like that, so focused on a child. But she knew he was protective of kids so maybe that shouldn't have surprised her.

"It's just the beginning. We have opened Pandora's box. These nightmares will keep coming to light, and I want to build something better for our children. Stand with me, yeah?"

"You don't even have to ask, Dante," Amara told him softly. "I'll always stand with you."

"I know you keep wondering what your role will be in this new order we have," Dante mused, looking at the boys. "You are the healer, Amara. You are the lighthouse guiding these lost souls to the shore. They need someone to guide them, someone who's emotionally intelligent, strong enough to understand trauma and survival and still be light. That's you."

He turned his neck, piercing her with his dark eyes, his voice dripping with conviction. "We'll find more children, more young boys and girls, in different conditions. We don't know how many. They'll need to be rehabilitated. They'll need help – physically, which I can arrange, but also mentally, which is your forte. We can give them a chance at life, Amara. We can leave a legacy in this godforsaken place. So, will you play with me, my queen?"

Amara looked at the innocent lives marred with this blip of darkness and felt her heart clench. She knew how much it took out of the soul to simply survive against the odds. She knew pain, and loss, and sheer force of will. And she knew she wouldn't be standing there without the help she'd had. There was no other option for her.

Turning her gaze back to the man she not only loved but felt truly proud to call hers right that second, she gave him her answer. "Yes, I will, my king."

Let the games begin.

It was late by the time the paramedics and the police wrapped up. Amara stayed behind as the two guys from social services showed up, helping them navigate the fate of the two kids at the hospital, ensuring they were also prescribed some form of counseling for their experience.

She had started to ask the same for the kid who'd been sitting with Tristan when Morana had given her a subtle shake of her head. Keeping that down for the time, Amara had walked with the guys as they took the other boys to meet with their guardians. By the time everyone was gone, there was only her, Dante, Tristan, Morana, and that kid left in the area.

Amara walked over to Dante's side as he sat down on the steps, watching her. He spread his legs and pulled her between them, pushing his face into her stomach, murmuring words in a tone so low she couldn't hear. She sifted her fingers through his hair, feeling the softness of the strands, feeling the warmth of his breaths against her tummy, and just held him as he held her, taking strength from her presence.

He tugged on her hips until she sat down on his lap, and snuggled his face in the crook of her neck, breathing in her scent. Amara felt her heart skip a beat, as it always did with him, and kept him close, her eyes lingering on the child who fell asleep with his head on Tristan's lap. She saw him look at Morana, saw them have a silent conversation, and saw Morana bend down, giving him a small kiss on the lips. It still awed Amara some days, the way Tristan allowed Morana so close into his space. He scooped up the kid in his arms and stood, the movement taking the attention of the man holding her.

Dante looked to the side at them while keeping Amara tight by his side. "You guys heading back?"

"Yes," Morana responded, taking her car keys out of her pockets. "Little Xander here is knocked out and Tristan wants to talk to him some more. We figured we'll take him with us, and figure stuff out later."

Dante gave her a nod, exchanging a look with Tristan. "Let me know if you need anything."

Tristan nodded, carrying the boy, Xander, in his arms to the car Morana had driven. He lay Xander in the backseat, got in the passenger's side while Morana got behind the wheel, and with a wave at them, drove out.

"How much do you bet they'll keep the kid?" Dante's voice had her looking down, his hand splaying over her stomach possessively.

Amara shrugged. "We'll see how it goes."

Dante gave her a little smile, and before she could take a breath, stood up with her in his arms, making her squeal lowly and grab his shoulders. Heart racing, she watched as he deposited her in the Rover, jogging around to the driver's side, and got in, pulling out of the eerie place.

"This place was so creepy," Amara muttered, watching it get smaller in the rear-view mirror. "How did the Morana's airport guy even know about this?"

Dante contemplated for a moment, driving them out of the woods and onto the dirt road cutting through the open fields. "He's the Shadowman."

Amara turned to look at him, seeing the full moonlight pouring in through the windshield, casting a soft, romantic glow over his features. She thought about what he'd said, interposing it with what she knew, and agreed. "It makes sense. That's why she never saw him."

The car jostled as Dante swerved the wheel, turning them back onto the highway. "He was there tonight."

Her eyebrows went up to her forehead. "You saw him?"

"No," he shook his head. "But he was there. One of the guys who escaped was found in the woods by our men, tied to a tree, a message taped to his chest."

"What message?"

Dante glanced at her. "It said 'good job'. He wanted us to find that place. He practically spoon-fed us this."

"He's playing with you guys," Amara inferred, turning the heating up as a chill went down her spine. "Why?"

Dante stayed silent. They passed a few miles in silence before Dante spoke up again. "Alpha is my half-brother."

That made Amara turn sharply towards him. Dante told her about his visit to Alpha's compound, about the information he had discovered, about the tragedies his father had made of people's lives. He told her everything, including not knowing if he entirely trusted the man or not. They were getting closer to the city, the roads still dark and empty, as the car flew by.

"He was nice to me," Amara reminded him.

"He wanted to fuck you," Dante amended, his jaw clenching.

Amara felt a laugh escape her. "That would've been funny though, what with you being brothers. I'd feel scandalous."

Before her last word was out, Dante pulled to the shoulder of the road, turning the vehicle off. He undid her seat belt, pushed his seat back, and pulled her over him, sending her heart careening through her chest.

"Say that again," he grit out.

Amara felt herself smile as she settled over him, her thighs straddling his hips, putting her hands over his chest. "You're being ridiculous."

One of his hands gripped her full breast, the other going to her ass in a hold that was nothing short of territorial. In the moonlight, his dark eyes gleamed like uncut obsidian, born of flames, cooled in winds. His masculine scent, that cologne she had loved since she first smelled it, permeated the closed confines of the car. He took over her senses – sight, sound, smell, touch – and she reveled in it, her heart pounding but desire coiling in her belly in known anticipation. This wasn't like it had been in the beginning. Their desire then had been a wildfire – unknown, unexpected, untamed. No, now it was a kindling, a bonfire in the middle of a snowy desert, melting the frost, warming the bones, lighting the dark. They had been together a hundred times before and they would be together a hundred times more. But their need for each other had evolved – from being lovers learning each other, they had become memories on each other's skin, every inch of her body knowing every inch of hers.

Given all that, all the years and touches between them, his hand holding her breast and ass sent heat curling through her spine, so familiar, so delicious, so wanted. Amara thrived in being desired by this man; she thrived even more in desiring him. For a long time after her assault, she had felt both undesirable and undesiring, not sure if she would ever find any sexual pleasure in her life, or get rid of the shame if she did.

Dante had introduced her to the spark of heat as a boy and taught her to master it as a man. He had been her first infatuation, her first love, her first kiss, her first lover that she had allowed into her body, her first everything.

But they had also spent all these years they had loved each other apart, across hundreds of miles, craving and needing but never having enough, loving in the shadows. While it truly was ridiculous that he would feel any kind of insecurity over her, she also understood. Their roots were strong but the tree had been cut, and now new leaves were sprouting. It would take time and nurturing for them to grow strong.

She leaned closer to him, pressing a kiss to the corner of his lips. "You're the beat to my heart, Dante."

His hand tightened on her ass. "And you're mine." He pressed his forehead to hers. "We'll be okay, right? With this life, with the baby, with each other?"

Amara rubbed her nose against his. "We'll be okay. We'll be together. That's what matters."

"And you'll love me when I'm old and grey?"

"You know I will. You'll be a hot silver-fox though," Amara grinned. "I'd do you."

"Fuck," he chuckled.

"Dante?" she whispered.

"Hmm?" he nuzzled into her.

"I'm feeling a little horny," she confessed, watching his eyes sharpen on her.

"Ask me to kiss you," he ordered, eyes dark on hers.

Amara felt her breath catch in the confined space of the vehicle. "Kiss me."

"My dirty fucking girl," he murmured, his hand moved from her ass, going under her dress, moving to cup her between her legs through her panties, as the other hand plucked her hard nipple. Heat shot through her breast, arrowing down right where his fingers were feeling her, wetness pooling on his hand.

"You're soaked," he growled, pushing her panties aside and plunging two fingers inside her.

Amara moaned, her head falling back as she gripped his head, hips moving over his fingers.

"Ride my hand, baby," he encouraged her, his voice low, husky, perfect.

Amara moved her hips in wanton motions, feeling his thumb settle on her clit, alternating between pressing it and rubbing it, and the coiled serpent of shameless pleasure tightened inside her, beckoning her to taste the ecstasy waiting for her.

"Soak my hand, dirty girl. That's it. This pussy is mine, Amara," Dante took her other nipple into his mouth over her dress, sucking it deep, making her arch back as a current zapped through her body. "These tits are mine." He moved up to kiss her neck. "This scar is mine."

Her legs spread as she settled even more, rotating her hips, and his mouth took possession of hers. He kissed her hard, devouring her mouth, sending electricity zapping through her nerves, her heart racing, her inner walls pulsing around his fingers. His tongue swiped over her lips, tangling with her tongue, before sucking it into his mouth. The wetness of the kiss, the dirtiness of the joining, the sloppiness of the sounds, just turned her on even more.

She pulled back to catch a breath, panting as she exploded out of nowhere, her orgasm crashing into her, making her keen and thrash and shake as her inner muscles clenched around him, shivers running up and down her spine, her eyes rolling back in her head.

Heart thundering, she opened her eyes as Dante pulled his fingers back, and brought them to his mouth, keeping their eyes locked, licking one digit, his tongue tasting her come, and heat coiled in her belly again, faster than it should have. He pulled her head down to his mouth, making her taste herself, their lips crashing and colliding together, before he pulled back, picked her up, and placed her back in her seat.

Amara gave a pointed look at his erection tenting his pant, and he grinned. "Not gonna fuck you here, baby. Not where anyone could sneak up on us and I'd be balls deep in you to notice."

Amara leaned towards him as he started the car again, sliding her hand down his chest, taking the flesh of his earlobe in between her teeth and tugging.

"Amara," he warned as her hand slid over his length, unzipping his pant. "Baby-"

"Keep driving, Mr. Maroni," she whispered, before bending down over the console and taking him in her mouth, giving her man pleasure as he somehow drove them home.

One of the things Amara was extremely grateful for was not having morning sickness through her pregnancy. After the initial few days of extreme exhaustion and sickness, she had bounced back and the babies had given her no trouble.

Her heart clenched, remembering there was only one baby now. She didn't know if that thought would always leave her feeling a little hollow but happy, but it was still fresh. Rubbing her still flat stomach, Amara looked in the mirror at her gown, feeling like she was going to burst out of it up top. The pink fabric which once hugged her breasts was now stretched to the last stitch, pushing her cleavage up high. A few more millimeters and she probably wouldn't even fit in the thing anymore.

Amara sighed, turning this way and that, trying to locate any changes on her body as Lulu napped at the foot of the bed behind her, the bed she and Dante now shared in the mansion. Her first night in that bed had been blissful sleep out of exhaustion. Last night, she'd been restless even though Dante had passed out cold. He was still asleep, as early morning light filtered through the room.

Dante was a heavy sleeper – always had been. Amara used to joke that an earthquake wouldn't wake him up. Once his head hit the pillow, he went out immediately like a light, no snores, no sounds, no movements. He rarely changed positions through the night, so still that Amara would've thought him a statue had he not been so warm.

She, on the other hand, was a mover. She turned and twisted a hundred times through the night, had vivid dreams or nightmares that usually woke her up, and had a hard time falling asleep. She also had a thing for pillows and blankets, the more the merrier, something Dante didn't understand. He didn't care so much – as long as he had a place to sleep, he'd close his eyes and crash.

Amara left him sleeping with Lulu at the foot of the bed, knowing he was tired, and put on the silk robe that went with her gown. Nighttime lingerie was a guilty pleasure of hers. They made her feel feminine and beautiful. As soon as she'd started earning, she had splurged on gowns and baby dolls to sleep in, and on the nights Dante had come to visit her, she'd broken out the special ones she reserved for the occasion, only to have him whip it off her. But it was that momentary pleasure, that flare of desire in his eyes that made it worth it.

Stepping out of the room, Amara closed the door and took in the corridor. Being on the east side of the mansion on the second floor, the master suite was slightly secluded from the rest of the house. The carpeted corridor was decorated with paintings on both sides – paintings Dante had brought down from the storage and had framed; paintings his mother had made.

They were oil paintings of vistas and abstract art – a familiar sunset over the Tenebrae hills, a river curving through the city, a leaf fallen on the grass, and disturbing shapes. His mother had been skilled, the shading and finish of her work incredible. She could see where Dante got his artistic bone.

Amara was about to continue when one painting caught her eye.

She stepped closer to it. It was plain except two shadows – one crouching to the floor, connected to the other looming over her. It was disturbing in its plainness, but that wasn't why Amara had stopped in her tracks. Back at university, one of her optional subjects had been the psychology of art and visual medium. She had spent a year studying it, enjoying it, analyzing different works by creators from over the world. It was that understanding of the psyche of the creator that had her pausing, considering all the paintings in the corridor in a new light.

Heart pounding, she ran back to the bedroom, going to Dante's side.

"Dante," she shook him awake, her urgency to know the answers fueling her blood. "Wake up."

His eyes opened, bleary, then took in her face. He shot up on the bed, alert, his hand going to the gun at the bedside table by instinct. "What's wrong? Is it the baby?"

Amara shook her head, taking a deep breath. "No, no, it's nothing like that. Relax."

She saw his hand come to her braid, wrapping it around his fist. "What has you waking me up at this hour then, my lady?" he asked, flirting.

Amara smiled, but her mind was still on the paintings outside. "I need to ask you something about your mother."

He frowned but leaned back against the pillows. "Sure."

"According to Alpha, she was an art student who was kidnapped by Lorenzo Maroni and brought here, right?"

Dante nodded in confirmation, his eyes narrowing at her question.

"And she used to paint with you and your brother?"

"Yes, but where is this going?" Dante asked, his voice thick from sleep.

Amara swallowed. "And you found her with Damien in the room with her wrists slit?"

His jaw clenched but he nodded.

"Does Damien remember anything from that time?"

The braid left his fist. "I don't know. He was too young at the time. If he did remember anything, he never told me, and I asked."

"Just answer one last question," Amara beseeched him, taking a hold of his big, rough hand in both of hers, her eyes earnest on his. "Do you have more paintings by her?"

He shook his head. "My father pretty much threw most of them out in his rage. The ones outside are the only ones I could save. What's all this, Amara?"

Amara bit her lip, not knowing how to tell him what she had learned. She inhaled, taking in the musky scent of his warm skin. "Your mother felt hunted, Dante," she whispered quietly in the space between them.

"How can you say that?" his voice came out hoarse.

"The paintings," Amara looked into his dark, chocolate eyes. "I studied them in school. Seeing them all together, it's all wrong. Was her death odd? Especially that she would kill herself with her child in the room?"

Dante's grip tightened on her hand.

"Could it be that she didn't slit her own wrists, Dante?" Amara felt her lips tremble. "Or if she did, something drove her to it? Could it be that she was murdered?"

They had no answers, even as more questions were born.

Dante

He called Damien.

After the suspicion Amara had shared with him, Dante hadn't been able to let it go. He tried to remember his mother, her sad eyes, her wide smile, her love for him and his brother. The more he remembered, the more he realized she never would have killed herself with one of them in the room. For years, he'd hated his mother slightly for abandoning them both, and now, standing with the phone to his ear, he was nothing but rage.

It wasn't his father. Dante knew that. For one, if his father had to kill her, he never would have married her. Once she became the wife of Bloodhound Maroni, she became untouchable. Her death had been a blow to his pride, and there had been nothing his father loved more than his ego. He had been angry, very angry, that she had thrown that insult at him, her suicide like a slap to his face.

The call connected and his brother's voice, one he hadn't heard in weeks, came on. "Dante!"

He could tell his brother was smiling. "How are you, Damien?"

"Good, good," Damien said, and Dante could imagine him nodding his head. He liked doing that. Nodding, shaking out his hands, tapping his feet. Dante had learned his brother's habits as a child, loving him as he was.

"How is Alia?" Dante asked, referring to the woman in his brother's life. They had met through a mutual friend. She was an interior designer, and from what Dante could tell, a sweet girl good for his brother.

"Good," Damien's masculine voice said over the phone. "We started a dance class together."

Dante smiled, imagining his tall brother and the tiny woman dancing, both uncoordinated as fuck. "How's that working out?"

"It's not," his brother chuckled. "But we have fun."

Dante was glad. "I'm getting married soon, by the way."

"To Green Eye Girl?" Damien asked. Even though he knew Amara by name, Damien had fallen in love with her eyes, so much so that he had spent a month obsessed with researching green eyes and that particular shade of green.

"Yes," Dante confirmed. "Do you want to come for the wedding?" he asked, even though he knew the answer.

"I want to," Damien sighed. "But it's better nobody know about me. I like my life here."

Dante hoped one day his brother would give another answer, but he respected his wishes. Given the chance, wouldn't he have chosen to stay out of this shithole himself?

"No worries," he said easily, knowing Damien got upset if he felt like he'd hurt Dante. "I actually called to talk to you about mom. Is it okay if I talk about her?"

He heard Damien's breathing pick up, and he waited.

"Yes, okay," his brother said. "I talked about her in therapy a lot back in Morning Star."

"You remember her?" Dante asked, surprised.

"A bit." The sound of something tapping came over the line – pencil on wood. His brother was tapping a pencil on wood. Not good.

"Hey, it's okay," Dante reassured him. "We don't have to talk about her."

"No, I should tell you," his brother said. "Dr. Sanders tells me I should tell you. It will help me. We were talking about these dreams I've been having forever but they're the bad kind. The good are mostly sex dreams or dreams where I build things you know, but that's not what the doctor told me to tell you."

Dante felt his heart begin to pound. "What did he say to tell me?"

"Dreams about mom," Damien spoke, the tapping of the pencil on wood constant in the background. "I don't have any memory of her but I always see this dream of this man holding me and mom crying and cutting herself and so much blood, and I wake up feeling really scared. Dr. Sanders said it could be trauma from what happened to her and I should talk to you about it, because in the dream sometimes you pick me up and get me out. You're my hero."

The tightness in his chest had his throat locking. "Thanks for telling me that, Damien. You'll tell me if you need anything, right?"

"Yes," Damien said. "Talk to you later, brother."

He hung up abruptly. Dante wasn't surprised, used to his brother being abrupt with the phone. He stood in his study, looking out at the lawns and the lake, his mind reeling from every piece of the puzzle that was coming to light. His brother had a high-functioning brain, so while it was possible that it could be his imagination, a vivid, recurring dream like that could also be a memory.

Their mother had wanted him to hide. She had felt hunted. She had been murdered.

Dante rubbed a hand over his face, trying to discern the threads of mysteries around him that just kept getting more and more tangled.

Over the next few weeks, things stayed quiet, or as quiet as they could be for a man leading the largest mob family in the underworld. Dante had truly taken over the reins of all businesses, surgically removed all liabilities, and strategically placed in assets – both people and things – that maximized their profit.

Tristan and Morana had gone back to Shadow Port with a young Xander, with the excuse that she would try to locate his next of kin herself while Tristan talked to the boy. Dante had scoffed at that, aware that just the act of them taking the boy meant they were thinking of keeping him. Dante was happy for them, but the shadow looming over the boy's appearance in their lives kept him skeptical, especially because it had been Xander who had coordinated their rescue with the Shadowman, even though he claimed not to have seen him.

Shadowman, or Morana's airport asshole, was an unknown entity. He had ties to the Syndicate, and that alone made him someone Dante was extremely wary of. He didn't know what game this guy was playing, or to what end, but he didn't like it.

Alpha called Dante in the weeks too, telling him that while he hadn't heard anything back from the feelers he'd put out, he was positive something would turn up. The call had been an update, but also a subtle hand reaching out, accepting the offer Dante had made to the man. It left him feeling good.

He had also begun looking into his mother's death, trying to find any reports from all those years ago, her history, anything. So far, he came up empty.

On the ground, he had restructured his father's resources, putting the army he'd been building over the years on the front and center of the fringe, men he had recruited and trained to make up the core of his organization. Vin, his most trusted man, he had assigned to Amara's security. That was a good move both because Amara was comfortable in his presence and because Dante trusted Vin with her. Having seen them attached at the hip for years, he knew his presence in her life was good for her.

And she was good for Dante.

Sleeping with her in his arms every night, waking up to her flush against him, knowing there was no need to hide his love for her had been the biggest, most beautiful change in his life. Some mornings, he woke up early, just looking at the woman he had wanted for years, unable to believe he had her.

Dante scraped the statue he was working on, early morning light filtering in the new studio on this side of the house, *Wuthering Heights* playing on audio, as he wielded the scraper over the rough surface of the dried clay.

'Be with me always – take any form – drive me mad! Only do not leave me in this abyss, where I cannot find you!'

Fuck, he should have listened to it years ago. The angst, the longing, the passion was reminiscent of his own tale of woe with Amara back then.

"Heathcliff was so swoon-worthy," Amara's voice from the door had him turning his neck to see her standing there, clad in one of his shirts.

Amara usually preferred wearing silk lingerie to bed, but one night when her gowns stopped going over her growing breasts, she had tossed them aside in a fit of pique, marched into his closet, grabbed his shirt, and put it on, claiming 'these won't outgrow me'.

He let his eye rove over her appreciatively; watching his large shirt hide her breasts and the small bump underneath, her hair braided to the side, falling over one shoulder, her beautiful eyes on his. He liked her in his shirts.

He put the scraper down as she entered the room, hitting pause on his phone to stop the book, and pulled her forward between his legs. Unbuttoning his shirt leisurely, keeping their gazes locked, he saw her pupils widen in the dark green orbs, her breathing picking up. She was horny, and she'd come to him.

They had visited the gynecologist twice over the last few weeks. On the most recent visit, Amara had confessed to being more aroused, more sensitive than usual. The doctor had simply told her it was natural, and sex was safe, and she should indulge herself as long as her hormones cooperated. It had been after that conversation that Amara had hopped on the bed for an ultrasound and Dante had seen their baby for the first time. It had been a blip, a tiny little bean on the black and white screen, and it had made something so powerful, so visceral rush through his system it had left him shaken. That was the moment the loss of their other child had hit him hard. Suddenly, that baby had become real too. He had seen that same joy and loss reflected on Amara's face, seen her struggle with her tears and lose the battle, and they had left the room, changed.

Dante parted the sides of the shirt, breaking their gazes to look at the little bump on her belly, stretching the scars on the sides of her stomach over her skin, rounding from the edge of her panties, and it hit him again.

That was his warrior child, inside his warrior woman.

Cupping the bump with both hands, the size still small enough that it fit the span of his fingers, Dante smeared the wet clay over her skin, marking both her and their child.

He pressed his lips to her tummy, feeling her hands come to his hair.

"You're going to be the most adored little princess in this whole world," he murmured softly to his baby, still not knowing if it was a girl or a boy technically, but knowing in his heart it was a daughter. "Daddy already loves you so much."

"Daddy Dante," Amara murmured in the voice he loved so much. "I like the sound of that."

"Be careful," he looked up at her breasts, feeling their heaviness in his palms. "It'll take me a second to make you dirty."

Her nipples pebbled, the visual enough to send blood rushing to his cock, constrained in his jeans. Fuck, he loved how her body responded to his words, his voice, his everything. It made him feel like the luckiest bastard on the planet.

Without another word, he took some wet clay on the side in his hands, smearing a thin layer of it over her breasts. He knew the cold clay would stimulate her, but it would be the immediate drying that would prickle her skin, make her nerves tingle everywhere it was spread.

Her quick intake of breath told him the coolness had hit her. Dante held back, watching, mesmerized as the thin layer dried over her peaked nipples, heaving with her little gasps. He stood up, pushing his shirt over her shoulders, letting it pool around her bare feet, leaving her clad in simple black cotton panties. The light from the rising sun hit her naked body, illuminating her perfection, her scars, her flesh, showing him the rivulets of moisture in the rapidly drying clay.

He wet his hands again with the argil, spreading it over her shoulders, hearing her shuddering breaths as he walked around her.

"I'm going to stand behind you, Amara," he leaned down to whisper in her ear, knowing it triggered her sometimes.

She nodded, her eyes closed, feeling his hands upon her flesh. Fuck, she was perfect.

He circled behind her, looking at the skin on her back, three thin strips of acid-burned flesh scarred diagonally across one hip to one blade. She probably didn't realize he had matched the structure of his back dragon tattoo to match her back scars, from one hip to one shoulder. If anyone looked at their naked backs together, they would see symmetry – a dragon breathing fire across her back in mirrored structure, side by side.

He bent to kiss them, before straightening, smearing the clay in his hand over them.

"Dante," she whispered, a tremor going down her spine, the vibration right under his fingers, and he continued to spread the clay all over, watching the layers dry, the scars immortalized in them.

Scooping more clay, he pressed up against her back, feeling the wetness smear over his chest, and spread his fingers over her stomach, ensconcing her bump generously with the argil, before moving it back up over her breasts. He plucked at her nipples, kissing the side of her neck, and felt her arch in his hands, her ass pushing into his hard cock. He pushed back, nestling himself between her cheeks over layers of their clothing, and her breathing stuttered.

His Amara was a breather. She moaned occasionally, screamed rarely because of her damaged vocal cords, and spoke sometimes, demanding his attention in the middle of sex. But she breathed – soft, slow, hard, fast, short, long, and so on. Dante had learned her breaths to learn her responses and anticipate her needs. He had spent years tracking the changes in them, understanding what each variation meant. He had memorized her like his favorite song.

That stutter in her breath meant she was getting close to coming.

Dante let go of her nipples and began circling his wet fingers around them, close but not close enough. "Can you come just like this, dirty girl?" he whispered into her neck, pressing his cock into her ass as she stood on her toes.

"Please," she begged softly, her breasts heaving in his palms, her head falling back over his shoulder, her hands coming to wrap around his neck, thrusting her heavy tits higher.

Dante sucked on her neck, taking both handfuls of her stunning breasts and squeezing them, before plucking her nipples again, extending them out, the clay on her drying over her skin, definitely adding to the sensation.

"Oh god, Dante," she mewled, her lips quivering as he continued his ministrations, humping her ass, pinching and pulling her nipples, and sucking her neck.

Her breath got shorter and shorter, her panting loud in the silent room surrounded by his sculptures, and Dante knew she was close. Opening his mouth, he nipped at the side of her neck, before biting down on her skin, hard enough to give her a hickey, and pinching her nipples hard.

She exploded, her mouth opening in a silent scream as her legs gave out, her weight supported by his hands on her breasts.

That was the first time she'd come just from stimulation above the waist and Dante felt good. There was nothing that fulfilled him more than giving this woman pleasure. It was when he took her to the stars that he felt most powerful, his own need secondary to taking her there, through any means necessary. Though nothing turned him on more than eating her pussy.

He turned her to face him and watched as she came back to herself – a vision of a woman smeared in his clay and her pleasure, naked, open, vulnerable, trusting, with heavy-lidded eyes and heaving breasts and divine beauty and carrying his child – and realized what muses were made of.

He cupped her face in his hands, overcome with the riot of emotions she inspired in him. "You're my magnum opus, Amara," he told her, pressing his forehead against hers, a move that always brought the turmoil in him to a standstill. "And I am your humble servant."

"No," she whispered, her words falling against his lips. "You are my emperor."

After making love in the shower cleaning up, Amara had accompanied him to his study, handing Lulu to him since she couldn't lift her anymore. The fucking cat loved to climb on his shoulder and if he stroked her, she purred right against him.

He watched Amara settle on one of the couches, taking Lulu in her arms, and begin talking as he walked around the desk, opening his suit jacket.

"So, I looked at the list of buildings you gave me," she told him, stroking the cat, dressed in one of her flowy dresses that still fit, a choker around her neck hiding her scar. She wore that or a scarf anytime she had to leave the compound.

"And?" Dante asked, taking out his reading glasses from the top drawer, looking down at the sheet she had handed him with annotations in her curvy, neat handwriting.

"You wear glasses? How have I never seen you in glasses before?"

Dante looked up at her question, looking at her surprised face over the frames. "Just for reading," he clarified. "You've probably never seen me read. I prefer listening to books, and any reading I do for reports and shit is at night here."

"You mean when you're here at night working, you wear those sexy glasses?" she asked.

Dante felt his lips turn up. "I wouldn't call them sexy, but yes."

"Hmm," she trailed off, petting the cat. "Anyways, Vin and I went to each of the sites and looked around," she leaned into a cushion, pulling her feet under her. "Only two of those buildings have enough space and seclusion that we'll need for the project. They're also both close to each other – about ten minutes walking – which I think could be a good idea for shared resources."

Dante nodded, reading her notes on the two properties she was talking about. She was thorough in her detailing of the pros and cons of both locations, adding the proximity to the compound as a pro. "What will you need in terms of manpower?" he asked her, looking up from the sheet.

"Depending on how many kids we're talking about."

Dante mulled for a second. "Give me an estimate."

Amara contemplated for a second. "I'd say one trainer and one counselor per five kids, one supervisor per twenty kids. That should allow each adult to give each child the attention they need without hampering their reserves. And security, of course, which you'll have a better idea about."

Dante nodded, looking down at the sheets again. "And can you arrange the trainers and counselors on our payroll?"

Amara nodded. "I should be able to. I have contacts in both the academia and training levels. I'll make the calls and interview each one of them myself. Vin can vet them. In case I can't, I'll let you know. It should take about a month or two to start."

His phone ringing interrupted them. He looked down, to see he had a meeting with one of his informers. Getting up from the seat, he pocketed his phone and buttoned his jacket, slicking his hair back from his face, and walked over to where she and the cat sat.

Placing a hand over the back of the couch, he bent down to see her raise her mouth up, ready to receive his kiss.

"You can handle it?"

"Yeah."

"And your practice?"

"I'll do sessions with those who need it the most."

"And your therapy?"

"I called Dr. Das for a monthly visit."

"And our wedding?"

"Let's set a date, yeah?"

"Good."

He gave her a kiss, pressed their foreheads together, and walked out to run the front of his empire, leaving her to take care of the back.

Amara

The date for the wedding was set three months away in spring, although she'd be in her eighth month of pregnancy by then. Initially, Dante hadn't wanted to wait that long, but she had reminded him that their wedding wasn't just their union, it was a statement in the underworld, and it needed to be a strong one. Dante Maroni marrying a housekeeper's daughter for love – the same girl who had been raped and tortured at fifteen – instead of a virginal beauty of a fellow family for power and connection was a big deal. People had to be invited, charades had to be put up, games of power had to be played.

Dante had agreed, and the next morning, she had connected with Morana and a wedding planner with her mother, getting the ball rolling. Her mother, who now lived in Dante's old house and had taken to tailoring baby clothes, had been overjoyed.

Amara swiped red lipstick over her mouth.

"You look like a goddess, Mrs. Maroni-to-be," her husband-to-be said from behind her, sending a thrill down her spine.

She gave him a once over, admiring him in his debonair black tux as he covered his suspenders with his jackets, the attire making him appear larger. She matched him, with a glittery sleeveless black Grecian dress, with straps that widened to cover her breasts and bunching under, before falling straight to her feet in layers, effectively hiding her growing belly, two slits on both sides till her thighs giving little peeks of her legs and tall heels as she moved. Hair loose and naturally wavy, she wore a plain gold choker on her neck, and gold bracelets on her wrists, the jewelry both hiding her scars and complimenting her warm-toned skin.

She did look good.

"It's Dr. Maroni-to-be," she corrected him, her low voice sounding husky even to her own ears.

"Mmm-hmm," he locked their gazes in the mirror, his hand holding hers as he slid something on her finger.

Damn, that was smooth.

Amara lifted her left hand, seeing the beautiful ring glint in the light. It was a gorgeous oval emerald, surrounded by a crown of diamonds, set in a beautiful platinum band.

Dante pressed a kiss to her lobe, showering her with affection. "There's an engraving on the inside that says 'my queen', so you always remember, no matter where you are or where I am, you're the beat to my heart."

Amara felt her eyes water and blinked rapidly since her mascara was not waterproof. "And your ring?"

He pressed a kiss to the back of her head, his eyes locked with hers, showing her a plain platinum band. "Matches. But I already know I'm your king."

"And a very modest one too."

He flashed a grin. "Ready to go?"

She nodded, taking the arm he offered her, grateful for it since wearing heels while pregnant was a different experience altogether.

It was a huge party in the mansion to celebrate Dante's official takeover of the Tenebrae Outfit. They hadn't wanted to do an engagement party since this was her official introduction into their world, and anyone who saw her on his arms with that giant ring would draw their meanings.

Over the last few days, Dante and his men had spent their time keeping and interrogating the man they'd caught at the creepy house and the guy the Shadowman had left pinned to the tree. One of them had bitten on a cyanide pill in his mouth and died. They stopped the other and took the capsule in his teeth. After weeks of refusing to crack, he finally confessed to his crimes.

Anyone working for the Syndicate knew they could never speak about it or hell would rain on them, their loved ones, anyone they remotely cared about. That was the reason most workers simply chose to end their lives before talking.

The guy had told them how the house had been a holding point for the kids between transport – a place where they stayed for a few days before handing the kids to the higher-ups in the organization. These were the low-level operators with one contact at mid-level who guided them on where to pick up the kids and where to drop them. That mid-level contact wasn't a name, just a phone number, and Morana had tracked it down to ping within the city limits.

Things were confusing and messy and made no sense – her abduction, MrX, Shadowman, the kids, Dante's mother. There were too many questions and no answers.

Walking down the stairs, she and Dante entered the huge hall that was usually used for hosting parties, her grip tightening on Dante's bicep as all eyes swiveled to them in the room, some friendly, some hostile, most guarded. There was a part of her that still found it surreal, that she would attend a party in the same halls where she'd once served. But that was the past. Straightening her spine, Amara stood tall beside her husband-to-be, proud of the woman she had become and the man he had grown into, and stepped in.

"Dante," Leo Mancini headed towards them, his eyes slightly shifty. "Can we talk in private for a moment?"

Amara saw Dante open his mouth before someone else from the Outfit demanded his attention, and Leo walked away to another side of the room.

Dante made conversation for a while then walked to the side, towards a man Amara recognized as the right-hand man of Maroni, and started to chat, his manner calm, cool, composed. Dante Maroni, the charmer, was taking the floor, and she doubted anyone could resist him when he got like that. She stayed by his side as he'd asked her to, looking around the room, her eyes coming to a halt on her half-sister Nerea.

Amara watched the older woman, dressed in black pants and sweater, and for the first time, she wondered about her. Nerea had come into the fold immediately after her abduction and Amara had been too distracted with her healing to pay her any mind. She had accepted the friendly hand the other woman had extended to her, and watching her now, she wondered if it had been a friendly hand at all. Over the years though, Nerea had done nothing but been good to Amara, checking in on her, giving her advice if she needed it, or even arranging her fake passport.

She wondered about her father. After he left her and her mother, they had never tried to contact him again, and Amara wondered if she should now. She saw Nerea catch her eye and give her a warm, genuine smile, and felt slightly guilty for feeling suspicious of her.

Giving her a little nod, they continued to circle the room, before the music came on and Dante turned to her.

"May I have this dance, my queen?"

Amara grinned up at him, taking his hand as he led her to the center of the floor, tugging her close. Once upon a time, his closeness to her had been reckless of him. Now, it was flaunting. He was flaunting her, claiming her, out in the open, and it felt glorious.

Pressing her face against his shoulder, he led her through the song, and if she closed her eyes, it transported her back to a decade ago in his studio, just the two of them, young, wild, unsure.

They had come so far.

One of his men cut through the moment, calling Dante's attention and Amara turned to let him go when the scent of raw tobacco hit her nose.

'What do you know about the Syndicate?'

Taking in a deep breath just made it worse. Amara closed her eyes, trying to push out the memories assaulting her from her mind, red stars behind her eyes as her lungs began to ice. Remembering the last time she'd had a panic attack, tied to a chair and losing her baby, Amara tried to get a hold of herself, wondering if this would ever end. She couldn't get anxious now, not when she was already high-risk. It was fine. She was safe.

Her fingers must have trembled because Dante paused in his conversation, turning to look at her, his dark eyes taking her measure within seconds.

"You need air?" he asked in a low tone, low enough that nobody else could hear. She gave him a nod, grateful that he knew her the way he did.

Alerting Vin, he put pressure on the small of her back, urging her to take a walk outside while he circled the party. Amara looked to see her friend, and now her head of security, waiting for her by the side door. He held the door open for her and Amara gave him a smile, walking out on her heels on short, sure steps.

The door closed behind her. "You okay?" he asked, leading her down a cemented path gilded with vines on the sides, ending a few feet away in a short gazebo.

Amara gulped in the fresh air on the hill, the scents of night blooms permeating the air, and felt her racing heart begin to calm. She took a seat on the marble bench and looked up at the stars, feeling Vin standing guard by the entrance.

The sound of footsteps had her leaning to the side to see Leo Mancini striding down the gazebo towards her, his eyes shifty, looking around to see if anyone was watching him. There were hardly any guards patrolling this side of the compound. Amara straightened as Vin blocked him.

"Move aside, boy," Leo spit out. "I have to talk to her."

Vin turned to look at her, asking silently if she wanted the man to be sent away. Amara didn't want to be alone with him, but she was curious as to why he sought her out. She gave Vin a slight nod, and he let the older man pass, putting his hand on the gun on his hip in case Leo did something he didn't like. Amara doubted he would, so close to Dante.

"Amara," Leo took a seat on the marble bench opposite hers, the relation to the Maroni gene evident in his jawline and distinguished looks. He looked around, hunching down a bit, and spoke. "Someone is going to kill me tonight."

Amara raised her eyebrows in surprise. "How do you know that?"

He shook his head. "It doesn't matter. I need to tell you something."

"What?"

"Ten years ago, you eavesdropped on a conversation you shouldn't have," he began, and Amara felt her heart begin to pound, her palms get clammy. She gave a look to Vin, who looked back at her, his body alert.

"Yes," Amara swallowed, remembering the exact conversation. "I was abducted because of that, wasn't I?"

"Yes," the man nodded. "But Lorenzo or I didn't give the order. We'd been working as affiliate partners with the Syndicate back then. Transporting…packages."

Amara felt bile rise in her throat. "But you worked as more before, didn't you? When the Alliance ended?"

Leo hesitated. "Lorenzo tried the shipment of one batch, but it ended in a fiasco with the Reaper and Gabriel's kids getting mixed up. The Syndicate told Lorenzo to just do damage control and stick to transport. Listen to me. I don't have time and I can't talk to Dante with the party going on. You're my only hope."

Amara didn't understand him. "Hope for what?"

"Redemption."

"What are you saying?"

"I've done terrible things. Terrible. With my hands but also with my silence. You coming to the compound again with Dante has made some people high up to take notice. I will be killed tonight and before I go, I want to confess. And Dante needs to know."

"Tell me."

Leo wiped his hand over his face, looking much older than his years. "The Syndicate is lethal about its privacy. Anyone who worked with them knew that speaking about it meant certain death. We had a contact, a handler, at the Syndicate during the Alliance when the first shipment was being planned." Amara felt ants crawling up her skin at the casual way he referred to innocent children as 'shipment'. She stayed silent, letting him continue. "We had a meeting with him to discuss further action. It was later that I discovered that Talia, Dante's mother, had overheard the meeting."

Pieces fell into place. "So you killed her."

He shook his head. "No. Lorenzo grew very fond of her actually. They'd had a rough start but over the years things became good for him. We decided to keep it quiet and protect her. She became antsy after that but we were containing the situation. Except we didn't realize another thing about The Syndicate – they always plant their people where they're dealing. One of our soldiers was their spy, and one day, he went into her studio and made her slit her wrists while holding the gun to her son's head."

"Oh god," Amara clapped a hand over her mouth, the shock of the words hitting her. She felt her heart bleeding for the woman, for little Damien, for Dante.

The wind swept over her exposed arms, chilling her to the bone, her eyes taking in the sincerity on the older man's face.

"I'm sorry," Leo said, his voice deep, and hesitated. "It was to teach Lorenzo a lesson, to keep him in line. There were bigger fish in the sea than he was."

"What happened to the spy?" Amara asked, her hand fisting the fabric of her dress.

"After the assassination and Lorenzo's cooperation, the spy got promoted in the Syndicate and became our handler. Any work, any news, any report, he was our contact."

The hesitation in Leo's demeanor had a rock lodging itself on Amara's chest.

This was bad. Whatever this was, it was bad.

"Say it," she whispered, hoping it wasn't what her mind was telling her. She felt Vin's hand come on her shoulder in support, and took a deep breath, steadying herself.

"When we caught you eavesdropping, we had to report it to him," Leo said, his eyes regretful. "He-"

A shot rang out, a bullet hitting him right between the eyebrows, and Amara screamed, her throat straining. Vin ducked, pushing her down to the floor, and Amara kept her eyes on the dead body of the man who had been partly responsible for her abduction.

A wave of dizziness swept through her, and she realized she'd been holding her breath for too long. Gripping the marble at her side, Amara felt her eyes begin to burn, her jaw shaking with the effort of keeping in the scream in her throat, memories, horrific memories, assaulting her.

What had he been about to say?

Guards came running to the gazebo, along with some guests from the party. Amara sat up on the floor, the chill from the marble seeping into her bones.

"Amara!" Dante's voice thundered through the ground as he ran towards her, his eyes panicked.

He dropped on his haunches as soon as he reached her, his hands going to her face, his eyes running over her body. "Are you okay? Is the baby okay? Fuck, Amara talk to me!"

Amara shuddered, hanging onto his hands. "I'm okay. We're okay," she reassured him and watched his eyes harden as he turned to Vin. "I want to know where the bullet came from and which motherfucker fired it."

Vin gave him a quick nod before running towards the mansion, and Amara turned to Dante, watching the deep pools of darkness in his eyes, wondering how she was going to tell him what she'd learned.

"So, wait, let me get this straight," Morana said over the video filling her phone screen. "This MrX dude who ordered your abduction was an Outfit soldier before he became a Syndicate spy? He got promoted for killing Dante's mom? Wow, that's a different level of fucked up. How did Dante take it?"

Amara sighed, stroking Lulu's fur in her lap. "How do you think?"

"Not well, I'm assuming?" Morana winced, the penthouse lit up behind her.

"He's been having meetings in his office for the last few hours," Amara told her. "I think my being so close to the bullet shook him."

"It'd shake anyone, Amara. Especially after finding out what he did about his mom," her expressive eyes softened in sympathy for him. She got distracted for a second on screen, looking to the side. "One second, Amara," Morana said before moving to the side. "No, no, that's not how you do it, Xander. Put the basic code in and open the file. Yeah, that's it. Well done, you! High five!"

Amara felt her eyebrows go up. Xander was what, eight? And he was talking code with Morana? What the hell?

Morana came back on screen, a huge smile on her face. "Sorry, Xander needed some help."

"How's he doing?" Amara asked, curious about the boy.

Morana shrugged. "Not the best, if I'm being honest. He's not talkative at all but boy, he's freaky intelligent. Like even I wasn't doing the shit he's doing at his age. He likes to sit with me when I'm working, seeing all the codes and stuff. But doesn't talk, except to maybe ask a few questions. Just my luck huh? Stuck with two guys who barely grunt," she ended on a little laugh, shaking her head.

"You should have him tested for his IQ," Amara pointed out.

Morana nodded. "Yeah, we will. I mean we're all just kind of adapting to being in the same space, you know? Tristan took to it like a duck to water, though. He loves him. He doesn't say it, but I can tell. I found them in the kitchen one night cooking pizza because Xander had a nightmare."

"That's big for Tristan," Amara admitted.

"I know right?" Morana nodded. "I'm still searching facial recognition for anything on him, but so far nada."

"Has he said anything about the Shadowman?" Amara asked, curious, settling back on the couch in the living room, sunlight filling up the space.

"Tristan said he mentioned him. Just that he always left Xander notes to communicate and stayed in the shadows. Last time he saw the guy was in the fog. I think you might be right, about him being the Airport Guy. He's been freaky about me not seeing him. By the way, have you tried this new peach milk moisturizer? I hear it's divine."

The sound of footsteps brought Amara's attention. "Listen, I'll talk to you later," she told Morana and they hung up.

Nerea walked into the room, her eyes coming to Amara.

"Hey," Amara said, concerned about the way the older woman stayed silent. Over the last few days, she'd not had the time to talk to the woman.

Nerea stopped at the edge of the room. "You're pregnant?"

Amara furrowed her brow. "Yes, why?"

Nerea shook her head. "No reason. I'll catch you later."

She walked right out of the room, the little interaction weirding Amara out.

Dante wore glasses, looking at his laptop screen as she and her mother sat on the office couch, discussing the wedding plans. Usually, they sat somewhere else and didn't interrupt her husband-to-be, but that day his input was required.

"So, gold or silver?"

"Gold."

"Different tables or buffet?"

"Different tables."

"Are we calling Al and his family?"

"Yeah."

That's pretty much how it had gone since the last hour. She and her mother would ask final questions, and he would give monosyllabic replies, all the while working on his laptop. It was a gorgeous day too, with the bright sun filtering in through the big windows of his office, Lulu napping on a particularly warm spot in the ray of sun. She'd made Dante's study her day place. If he was there, she'd be there. If he wasn't there, then she'd find Amara. If neither of them were there, then she'd snuggle somewhere in a huge mansion and sleep.

Amara looked at him in his zone, with the scruff that had become an almost beard, the glasses on his handsome face, and felt her belly flutter the same way it used to when she'd been a teen, watching the unreachable boy. She rested her face on her hand stared at him.

"Why are you staring at me?" he asked her, not looking up from the screen.

Her mother looked up at them. "She has always stared at you, Dante," her ma said with amusement. "You shouldn't be surprised anymore."

Dante grinned but kept working. The vibration from his phone had his face turning to the side.

"Morana," he greeted. "I'm putting you on speaker. Hold on."

He placed the phone on the table and went back to looking at his screen.

"Okay, so you know how I've been keeping my eye on Nerea for months? She disappeared so I tracked her and guess who she led us to?"

"Who?" Dante asked absently, still looking at his screen.

"MrX," Morana's excited voice came from the speaker as she talked fast. "So, I went down under, digitally speaking, looking for more info on the guy she met and I just hit jackpot!"

Dante stilled, his focus on the call now. "You have a name?"

"Oh no," Morana spoke, enthused. "I have a first name and a photo. How amazing is that? I'm running facial recognition as we speak. Check your email. I've sent it to you. It's encrypted for protection so I've sent the code you'll need to decrypt it as well. Okay, that was it. I have to go now."

"Tell Tristan to give you a hug from my side," Dante smiled.

"Fat chance of that," Morana chuckled. "I'll just take it myself. Talk to you later."

The call cut off and Amara felt amazement wash over her again at the crazy stuff her friend did, which she'd never been able to understand. She stood up, her back slightly aching as her bump grew, and walked to his side, curious to see the photo.

Dante opened the email, put in the code, and a flurry of text came on the screen for a split second before the folder opened.

"Xavier," Dante mused. "MrX. Seriously?"

Shaking his head, he clicked on the photo, enlarging it. It was the headshot of an average looking, clean-shaven, balding man wearing gold-rimmed glasses.

Amara frowned, the photo nagging something in her brain. "I've seen him before."

Dante turned to her, his eyes sharp. "Where?"

She shook her head, trying to remember, his face familiar but stranger. And suddenly, it hit her.

"They showed me his photo," she rasped out. "During my interrogation, they showed me his photo and asked me if I recognized him. That's where I've seen him!"

Dante clenched his jaw, his hand settling on her hip. "We already know he's the one who gave the order. And that he was possibly there."

She felt her mother come to her side, rubbing her back in comfort before suddenly her hand stopped. Amara looked down to see her mother staring at the screen, a look of shock on her face.

"Ma?" she asked, concern washing over her. "You okay? You know him?"

The older woman looked like she was reeling, looking up at Amara with the same green eyes.

"That-that's your father, Mumu."

Amara felt her heart stop.

No.

No way.

What the hell was she talking about?

"No," Amara whispered.

She felt Dante's grip tighten on her hip, his eyes on her mother.

"Are you sure that's the same man? Amara's father?"

Her ma nodded, looking closely at the screen. "He's aged but it's definitely him. He ordered your abduction? That's not possible. No. He's your father!"

Her father? She'd never had a father. He had left so early in her life she didn't even remember him anymore. It hadn't traumatized her or anything. Her mother had been more than enough for Amara. But what the hell?

"I don't understand," Amara croaked, confused, scared, not good.

"I kicked him out soon after you were born, Mumu," her mother told her. "He had been... toxic and I didn't want that in your life. So I asked him to leave and he left. I was prepared to tell you about him but you never asked in any detail."

She hadn't seen that one coming.

She had absolutely *not* seen that one coming.

It felt surreal. She couldn't believe this. She wouldn't believe this. Because believing this meant believing that her father had been the one to sanction her trauma, her torture, her rape. Believing this meant believing he'd been the one to hold Dante's brother hostage while making his mother bleed. Believing this meant believing he was a monster and not just a stranger who never wanted to be a part of her life.

It was the silence in the room that slowly made it real to Amara. She felt the tar in her lungs again, dripping, pulling her under, weighing her down as she started to breathe faster. Her mind started to process but failed. Her heart started to hammer and her stomach got tight.

She felt something heavy on her chest as her vision blurred, swaying slightly on her feet. Something pulled at her arms, making her fall and sit on something warm. The scent of masculine, musky cologne cut through the fog, seeping into her lungs, dispersing the tar with the feeling of safety it brought.

Amara focused her gaze to find herself sitting on Dante's lap, his strong, muscular arms around her, squeezing her tight.

Lulu jumped on the table, coming towards her, years of being with Amara having made her sensitive to an anxiety attack.

Amara took a deep breath and pulled the pet into her arms, hugging her to her bosom, stroking her as the cat started vibrating like a little motor against her, calming down her racing heart.

"So, MrX is my father," she whispered, her voice breaking on the last word as she felt her man still, before he relaxed again, giving her a soft squeeze before staring at her mother.

"What did he do when you were with him?"

The words were quiet, permeating the air in the room.

Her ma inhaled, her slightly wrinkled hands shaking as she absorbed the news. Amara couldn't even imagine how she must have been feeling. "Xavier was a soldier in the Outift at the time. It was right around when I joined the staff as a cook. He was very brazen, and we spent a night together, and it got very toxic, very fast. He'd had a horrible upbringing and the more I saw him, the more I realized just how... wrong he was. Your birth gave me the push to throw him out of our lives. I never wanted his shadow to touch you."

Amara felt her throat get tight at the love her mother had for her, relating to it now in a way she never had before. Hadn't she done the same when she'd found out she was pregnant? Hadn't she run away to protect her child from this world?

Amara took a hold of her mother's hand, her eyes shimmering. "I love you, Ma."

Her mother's gaze softened. "I love you, Mumu. Are you okay, baby?" she asked her.

Amara shrugged. She didn't know.

Dante kept his arms around her, his voice kind as he spoke. "Will you give us the room, Zia? And please get yourself some tea and come back."

Her mother nodded. "I'll leave you two to talk."

Amara watched her walk out and close the door behind her, and she let the cat down on the floor, turning in Dante's lap to look at him.

"Now I know how Morana feels," Amara told him softly, her heart hurting. "The sins of our fathers do stay with us. I'm sorry for what he did to your mom, Dante."

Dante's jaw clenched under his scruff, his dark eyes closing as he put a hand behind her head and pulled her forehead to hers, just breathing her in, their chests rising and falling in the same rhythm.

"I'm sorry for what he did to you," he told her, his voice gruff.

Amara swallowed. "He was there. He came to see me there and let it happen. What kind of a monster does that?"

His hand on the back of her head tightened. "Promise me something, Amara."

Amara opened her eyes to see the dark chocolate pools of his, waiting for him to continue.

"If I ever lose my way, lose my soul to this place-" he told her, his eyes fierce "-and become toxic to you or our children, promise me that you'll end me."

"Dante-"

"Promise me."

Her mouth trembled. "You won't. I won't let you."

He pressed his forehead to hers deeper, and they stayed silent, absorbing the dark drop of ink that swirled in their lives.

Amara

"Any soreness?" the gynecologist asked Amara, rubbing cold gel over her lower abdomen.

Amara shook her head, Dante holding her hand. "I'm feeling tired though. I don't know if it's everything going on mentally or because of this little one."

The doctor smiled. "Your body is creating another human being, Amara. It's taxing. You need to rest more if you feel like it. In fact, I recommend you don't get yourself in stressful situations given your risky pregnancy."

Amara nodded and she and Dante both looked at the screen as the wand moved over her skin, the black and white flaring to life.

"Ah, look at that," the doctor told them. "Do you want to know the gender? I can see it."

"It's a girl, isn't it?" Dante asked from her side, rubbing her ring.

"Indeed it is," the doctor confirmed, pointing to a white shape on the screen. "That's her right there, nestled in her mother's womb, all comfortable and safe. And she looks healthy. Congratulations."

Amara felt her throat lock as emotion clogged her, the reality of the life inside her crashing over her, the reality of the life that should have been there but they'd lost weighing her down. She could feel the same emotions rolling over the man at her side, his fingers flexing against her hand, his eyes surprisingly moist.

"Could you take some pictures please?" Dante asked in a heavy voice.

The older woman nodded. "Sure."

Dante looked at her, pressing their foreheads together.

One baby there, one baby missing. Amara didn't think that would ever not hurt.

"How are you dealing with it, Morana?" Amara asked as they talked on video again, her with a hot chocolate in her bedroom and her friend with some wine in the living room.

Morana sighed. "I don't know, honestly. I guess I'm not thinking about it too much right now. It can be overwhelming, you know?"

Amara nodded. She knew exactly what she meant. "What do I even do? My father ordered my abduction. He killed Dante's mother. It's just-I don't know how to wrap my head around that."

"I had a great biological father who protected me and died five minutes after I knew him. And the man I thought was my father my whole life hated me for replacing his daughter. I think about her too, you know. The real Morana. If she's okay. If she's alive."

Amara felt her heart clench. "Are there no good fathers alive in our world?"

"Dante will be a good Daddy," Morana gave a cheeky wink, making Amara sputter.

"So would Tristan," Amara pointed out.

Morana raised her glass. "To finding good fathers for our kids. We scored in that department."

They sure did.

Nerea had gone off the radar.

After that weird as hell conversation with her, she had dropped out of the Outfit without giving any reason, and Amara's suspicions started to solidify. The possibilities of her working with MrX were high, but Amara didn't understand why she'd spent years trying to bond with her.

After a week though, Morana had come through with his last known location a few miles out of the city, following the breadcrumb Nerea had left knowingly or unknowingly.

Dante had gotten his men together, and Amara had waited the nail-biting hours as he'd returned, telling her they had him.

It was close to midnight and as he got ready to interrogate him, Amara fumed.

"You're out of your mind if you think I'm staying behind, Dante," she told him in no uncertain terms.

Dante just stared at her evenly, not her man but the leader of the Outfit right then. "You being there makes me look weak. You being there would stop me from interrogating him if push came to shove. I'm not going to torture him, Amara, not in front of you, not when it can trigger you, not when you're high risk."

Amara took in a deep breath. "I need to see him."

"And I need to make sure this doesn't touch you or our baby."

He didn't get it. She needed the closure. She needed to find why.

"I'm coming, Dante," she told him in the same tone, standing in his office. "You can't order me around."

He tilted his head to the side. "No, but I can order my men not to let you out of the room. Don't make me do that, but don't think for a second I won't. Not if it's to protect you."

Amara grit her teeth in frustration, watching him walk out of the room. He was crazy if he thought she wouldn't get to Xavier. She needed to know, to ask for herself why he had destroyed her when she'd done nothing. Giving him a head start, Amara waited for fifteen minutes before slowly walking out of the study, only to see two guards at the front door out of the mansion.

He'd fucking done it.

Gritting her teeth, Amara turned to the back, using the kitchen entrance his majesty would probably not have thought of, and escaped out into the lawns.

Night enveloped the hill and guards patrolled the area, giving her curious looks as she made her way towards the training center in her bohemian dress that hid her belly.

Two guards stationed outside stopped her. "You can't go in, ma'am."

Amara gave them a smile, showing them her phone. "Dante forgot his phone in the bedroom and it's been blowing up with calls. This late at night, it has to be urgent. If I were you, I'd just let me pass for a quick second so I can give him the phone and walk out. He'd get really angry if they were important calls, you know."

The guys exchanged a look, hesitating.

Amara added more. "Honestly, what do you think I'm going to do, gentleman? Lift weights at midnight?"

One of the guys nodded. "Five minutes, ma'am."

Amara gave him a bright smile and slipped inside. While they hadn't announced their engagement per se, people weren't idiots. Even if she didn't have a giant green rock on her finger and he didn't have a band on his, the preparations for the wedding and the fact that she'd taken over the household after Chiara left right after Leo died, people knew she was going to be the mistress of the mansion, and as such, they'd begun to treat her with the respect that title demanded.

It was the first time she had ever come into the training center. From everything she'd heard about it growing up, she had imagined dungeons and torture chambers, not state-of-the-art facilities, a boxing ring, a fitness center, weapons locked behind glass cabinets at this time of the night. Amara had spent the last few hours preparing herself for this confrontation with a man she had never met but whose blood ran through her veins, and she was not going to be denied like a child who didn't know what was good for her.

She knew from what Dante had once told her that the interrogation room was in the basement. Heading to her right, she opened the sole door and descended the steps of the training center down to the basement. The space slowly came into view, along with the people. Vin stood off in one corner of the room, and Dante sat in a chair opposite another man.

All eyes came to her as she entered.

Dante's narrowed, a bright flare of annoyance and anger going through them, and Amara lifted her chin, daring him to say something. The vein on the side of his neck ticked, but he stayed silent.

Amara felt a calm wave of strength pass over her. This was for herself, for her child, for the world she was bringing her into. While their world would never be good and clean and straight, she could do her part in making it better. She had survived so much, she could handle this confrontation.

Feeling Dante's silent presence there emboldened the strength inside her. He had always done that, since the day beside her hospital bed to this precise moment when he was pissed at her – he made her stronger, made her feel safer, made her feel supported. He was one of the biggest reasons she was as sane as she was, that she had held onto life through the worst of her trauma, that she had healed. He called her his lighthouse but he had always been hers, standing tall through the worst of the stormy nights, lighting up the dark, letting her know that shore was close.

The basement looked more like the dungeon she'd imagined – dark, dank, and destitute. The walls were a bleary grey, the high ceiling supported with stone pillars, yellow bulbs hanging every two feet, giving the place a miserable glow.

Vin stood to one corner - face hard, arms folded across her chest.- by a table with several weapons, seeing which twisted Amara's stomach.

Amara removed her gaze from them to the man sitting on a chair in the middle, untied, and watching them all. A clean-shaven, well-dressed, bald man with horn-rimmed spectacles. The same man whose photo her kidnapper had shown her on the phone all those years ago. Her father.

Amara came to a stop a few feet from him, locking her eyes with his olive ones, every memory of her assault coming to the forefront of her mind.

'MrX is here.'

He had been there.

"Why?" she asked, her voice raspy. That was what she wanted to know. Why.

Xavier smiled at her, his eyes warm. "Their first order had been to kill you, girl. I hadn't known it was you. But when I saw you there, looking so beautifully broken, I had you live."

Beautifully broken? She'd been assaulted, tortured, raped. She'd had her skin flayed from her flesh and acid drip over her muscles and blood cover her being. There was nothing *remotely* beautiful about everything that she had survived.

"So, had it been any other innocent girl, she would have been tortured and raped and killed?"

"Yes."

He was sick in the head.

Absolutely *sick.*

Amara felt acid from her stomach rising in her throat. "And Dante's mother? You killed her for the same reason you had me taken? That she overheard a conversation she wasn't supposed to hear?"

He smiled, a warm smile that made Amara's skin crawl. "Do you have any idea how vast, how deep our organization is? There are some very powerful people connected to some very powerful places with us. That's why we have a simple policy to protect ourselves – no witnesses. Anyone who's not working with us knows nothing about us."

"So you've killed other innocent people over the years?"

"Of course."

Amara swayed on the spot as the entirety of it hit her. She was just one in a line of many. Dante's mother had been just one in a line of many. There were many who died and no one even knew a thing. Who the hell were these people?

She felt Dante put his big hand behind her, holding her just on the curve of her waist, and she leaned into it, glad to have the support.

Once she was steady, he got up, pushed her into his vacated seat, and walked to the side towards another chair.

"I want to kill you, Xavier," Dante told the man who had sired her calmly, pulling up that chair next to hers. "I want to kill you for what you put my mother and brother through. I want to kill you for what you put my woman through. I want to kill you for what you've put so many innocent people through."

"But you won't." Xavier relaxed back in his chair.

"But I won't," Dante agreed. "A few years ago, I would have. Now, you are more useful to me alive than dead. The day you stop being useful to me? You'll perhaps go to sleep and never wake up. Or maybe you'll pour yourself a glass of water and instead drink acid that melts your organs from the inside. Or maybe you'll wake up tied to a chair with knives in your skin. Or hell if I'm in a merciful mood, maybe you'll go to the grocery store and have a terrible accident. I mean, who knows?"

Damn, he was good. Amara saw her father stiffen a bit at each word, even as he stayed silent.

"Are we clear?" Dante asked, taking his jacket off.

"Yes," her father said quietly.

Dante nodded, slowly folding the sleeves of his shirt over his forearms. "Now, let's talk like adult bad guys. The kids my father sent twenty years ago, where are they?"

Xavier shrugged. "I wouldn't know. I was just a foot soldier then here in the Outfit. They promoted me to the ranks afterward."

"Can you find out?"

"Possibly, yes. But the young ones rarely survive."

"Hmm," Dante finished rolling up his sleeves, looking back at Vin. "Hand me the gun please."

Vin quietly went to the table and picked up a gun, passing it over to her man.

Dante placed it on his lap and took out a cigarette. "In that batch of kids, there was a three-year-old redheaded girl," Dante began. "I want her and you will get me her information."

Her father stayed silent.

Dante blew out a puff of smoke. "Why kidnap us a few weeks ago and take us to the same location?"

Xavier looked down at his hands. "It's a place we started using again a few years ago. She wasn't supposed to be taken, just you. The guys thought she was collateral."

Amara's disgust was probably plastered all over her face because Xavier looked at her and said, "I was never meant to be a father. Some men just aren't."

"That's your excuse?" her tone was disbelieving.

"It's the truth. Children become what their parents are. Nerea had a shitty mother who left her with me, and she grew up hard; you got a good mother who raised you, and you grew up kind. Me? I was raised by a monstrous man, so that's what I became."

Amara shook her head, unable to believe what she was hearing. "We are not our parents, Xavier. Children are… like wildflowers. They may be planted in one place but they grow where their hearts lead. It's not where we're planted but where we bloom that defines us."

A laugh escaped the man. "Oh, you naïve girl. What a luxury that innocence must be. Yes, you've been through hell, but my dear daughter, hell is much bigger than you ever thought it was. This world is much bigger, much deeper, much darker than you thought it was. The places I've been, I couldn't be anything else but who I am."

A shiver went down Amara's spine at his words.

Xavier grinned at seeing her shudder. "Let the sleeping monsters lie, girl. They already have their eyes on the Outfit because of Lorenzo's death, which they're writing off as an internal thing. These people have no conscience. No humanity. You will unleash something upon your family I don't think you truly understand. You'll see when your child-"

A wave of protectiveness crashed over her so intensely it made her heart stutter.

Amara took the gun from Dante's lap, her hand gripping it hard. She wanted to shoot him. She wanted to shoot him and remove his essence from a world where her child would be born. But doing that would lose them a lead. He could give them information that could save countless other children. But he didn't deserve to live.

The indecision between her maternal instinct for her child and her protective instinct for other children warred inside her. Amara put her nose on the gun, breathing in and out, trying to contain the rage his words unleashed inside her.

This man had made so many people suffer, and she couldn't make him pay because he had the power to stop others from suffering.

Win. Dante always said when dealing with his father – lose a battle, win the war. She needed to lose this.

Amara straightened her arm, her eyes flickering to Dante once to see him watching her, and she unlocked the gun as Vin had taught her, and pointed it to the man grinning at her, her arms slightly shaking. The proximity to him allowed her to aim better, and she pulled the trigger over his kneecap.

The loud shot and the recoil hit her hard, pushing her back into the chair as Xavier screamed in pain, clutching his knee.

"That's for fifteen-year-old me, you bastard," she rasped out, the satisfaction of watching the blood leave him acute in her. Dante didn't say a word, just watched her like a hawk as she watched her father, her chest heaving.

Aiming to the other knee, she blew it out too. "And that's for Dante's mother and countless other innocent people you've destroyed."

She stood up, walking to the chair he was howling in and pointed the gun to his head.

"Listen to me, and listen well, Xavier," Amara said, her voice firm, bringing his attention to herself. "Your organization has spies here? It's time we plant our own there. You will help us plant a spy in your ranks. You will help us find the missing kids. You will give us answers. And you will keep your mouth shut about it. If at any point, you betray us and bring danger to my door, if anything you do directly falls on my family, forget anyone else," Amara stated, digging the gun into his forehead, seeing his eyes widen slightly. "I will make them hurt you, over and over and over, and I won't let them give you death until your skin is flayed from your bones. Am I clear?"

He nodded.

She turned to Dante. "Promise me, if his shadow ever falls on our children, you will make him suffer."

"With pleasure," Dante promised, blowing a ring of smoke in her father's face.

Amara nodded and walked back to the chair. "So, who's going to be our plant in the Syndicate?"

"I am," Vin said from the side.

Amara looked at him, her heart racing. "Vinnie."

Vin's eyes came to her. "I couldn't protect you then, but I can now. Let me do this."

Amara stared at her lifelong friend, seeing the man he had grown up to be, and felt her heart soften.

"We'll discuss this later in my office," Dante said to him, standing up from his seat and extending his hand to Amara. "As for this bastard, lock him up here for now."

Amara took his hand and began walking away from the scene, climbing the stairs, walking out of the center.

Dante smoked the last of his cigarette, taking a drag, staying silent. Amara knew he was fuming at her so she stayed silent too. They walked to the mansion and headed to his study, him closing the door behind her and pushing her up against it, his hand holding her jaw, his eyes blazing. "Defy me like that again when it comes to your safety, and I kid you not, I will lock you up, Amara."

Once upon a time, that statement would have possibly triggered her. Knowing this man now, Amara rolled her eyes. "Why would I defy you if it doesn't make sense? I'm not a thrill-seeker. I like my life quiet. And I like being safe. But when you deny me a chance for closure, I will take matters into my own hands, Dante."

"You don't see him anymore. You don't deal with him anymore. You don't even think of him anymore," he growled an inch from her lips. "I will deal with him and I will take care of him when the time comes."

Amara stroked his chest. "Okay."

"The spy planting was a good idea, by the way. Well done."

Amara looked at his face, the beard covering his jaw, the scent of his cologne and smoke mingling together in a concoction she liked. "What if he's right, Dante? How do we stop this from tarnishing our children?"

He looked down at her and cupped her face, pulling her flush into him. "He was right to an extent, Amara. We are our parents to an extent. I have so much for my mother in me, and I know that. You have so much of yours. Our kids will have bits of us too, but we're more than our parents. Look at Tristan. Look at Morana. Look at us. Our kids will be more than us too. And we'll do it as we do everything. Together, you and me. We make this kingdom what we want. Tonight was a big step towards that. We have answers and we have a lead. We're building a new house on the foundations of an old one, and if need be, we'll paint it with blood."

"So, what, we play them, my king?"

He chuckled, his fingers flexing on her face. "We play them, my queen."

24

Amara

She was going to explode, and not in a good way.

Amara winced, walking the length of the big party hall in the mansion, her ankles swollen, her spine bent back, her hands on the back of her hips – all because she'd become a whale. The doctor had told her that the eighth month of pregnancy would be hard on her body but she hadn't warned how hard. She was running to the bathroom every five minutes to relieve her bladder, she was swollen all over like a pumpkin, and her joints had started to crack. She was nothing but a giant stomach at this point.

"No, don't touch the chandelier," she told one of the staff who was on a ladder, stringing lights across the room in preparation for the wedding ceremony in one week. It was going to be a grand affair, and not because either she or Dante wanted that.

She'd never thought as a child how her wedding was going to be. Back then, all she'd seen had been Dante and he had been unreachable, so wedding days weren't really something that she'd given any thought. She liked how the preparation was going though.

The garden behind the mansion, from the wall to the gazebo, had already been decorated. Poles had been set up and canopies of sheer white and gold had been put up, covering the entire open space. Seating places were being set up, flowers had been booked, and basically, the entire lavish ceremony was good to go. And since it was almost the summer, there was no possibility of rain for the week, only bright sun and cool winds.

Amara couldn't remember ever having seen a party of this scale on the compound. Including the acquaintances of Mr. Maroni and the families of the Outfit and its partners, well over seven hundred people attending the wedding of Dante Maroni and his outsider bride. Most of them didn't approve, from what the grapevine said, but they were all supportive of Dante's ascension and his new reign, and what he would bring to the table.

"Ouch," Morana's voice said from behind her, her hazel eyes behind the glasses on Amara's ankles in the flats. "That looks nasty."

"Feels worse," Amara groaned. "I swear she feels like a giant even though I know she's small."

"I mean both you and Dante are vertically blessed, so I wouldn't be surprised if she's tall too," Morana commented. She and Tristan had flown in last night, a week before the wedding, so they could help out. Since Damien wasn't attending, Tristan had agreed to stand with Dante and Morana with her. Amara knew they weren't getting married anytime before they had answers about Luna, but secretly she hoped one day soon they would. The biggest surprise though had been the little boy they'd brought with them.

Xander was a quiet kid, but he'd already weaved his way into Tristan and Morana's life. Amara had seen both him and Tristan playing cards at night and she understood what Morana meant. Tristan loved the boy. It was evident in the way he stood close to his side, or always kept his eyes on him when he was in the room, or ruffled his hair. Amara recognized the ways Tristan fell in love, the same way he had with Morana, just with much less turmoil. As for Morana herself, she had taken to Xander like a pro. And given both their histories, Amara was certain they would make incredible parents to the little boy if they chose to keep him.

"Your dress is here, by the way," Morana grinned, her excitement infectious. "It's so gorgeous, Amara. You're going to blind Dante."

Amara snorted. "I hope not. Any news about Nerea?"

Morana shook her head, watching the giant chandelier being sparkled. "She's gone underground, but I'm not surprised. She had to have known your father was MrX."

Amara shrugged, still willing to give her the benefit of the doubt. "Maybe, she didn't, Morana. We don't really know anything about her or her past. And she's been good enough to me over the years that I won't throw it out, not without proof."

Morana nodded. "I like that about you, you know? Your openness. Damn, who has these huge ass chandeliers in like every non-bedroom room? Crazy rich people."

Amara laughed, felt the pressure build in her bladder, and sighed. Few more weeks. Just a few more weeks.

On her way back from the bathroom off the living room, Amara climbed the stairs to the second floor where Dante's mother's painting studio had been. She had never had the chance to go there before, and she'd always wanted to.

The huge room was empty except for a few boxes and art supplies under a large window, right opposite the entrance that had the entire vista of the hills and the river running through it laid there for her viewing. Amara headed to it, taking in the view. It was beautiful, and she could see why it had been artistically inspiring.

"This is where he killed her, you know," the feminine voice behind her had Amara spinning on her swollen feet, wincing at the throb in them.

She looked as Nerea slinked out from behind the door, dressed all in black, looking far older than Amara had ever seen her look, lines of stress on her face.

"Sister," Amara rasped out. "We have been looking for you."

The other woman nodded. "I know. I've been hiding."

Amara blinked. "Why?"

Nerea gave a smile, one that sent a chill down Amara's spine. "You have an amazing mother, you know," she started, stepping closer into the room.

Amara instinctively took a step back, staying silent.

"You have an amazing friend," Nerea continued, her tone soft, slithering between them like a serpent. "You have an amazing man. And now, you'll have an amazing child. Amazing Amara."

Amara felt her chest go tight, her hands protectively covering her belly.

"And you know what I had?" Nerea took another step, her hand stroking the gun at the side of her hip. "I had an abusive father who let his friends rape me. I had a shittier mother for leaving me with him after she knew what he'd done. And I had no friends because he started training me to be a spy."

Her heart hurt for the woman, even as her senses stayed alert. "I know how the shame feels, Nerea. I know how it stains your soul."

"No, you don't," Nerea shook her head with a laugh. "What, you think you get tortured for three days and raped by three men, you know how it feels? You can never know, Amara, because after he ordered them to let you go, you had people who coddled you and sent you to fucking therapy, for god's sake. I had a cold room and training to attend in the morning. So, no, Amara, you'll never know how it feels. The dark in your soul is but a blemish. The dark in mine is an eclipse."

The pain in her voice, the anguish in her face, the torture in her eyes made Amara's heart bleed, her pulse pounding in her veins as blood rushed to her ears.

Nerea chuckled at her silence. "I was fine, you know. I was coping. Until Xavier gave me the assignment to be the spy in the Outfit, and get close to you on the side, just to make sure you didn't blab anything. They accepted me because I was his daughter, and I came here happy that I had a sister, happy we didn't know our father, happy that she could understand my pain, hoping to connect. And I saw you – beautiful, scarred Amara who had a mother who loved her, a friend who protected her, and the fucking prince of the Outfit in the palm of her hands. That upset me, Amara."

Amara felt a tightening in her stomach, her breathing getting a little labored. "I'm sorry," she told her sister, her heart clenching in pain. "I'm so sorry for everything, Nerea."

Nerea tilted her head to the side, considering her. "You know, I think you might actually mean that. And that just makes me hate you even more."

The intensity of that emotion emanating from the older woman hit Amara square in the chest, sending pain down her stomach. Amara gripped her bump, willing herself to stay calm and not stress the baby, but fuck it was hard. She needed to get out of the room.

Amara went to take a step to the side, only to have the other woman block her, and her heart began to pound uncontrollably.

The baby. She had to stay calm for the baby. She couldn't lose her too. Not now.

Amara took a deep breath in, willing her body to listen to her brain. "Let me out, Nerea."

Nerea smiled. "We're just having a long-overdue conversation, sister."

Amara glanced at the gun on her hip, swallowing. "I don't understand. You were so nice to me, especially when I was exiled."

"Oh, I was happy when you got exiled," her sister mentioned, playing with the gun on her hip. "Lorenzo didn't really care about what Dante was doing with you. You were an insider and a servant's daughter, and he didn't care where Dante stuck his dick. It wasn't until I whispered to him how emotionally attached Dante was to you, how you were seeing dreams of taking over his empire, how you would bring the Maroni name to shame. Oh, he ate it up, the egotistical jackass."

She remembered the day she'd been called to the mansion out of the blue, the entire conversation in the room, the way her heart had broken.

"I thought you'd be in pain and I was happy," Nerea shook her head in disbelief. "But no, you're Amazing Amara. You got a full fucking ride to university to study what you wanted, you got a beautiful apartment, you got a car, you even got a fucking cat. Guess it pays to fuck the prince, huh."

Rage, so deep and vicious and old, flooded her system. Amara had always chalked everything that had happened to fate but staring at this woman she shared half her blood with, realizing that she was responsible for the pain and loneliness she had suffered, that Dante had suffered, pure, unadulterated rage engulfed her.

She stayed silent, seething, pieces clicking into place.

Nerea took the gun out of the holster, and Amara turned slightly to the side, instinctively shielding her womb. This woman might have destroyed her but she would not destroy her daughter, not as long as she had a breath in her body. She needed to buy time.

Pretending to be afraid and half-afraid, Amara softly asked her. "You're the one who sent those guys to Los Fortis, didn't you?"

Nerea smiled. "How do you think Dante found you so quickly? I got you the fake passport, remember? I knew exactly where you were, and I told him that you'd mentioned going there."

Amara nodded. It made sense. "And Alpha? You went to see him?"

Nerea laughed. "Lorenzo told me about his bastard son a few days before he died, and I was curious. And since I was already in Los Fortis, I set up a meeting with him. He's a suspicious bastard though. Knew something was up immediately. I was sloppy, flying from Shadow Port. He connected it to you, I guess, and his men almost saved you and Dante."

Amara made a note to invite him to the wedding, just to thank him for being good to her and trying to save them.

"Thankfully, my men got you out before he could interfere," Nerea sighed. "They all thought you weren't supposed to be taken, that Dante was the target, but he wasn't. It was always you. Taking you two to that place was for you. It was a nice touch, wasn't it?"

The memory of being tied to that chair again, bleeding between her legs, losing her child assaulted her, the fear, the pain, the anger revolting everything inside her. Amara felt hatred, true hatred, seep into her pores.

"I lost my baby," Amara whispered, the muscles in her body tight, her hands fisted on the side. "I lost my child because of you."

A smile came over Nerea's face, the sight sending revulsion through her system. "I'm glad."

Oh, the bitch was going to die. The bitch was going to die with pain.

For the first time in her life, Amara felt true, murderous hatred fill her entire being.

A contraction hit her stomach, making her gasp as she gripped her stomach.

Braxton Hicks. That's what they were. She'd read about them. Yes.

"Oh, is the baby coming?" Nerea asked with mock-concern, her pretty face twisting into something ugly.

Amara shook herself. "No." It couldn't be. It was too soon. She wasn't ready. There was no way the baby was ready either.

Nerea pointed the gun at her, and Amara felt panic, true panic, fill her system, her anxiety hitting the roof as she tried to fight it and contain it inside herself. Fear, fury, and fire mixed inside her, twining around each other so closely she couldn't even differentiate which was which anymore.

Protection came to the fore.

She had to protect the baby. She had to protect herself. She had to live a long and happy life with the man she loved. She deserved it.

But she was on the second floor in a room nobody ever visited while most people were downstairs preparing for the wedding. Amara took a step back, her hand going behind her. She made it look like she was searching for the windowsill to support herself; instead, her fingers came into contact with the surface of the boxes behind her, searching for a weapon, anything to help her.

Nerea stepped closer once, twice, three times, until her gun was right over Amara's stomach, barely an inch away.

Her heart stopped, before thundering inside her chest, the flush of adrenaline wild in her veins, her entire being acutely aware of every single breath she took that pushed her stomach out, closer to the mouth of the gun. She tried not to breathe too hard, and another violent contraction hit her, hard.

No. No. No.

Fight with me, baby, she begged mentally to her unborn child, her heart racing.

"I'm sorry, Amara," Nerea said, her words building up inside Amara until her hands started to shake. "You can't have everything. You won't have anything. I won't live knowing you got happiness. I can't."

Nerea's thumb clocked the top of the gun, unlocking it, her finger tightening on the trigger.

Amara went wild on the inside, searching behind her, her hand hitting a small can of paint.

Another contraction hit, faster than the one before.

Just a little more, baby.

"You don't have to do this, Nerea," she urged the other woman, buying some more time as her hand worked to lift the lid of the can. Amara felt a nail break, the pain in her finger making her wince which thankfully got masked with another contraction.

Amara gasped, exhaling loudly, covering her stomach with the other hand, the back of it touching the gun.

She just had one shot at this. Just one shot and she couldn't miss.

Swallowing, Amara picked up the can of paint with one hand, swinging her arm around to throw it on the woman's face, while pushing the arm of the gun to the ceiling with the other. A shot rang out just above her shoulder, and Amara felt her water break at the sound, her heart palpitating as she slugged through the pain.

Nerea went down with a gasp, her free hand trying to wipe her eyes. Amara bent even though she shouldn't have, grabbing the gun from the woman's hand, and turned it around.

And then she emptied the entire clip into her half-sister.

The bullets emptied.

Someone came rushing into the room.

Amara felt her knees give out as a cramp hit her, all the pain she'd been holding crashing into her, her low-pain threshold making her vision blur with the red stars that started to dance behind her lids.

Everything became a blur. She felt someone pick her up, carry her, move her. She felt the movement of the car and then the stench of the hospital. The thing she felt most was the endless *pain.*

Dante's hands came to hers at some point, his voice whispering and shouting words of encouragement to her. Sweat drenched her. Lights came in and out of focus. And it went on and on and on and on.

And hours later, Tempest Talia Ava Maroni slid out into the world with a scream louder than her mother's. Her lost sister never followed.

EPILOGUE

Dante

D ante looked down at the little warrior princess in his arms, his little storm, and felt something shift inside him, fall, click into place, locked tight. With the names of both women who had protected their children in their own ways – his mother and Amara's – Tempest was a wrinkly, scrawny little thing, with a head full of dark hair and eyes squinted closed, looking nothing like the babies he saw in the media. He'd never seen anything more beautiful.

With her rump on his palm and her entire body – waddled in a blanket – fitting in the crook of his arm, Dante felt his eyes begin to burn.

"Dante-" the voice croaked from the hospital bed, bringing his attention to the woman he didn't even know what he felt for anymore. Love was too tame a word, adoration too juvenile. Broken and bleeding at fifteen, she had made his world tremble; exhausted and spent now, she owned it.

He went to sit beside her, putting his precious bundle over her chest, watching as the woman his entire life belonged to gave a tearful smile, sobbing as she brought up a scarred hand to hold her, her ring glinting in the muted light.

"She made it," Amara rasped out, her liquid eyes taking her in, before coming to his, shimmering with such endless emotion he felt himself falling into them again. Her eyes, those unique, beautiful, expressive eyes, had always been the hook into his chest.

"She's a fighter," Dante said, his voice sounding rough to his ears. "Like you."

Amara's lips trembled. "She ours, Dante. Ours. After all this time."

Dante pressed a kiss to her wet lips. "My warrior queen. I'm so proud of you."

Amara nuzzled her nose against his. "Did you count her toes?"

"Every one of them."

The princess made a *mou* with her lips, a mewl coming from her little body.

"We will keep her safe, won't we?" she asked him quietly, still looking down at their miracle. Dante rubbed the baby's soft skin with a finger, his heart clenching as she gripped it with her tiny hands, the trust in the action the same unconscious trust fifteen-year-old Amara had shown him. It made everything inside him vow to shield them.

"Yes, we will," he vowed.

"And if she ever cracks?" Amara locked her gaze with his.

"Then we fill her up with gold."

She smiled, and Dante pressed his forehead to hers.

"Oh my god, she's precious," Morana cooed at little Tempest as Amara sat up on the hospital bed with her in her arms while Dante sat on a chair by the side.

They had just told Amara the story. Morana had been the one to find her in the room, having heard gunshots, and she had been the one to scream for help. Tristan had been the one to rush in, pick Amara up and carry her to the car while giving out instructions to get Nerea's body away. Morana had sat in the back with her while Tristan had driven like a madman to the hospital, calling Dante on the way. She had been in labor for five hours with Dante by her side before Tempest came out, screaming like a banshee at being inconvenienced out of her mother's snug womb.

The baby blinked around, her eyes a little more open.

"She has your eyes," Tristan noted, standing behind Morana. Yes, and Dante loved that. Just like Amara had inherited her eyes from her mother, Tempest had inherited them from her.

Amara looked around the room, her face falling a bit and he realized she missed Vin. Dante felt bad about that. He should have been there with them in this important moment, but he was deep underground with Xavier, having been taken into the fold on MrX's recommendation. He contacted Dante once a week with updates and Dante was expecting his call today. He looked down at his watch, to see it was early yet.

His eyes went to Tristan's hand as he slowly put a finger over the baby's cheek, and the tattoo on his ring finger caught Dante's eye. It was too good an opportunity to pass.

"That tattoo," Dante said, grinning. "You're so romantic, Tristan."

Tristan gave him a middle finger that Morana immediately slapped. "There are children here. No weird gestures."

"Tell him not to piss me off," Tristan said, giving Dante a look.

"No cursing either," Morana pointed out.

Amara's soft laughter rang from the bed. "You'll be her godparents," she said softly to the two people in the room, her mother having left just a few minutes ago after seeing her granddaughter.

"Are you sure?" Morana asked for the hundredth time.

Amara nodded, rocking Tempest in her arms. "There aren't two people I trust more with her life besides Dante. If anything were to happen to us, I'd die knowing she was safe and loved by someone who would lay their lives for her."

Morana went teary-eyed. Tristan put a hand on Amara's shoulder in silent acceptance. And Dante smiled.

"Who's on Amara now that Vin's gone?" Tristan asked quietly, standing by his side as they waited for Amara to walk out into the lawn.

Trust him to ask the most non-romantic question during one of the most romantic moments of his life. Dante almost chuckled but stopped himself.

"Sav," Dante replied, looking around at the garden that had been transformed into something out of a crazy fairytale. They hadn't delayed the wedding, but he'd brought Amara home and not allowed her to lift a finger while she recovered. Call him overprotective, but that's where he was at.

Dante stood in a tux, looking around at the guests who had come in for the wedding, the who's who of the Outfit, the underworld, his father's acquaintances, and his.

"I think Xander's like Damien," Tristan said out of the blue from his side, his brows slightly furrowed. "Not exactly the same, but similar. You have any tips for me?"

Dante turned to follow his gaze to the young eight-year-old boy who sat in the front, looking down at a tablet. Combined with what Morana had told him about his high intelligence, Dante could see why they'd think that.

"Don't think," he told Tristan. "Know. Get a diagnosis so you can do what's the best for him. Assuming you're keeping him, of course," he added with a sly grin.

Tristan gave him a look, before looking forward again. "He reminds me of myself when I was that age. I don't want him to be alone. Morana and I, he's happy with us."

Dante smiled. "Then don't. Are you happy?"

"I think so."

The music beginning stopped their conversation. Dante turned to see Zia walking down the aisle arm in arm with his woman is a stunning dress of white gold that shimmered in the sunlight, the lacy full sleeves covering her arms, the high neck covering her scar, her hair in some kind of an up-do, his little warrior princess nestled in her arms.

Dante felt something move inside his chest, something so soft and fierce and alive, something that only resonated with and for this woman. His magnum opus. His warrior queen. The mother of his child.

She came to a stop beside him, a wide smile on her red lips. "Hi."

"Hi," he murmured, his eyes taking her in, savoring this moment he'd never thought he'd have with her over the years of wait, his eyes flickering down to the curious little girl wiggling and looking around in awe.

He bent down and planted a kiss on her head, before pressing a hard kiss to his woman. "You're the beat to my heart, Amara. Now, she's a beat too."

She wiped the lipstick from his mouth. "And mine."

The ceremony began.

And though their world kept getting darker every day, empires he hadn't known about coming to light, the one he was building nascent and dangerous and terrifying; though there were mysteries unsolved and questions unanswered and futures unknown; though there were possibilities of danger lurking in every corner, Dante looked around at his chessboard, and with his queen by his side, he felt ready to play them all.

The man watched from the shadows as the wedding commenced.

Dante Maroni got married to an outsider, his heir already born.

The Predator stood by his side, Morana Vitalio on the other.

The kid he'd led them to sat in the front.

And Alpha, the king of the south, sat in the back with a tiny woman.

It was perfect for all of them.

The man flicked a lighter on and off.

He would give them a week, and then it was time to leave more breadcrumbs.

It was time.

The Dark Verse series continues with the story of The Finisher, coming 2021.

Thank you for choosing my book. I hope you enjoyed Dante's and Amara's journey. Though it is not the end and you will see them again, it makes me emotional nonetheless Please consider leaving a review/rating before hopping on to your next book adventure. I would truly appreciate that so much.

ABOUT THE AUTHOR

With stories in her veins and words in her blood, RuNyx began her writing journey online five years ago. Since then, she has devoted her life to story-telling and made a career out of the same. She believes that the best of stories come from the best of conflicts, and has made it her mission to find love in the darkness.

To stay updated about her books and connect with other readers, join her reader's group on Facebook – *RuNyx's Firebirds.*

Find her on her Twitter, Instagram and Facebook. She loves to hear from her readers. To stay updated about upcoming books, sign up for her newsletter. All information can be found on **www.runyxwrites.com.**

The Finisher will release worldwide in 2021.

Other titles by RuNyx

The Predator

The Reaper

Milton Keynes UK
Ingram Content Group UK Ltd.
UKHW021302080923
428306UK00023B/738